Coming Home

a novel

Coming Home

a novel

ROBERT EZELLE

COMING HOME

To my Special Angel:

You are the wind beneath my wings.

Author's Note

Many books have their genesis in the author's mind as a what-if—a premise around which he or she constructs a story. Sometimes, when the author puts pen to paper, the story just seems to construct itself, as happened in the case of this book.

Coming Home is a fantasy, but it is not your typical tale about elves and dwarves, dragons and treasure, kings in castles, or lost princes. Rather, it is a story of what-ifs.

God expresses his love to people in many ways, the greatest of which is the gift of his son so mankind might have forgiveness of sins and reconciliation with him. There are many other ways he shows his love. He has healed the sick, made the blind to see, and caused the lame to walk. The Bible and Church histories are replete with examples of his supernatural intervention in the lives of everyday people.

Angels are another form of God's supernatural intervention. The biblical record verifies their existence and describes several instances in which they have appeared to people. Additionally, throughout history, there have been men and women who claim to have been visited by angels. In these instances, the angelic visitor has provided comfort, provided for a physical need, or rescued someone from danger.

But what if, instead of sending angels, God bent the laws of physics and sent a man or woman across space and time? What if God's creation is richer and more varied than we can perceive with our five senses?

God's creation operates according to certain physical principles, which we are still in the process of discovering. According to our perception, time marches forward in a linear fashion, and once an instant is gone, it is forever gone, never to be retrieved or touched again. Our experience leads us to believe that God does not bend the laws of space and time in advancing his purposes, but what if . . . ?

Yes, God is sovereign. He created the heavens and the earth and set the stars to roam in their courses. He always deals with mankind according to his character and his nature as revealed in his Word. He is fair, kind, and infinitely loving. He has the best interests of his people in mind at all times.

All that being said, what if . . .?

"For I know the plans I have for you," declares the LORD, "plans to prosper you and not to harm you, plans to give you hope and a future."

—Jeremiah 29:11

"You did not choose me, but I chose you and appointed you so that you might go and bear fruit—fruit that will last—and so that whatever you ask in my name the Father will give you."

—John 15:16

"It is for us the living, rather, to be dedicated here to the unfinished work which they who fought here have thus far so nobly advanced. It is rather for us to be here dedicated to the great task remaining before us—that from these honored dead we take increased devotion to that cause for which they gave the last full measure of devotion—that we here highly resolve that these dead shall not have died in vain—that this nation, under God, shall have a new birth of freedom—and that government of the people, by the people, for the people, shall not perish from the earth."

—Abraham Lincoln, 16th president of the United States, the Gettysburg Address

"Fight on and fly on to the last drop of blood and the last drop of fuel, to the last beat of the heart."

—Baron Manfred von Richthofen, leading ace of WWI (80 air combat victories)

"Fighting in the air is not sport. It is scientific murder."

—Captain Edward Rickenbacker, leading American ace of WWI (26 air combat victories)

"Of all my accomplishments I may have achieved during the war, I am proudest of the fact that I never lost a wingman."

—Colonel Erich Hartmann, leading ace of WWII (352 air combat victories)

The fighter community is a subculture of the greater US military. It has its own acronym-laden language that the uninitiated would find almost impossible to understand. For your convenience, I've included a glossary at the end of this novel.

Chapter 1

Transition

Morgan Michaelson glanced at the twinkling lights of Fallon in the rearview mirror of his speeding truck. The small Nevada town and its namesake naval air station had been his home for the past year. Every turn of the wheels increased the distance between him and the woman who had captured his heart so completely.

A scream of anguish formed in his throat. "Lord, why are you doing this to me?" he demanded. "I've served you faithfully for more years than I can count! In all that time, I've never asked anything for myself. Now, when I've finally found someone to love, you tear me away from her. Can't you find some room in your grand purpose so we can be together?"

Something deep within him wanted to curse the unfairness of it, the hard-heartedness of God for demanding this of him. But the rational part of his brain argued back that, in all fairness, he could not blame God. It was his own fault. He had violated the sacred trust placed in him, and now he would have to suffer the consequences.

An irrational thought flashed through his mind: *Turn around; go back to her.* But as fast as it came, the thought was gone. Staying was not an option. Kate was already back in her own time and place, and soon this shadow of reality would cease to exist. He had to keep moving, moving fast, if he did not want to be caught up in its dissolution.

He pressed the gas and watched the speedometer creep up to eighty. Glancing again at the rearview mirror, he saw the town's lights continuing to burn brightly.

A billboard winked out of existence, then another. Transition was beginning—the shifting of time and space that would take him from one assignment to the next, from one corner of God's creation to another. Not for the first time he wished it was something he had some control over, but it wasn't. It was just something that happened. And he was along for the ride.

The subtle changes had probably been taking place since he left Fallon, but now they were becoming increasingly noticeable. The westbound, divided highway suddenly became a two-lane road. Before his eyes the truck's digital instrument display became round, analog dials. The steering wheel grew larger but thinner in his hands, hard plastic replacing padded leather.

He didn't need to look at his wrist to know his smart watch was gone, probably replaced by something mechanical. He glanced down by his knee. The cup holder was gone and along with it, the iPhone he normally kept there when he drove.

His stomach tightened. The familiar rules were playing out. He could not take anything to an earlier period of history or to a different corner of creation that did not belong there. Things shifted to match the time and place or they vanished outright.

All indications were that he was going back to an earlier time. If the truck stopped working, it would be a sign he was going way back.

A road sign flashed past, blue on white, the script cursive. He glanced in the mirror again. The town looked much different now—smaller, fewer lights.

He'd done this all before, many times. There would be changes, details subtracted, others added, until the accumulated whole brought him to an entirely different place, the place God wanted him to be.

The truck jolted hard on a pothole, causing Morgan to ease his foot off the gas. He tried to concentrate on the twin pools of yellow light cast by his headlights, but despite his best efforts to keep his mind on the present, it seemed determined to reach back through the long, dark years of the past.

Memories of previous assignments cascaded through his mind, deepening his despair. Bringing a lost child home to his family. Standing in an infantry square, bayonets facing outward, ready to receive a cavalry charge. Serving the poor in a teeming slum. A desperate sword fight in the dark, snow swirling. Men hunkered down in the mud beside him, cowering, as an artillery barrage walked toward their trench. Fleeing through a war-ravaged countryside. Prison cells. Hunger. Hardship.

Lord, is that all you have in store for me? More pain? More suffering? I thought this last assignment might be a break, something different. But I guess it wasn't that different after all. When it comes right down to it, it seems you had me preparing Kate for war.

A jolt of adrenaline surged through his veins. Now he had to cope with fear on top of the other emotions tearing him apart— not fear for himself, but fear for Kate. She was going into danger. He had known it deep down but had buried it in the delight of time spent with her.

The road to Reno suddenly curved eastward where there should be no curve. A flurry of snow swirled in the headlights. Within moments it gave way to rain and then to dry flakes again.

The adrenaline faded, leaving him tired, drained, spent. *Lord, how long have I been doing this? It feels like I've lived a lifetime of years, but how do you possibly measure time when it really has no context, when you shift me from one corner of your creation to another, and dip me into and out of the flow of time. When I'm in one place for many years and in others for just an instant and there is no regular passage of seasons?*

The crunching of tires on gravel as the pavement ended snapped him out of his reverie. The pitch of the truck's engine grew higher, tinnier, the suspension hard, jolting him painfully as it bounced over ruts. It would die soon. He knew it. When it did, he would call for Midnight.

He didn't know exactly what Midnight was. It was just one more thing about his life that was uncertain, unknowable. In any case, the striking black horse was another provision made for his need,

3

sent to accompany him on assignments where there were no cars, no electricity, no phones.

His mind ran with the thought. No ability to call. No ability to text. No ability to even send a letter. No ability at all to connect in any way with Kate. The thought was pure anguish.

The engine cut out, startling him with the sudden silence, then the headlights died as the truck rolled to a stop. The stars were back, blazing overhead. A full moon, a brilliant white orb, hung high above the horizon, bathing the countryside in silvery light. Where there had been desert, there was now grass.

He opened the door and climbed out. It was warm, the grass soft under his feet. A dark shape—a horse—whickered a greeting. It came over to him, hooves thumping hollowly on the turf, and nuzzled his chest.

"Hello, old friend," Morgan said softly as he ran his fingers through the horse's mane. "Where are you taking me to this time?"

There was no answer. There never was.

But before he continued his journey, there was one crucial thing he had to do. He had to take his inner wrestling to the Father and lay it down. Morgan had broken the rules. He had tried to change the outcome of God's plan. He had sinned, plain and simple. And he had learned through bitter experience that unconfessed sin corrodes. It corrodes soul, it corrodes spirit, and it corrodes relationship with God. He had to deal with it, and deal with it immediately.

He dropped to his knees and began to pray. Ignoring the dampness that soaked through his jeans, he tried to pour out his heart to God. But the connection he usually felt when he prayed was not there, and he knew why. He had broken it with his disobedience. Yet, despite the lack of connection, he knew he must unburden himself and seek forgiveness to be right once more with the one he had served with all his heart.

What seemed like an eternity later, he started to rise to his feet, but a thought struck him. This was not just about him. There was another who had been touched by his disobedience.

Lord, please bless Kate. Protect her as she does the work you had me prepare her to do. If you can find it in your heart to do so, let her remember me. And let me honor the promise I made to come back to her. Release me from this life of mine. Take me back to Kate. Let me live a normal life once more—a life with the woman I love.

The still, small voice he longed to hear did not speak. He felt no sense of God's presence, no feeling of affirmation or negation. No peace, no calm, no sense that things would work out—just silence, as if the door to heaven were closed in his face.

Totally spent, he climbed to his feet and called Midnight back to him. As he wrapped his fingers around the horse's silky mane, pain stabbed through his left hand. Startled, he looked at the bandana wrapped around it. He'd almost forgotten.

The black stain on the cloth was evidence the wound had bled through. But it was not just his blood—Kate's was there, too, comingled with his. He felt a momentary surge of nausea at what he had done. But, he reminded himself as he climbed onto the waiting horse, he'd had no choice.

As Midnight carried him away from the abandoned truck, Morgan felt around in the breast pocket of his shirt, afraid his fingers would find it empty. It was not. Kate's picture was still there. It had survived the transition so far. There was still a connection. There was hope.

Chapter 2

Graduation day! Heart racing in anticipation, Lieutenant Commander Kate Trenary snapped instantly awake, images of yesterday's massive dogfight playing in her mind as she relived the thrill of leading fifty aircraft deep into simulated enemy territory.

She shot a glance at the clock on her nightstand and felt a wave of disorientation wash over her. That couldn't be right. The numbers were red. The clock in her BOQ room at Naval Air Station Fallon was green.

She fought momentarily to overcome the feeling of being in two places at once, but then reality crashed over her, and with it came a surge of bitter disappointment. She was home—not at Fallon. It was only a dream—but what a dream!

Another image from her dream surfaced, rocking her to her core. Soft music played. She swayed to the beat, her head resting against the chest of the man she loved. His strong, muscular arms surrounded her, holding her tight. She breathed in his masculine scent. Her emotions whirled. Her feet hardly seemed to touch the floor. She tilted her head back to look into his eyes. They were soft, intense, full of emotion. She felt as if she were drowning in their depth. Gradually he tilted his head toward hers. When their lips met, a volcano erupted inside her, causing her knees to weaken.

She clung to the memory, playing it over and over in her mind, focusing on every detail, anchoring each in her memory. Every line of his face. The curve of his mouth. The angle of his jaw. The feel of his strong arms holding her close. Most of all, what she read in his eyes and what she felt in her heart.

Surprised at the sudden moisture welling in her own eyes, Kate snuggled under the covers and replayed the delicious images, but a dull throbbing in her hand made concentration impossible. Baffled, she switched on her bedside lamp. She winced at the penetrating brightness and pulled her hand from beneath the covers, frowning at the dish towel wrapped around it, a dark stain showing where blood had soaked through. Her stomach contracting painfully, she fought to remember. How had she hurt herself? But hard as she tried, the memory remained buried.

She turned off the light and struggled to focus, directing her mind to take her back into the dream, back to Fallon.

She'd just finished a special TOPGUN course, one designed just for her. But why would she be dreaming of TOPGUN? She'd done it years before, when she was a lieutenant. Nervous tension, she told herself. Probably brought on by the stress of the day to come.

Everything was a fading jumble, hazy and unreachable. *I hope I remember something in the morning,* she thought just before she surrendered to sleep.

Words bursting into her mind with the intensity of a gunshot jolted her awake again. "This is real, Kate. You must hold onto three things and don't let go: your memory of us, the scar on your arm, and the cut on your hand. Whatever happens, don't lose faith. Our time together has been real."

The urgent words triggered another memory. This one at least was clear: two cuts, comingled blood. An archaic ritual. An unbreakable commitment, binding her to the man she loved more than life itself.

But her heart fell at the remembering. He'd said he couldn't stay for graduation. He had to deploy. But the emotion in his voice, bordering on panic, was unmistakable.

She ran her fingers down her right forearm and felt the small ridge where the sword had cut her. How long ago was that? Seven months? Eight? She couldn't remember.

Scar on arm, cut on hand, our time together has been real. She repeated the words several times in her mind, anchoring them in her memory, refusing to let them fade.

Dabbing at the moisture threatening to spill from her eyes, Kate struggled to retrieve what she could of the dream. She must remember! She tried to weave what little she had into a coherent whole, but there wasn't enough to work with. Only fragments floating gently away like soap bubbles on a gentle breeze.

Soon she was left with just a face. Brown hair, hazel eyes, rugged features. He was beautiful and she loved him. As she slipped back into sleep, that image fled too, and she felt her heart breaking at its loss.

Kate struggled toward consciousness, accompanied by the insistent chiming of her alarm.

As she swung her legs to sit on the side of the bed, mind still fogged by sleep, she had a sense of having dreamt something, something deep and complex. Something meaningful. She paused for a moment, trying to recollect, but nothing was there.

After a moment or two she gave up. The dream was gone, and she mourned its passing, knowing it contained something precious, important, a purpose to be realized, and most important of all, a love unlike anything she had ever experienced.

Get real, she thought as she staggered into the bathroom and snapped on the light. *It was only a dream.*

As she turned on the water to brush her teeth, a twinge in her hand arrested her. She looked down, saw the cut at the base of her thumb, and felt her pulse quicken. *How on earth did that get there?* She held her hand under a stream of warm water and watched a faint cloud of pink swirl down the drain.

It probably needs a stitch or two, she thought, but dismissed it. *Too much at stake today. A couple Band-Aids will have to hold it. Can't miss my first flight back after the accident.*

The accident. Adrenaline surged as she relived the moment. The panicked radio call. The column of smoke rising from Banger's funeral pyre on the desert floor. Two men had died, and the pain of it left an aching feeling of loss in her gut. Worse, she couldn't shake the nagging feeling that it was all her fault. Somehow, she should have seen the Air Force F-16 transiting her division's altitude block and warned Banger of the impending midair collision. There were those in the squadron who felt that way too. She'd heard the muttered comments. Seen the averted eyes.

Stop it, Kate. This is going to get you nowhere. The accident board absolved you of all responsibility. You need to focus on today. Another adrenaline surge. A month was a long time to sit on the ground. Skills atrophied, and this morning she was flying with Lieutenant Commander Animal Harnish, the operations officer of—and arguably the best pilot in—Strike Fighter Squadron 56, known to one and all as the Outlaws. They were taking up the squadron's two nuggets for a basic air combat tactics hop. She was going to need every ounce of her skill and concentration if she was going to put up a good showing against Animal. If she didn't, not only he, but the entire squadron would know. He would ensure they knew, rubbing her nose in it and solidifying his position as king of the hill.

As she quickly showered and dressed, the dream she no longer remembered continued to clamor for attention. Putting the finishing touches on her hair, she lectured herself in the mirror. "Focus, Kate. You're not some teenager moping over lost love. Today could be the most important day of your life. You have to get past this flight and then re-earn the trust of the squadron. If you don't, you're finished as a naval aviator."

Stomach sour with fatigue and tension, she strode into her kitchen, rummaged in the pantry for a protein bar, snatched her keys off the counter, and slipped out into the cool morning air. Time to go do battle.

Chapter 3

Transition

D awn found Morgan riding along a beach. Waves whiffing faintly of ammonia crashed on blood-red sand. A russet sun rose slowly, its orb stretching almost from horizon to horizon, but there was no warmth in its rays. He shivered and pulled his jacket tightly around him, tamping down a feeling of disquiet that rose within him at this terrible place. But with each step Midnight took, the sun shrank, became red then yellow, growing warmer in its change. He loosened his jacket as the sea retreated and sand gave way to a boreal forest.

As Midnight plodded slowly forward, a dizzying sequence of landscapes and seasons assaulted Morgan's senses. Mountains sprang up and retreated. Trees gave way to desert and then to savannah as summer became winter and then summer again.

With time, the dizzying changes slowed, and he found his path taking him through low, rolling hills dotted with oak trees and a few pines, punctuated by an occasional stone outcropping.

No contrails crisscrossed the sky. No engines revved. No horns honked. That much quiet could only come from the complete lack of human habitation. The occasional bird called from a tree, and he appreciated the company, such as it was. The only other sound penetrating the stillness was the rhythmic thump of Midnight's hoofs as he carried Morgan steadily eastward, away from Kate.

He made camp for the night by a crystal-clear brook bubbling up from the base of a rocky scarp. He gathered brush and built a fire as the sun dipped below the horizon, turning the sky into a riot of pinks, mauves, and reds. He was alone in this place, but still he kept the fire small, shielded behind a pile of boulders. Midnight grazed nearby. He would give the alarm at any approaching danger.

Miserable, with a heavy heart and a knot in his stomach, the last thing he wanted was food, but he forced himself to down some jerky. A whisper deep in his soul told him he would be needing his strength.

He pulled Kate's photograph from his pocket, stared at it in the failing light, his heart lurching as his eyes met hers. The camera had caught her in semi-profile, head tilted back, a laugh forming on her lips, white teeth gleaming, reddish-blond hair tucked behind her ear. Smoky blue eyes flashed with amusement.

Grief and regret welled up within him. How could he have let things get so out of hand? How could he have lost his heart and risked hers so badly?

Sitting alone in the semidarkness, staring into the fire, he wanted more than anything to go back to her, to hold her in his arms again, to beg her forgiveness. But it was way too late for that. There was no going back—only forward.

For the first time since he had been called to this strange life, hopelessness crashed down on him. In the past, he had been perfectly willing to go where he was led, face any hardship, stand up to any danger. If it cost him his life, he was content. But now, he had something new to live for, something he wanted but could not have.

And that's the whole point, Lord, he thought bitterly. *I sinned by seeking what I wanted and not what you wanted. You didn't prohibit me from falling in love. You encouraged me to love Kate, to reflect your love to her, but I chose to do much more than that. I interfered in your plan, tried to bend it to my will by binding her to me instead of simply letting her go as I should have.*

He stared moodily into the fire, stirred it with a stick, and watched embers soar, carried aloft by the heat of the flames.

He paused for a moment, hoping the still, small voice would speak to his spirit, but it remained obdurately silent. He began to whisper a prayer but stopped himself as awareness blossomed. *Stop focusing on yourself. You need to be praying for Kate.*

In the thickening darkness, he prayed for her safety. He prayed for God's blessings on her. He prayed that God would give her power to do his will. He did not pray that God would help her forget him. That was too much to ask.

Numbed to somnolence by the flickering of the flames, Morgan found his mind drifting, drifting to the moment it all began, the moment the Lord first spoke to him about his assignment with Kate.

He had left his previous assignment days before. Exhausted, he sat on a boulder beside the dusty road he was traveling and took a sip from his nearly empty water bag.

Listen, I have something to tell you. The whisper in his mind was quiet, soft, barely noticeable, but he was so attuned to the moving of the Spirit, his attention snapped to it. As he listened, instructions began to flow through his mind. He tried to slow his racing heart as the implications of what he was being told sunk in. He was being sent to a corner of creation that was just like his own time and place. He would be flying again—his task to prepare a young Navy pilot for a mission on which much depended.

But, Lord, it's been an entire lifetime since I've been back to my own time, Morgan protested. I barely remember my life as it was. You've had me flying any number of times during my assignments, but never the high-performance jets of my own time. I've forgotten everything I knew.

Have you? was the gentle reply, and with it came a warm, caressing wave of reassurance.

Morgan strode confidently into the classroom feeling a lightness he had not felt in more years than he could remember. A year of flying. Training, not combat. No hardship. No hunger. No danger. *This should be a piece of cake,* he thought. *And fun to boot. I can't wait to get in the air again.*

He stopped dead. In his wildest imaginings, he had not anticipated the slender figure at the front of the room rising to greet him. It had never once occurred to him that his subject would be a woman—even worse, a drop-dead gorgeous woman at that.

His first impressions were indelibly burned into his mind—reddish-blond hair, cut in a collar-length bob. About five eight or five nine, slender, soft curves only hinted at under her olive-drab flight suit. Smoky blue eyes that studied him intently, assessing him, measuring him, challenging him. Red lips slightly parted.

Adrenaline coursed through his body, and he had an immediate and inappropriate thought, wondering what it would be like to kiss those lips.

"Morgan Michaelson," he said, extending his hand. "I go by Merlin."

He could have sworn he felt a bolt of electricity cross the gap between his fingertips and hers, a jolt so strong it caused his heart to miss a beat.

A momentary startlement in her eyes, quickly masked, told him she had felt it too. "Kate Trenary," she replied, her grip firm. "Elsa."

Realization washed over him. This assignment was going to be anything but a cakewalk.

"Take a seat." He indicated the chair at the end of the table and, heart hammering, plopped down opposite, putting as much distance as possible between them.

He forced a mask of calm on his face as he tried to rein in his raging emotions. *Knock it off, for Pete's sake. You're no teenager experiencing a wild crush.*

"You and I are going to spend a lot of time together," he said, trying to keep his voice steady, "so we can save the pleasantries for later."

If she was put off by his tone, she didn't let it show. Her eyes locked onto his, staring disconcertingly at him like she was reading every emotion raging through his heart—no, deeper than that, reading his very soul.

His mouth was uncharacteristically dry as he fought the sensation of drowning in those infinitely deep pools of blue. He continued, "Let me explain how this program is going to work. We're going to go through all the phases of flying, starting with basic fighter maneuvers, similar, then dissimilar. We'll progress to air combat maneuvers, and air combat tactics, then do the same

13

with air to mud work. The main difference between this and a regular TOPGUN course is that we'll also be doing large force employment. A year from now when you graduate, you're going to be the best of the best. The pace is going to be grueling and I'm going to be hard on you—very hard—so get used to it.

"You'll fly almost every day, except weekends, spend lots of time in the books, and when you're not flying or studying, you're going to be working out, making sure that you can physically handle everything we throw at you."

He took a slow breath and looked for a reaction. If his words gave her pause, it didn't show. Her gaze remained cool, measuring, assessing. Perhaps it was his imagination that caused his throat to tighten, but was he getting the vibe that she liked what she was seeing as much as he did?

He spent the next hour walking Kate through the details of the program and what would be expected of her.

"There you have it," he said, wrapping up. "Two years' worth of flying packed into one. It's going to be tough, but you'll leave here flying better than you ever thought possible."

God, she's beautiful, he thought as he pushed back his chair and stood. *Have to keep this professional or you're going to be in a world of hurt.*

"You're free for the rest of the day. First hop tomorrow. BFM. Briefing is at oh six hundred."

He turned abruptly and left the room, not letting his eyes linger on her a moment longer. *Idiot,* he thought as he strode away down the hall.

From that moment forward, he had done everything he could to bury his growing attraction, but like a moth circling a candle flame, he found himself drawn inexorably to her.

*** *

Morgan rode eastward for several more days. Unaccustomed to the saddle, his muscles screamed at him to stop, but transition pulled him inexorably forward. The hills had ended a few days before, and now he rode toward the rising sun over a featureless plain of grass that extended from horizon to horizon.

It was already hot. He sipped carefully from his canteen, preserving the couple of inches of remaining water. The food he had brought with him was almost gone. He had never taken much with him on previous transitions. What he needed God provided. Whether it was a meal shared by hospitable strangers or an animal he was able to snare, he almost always had enough to fill his belly.

Since leaving Fallon, he had seen no sign of human habitation or any indication that people travelled this sea of grass. No house, no fence, no wheel print, no smoke, nothing. He was completely alone.

All the familiar rules of transition were in play. His jeans had given way to rough homespun wool. His denim jacket was now buckskin. The money he carried in his wallet had become a handful of coins. His ID and credit cards were gone.

Kate's picture had disappeared a couple of days before. He mourned its passing, but her face was so fresh in his mind that he knew he could recreate it in a few moments if given a pencil and paper.

Other changes were more telling, ominous. The Glock he had left Fallon with was now a Remington ball and cap revolver, his sleeping bag now a bedroll.

He saw his first sign of human habitation two days later. Trees began to spring from the prairie. He forded a stream, and a short distance later came across a dirt track. There was a hoofprint in the dirt—a shod hoofprint. He saw the first house long before its inhabitants saw him. It was a mean affair, with sod walls and a plank roof built into a hillside. A mother and two children silently watched him as he rode by.

That day he passed more houses and a small village. Everything he saw, the character of buildings, the rough clothes of the people, the tack of the horses, told him he was in America, not Europe. He guessed the time to be somewhere around the middle of the nineteenth century. It was not a comforting thought. A sudden premonition settled into his gut, causing a shiver to run down his spine.

Oh God, he prayed. *Don't let it be that. Please don't let it be that.*

He received his confirmation three days later. Midnight led him along a muddy road beside a river. Farmlands dotted the countryside. The warmth of the previous day was gone, and his breath fogged in the early morning dampness. A feeling was growing in his heart—a familiar feeling—that he was nearing his destination. A thought flashed across his mind. He had been dwelling on Kate. If he was where and when he thought he was, he was almost certainly going into danger. Grave danger. He had better start dwelling on the present, on this assignment, and not on the past.

He paused for lunch in a ramshackle roadside inn he figured would not deplete his small collection of coins too much and found a seat in the plainly furnished common room. A dour, stick-thin woman brought him a plate of greasy eggs and ham and a slab of bread. As she left, he asked her for a newspaper.

"I'll see what I can do," she replied.

He had only taken a couple of bites of the unappetizing mess before she slapped a grimy, well-worn paper on the table in front of him. "It's yesterday's," she said, forestalling his question.

The headline "Terrible Battle, Immense Slaughter" jumped off the page at him, causing his stomach to lurch and bile to rise into his throat. He pushed the plate away and read more closely. The story described a battle in which a Union army under General Grant had defeated a Confederate army in a place called Pittsburg. A long list of casualties took up almost an entire column. He stopped reading and looked at the date at the top of the paper: April 12th, 1862. His fear had just become reality.

Chapter 4

"Outlaw 11's ready." Animal's voice over the radio was hard, metallic.

"Outlaw 13's ready," Kate replied, pushing her throttles forward while snapping a quick glance at Lieutenant Junior Grade Justin Banks, call sign Jethro, hanging in position a couple hundred feet down her right wing line.

Twenty thousand feet below them the Panamint Range thrust northward to where Animal and Lieutenant J. G. Albert Otis, call sign Spud, were orbiting over the Saline Valley, defending an imaginary point on the ground. From her vantage point above Death Valley, the stark grays and whites of the desert floor looked more like the surface of the moon than any place on earth.

She bumped her radar out and immediately found them turning toward her from the back side of their orbit.

"Outlaw 13, contact three three zero for forty, twenty-five thousand, turning hot," Kate transmitted over the discrete frequency she shared with Jethro.

"Outlaw 14, same." Good. Jethro saw them too. She felt a surge of satisfaction. So far, the mission had unfolded just as planned. Spud and Jethro had performed almost flawlessly in their long-range radar work and tactics. Now, for the final engagement, Animal had upped the ante, requiring a visual identification before anyone could take a shot. This would bring the fight in close and result in a four-airplane dogfight that would quickly consume their remaining fuel.

Kate's ALR-67 radar warning receiver, or RWR, shrilled. She scanned her displays, noting the illuminated AI light and air-to-air threat symbology at twelve o'clock. Animal and Spud had found them on radar.

"One Three's spiked."

"Two same," Jethro replied.

She began a gentle climb, careful to stay subsonic as she watched Animal's track march down her right DDI. Those on the ground below took a dim view of having their peace disturbed by a ground-shaking sonic boom.

There was no need to lock on as Animal or Spud had done. She knew exactly what they were doing. Besides, she would lose them off her radar when she and Jethro began their evasive maneuvering designed to complicate Animal's and Spud's radar problem.

Closing at almost twice the speed of sound, their action point was upon them in seconds.

"Outlaw 13, action," Kate transmitted while hitting the chaff button several times, dispensing bursts of small strips of aluminum-coated glass designed to confuse an adversary's radar. As she did so, she yanked her jet into a hard, descending, left-hand turn. Without checking, she knew Jethro would be starting a right-hand, climbing turn away from her. If he remained targeted, he was to leave the fight. If untargeted, he was to swing wide around Animal and Spud and come in behind them.

Pointed almost straight at the ground, Kate pulled her throttles back to prevent her airspeed from building. Maintaining Animal's last known position at her three o'clock position, she was lost in the ground clutter, blind to his radar. To further confuse it, she deployed several more chaff bundles. Approaching the hard deck, she set her wings and pulled to where she instinctively knew Animal and Spud would be. Her RWR was clear. They had not found her.

Scrolling her radar up, she found Animal's flight almost instantly. Her eyes straining to catch sight of them, she held off locking on until the last minute so as not to give them a warning in their cockpits.

"Outlaw 14, double spiked, dragging." Jethro's radio call confirmed their plan was working. Animal and Spud were both chasing him. Kate was untargeted. This was playing out perfectly to her advantage.

She picked out two dots far above her, highlighted against the desert haze. Time to lock. Throwing her radar into boresight, she allowed the radar's automatic mode to lock the closer target but was still too far away to visually identify the type of aircraft and take her shot.

A string of red dots—flares—streamed behind the jet as it turned toward her. For a moment an F/A-18 Super Hornet hung in the air in perfect planform. She mashed down on the pickle button, sending an imaginary AIM-120 AMRAAM missile winging toward it.

"Fox three kill, F-18 right-hand turn, twenty-two thousand," she transmitted as she broke lock and acquired the farther jet.

This one was tougher prey. It had seen her and was turning hard to bring its nose to bear. The range decreased rapidly. Too close for a second slammer, she thumbed back to select her AIM-9X Sidewinder heat-seeking missile, while pulling her throttles to idle to cool down her jet, preventing his missile from locking and tracking her heat signature. Her missile refused to track, indicating he had done likewise.

Her target's response was quick, efficient, perfectly executed. She had no doubt she had removed Spud and was now up against Animal, who would undoubtedly give her a much harder fight.

They passed almost canopy to canopy, each in a hard turn toward the other's six o'clock, to all intents and purposes, neutral. Kate's heart hammered with exhilaration as she slammed her throttles forward and pulled hard on the stick. G-forces crushed her into her seat as she craned her neck back over her shoulder to keep sight of Animal, who suddenly reversed his turn back toward her, keeping it a close-in fight.

She pulled back into Animal, now well behind his wing line. She had gained the advantage, was on the offensive. *Come on, Animal. Let's see what you've got.*

Her mind was operating with a clarity she had never experienced before. With minute adjustments of nose position and g-forces, she anticipated and countered his every move.

She was far too close for a missile shot. The only option remaining was her gun. She settled into his plane of motion, aligning her flight path with his. Now all she had to do was control her speed to stay behind him while pulling her nose to point in front of his to establish lead.

Animal saw the inevitable and jinked violently downward, spoiling her shot at the last possible moment. Careful not to overtake him, Kate followed him through the turn, once more aligning flight paths and establishing lead.

Animal jinked again, but a slight preparatory wing dip had telegraphed his intentions. Anticipating his move, Kate rolled with him, keeping her nose in front, and as Animal's wings settled, she felt a surge of satisfaction as she squeezed the trigger. Pipper rock-solid on Animal's canopy, she transmitted, "Guns, guns, guns. Guns kill F-18 left-hand turn fifteen thousand," and pulled away sharply from Animal's jet.

"Outlaw 11, knock it off." There was no concealing the anger in Animal's voice.

In sequence, Spud, Kate, and Jethro crisply acknowledged the terminate-engagement call.

Animal's voice came clipped and terse on the radio as he directed his flight's rejoin and exit from the airspace.

Cresting the snow-capped ridge of the Sierras on the way back to NAS Lemoore, Kate dreaded the debrief that was to come. Animal was not going to forgive Spud's error in radar work. Even worse, he was not going to forgive her for having the temerity to outfly him.

Twenty minutes later, heart in her throat, Kate watched Animal stride toward her across the parking ramp. Tall, muscular, hair slicked back with perspiration, face dark with anger, he approached her with the menacing force of a tornado. She opened her mouth to say something, but he wordlessly brushed past her, forcing her to take a step back or fall to the concrete.

Kate bit back the angry words that sprang to her lips as she hefted her helmet bag and began to follow him toward the maintenance building. She shot a glance to her right. Farther down the ramp, Jethro, despite being parked next to Spud, abandoned his fellow nugget to a solitary walk to maintenance. Watching Jethro's retreating back, Spud shrugged and walked slowly across the expanse of concrete, a picture of isolation.

How on earth was I able to outfly Animal? she mused. Animal, one of those few pilots whose call sign so matched his personality that everyone forgot he had a given name, was a legend among the fighter community—truly one of the best of the best. She knew she was good, but not in his league. Given her rustiness, he should easily have humiliated her, not allowed her to outfly him. With a sense of dread, she knew he would find a way to make her pay.

She furrowed her brow as a niggle of worry grew in the back of her mind. First the dream she couldn't remember, and now this. What on earth was going on?

"It's great to have you back, Elsa," Commander Steve Nelson, known informally as "Digger" or slightly more formally as "Skipper," stopped her outside the briefing room in which Jethro and Spud were waiting for Animal.

"We've missed you up in the air," Digger continued. "I had no doubt the accident board would clear you. There was no way you could have seen that Viper nose-on miles behind you."

"I wish everyone would see it that way," Kate lamented. "I'm not sure I do myself."

"Listen," Digger's voice firmed. "Don't take on something that's not your fault. The squadron respects you. They'll move on."

Kate felt the claws of recrimination and regret loosen their grip, slightly. "Thanks, Skipper," she replied, forcing a thin smile to her lips. She found herself liking this handsome man who had taken over the squadron only a month before the accident and was still trying to navigate his way around the Outlaws' competitive culture.

21

"By the way, Animal's not too happy," Digger added, a broad grin creasing his deeply tanned face. "Sounds like you cleaned his clock out there."

The briefing room was sterile, utilitarian. A large whiteboard for reconstructing the flight took up one wall. Another was taken up by a large console with slide-out boards for briefing guides, emergency procedure of the day, and training rules. A rectangular table and chairs could seat a division of four pilots. Jethro and Spud sat silent across the table from each other.

Kate took the seat at the foot of the table and looked impassively at the two nuggets. Despite having joined the Outlaws at approximately the same time, they were a study in contrasts. Jethro—boyish faced, lean, bursting with nervous energy—struck her as a whippet, but a whippet with the personality of a Yorkie. Spud was something else entirely. Other than Animal's, Kate could not think of a call sign that matched its owner more perfectly. He had the personality of a potato and, unlike most fighter pilots who were lean and trim, he had the physique of one too—squat and solid. His eyes met hers and flicked rapidly away, his broad, meaty face expressionless. Wide and muscular, she had seen him in the gym effortlessly lifting weights she would not have been able to budge. Just another of the many ways he was . . . different.

Animal blew into the room five minutes later, his face a mottled shade of red, his neck muscles rigid cords. He reminded Kate of a bull pawing the ground, all aggression with little restraint.

A bull, dangerous and clumsy compared to Merlin's wolf but no less lethal. The thought flashed across her mind, just as quickly followed by, *Who's Merlin?*

"That was pathetic," Animal growled, his voice thrumming with barely suppressed anger. The words were addressed to all of them, but Kate felt an uncomfortable feeling grow in the pit of her stomach as she realized where the bulk of Animal's ire would be directed.

"Getting out to the area should be uneventful." Animal's eyes fixated on Spud and his face darkened. With that, he began flaying his hapless wingman for everything from his radio check-ins to his formation position.

Kate shot a sidewise glance at Spud who, face impassive, shrunk in his seat and retreated into himself. *Doesn't he care? Where's his pride? If Animal treated me like that, I'd be hopping mad.*

Animal covered the return to base in much the same way, continuing to flay Spud mercilessly. *Interesting. Jethro wasn't perfect out there. No criticism for him. He's one of the boys.*

Animal paused his tirade and fixed Spud with a withering glare before walking over to the whiteboard. Picking up blue and red markers, he reconstructed the mission in minute detail, drawing each engagement on the board, blue lines depicting his and Spud's flight path, red lines depicting Kate's and Jethro's until the board looked as if it were covered by spaghetti. Although he highlighted the correct decisions and errors each of them had made, the bulk of his attention was focused on Spud, dissecting his radar work and his air-to-air maneuvering, homing in on each error with the tenacity of a missile seeking its prey.

Kate gnawed her lip. Despite her dislike of Spud, Animal's incessant attack piqued her sense of fairness. She began to tally the times Animal glossed over Jethro's errors while savaging Spud's, but gave up the exercise after it became obvious that this was all about Spud.

Spud hunkered down under Animal's verbal lashing like a boulder weathering a hurricane. Kate debated speaking up, but that would violate the unwritten rule—he who has the chalk, or in this case the dry-erase markers, is the only one who gets to speak.

Animal drew himself up until he was nearly towering over the three aviators seated at the table. "We can cover the final engagement in our individual section debriefs." He glared at Spud again. "Your inept radar work got the two of us killed. You're going to have to do a whole lot better than that if you expect to survive in a combat situation."

In turn, starting with Kate, he looked the other aviators in the eye. "Given everything that's been happening in the Middle East, if the news that leaked out of Iran last month is true and they're about to test a nuclear weapon, then we're going to have to do something about it. The world cannot live with a nuclear-armed Iran." He fixed Spud with a baleful glare. "Think about that,

Nugget. If you believe you're even remotely ready to fly one of Uncle Sam's shiniest toys in combat, you got another think coming."

He turned to Kate. "You and Jethro are cleared off for your own section debriefing."

As she and Jethro rose to find their own briefing room, Animal turned his attention back to Spud.

How like Animal to engineer things so he doesn't have to address his own mistakes, Kate thought as the door closed behind her, cutting Animal's tirade off midsentence.

The debriefing with Jethro was a blessed relief compared to the misery of sitting through Animal's tirade.

"There you have it," Kate declared thirty minutes later. "You employed well today. If you practice the things I pointed out, your radar work will continue to improve. Between flying the jet, working your systems, and communicating, there's an awful lot going on. It's like a quarterback reading the field. With time, you'll do better and better at digesting all the information coming at you, and you'll make fewer and fewer mistakes."

Jethro looked pleased at the compliment, his eyes meeting hers for only the second time during the debriefing. *He's one of those who doubt me,* Kate thought and tamped down a slight surge of irritation.

As Kate stepped out into the hallway, exhausted, she heaved a sigh of relief. Time to hit the gym. Time to work off some of the stress that had been building since she woke up from that dream or whatever it was. But as she walked back to her office, a niggling thought crossed her mind. *What are you doing to make Spud part of the team?* She dismissed it impatiently.

Kate collapsed onto the sofa in the living room of her small rambler, almost too tired to move. She looked down at the bowl containing the Caesar salad with extra chicken she'd picked up on the way home and debated pushing it aside. *Nope. You've had a long day. You need to eat,* she admonished herself.

The blue numbers on the cable box caught her attention. 9:20 p.m. Where had the day gone? She never made it to the gym. With pre-deployment workups wrapping up, there was so much to do, and the days were just getting longer and longer.

She took a tentative bite of her salad and was surprised to find her appetite suddenly return. In moments the bowl was empty.

Lord, what are you doing to me? She unlaced her boots, pulled them off, and kicked them aside. Closing her eyes, she began to grapple with the problem that had bothered her all afternoon. Even on her best day, she could only hope to hold her own against Animal. She should never have been able to outfly him so easily. It wasn't that he was off his game. He clearly wasn't. She had just flown better. Where had she developed her newfound skills?

She fingered the Band-Aid covering the heel of her hand. Did it have something to do with that and the scar on her forearm she had no memory of receiving? If so, what? Was it tied to the dream she'd had the night before? The dream that lay just beyond the edge of her memory and left a raw, aching wound in her heart?

Was this something to do with Nick? The thought of her ex-fiancé caused her stomach to tighten. But no sooner had the thought crossed her mind than she dismissed it. Nick was blond, blue eyed. The man in the dream had darker hair and soft, luminous brown eyes.

Kate's heart jumped. There, she had something—something she could grasp. Perhaps she could leverage it into another memory. She closed her eyes, and with her fingers softly caressing the scar, searched for something, anything that might give her a clue. But there was nothing there. Her memory remained maddeningly closed.

Frustrated, Kate refused to give up. She pictured herself lying in bed, reliving that moment of waking up from the dream and tried to force herself back, yet again, into the recesses of her memory.

This time she found something and latched onto it, refusing to let it squirm away. Breathless with anticipation, she hauled it forward and let it blossom into her mind.

She sat in the front seat of a car—no, a truck, she realized. Her seat was reclined, her bare foot on the dash. She was relaxed, at ease, casually comfortable in a way she seldom experienced. Classical music played quietly but she could not identify the piece.

She looked over at the man driving. Strong profile, clean-shaven, not like the current trend of beards or a two-week growth of facial hair. Brown hair with a few strands of gray at the temples. Uncalloused, well-formed hands gripped the steering wheel.

"What's this one?" she asked, intrigued by the layered harmonies of the piece streaming through the speakers.

"Another movement from Bach's Brandenburg Concertos," he replied in a pleasant baritone. "It's not used in the movies as often as some of the other pieces we just heard, but it grabs me for some reason I can't explain." His face took on a far-off look as if the truck and the road in front of them were a million miles away. "Trust me, it's far better live than playing on one of these gadgets." He motioned to his phone nestled in the cup holder in the console between them. "Can you imagine living in a time when all music was live? When it was only ever played by real people on real instruments? When you didn't have it at your fingertips every moment of the day and night, when every music experience was a concert?"

Kate found herself bemused by the insight, and opened her mouth to speak, but as the uplifting strains faded, she found herself captivated by the dark, haunting strains of the next piece on his playlist.

"Let's skip this one." He tapped a button on the dash and another light, airy piece filled the truck's cab.

"No, go back," she said. It suddenly seemed important that she know why that particular piece bothered him, especially if he had chosen to put it on his playlist.

He obliged, and once more the organ and strings picked up their melancholy melody. "What's this one?" she asked.

"'Adagio in G minor' by Albinoni," he replied. "Even though it wasn't really written by Albinoni."

"It sounds really sad," she said, her heart growing more captivated by the somber tones. "What movie was it used in?"

"Several," he replied, his face subtly contorting as some memory seemed to cross his mind. "*Flashdance, Gallipoli.*"

"What's *Gallipoli?*"

"A movie about a failed British expedition against Turkey during World War I." His voice was low, strained, the words difficult to make out.

"I thought you didn't like to watch movies like that," she asked, puzzled.

"I don't," he replied. "I have it on the playlist because it's a beautiful piece, but it brings back memories." He turned his head toward her, and his dark eyes were full of pain.

"Care to share?" she asked, and reached out to lightly brush her fingers against his hand resting on the console.

"Maybe later," he replied, turning back to the road. "It's a long story. We've had a great day and I don't want to spoil it."

Just as fast as the memory had come, it turned itself off. She wanted to shout with frustration as she tried to prevent it from fleeing, to extract more, but nothing came. The vault door had slammed shut, the wheel turned, the locks firmly in place.

But she had something, she tried to encourage herself. While it wasn't the overpowering feeling of being madly, passionately in love, there was a sense of easy comfort in the memory. Of closeness. Of discovery. Perhaps of growing love not yet realized.

On impulse she pulled her laptop toward her and began to write, jotting down every bit of the memory she could recall. She had no idea how long she wrote, but as she hit save, she stifled a yawn and looked down at her watch.

Her heart lurched. Eleven thirty—way past her bedtime. She had to be up at five. How on earth had she just sat there for a couple hours daydreaming?

She shook her head to clear it. Tomorrow is another day. What new surprises is it going to bring?

Chapter 5

S tomach knotted with tension, Morgan allowed Midnight to set his own pace down a road that was little more than a ribbon of mud crossing the countryside. Albany, New York lay just a few hours' ride ahead.

Albany. Kate had said her family was originally from upstate New York. The thought triggered a memory, slewing his thoughts back to the early days of his relationship with Kate, a time filled with raw emotion and anger—when, to preserve himself, he subtly encouraged her growing rage toward him. When he fought to prevent himself from being captivated by those astonishing blue eyes. When, if he were honest with himself, he knew he was fighting a losing battle.

"You want me to do what?" Kate exclaimed, looking dubiously down at the bell-guarded dueling swords lying on the table before them.

"Ever handled a sword before?" Morgan answered, dodging the question.

"No." Kate shook her head slowly, a look of bewilderment mixed with anger on her face.

"Consider it a focusing drill. You fence standing in a fixed position—"

"With sharp blades? Are you out of your mind?" Kate cut him off.

Exactly the thought he'd had when he'd first been taught to use to the sword all those years ago. The scars left by the experience were long faded, but the lessons learned had lasted him a lifetime. Now, despite his misgivings, he was about to teach them to Kate.

He regarded her coolly. Pink spots burned high on her cheeks. Her chest heaved with barely suppressed anger. *Man, she's beautiful,* he thought. *Thank God she hates me so much. I wouldn't trust myself one iota if that anger wasn't there—if, God forbid, she was interested in me. No, don't go there.* He forced the thought away.

Centered again, he continued. "It used to be common in some student circles. The idea is to cut, not thrust. You can do it that way, too, but it's more dangerous. The drill will increase your ability to hold a single thing in your mind to the exclusion of all else. It will also help you to stand strong in the face of personal danger and not shrink."

"I've been in combat before," Kate snapped. "I don't give up and I don't shrink."

Morgan had no doubt she was telling the truth. "I have too. Trust me. This is different. When you see a sharpened blade coming at your face, you'll want to back up, keep the danger at arm's length. This will help you take it head on."

Kate's eyes met his in an angry, defiant glare. "I'm not interested in getting sliced up just to give you another way of lording it over me."

He fought back the urge to relent and broke contact with those angry blue eyes.

"I'm very good at this," he replied, trying to keep his voice level. "I'm not going to slice you up."

Kate looked at him, incredulous. "You're telling me you've actually done this before?" She picked up one of the swords, weighing it in her hand.

Morgan nodded.

"When?" she demanded.

"Off and on," Morgan dissembled.

"Ever been hit?"

29

"Yup." He touched the fading scar on his right cheek. It wasn't exactly the truth. He'd received it in a vicious hand-to-hand melee many years before. The blow intended to split his skull had merely grazed him, but Kate didn't need to know that.

"Then you aren't perfect." There was a slight tone of satisfaction in her voice, and Morgan knew that even if it was going to require a little more persuasion, she was eventually going to pick up the gauntlet he'd thrown down.

"No, I'm far from perfect," he admitted sheepishly. *More than you'll ever know.* "I bleed like anyone else, but you won't hit me. I know what I'm doing."

Kate took a couple of tentative swings with the sword. She had no concept of stance or form, but he had no doubt she would pick this up quickly.

Problem was, he had no idea at the time how adept a pupil she would prove to be—how terribly wrong it would all turn out.

It was late afternoon when the road crested a hill overlooking Albany. He paused for a moment looking out over the town, its church spires standing tall, streets laid out in orderly rows, the Hudson River lapping against its feet. How much larger, more sprawling it was than when Morgan had last seen it a couple dozen years ago in his own life—but eighty years earlier in *this* time. A different war had gripped the country then, a time when all hung in the balance, much as it did now.

He forced the thought from his mind as certainty grew in his heart. This was the place. He had arrived. Now all he had to do was find the person he was sent to mentor, get the job done, and, God willing, get home to Kate. Simple, right? A twist in his gut warned him that, given the times, it might be anything but.

He found an inn and looked ruefully at the few coins he had left. At best, he had a night or two before his resources would be depleted and he would be on the street. "Lord, you'll provide," he whispered. "You always do."

Albany was the first sizable town he had come across since parting from Kate. After settling into his room, before he did anything else, he had one important task to accomplish, one that had been constantly burning in his heart.

Kate, I made a commitment to you when we parted. I promised to write to you faithfully, to keep the letters for you when we're reunited. You promised to do the same. By golly, I'm going to honor that promise.

As evening fell, he went out into the streets, found a shop that sold stationery, and bought a leather-bound notebook, a pencil, a dip pen, and a bottle of ink. Returning to the inn, he ate a light meal, purchased a candle, and went up to his room. It was small, plainly furnished, but at least it had a table and chair in addition to the bed.

He lit the candle, tore a sheet from the notebook, and spread it flat on the table in the soft pool of light. He held the pencil for a moment, visualizing the photograph he so wished he had been allowed to keep. With deft strokes, he outlined the shape of Kate's face and the flow of her hair. Pausing every so often to probe the corners of his memory, he filled in the details. An hour or so later, he was satisfied. Kate's portrait, in pencil now, filled the paper. Her eyes laughed at him. Her smile beckoned. He longed to somehow be able to reach into the paper and run his fingers over her soft cheek.

He stared at it for long moments, allowing memories to cascade through his mind. Good memories. There were a lot of them—far more of them than there were bad. Lord, how he missed her.

How was she handling the surprising change in her flying skills? How was she handling her emotional turmoil? Was there any turmoil? He had done what he could to provide her anchors to him, anchors deep into the vaults of her memory. Had they held? Was he real to her or was he nothing more than a dream dimly remembered, the way God had planned for it to be? The thought caused a surge of anguish in his heart.

With an effort, he brought his raging thoughts under control. He had to believe, had to have faith. He needed to write. It would help him maintain the connection.

But what to write? he wondered as he pulled the notebook toward him. Pour out his heart or be a little more restrained? Did it matter? After all, there was no guarantee that she would ever read his

31

words. For several long minutes he wrestled with himself and then began to lay his thoughts out onto the paper.

April 14th, 1862

My Dearest Kate:

I am writing you by candlelight from a small inn in Albany, New York. I pray that one day the Lord will allow me to give this journal to you, just as I pray he will allow me to read the letters you will have written to me.

Parting from you was the hardest thing I have ever done. I would have given anything to stay with you, but God had other plans.

The last thing I intended was to fall in love with you, but I couldn't help myself. Looking back, I think it happened the moment I first saw you. Your confidence, your smile, your spirit drew me in like no one else has ever done before. And, of course, it does not hurt that you are gorgeous. There you were, the girl of my dreams, sitting in the classroom before me. The rest was inevitable.

I have been traveling for days to get to where I am called to be. Each day has been agony, knowing it has taken me farther from you.

I hope there are not too many letters in this journal before we are finally able to see one another again. Each day apart from you is like a day without sunshine. God is my light and my life. You have become my hope and my dreams.

I pray Isaiah 40:31 for you:

but those who hope in the LORD will renew their
strength.
They will soar on wings like eagles;
they will run and not grow weary,
they will walk and not be faint.

When you sleep, Kate, dream of me. I love you.

M

He stared at the page. It could not even begin to contain the
depth of his feelings and the emotions roiling his heart, but it
would have to do. He hoped the journal was not too full before he
could present it to Kate. *If* he could present it to Kate, his fears
reminded him.

He blew out the candle and crossed to his bed. In the soft
moonlight streaming through the window, he knelt to pray. As he
did, it occurred to him that as much as he prayed for Kate's safety,
he should also be praying for his own.

Chapter 6

K ate heaved a sigh as she finished the safety report she had been reading and glanced at the clock on the wall of her cramped office. Fifteen thirty. Another week down, a little over three weeks left until deployment. She had just enough time to catch a quick workout before heading over to the club for an evening of alcohol-fueled camaraderie and storytelling.

It was the last thing she wanted to do, but it was tradition. Fighter pilots always gathered on Friday nights to swap war stories and talk tactics. Alcohol flowed freely and air battles were fought and refought with hands taking the place of jets. The bonding ritual went back to the earliest days of aviation, but she could certainly have done without it today.

She arranged the folders on her desk into a neat stack, locked her computer, pulled her flying jacket from the back of her chair, and made a beeline for the front door of the squadron building.

On the way out, Kate stuck her head into the XO's office. Commander Dave Jenkins, her boss, was seated at his desk, his ebony face twisted into a scowl as he stared into his computer screen.

She knocked softly on the doorjamb so as not to startle him. "Torch, I'm outta here. See you at the bar."

A loud commotion in the hallway behind her caused her to miss his reply. She turned to find Animal emerging from his briefing room swearing loudly. "FNG's dumber than a sack full of hammers. He has no business wearing a flight suit and flying a multimillion-dollar jet. He's going to get himself or one of us killed someday."

Face flushed with rage, he strode toward her.

"Out of my way, Elsa." Animal pushed past her into Torch's office and flopped down on the vinyl sofa opposite Torch's desk.

She felt a surge of irritation but quickly squelched it. Confronting Animal when he was like this was a losing proposition.

"Torch, Spud's gotta go." Animal's voice vibrated with frustration. "When's Digger going to realize it?"

Wanting no part of the conversation, Kate turned to leave and almost bumped into Digger, who had come out of his office to see what the commotion was.

"No, Elsa. You stay," he said as he strode into the office. "Close the door behind you."

Torch and Animal both rose to their feet. Kate trailed in behind, already feeling uncomfortable at the conversation she knew was coming. Digger dropped heavily into one of the armchairs flanking the sofa and shot a pointed glance at Torch, who was starting to sit back down at his desk. Torch sighed, came around his desk, and flopped into the other chair. Wishing she could be anywhere but here, Kate took the vacant seat on the sofa beside Animal.

She looked at her two bosses, comparing them. Digger—tall, lean, closely cropped blond hair already showing streaks of gray, accentuated by a deeply tanned face. Torch—equally tall but muscular, bald head cleanly shaven. Both radiating power and authority but also a subtle, ever-present tension Kate often wondered if anyone else perceived. The two men clearly did not like one another, but for the most part, they did a good job of not letting it show before the rest of the squadron.

She felt a growing sense of unease. How was she going to navigate the conflict between them? Would they force her and the rest of the Outlaws to take sides?

No, don't go there. She dispelled the thought and shot a sideways glance at Animal, who was leaning forward, red-faced, obviously still in a rage.

"Ok, Animal. Out with it," Digger said calmly.

In a lengthy, profanity laced tirade, Animal eviscerated the newest addition to the squadron, tearing apart everything from his flying skills to his awkward personality. Kate's stomach tightened painfully. Animal had a reputation for being hard on the squadron's pilots, but this was way over the top.

"Today's mission was the frosting on the cake," Animal declared, deflating, his rage spent. "His radar work sucked, and he's absolutely useless at ACT. He's a worthless toad and needs to go, before he kills someone."

Digger surprised Kate with his quiet, measured response. "You finished?" he said, ice dripping from each word. He paused, giving Animal the opportunity to respond. He did not, but she clearly saw the pulsing bulge at his temple.

"There's a process to take an aviator's wings," Digger continued, "and I initiate it, not you. Understood?"

Animal angrily met his gaze, but after a moment dropped his eyes. "Understood," he replied, resentment dripping from the single word.

Digger turned next to Kate. "Elsa, there's a reason I asked you to stay in here. You're safety officer and one of our most gifted instructors. You've flown with Spud a lot. Given the noise coming out of the White House, instead of showing the flag in WESTPAC, we may find ourselves deploying to Iran instead. Things could turn ugly quick. Can Spud hack it?"

Kate did not want the responsibility being thrust upon her. Animal was right. Every pilot deploying needed to be a full-up round. Spud was weak. He was awkward. He wasn't measuring up. Her gut told her he needed to go. She opened her mouth to say so, but she owed Digger an intellectual assessment, not an emotional one.

"Spud's basic flying skills are okay," she said, slowly, as she scrambled to marshal her thoughts. "He knows the fundamentals but struggles with employment. His BFM skills are marginal. His radar work needs improvement, but he's a nugget making nugget mistakes."

She shot a quick glance at Animal, whose eyes were boring into her, the red flush returning to his face. Torch's hooded eyes were impassive, unblinking.

"Performance-wise," she continued, forcing her voice to remain steady, "there's not a lot of difference between Jethro and Spud, but Jethro's doing a better job fitting in. The challenge with Spud is his personality. He's not very likable and the more we hammer him, the harder it's going to be for him to want to become part of the squadron."

Butterflies dancing in her stomach, she ignored Animal's venomous glare, focusing on Digger instead.

Digger returned her stare for a moment, then shot a quick glance at Torch. Kate could almost hear the unspoken *"back off"* before Digger turned back to Animal, his mouth set in a hard line. "Animal, as ops officer, it's your job to make Spud an Outlaw and get him ready for deployment."

Digger paused for a moment then continued, his tone firm, measured. "As a leader, there's only so much you can do through fear and intimidation. You can coerce compliance, but people will follow you only so far. If you want to sit in Torch's and my chairs someday, you're going to have to learn how to modulate your approach. Got it?"

"Yes, sir," Animal's reply came out as a strangled gasp.

Digger turned back to her. "Elsa, could you excuse us, please?"

As she obediently rose and headed toward the door, she realized Digger was not finished with Animal. "What is it about this you don't get?" Digger's voice was harsh. "I will not tolerate your publicly ripping apart my pilots . . ."

As she walked out to her car, a thought played over and over in her mind: *I'm so glad Spud's Animal's responsibility and not mine.*

As Kate climbed out of her midnight-blue Mustang in the gym parking lot, her anxiety over the conversation in Torch's office was suddenly sidelined by a burgeoning ache in her heart that was almost physical in its intensity. Something was missing from her life, something precious. But it wasn't just missing—it had been ripped away, leaving an agonizing, gaping wound.

Fighting the temptation to sink back into the seat, she hefted her gym bag over her shoulder. An exercise-induced surge of endorphins was just what she needed to settle her churning mind and emotions.

Entering the crowded base gym, Kate wrinkled her nose at the smell of sweat laced with disinfectant. Lisa McKay, her best friend since their Norfolk days, was not hard to spot. Taller than Kate, willowy, with long, black hair pulled back in a ponytail, she was a head turner wherever she went. Although Lisa was not an aviator, their shared faith and love of horses made them inseparable.

They started with chest presses. Mechanically, her mind still in a fog, Kate loaded the bar with two twenty-five-pound plates and slid onto the bench. The bar moved easily—too easily. She added twenty pounds and prepared to strain. It moved easily again. She frowned and swapped the ten-pound disks for a pair of twenty-fives. This time she felt her muscles begin to burn. She did three sets of twenty and finally felt the sweat beginning to drip from her forehead.

Lisa shot Kate a speculative glance as she helped her remove the added weights from the bar. As Kate spotted while Lisa cranked out her reps, a memory exploded in her mind.

It wasn't Lisa's face she was seeing but someone else's. The man from her dream, the one who had held her in his arms and kissed her so passionately. But the positions were reversed. She was the one under the bar straining. He was the one spotting. Her arms felt like overcooked spaghetti. "One more," he had demanded.

She complied. Trembling, burning, her arms forced the bar upward.

"Now another; don't give up," he said, an edge in his voice.

She was not going to let him have the satisfaction of seeing her quit. Hating him with every fiber of her being, she lowered the bar and groaned with effort as, muscles protesting, she raised it again.

It wobbled dangerously, but he put his hand on it, steadying it. Slowly, painfully, her arms reached full extension.

"Well done," he had said as he guided the bar back into its supports. Her chest heaving, she slid out from under the bar and stood facing him, defiant.

"Kate, you okay?" Lisa's voice jerked her back to the present. "You spaced out on me there."

Kate shook her head to clear the cobwebs of memory. "Sorry about that. I was thinking about something," she muttered as they moved over to the shoulder press.

Kate found she needed to add weights there as well. Same with the biceps and triceps machines. Same with all the lower body machines.

"What's going on?" Lisa asked as they started on the treadmills. "Animal get under your skin today?"

Kate's thoughts were a tangle of confusion. How to even begin to answer Lisa's question? "No, it's not Animal," she answered softly, her voice barely audible over the blaring music in the gym. "Just a lot on my mind, okay?"

Lisa shot her a sympathetic glance. "I get it. We'll talk tonight in the bar. Give us something to do while everyone else drinks themselves silly."

Muscles aching slightly, Kate climbed onto a treadmill and slowly cranked up the speed. She was surprised to find her normal eight-and-a-half-minute pace failed to get her heart rate up. She added speed until, astonished, she found herself settling in at a six-and-a-half-minute–mile pace. She never ran that fast unless sprinting. Yet, it was comfortable.

On the treadmill beside her, Lisa leaned over. "Trying to get something out of your system? Save it for next weekend's ski trip."

Mind whirling, Kate just shook her head.

Lord, what are you doing to me? First the flight, then the weights, now this. She felt a stab of fear. How could her body have changed so completely that she was easily doing something she would never have thought possible?

As Kate tried to process her thoughts, one mile became two, and another memory percolated to the surface of her mind.

It was fall, the temperature a pleasant seventy-five degrees—cool enough to run outside. Her dream guy was running beside her. She was tired and angry, having already run far past her normal stopping point.

"Another mile. You can do it," he demanded. "Dig deep. Find that inner reserve of strength."

"I can't." It took her two breaths to force the words out. Her legs felt like rubber. A blister burned on her big toe. Her chest was on fire.

"Yes, you can. Don't give up on me."

She stopped and, chest heaving, tried to fill her oxygen-starved lungs.

"Kate, if you make a habit of quitting, you'll never know what you're truly capable of. Keep running."

She raised her head to look at him. He was jogging in place, T-shirt soaked, face red and dripping with sweat. The look of censure in his eyes struck a nerve. She started running again.

With each step, she felt her resentment grow. In the air or on the ground, nothing was ever good enough for him. He was always pushing, always demanding more. As she ran, her thoughts focused down to one laser-sharp point—no matter what it took, one day she was going to beat him.

"Kate, time to go." Lisa's voice snapped Kate abruptly out of the memory into reality. She looked down and was shocked to see she had already put three and a half miles behind her.

Mind whirling, she stepped off the treadmill. What on earth had just happened? More intriguingly, how could she both love and hate the same man?

Chapter 7

Lord, lead me to the person you want me to help. Morgan breathed a silent prayer as he closed the inn door behind him and stepped out into the street. He paused and took a deep breath of early morning air, redolent with once-familiar smells. Smells of animals and of people living close together with inadequate sanitation.

For the better part of the morning, he prayerfully walked the streets of Albany, waiting for the gentle nudge, the quiet whisper that would lead him to the one he was to serve. He felt nothing. He walked past bustling shops and strolled along quiet, prosperous streets fronted by yellow-brick row houses. He passed the vast, columned portico of the capitol building and studiously ignored the entreaties of a handful of soldiers in blue who were raising a regiment for the state. No pull. No nudge. Silence.

By early afternoon, clouds had driven the sun from the sky and were threatening rain. His stomach growled from the lunch he had forgone so he could save a few pennies. He walked by the river swirling brown, a myriad of boats anchored along the waterfront, a forest of masts rising above them. He jostled with the stevedores loading and unloading. He elbowed his way through crowds. No pull. No leading.

He glanced uphill. Maybe it was time to walk the newer residential areas again. Head down, he started the trek upward. It was too early to be discouraged, he tried to tell himself. These things took time. God would lead him to the one he was to serve, as he always did. His foot slipped in something wet, and his nose crinkled at the smell.

How he would have loved to exchange it for the pungent, slightly sweet smell of jet exhaust—to be walking the flight line, ready to take to the sky.

He felt an occasional drop of moisture on his face as he walked past rows of snazzy two- and three-story brick houses. The streets were cobbled and lined with young trees that in a generation or two would provide a canopy of shade over the neighborhood. Still nothing. With an effort of will, he pushed back a growing feeling of panic. Perhaps he should go to the other part of town where the less fortunate lived, those who earned their living off the strength of their backs.

He walked along unpaved streets with houses jammed together and a myriad of smells that would have gagged a maggot. Worn, tired women hurried to haul washing off lines as the rain began in earnest. People scurried past him, heads down and collars up against the rain.

He prayerfully walked the streets until late afternoon. The rain stopped, the clouds dissipating as fast as they had formed. The sun dried the streets and rooftops in a haze of rising steam.

He walked the waterfront again. Once again there was nothing. He turned his back to the river and started toward the hill yet again, ready to call it a day. As he did so, a memory of Kate began to surface, causing his mounting panic to subside. They were standing together in church, sharing a hymnal, joy shining from her face as she sang. He would have loved to have opened the memory fully, drawn comfort from it, lost himself in it, but he was here for a purpose. A stroll down memory lane would only serve to distract him. He impatiently tried to push it away, but it refused to leave.

He suddenly felt an overwhelming urge to find a church and pray. A double-spired building several blocks away caught his eye.

He studied the church as he approached it. A red-brick affair with tall, arched windows, it sat several feet above street level. A wide flight of steps led upward toward double doors situated between the two steeples. A cluster of people stood outside talking animatedly. A couple of men sat on the steps taking in the last of the afternoon sun.

He started toward the door, thinking to spend time kneeling at the altar. He was about to brush past a hunched-over figure seated halfway up the steps when he felt the nudge he had been waiting for. As always, it was nothing strong, not an *aha* moment—just a quiet sense in his spirit that here was a person who needed him.

He did not immediately react but continued to the top of the stairs and examined the figure from a distance. The style and cut of his clothes indicated affluence. This was not a laborer but somebody from the upper class, probably educated, certainly wealthy. His shoulders shook and Morgan felt a stab of shock. The man was crying.

Just as quickly, compassion welled up inside him. What tragedy would make a man break down in public, especially in a society where emotions were normally rigidly controlled?

Lord, you brought me here. Show me how to approach this man. Show me what you want me to do.

The still, small voice did not answer, but the feeling of compassion in his heart continued to grow. Unable to hold back any longer, he went back down the steps and sat down beside his newest protégé. Seeking to offer comfort, he extended his hand to touch his shoulder.

The other started and turned toward him. As he stared into the familiar face, shock and adrenaline coursed through Morgan's veins. It was Kate! His heart lurched painfully. Then common sense stepped in. It could not be Kate. This was a young man, hardly more than a boy, but he had Kate's eyes, her features, her reddish-blond hair. A closer look showed him differences. His face was fuller, the nose different. Yet, the resemblance was striking. He looked to be about ten years younger than Kate. About twenty, Morgan guessed, twenty-one at most. A few faint wisps of hair clung to his upper lip and chin. His eyes were red-rimmed. He reeked of alcohol and cigar smoke. His breath was sour with vomit.

"I'm sorry if I'm intruding," Morgan said gently. "I saw you sitting there, and it looked to me like you could sure use a friend right now." He extended his hand. "Merlin Michaelson," he offered, and, after a quick internal debate, elected not to correct the automatic use of his call sign.

The young man made a visible effort to draw himself together. Habitual politeness caused him to grasp the proffered hand. "George Maxwell." His voice was baritone, well-modulated, educated. His eyes narrowed as he searched Morgan's features, ran his eyes down his unkempt, ragged clothes.

"I'm sorry, but I don't feel much like talking." He withdrew his hand sharply and rose to his feet. He stumbled, and Morgan reached out to steady him, but the young man shook off his touch with an irritated "I'm all right."

Somewhat unsteadily, he descended the steps and turned up the busy street.

Nobody said it would be easy. Morgan sighed to himself as he rose to his feet to follow him.

Wait. The command in Morgan's mind was sharp, insistent. *Let him go. I will bring you to him later.*

Morgan stood on the church steps, a sense of exhilaration growing in his heart. God had spoken to him. What to do now? There was only one thing he could do. He climbed the steps and went into the church to pray.

It was dark when Morgan finally made his way back to the inn. He wasn't hungry but forced himself to eat something before retreating to his room. By the light of a sputtering candle, he sat with the journal open on the desk before him. It was time to write Kate another letter. But what to write? That he had met a man who could be her many times great-grandfather?

Instead of an answer, a memory slowly coalesced in his mind, bringing with it a world of recriminations. A memory from the early days when his emotions were on fire and desire warred with restraint.

Morgan impatiently leaned against the front fender of his truck, parked outside the bachelor officer quarters. Although the sun was only just separating itself from the horizon, it was already warm—very warm. A trickle of sweat worked its way slowly down his back as he dropped his sunglasses into place over his eyes, cutting the glare. Where was she? Was she going to stand him up? He'd been hard on her the previous day and wouldn't blame her if she did.

He closed his eyes and tried to relax, let some of the tension brought on by constant proximity flow from his body. But it was no good. All he could see in his mind's eye were those extraordinarily blue eyes of hers, her lips, the stray strand of reddish-blond hair she repeatedly brushed away from her eyes.

A door closed and his head jerked in that direction. His mouth went dry as he spotted Kate walking toward him. She wore a faded red plaid shirt half-unbuttoned over a white camisole. Tight jeans covered long, trim legs. Well-worn boots, a battered belt, and wraparound Oakleys completed the outfit. Her hair, too short for a ponytail, was gathered untidily at the back of her head. She looked as if she were out for a day of work on the ranch. All that was missing to complete the ensemble was a Stetson, and he knew without a doubt that if she didn't have one here, she certainly did at home.

As hard as he tried, he could not stop his eyes from lingering. From slender hips to flat stomach to the slight rise of her chest, she portrayed an image of lithe, athletic grace. *God she's beautiful*, he thought. *But also more than a little intimidating*, he quickly added.

"Where are we going?" she asked curtly, in reply to his greeting.

"Reno," he answered as he opened the door for her.

She climbed into the cab and slammed the door a little harder than was necessary. "Why?"

"Marksmanship training."

"Why Reno and not on the range here?" she asked as he settled in behind the wheel. She turned and gave the duffle in the back seat a meaningful look. "Looks like you have an arsenal in there." If there was any hint of warmth in her voice, he couldn't detect it.

"Tactical range," he replied, sliding the truck into gear. "I figured we could take a down day from flying, and my muscles could use a break from working out and fencing. Besides, punching holes in paper is a great way to relieve stress."

45

She muttered something unintelligible, turned her head, and stared out the window in silence as he exited the base and sped north toward town.

Good. She's not in a mood for conversation. That'll help me keep some semblance of distance, stop me from saying something stupid.

Then why are you engineering an activity that will put you together for an entire day? his mind argued. *Admit it, you wanted to do something fun with her.*

Yes but, the coldly logical part of himself argued back, *it's all part of the plan. By nursing that competitive spirit of hers, I can keep her mad at me.*

He concentrated on driving. Kate sat motionless, head turned away from him. He couldn't tell if her eyes hidden behind those dark lenses were open or closed. Sitting next to her in painful silence was torture. It was his fault. He'd nurtured her resentment. A burning tightness that was more psychic than physical grew in his chest.

His mouth betrayed him. "I bet you're pretty good with a gun. Had to be, living on a ranch, riding the range." As soon as he'd spoken the words, he wished he could take them back.

She turned her head, and he was confronted by those mirrored walls covering her eyes. How he wished he could see them, take his cue from them, but he couldn't. He was adrift, would have to feel his way blind.

For an instant he thought she was not going to say anything, but finally she did.

"I'm not bad," she admitted. "Dad made sure I knew how to use one. Got me a Colt Python for my sixteenth birthday. We never rode out without a Marlin either. I can hit what I aim for."

There it was, the implicit challenge. She'd just upped the ante. Now he had a decision to make. He had no doubt he could outdo her on the range. He had years of training and practice on her. He could accept the challenge and add another brick or two to the wall between them. Or he could try to make it a fun experience and run the risk of causing the wall and his heart to crumble.

He sensed the tension in her, taut like a vibrating bow string. It wouldn't hurt to take away a little, would it?

"I'm sure you know basic marksmanship, but today we're going to do something different. Shoot/no shoot drills, shooting on the move, team drills. That sort of thing. We'll do this a few times throughout the course so that when you graduate, you'll be reasonably proficient at taking care of yourself."

She lowered her glasses and fixed him with a measured stare. "And why would I need to do that? Is this another one of those things like fencing? Teaching me something I'm never going to need?"

He took his eyes off the road and met her gaze for an instant. "You never know when you're going to need it. Hopefully you never will."

Kate lapsed into silence and looked back out the side window.

An irrational thought crossed his mind. Perhaps when the day was over, they could have a quick dinner in town before they headed back to base. *No.* The answer was firm and immediate.

But the image refused to leave his mind. A relaxing evening. A nice meal with a beautiful, intriguing woman. What could it hurt?

A shout in the street outside jerked Morgan back to the present. He stifled a groan as he banished the memory and tried to tamp down the wave of regret welling up inside him. *Don't go there. What's done is done and there are no do-overs.*

He looked down at the notebook. A blank sheet stared back at him. He closed it with a snap. No words would flow tonight.

While it would have been infinitely more pleasant to dwell on the blonde aviator who occupied practically every waking thought, he forced himself to put her aside and instead think of what the morning would bring, and of the man who had been placed in his charge. Thoughts churning, he slept little that night.

Chapter 8

31 January
NAS Fallon, NV

"Animal, give me your keys." Kate kept her voice low while projecting every ounce of authority she could muster. Animal towered over her, waving unsteadily on his feet, a glass of beer—his sixth, if Kate had counted correctly—clutched tightly in his hand. He normally relinquished his keys to her willingly at the start of a bar night, but tonight he had refused, his gimlet eyes meeting hers with a defiant glare. "I'm not going to drink that much tonight," he'd said. But he had. In addition to the beers, no less than a half-dozen tequila glasses lined the table where he had been sitting. Animal had consumed a quantity of liquor that would have felled an ox, but like his flying abilities, his capacity for drink was legendary.

Kate was aware of Animal's cronies' eyes fixed on her back. Trojan and Spanky, the Outlaws' maintenance and admin officers were both there, making her the only department head not in Animal's immediate circle. Then there were Toad, Mogas, Jasper, and Nemo, some of the Outlaws' younger pilots. And rounding out the tally for the evening, Jethro, who was doing everything in his power to become one of the gang.

"Animal, you're in no shape to drive." She kept her voice calm, trying to sound reasonable. "With everything you've had to drink, you're way over the legal limit."

Animal's eyes hardened. "I'm all right, dammit," he spat from behind clenched teeth. "Are you my mom? I don't need you or anyone else to drive me home." He teetered dangerously and clutched a chair back for support.

"Animal." Kate couldn't keep the exasperation from her voice as she held out her hands. "Just give me your keys or I'll call the SPs the moment you walk out of the club."

"You wouldn't dare." Animal glowered at her, still swaying unsteadily. "You do that, and you're done as an Outlaw."

"You drive drunk, you're done as a naval aviator," Kate retorted. She saw a flicker in Animal's eyes and pressed home her advantage. "Give me your keys."

"Oh, come on, Animal. Just do it," Trojan chided. "You're pissed because she tracked you yesterday. Don't take it out on her."

Animal opened his mouth as if to argue but then snapped it shut into a firm, angry line and fished in his pocket for his keys. He slapped them into Kate's hand so hard her palm stung. "I don't need no friggin' babysitter," he muttered as he turned back to where his cronies sat, huge grins on their faces.

Kate seethed as she made her way back to her seat at the bar. *You need to be able to fight your own battles, not have Trojan fight them for you.*

"That went well," she muttered sarcastically to Lisa as she flopped onto her stool and scanned the rapidly diminishing crowd of aviators. Normally she loved being around them. Their exuberance and zest for life was compelling. She was a fighter pilot to the core of her being. Flying defined her, and she loved being part of that small, exclusive community of like-minded souls. But there was a downside to the fraternity-like atmosphere of a fighter squadron. The wild partying and heavy drinking clashed head-on with her faith. She and Lisa had come up with a compromise. Although they enjoyed an occasional glass of wine, they would not drink at the bar, but instead would serve Kate's fellow aviators as designated drivers.

Kate looked at her watch and stifled a yawn. Although it was late, the hardcore drinkers would be at it for at least another hour or two.

"What was with you at the gym this afternoon?" Lisa popped the question Kate knew had been on the tip of her tongue all evening.

Kate tried to marshal her thoughts but was interrupted by a raucous shout from the far side of the room. Jethro raised a full shot glass of tequila and downed it in a single swallow to the cheers of his compatriots.

She turned back to Lisa, who was observing her shrewdly, one eyebrow raised in anticipation. "I know you too well, Kate," she said drily. "You're not going to dodge the question this time. Out with it."

What to say? That I've had some dream and, all of a sudden, I fly better and I'm stronger and faster because of it? That I met some guy I'm in love with, even though I hate his guts? That makes no sense.

"There's something different about you—a glow that hasn't been there for a long time." Lisa paused and studied Kate's face. Something in it must have revealed the truth because she clapped her hands and declared gleefully, "You've met someone. I was beginning to wonder if you'd ever get over Nick. Is the Ice Queen finally starting to thaw?"

Kate felt her face begin to burn, not just for Lisa's use of Kate's hated call sign, but also for bringing up her ex-fiancé—he who was never to be mentioned.

Her throat tightened as a memory she'd kept firmly buried resurfaced in her mind. Nick, red-faced, his voice trembling with fury as he spat out the words: *"Elsa is the perfect call sign for you. The Ice Queen. How appropriate. I can't compete with your career and your rigid perfectionism anymore. I'm done."*

"That's not fair," Kate snapped back at Lisa. But her anger vanished at the hurt expression that flashed across Lisa's face.

"Sorry," Kate said sheepishly. "I guess I'm more on edge than I thought." But how on earth could she tell her friend who knew her better than anyone else in the world what was really happening inside of her?

As if sensing her discomfiture, Lisa relented. "If it's a guy, we can talk about that later. If it's Animal, well, look at him . . ." Her voice trailed off and Kate followed her gaze. The line of shot glasses in front of Animal was steadily growing. Red faced, still gripping his chair, he regaled his crowd of admirers with another war story. He paused to down another shot and slammed the glass down on the table so hard Kate was surprised it didn't shatter.

Jethro, standing at Animal's side, mimicked him and staggered backward as he lost his balance. Trojan shot out a hand to steady him, and Jethro, balance restored, slammed his glass on the table beside Animal's.

"That's a competition he's going to lose," Kate commented.

"Where's your other nugget?" Lisa asked, her eyes quickly flicking over the crowded room.

"Spud?" Kate snorted, feeling her mouth curl with distaste. "You won't find him in here," she said dismissively. "Hanging out with the bros is the last thing he wants to do."

Lisa twisted her mouth into a wry smile. "I just push paper—I'm glad I don't have your problems."

"Not really my problem," Kate responded flippantly. "He works for Animal, not me."

"The president made it perfectly clear on the news this morning he will not allow Iran to have nuclear weapons. If we end up in a shooting war, maybe Spud really is your problem," Lisa commented drily. "After all, you'll be leading missions he'll be flying in."

As Kate let the thought circulate in her mind, she did not find it sitting well at all.

Lisa covered a yawn with the back of her hand. "Kate, I'm really tired." She looked around the room, surveying the handful of remaining pilots. "I think you've got this. Mind if I head out? You want to get together for breakfast tomorrow?"

Kate shook her head. "Wish I could, but I need to come in and plow through a bunch of paperwork if I'm going to have a chance of making our trip next weekend."

Her friend shot her a sharp glance. "Kate, you promised. It's Whistler. We won't get our money back if you cancel. Besides, it's your last chance to unwind before you're gone for the better part of a year."

"I know," Kate replied, dropping her head and staring down at the condensation surrounding her glass of club soda. "Look, even if I have to work all day tomorrow and later every night this week, I'll be there, barring some catastrophe." Kate shrunk slightly under Lisa's assessing gaze. "Listen, I mean it," she hastened to add.

Lisa held her eyes for a moment before sliding off her stool. "I'll hold you to it. See you in church Sunday."

Alone at the bar, Kate surreptitiously touched the Band-Aid on her hand before gliding her finger along the hard ridge of skin on her forearm. "How did you get there?" she whispered softly.

These things were supposed to be indicators that something was real, but what? A dream? Dreams aren't real. Then how do you account for lifting more weights than you've ever lifted before? Or running faster than you ever thought possible?

Another thought bubbled to the surface of her mind, adding to her discomfort. Was Lisa right? Was Spud really her responsibility? *God, I hope not.* The thought was automatic, visceral.

She looked at her watch again. Almost closing time. Mission accomplished. She had Animal's keys and would keep him and Jethro off the road tonight. Being a good wingman was all about watching your buddy's six.

***

"When are you going to tell me about this guy you met?" Lisa whispered in Kate's ear as they waited for church to start. "You seem distant, preoccupied."

If only Lisa knew the truth of it. Too bad he was only the stuff of dreams, but as good a friend as Lisa was, Kate wasn't quite ready to share the truth with her.

From their spot near the front, Kate watched the band members tuning their instruments. She would have to dodge the question for only a moment or two longer.

She shook her head. "Just thinking about work and all the things going on in the squadron," she dissembled. "It's good to be back flying again, but some of the guys are still holding the accident against me."

A sudden blast of music drowned out Lisa's reply.

Lord, between the squadron and the dream, I've been tied up in knots these past couple days. Help me lose myself in you. Help me find just a little bit of peace, okay? Kate raised a hand, closed her eyes, and swayed gently to the music, reveling in the presence of God. The majestic melodies of "Forever" washed over her, entwining her, lifting her up.

Deep in her soul she felt a flood of love and affirmation filling her, and she gave herself to it fully.

"Forever" gave way to "Break Every Chain," and the incredible feeling continued to grow in her heart.

Lord, break every chain in me that holds me back from being closer to you. I want to know you better, to be closer to you. She was bouncing on her feet now, giving herself totally to the feeling of worship growing and burning in her heart, stretching her hands high, continuing to bask in God's love.

Without warning, the feeling was shattered, driven away by a discordant memory . . .

She frantically manipulated the controls of her Hornet to get away from the jet camped at her six o'clock, but no matter how hard she tried, it stuck behind her. A voice she was coming to hate—Merlin's voice—came over the radio. "Tracking kill, Hornet right-hand turn, twenty thousand. Hammer One, knock it off."

"Hammer Two, knock it off," she responded automatically to the terminate-engagement call as she leveled her wings and pulled her nose up to the horizon.

In church, Kate's hand came down and the music faded away as memories continued to crash over her—whole waves of them.

In her dream, she was back at TOPGUN, the only student of a yearlong course when the normal course was nine weeks. It was the most intense, demanding flying she had ever done. It tested her and honed her skills until she was flying far better than she had ever dreamed before.

More engagements flashed through her mind, the outcome always the same. At times, she would come close to winning, but at the last minute, Merlin would defeat her shots and then, through some skillful manipulation of the controls, end up behind her.

She asked him about his call sign. He'd earned it, he said, because he could do magical things with a jet. She could believe it and vowed that one day she would outfly him. It never happened.

With each passing sortie, her frustration grew. Almost as if watching it on a movie screen, she saw the ugliness of her attitude toward him, her resentment, her growing dislike. It horrified her.

"Was I really like that, Lord?" she whispered.

She sank to the pew and buried her head in her hands. Is this how I really am—petty, resentful, jealous? How could I be so consumed by hatred? I'm not like that, am I?

Tears ran down her cheeks as she tried to come to grips with her feelings. An undercurrent of thought ran through her mind. *This is not real, this didn't happen.* But she couldn't make the excuse stick.

Lisa sank to the pew beside her, put her arm around her, offering comfort. But Kate's overwhelming horror made comfort impossible.

Deep inside her heart, she knew this was not all there was. Something worse lay buried, waiting to be dug up. She tried to find it, to pull it to the surface, but it eluded her, like a frightened animal, burrowing deep to avoid any possibility of being brought into the light.

Chapter 9

S un was streaming through the chinks in the shuttered
windows as Morgan sprang awake. He felt a sense of lightness
in his soul that had been absent for a long, long time. At
Fallon, his optimism had been crushed by the knowledge he would
be parting from Kate. But now it was back. He was admittedly in
a time he would have given anything not to have visited, but at
least he had found the man God was sending him to. Now all that
remained was to discern and accomplish his task.

As he dressed, he considered the coins on the table beside him.
There were only enough for another night, two at most. Last
night's meal would have to carry him until evening. If the Lord did
not bring him to George soon, he was going to have to find
cheaper lodgings, and a job.

Morgan began the day by pacing the streets once more. As with
the day before, there was no pull. No leading. No gentle whisper
to his spirit. He prayed as he walked but could not dispel the faint
glimmer of anxiety hovering in his gut. How long was this going
to take? What was his real purpose in this time? What need did that
young man on the church steps have that only he could meet?

George had been well-dressed. Could Morgan catch a glimpse
of him by walking the streets of the better neighborhoods?
Perhaps. So for the better part of the morning, he walked streets
lined with mansions and neat, tidy rows of houses. Nothing.

Perhaps the young man worked in one of the businesses toward the heart of town. His sense of anxiety growing, he tried there. Again nothing.

At noon he paused by city hall, attracted there by the sound of a drum. The soldiers were back. A burly, dark-haired man, eagles on his epaulettes, sword at his side, climbed a makeshift platform and began to harangue a gathering crowd of onlookers in a fervor of patriotism.

Oh man, you have no idea. Morgan hung back by a spreading elm just starting to send out tender shoots of green. *What are you going to do the first time you hear a round go past your ear, hear the roar of cannon fire, and see your men dropping all around you?*

A wave of compassion washed over him as he saw a handful of young men step out of the crowd and up to the table. He did a quick calculation. *Three years before you come home, if you ever come home.* Too much lay before them to ever make that likely. The Civil War was the deadliest war in American history—a war in which old-world tactics crumpled in the face of evolving technology. He remembered the names of battles, names linked with unimaginable slaughter: Antietam, Fredericksburg, Gettysburg, Cold Harbor, some of the bloodiest battles in American history. All these lay ahead. Would any of the men so eagerly stepping up to the table live to see their families again?

He could bear to watch it no longer and turned quickly away. He'd only taken a couple of steps when he caught movement out of the corner of his eye. Perhaps it was the disheveled, once-natty clothing that had caught his attention, perhaps it was the flash of red hair under a hat pulled low. The blood drained from his face as he spun and tried to force himself through the crowd of onlookers, but it was too late. George Maxwell stood before the recruiting sergeant, the colonel looking on, his face beaming.

"George!" Morgan shouted, but the young man did not hear him over the noise of the crowd. He elbowed his way frantically toward the table where George was adding his name below those who had joined the regiment earlier. "Stop!" he shouted again, fear causing his voice to raise. He clutched at the younger man's elbow, but George impatiently shook him off.

"Back away," a soldier ordered, stepping between them, musket held across his chest as a barricade. This scene had obviously played out before as wives and lovers had tried to stop their men from enlisting.

Morgan could have dealt with the man easily, taken his musket away, used it as a weapon against him, but to what purpose?

Sick at heart he turned away. Feet dragging, he made his way back to the church where he had first found George, the church where the previous day he had found a modicum of peace. But that peace was gone, driven away by George's foolishness.

Morgan stood outside the church, despairing. He sat down on the steps, just a few feet from where George had sat the day before, and buried his head in his hands. But there was no one to minister to him as he had done to George. He was completely and totally alone.

What makes you say that? It was not so much a voice in his head, but a thought, barely imagined, soft, almost humorous. *Have you ever been alone since you started walking with Me?*

Of course I've been alone, Morgan snapped back churlishly. *You've left me alone plenty of times and in a lot worse situations than this.*

Really? There was amusement in the voice now, amusement colored with a love Morgan found impossible to ignore.

I'm sorry, he replied. *Please don't ask me to do this.*

But you must. It's the only way.

Can't you find some other way? Break his enlistment, something like that?

What's done is done. It cannot be undone. An old thread has come to an end. A new one is being woven into the tapestry of creation. You have a part to play in the weaving of that thread.

But this? You can't ask this of me. I've done enough already. Please just let me go home, find Kate somehow. Can't you send an angel to take care of this guy?

Morgan felt a flicker of love caress his mind. *Of course I could, but that is not My choice. My choice is for you to be the one who leads him to me. If he will come,* the voice added.

Every fiber of Morgan's being rebelled against what was being asked of him, but he felt his objections draining away before he could begin to frame the thoughts. Yes, the Lord had asked much of him over his many years of ministry, but at the same time, he had always provided.

"Lord, I don't want this," Morgan muttered under his breath, forcing his mind to form the words, "but your will be done. Where George goes, I follow. Just help me do what you're asking me to."

The voice chose not to respond, but Morgan felt the faintest tickle of a caress in the deepest recesses of his mind.

Words from the twenty-third Psalm filled his mind as he got to his feet: "Even though I walk through the darkest valley, I will fear no evil, for you are with me . . ."

The next morning as the sun broke the horizon, Morgan gathered his meager belongings, collected Midnight, and rode into the countryside. In an isolated glade, he threw his arms around the horse's neck and buried his face in his mane, breathing in the animal's scent. He felt strangely reluctant to release him, but where he was going, he had no need of a horse, at least not for now.

He pulled back, stroked the horse's soft nose, and looked deep into his placid, dark eyes. He touched his forehead to Midnight's muzzle. "Goodbye, my friend," he whispered. "God bless and keep you."

Midnight nuzzled his chest briefly, snorted, then turned away into the woods.

Morgan trudged back to the city, fear weighing down his heart. Over and over, he prayed the words of Isaiah 43:1:

"Do not fear, for I have redeemed you;
I have summoned you by name; you are mine.
When you pass through the waters,
I will be with you;
and when you pass through the rivers,
they will not sweep over you.
When you walk through the fire,
you will not be burned;
the flames will not set you ablaze.

For I am the LORD your God,
the Holy One of Israel, your Savior."

Rivers of difficulty and fires of oppression were certainly before him. *Dear God, don't make me do this.* It was an anguished cry from the depth of his soul. There was no answer. With each step he took, the conviction grew. There was no other way. He must do what the Lord called him to do.

The recruiting table was still there in front of city hall. He walked up to a massive, bearded sergeant. "I want to enlist," Morgan said simply, the words belying the heaviness in his heart.

The sergeant looked him up and down, asked a few cursory questions in heavily accented English. *Only a few years off the boat from Germany*, Morgan thought.

Finally, the sergeant seemed satisfied the man standing before him was suitable grist for the mill of war. "Name?" he asked.

The reply was as natural to Morgan as it had been in his earlier conversation with George. "Merlin Michaelson," he said without hesitation. It was the name Kate knew him by. It seemed fittingly ironic her ancestor would too.

The German scratched something on a piece of paper and pushed it toward Morgan. "Sign here," he demanded.

Only after he had scrawled his signature did he notice the sergeant had spelled the forename, "Merlyn." He felt a flash of amusement. That was different. But it felt right somehow. He let it stand. A moment later the paperwork was done. He was a private in New York's newest regiment, the 172nd New York Volunteer Infantry.

Chapter 10

Totally exhausted, Kate lowered herself into the hot tub. She and Lisa had skied Whistler's near-vertical mogul fields until the lifts closed and then made a high-speed dash all the way down to the village. "I hurt all over," she proclaimed as she sank to her chin in the steaming water.

Lisa let out a loud groan beside her. "You're crazy. If you're going to abuse me like that you can ski alone next time."

"Nobody forced you," Kate replied. "If I recall, you were the one who suggested we race to the bottom."

"I know, I know. I'm just so tired I want to go to sleep right here."

Kate put her head back and closed her eyes. *Lord,* she breathed as the heat and pulsing water worked its magic on her aching muscles. *I'm so tired, but it's a good tired. Thank you for this last weekend away.*

She allowed her mind to go blank, just enjoying the moment of intimacy with God.

With a nudge of her foot and one simple question, Lisa shattered her moment of peace. "Kate, what's that on your arm? I don't remember you having a scar there before."

Kate moved her arm from where it had been draped over the edge of the hot tub and looked down at the scar, pink, prominent against the tan of her forearm.

"Fencing accident." The words crossed her lips before she could form a conscious thought.

Lisa's eyes widened in surprise. "I didn't know you fenced."

Kate's mind almost shut down in her confusion. Where did that come from? "I—I don't." The words were more of a question than a declaration.

Suddenly she was a million miles away from the Coast Mountains of British Columbia, reliving a memory, sharp, defined—something experienced, not dreamed. Yes, she did fence. Morgan had taught her well. Too well.

This is dumber than dirt, Kate thought as she hefted the sharpened saber while wishing she had the rudimentary protection of a fencing mask and jacket. Every time they engaged in this exercise the same thought flashed through her mind: *I don't care how good he says he is, one of these days one of us is going to get seriously hurt.* But the anger and resentment burning inside her drove her fear away.

Despite her having executed perfectly during the morning mission, Morgan had still found areas to criticize, things so ridiculously trivial they were hardly worth mentioning. As he raised his sword in salute, she resolved today was the day she was finally going to beat him.

She launched her attack as he settled into his stance. With no conscious thought, she threw herself at him, letting reflexes and muscle habits drive her movements. Her attack was completely uncoordinated, but he had not been expecting it and staggered back, fighting to regain his balance. Time slowed to a crawl as she watched the point of her blade driving, inch by inch, toward his unguarded face. His sword, blindingly fast even in her time-compressed perception, drove hers away, but as it did so, she felt a burning sensation on her right forearm. In shock, she disengaged, fell back, and looked down at the line of red beginning to well.

He stepped forward, an apology on his lips, but she angrily motioned him away. Her pent-up frustration burst like a dam. She excoriated him for his fault-finding, his criticism, for nothing ever being good enough. Her rage drove her tongue, causing her to use

ROBERT EZELLE

words she had never before uttered in her life, but as she spoke them, she felt diminished, soiled, unworthy.

He faced her wrath calmly, his expression contrite.

"Let's call it a day," he said.

She felt lower than she ever had in her life, but she was not going to let it end there. "No," she replied, putting steel into her voice. She was going to finish this on her terms.

With her sword, she motioned him *en garde*. He demurred, but she insisted, rage still coursing hot in her veins as blood dripped from her arm. Slowly, reluctantly he raised his sword. She attacked again. Metal clashed loudly as she tried to find a way past the impenetrable wall his sword made in front of him.

She detected an almost imperceptible opening and slashed hard, putting every ounce of her strength into the blow. As fast as she was, he was faster, his sword flashing upward to protect his head. Her sword met his with an impact that jarred her arm all the way up to her elbow. Her rage evaporated in a nanosecond as she felt rather than saw her blade snap, the jagged stump now free, driving toward his heart. Off-balance, she tried to deflect it, but her momentum drove it inexorably forward. She watched in sickening horror as it pierced his chest just below his left shoulder. He sank to his knees, his eyes locked with hers, the unfathomable expression in them penetrating her soul.

Her remorse almost caused her to come unglued, but she hung on as best she could while waiting for the medics to arrive. She cradled his head in her lap and tried to staunch the bleeding. "I'm sorry, I'm so sorry." She repeated it over and over. Tears flowed down her cheeks and fell on his upturned face, but she didn't care. His eyes stayed locked on hers. There had been no anger in them, no accusation. As the medics arrived, he slipped into unconsciousness.

The long night waiting in the emergency room had been the worst of her life. How could she have let her rage control her so completely these past several weeks? She was a Christian. She loved the Lord. How could she have allowed anger to overcome the love she was supposed to feel for another human being? She felt

62

wretched—worse than wretched. She felt ashamed. Unable to bear it, she rushed to the restroom and emptied her stomach.

It was long after midnight when her mind at last began to calm and her thoughts came back into focus. She had known Morgan for, what, four months? Five? If she thought dispassionately about it, she had to admit that while he had driven her hard, he had always been patient, respectful. He had never put her down. He had never criticized her harshly. He had not participated in the dog-eat-dog environment of a fighter squadron where the strong were adulated and every hint of weakness was seized upon and savaged mercilessly. Yes, he had pushed her to the limit of what she could endure. Yes, he could fly better than she, but he had not lorded it over her as others would have done. In fact, he frequently complimented her, praised her when she had done well.

With another wave of shame, she suddenly realized she had not heard the positive words—had only zeroed in on those she had perceived as criticism. Her animosity toward him was entirely unjustified. It had been her pride, her need to win that had brought her to this, the lowest point in her life.

They let her see him as the early morning sun started to bathe the waiting room.

Morgan lay sedated but breathing regularly. She stood there looking at him for long moments, not knowing what to do. Finally, she crossed over to the bed, bent down, kissed his forehead, and whispered in his ear, "I'm so sorry. Please, please forgive me."

As her lips touched him, a shocking question burst into her mind—was all her rage and anger masking a completely different emotion? Something deep, something special? She reeled under the implications.

"Kate, what's going on?"

Lisa's voice impinged on the stream of memories, snapping Kate back to the present. "You completely checked out on me."

Kate fought a wave of disorientation. The sudden transition between memory and the present was too much. She shook her whirling head to clear it. "Sorry, Lisa," she replied. "Just trying to wrap my brain around something. Give me a moment, okay?"

Lisa relaxed back into the hot tub, but the expression of concern did not leave her face.

Kate closed her eyes again. How to process this sudden influx of memories? How to sift through them and make sense of them? As she succumbed to the massaging comfort of the water surging around her, one thought became crystal clear: Her imaginary dream guy now had a name to go with his call sign. Morgan. Morgan Michaelson. More than that, she realized with a shock, he was someone she could happily spend her life with.

***

19 February
NAS Lemoore, CA

"What an unmitigated disaster." Kate pronounced the words slowly, deliberately, struggling to keep her anger from creeping into her voice. She looked at the other three pilots in the briefing room, sensing their frustration.

Gator, her section lead, wore an angry flush on his face while studiously ignoring her gaze. Nemo, her wingman, squirmed unhappily in his seat. There was no question where their animosity was focused. It was not directed at her, who as leader of the division of four aircraft should bear the blame, but rather at the junior member of the flight—the nugget who had let them all down.

It was going to be a long and painful afternoon as she dissected the mission, engagement by engagement. This should have been Animal's flight, but he was mysteriously absent. Had been since the weekend.

Taking a deep breath and trying to keep her voice level, emotionless, she began the debriefing. "Start, taxi, takeoff, and to and from the area were all standard," she began. "Spud, you took forever to get on board. We were halfway to twenty-five oh eight before we had the formation together." Kate paused momentarily to frown at him. "The rest of the flight to and from the area was uneventful—"

"I was conserving gas," Spud said, cutting her off.

"What are you talking about?" Kate snapped, caught off guard.

"The rejoin," Spud replied, his high-pitched, nasal voice grating on her ears like fingernails on a chalkboard. "I couldn't catch you and didn't want to use gas we needed later."

Kate felt a hot flush suffusing her face. "Spud," she said, making only a token attempt to keep the irritation from her voice. "We've moved on. Don't interrupt me. I don't care what you have to do to rejoin expeditiously. Tap burner if necessary. Just be where you're supposed to be."

Spud sat back abruptly in his chair, his face turning a dull red.

Kate tried to slow her racing heart. "This was supposed to be a simple four v. four DACT mission against Fresno F-15 Eagles. Because of a number of execution errors on our part, they handed our butts to us."

She took a deep breath and started to draw on the whiteboard, using red markers. "The first engagement they came at us in two groups, lead trail separated by five miles with a 15,000-foot altitude split."

She turned away from the board, paused, and glared briefly at each of her wingmen in turn. "A simple presentation that we should have been able to deal with easily."

Picking up a blue marker, she began to draw, her voice vibrating with aggravation as she reconstructed the fight. "We came at them in a wall. Nemo and I correctly targeted the leaders. Gator, the trailers were yours and Spud's responsibility . . ."

Fifteen minutes later, she turned to her flight. "To summarize, Spud, you locked Gator's bandit. Gator, you didn't recognize it. You both died because of it. Let's look at the radar recordings and see how this mess happened."

In the air, she had clearly seen the debacle unfold on her radar, had formed the three-dimensional picture in her mind of where all players, both friendly and adversary, were at all times. Now it was just a matter of looking at the recordings to validate it. With all

65

four radars displayed on a large flat-screen TV, she played the recordings in slow motion, letting the air picture develop.

"There." She hit the pause button. "This is where it went south. We have all four targets on our scopes." She pointed at the four symbols clearly visible on both Gator's and Spud's radar displays.

Advancing the player a few frames, she paused again. "There, you see both of you are now locked to the same target. Spud, you have Gator's bandit. Yours is untargeted and neither of you recognize it. We only had a couple of seconds to rectify the situation and it didn't happen."

"I saw the picture and tried to lock my guy," Spud interjected, "but the radar must have jumped to Gator's target." The look exchanged between Nemo and Gator was unmistakable.

Kate's jaw muscles tightened painfully. "Spud, radars don't jump targets. These guys were not that close." She backed the player up. "Look, you can see your acquisition symbols right there under Gator's target. You picked and locked the wrong guy."

Spud opened his mouth to argue, but Kate turned her back to him and advanced the player. She quickly, deftly broke down the rest of the engagement, pointing out the other mistakes that had contributed to the fiasco while trying to find something positive to emphasize.

Kate suppressed a sigh and glanced at the clock as she began the painful dissection of the second engagement. Gator and Nemo took their licks stolidly while she spared herself no criticism. But again, Spud continued to argue away his mistakes. Every time he opened his mouth, she could sense Gator's and Nemo's frustration growing to match her own.

An hour later, her throat tightened as she summarized the third engagement. "Our adversaries gave us a harder problem this time. We all targeted correctly, except for you, Spud. You didn't lock anyone and didn't make a radio call to let us know. That put everybody's situational awareness into the toilet and left an untargeted bandit in the area."

"I just didn't have the picture," Spud said sullenly. "And I was heads down in the radar when Gator turned—"

It was the final straw. "Would you stop your whining?" she shouted as her anger boiled over. "I'm sick of listening to your excuses and so is everybody else. Own your mistakes. Even better, don't make them. You're going to have to up your game if you want to make it as an Outlaw."

Seeing the shocked looks in her wingmen's faces, her anger dissipated as quickly as it came. Exhausted, mouth dry with frustration, she slammed down the dry erase markers she had been holding. "We're going to have to do better when we sail in a couple weeks," she said forcefully. "There's a strong possibility we're going to end up near Middle East instead of off the coast of Korea. If intel has it right about Russia getting involved if war breaks out, things are going to be a whole lot tougher than they were today when four thirty-year-old F-15s ate our lunch."

She took a deep breath. "Unless anyone has anything else, we're done."

Nobody did.

One thought burned brightly in her mind as she strode back to her office. Animal was right. Spud had to go. He was a danger, a liability. He didn't fit, and he was going to pull the squadron apart if Digger didn't do something fast.

"Elsa, Skipper wants to see you." Startled, Kate whirled to find Torch standing by Digger's office, face grim.

Digger was seated at his desk, his face an expressionless mask. Wordlessly he motioned to the two chairs in front of it. Kate perched at the edge of one while Torch flopped into the other. Her breath caught in her throat. Had word of her outburst already made its way to Digger? Kate searched his face hoping for a glimmer of reassurance, but his features wore a deep scowl—no help there.

"I have a challenge for you," Digger said after an uncomfortable moment of silence. Kate allowed herself to relax slightly. Good, this wasn't about her outburst, but why was her normally congenial boss so serious?

"Animal got a DUI last Friday," Digger continued, his voice flat. "He will not be deploying with us."

Kate's heart sank. She had not been there to grab Animal's keys and nobody else had done so. The Outlaws had failed to take care of one of their own. The navy had zero tolerance for officers who drank and drove. Animal was done, both as an aviator and as an officer.

Digger's next words had caught her completely by surprise. "You've done a great job in the short time you've been safety officer. I want you to take over ops for this deployment."

Her heart lurched at his unexpected words. Objections flooded into her mind. She was too junior. She wasn't ready for the crushing responsibility. Animal had at least another year and another deployment on her.

Digger calmly cut through her panic. "It's a big job, but I know you can do it. Torch and I will help you. So will the other department heads. You're more than capable."

He paused, and Kate felt herself shrinking under his penetrating gaze.

"It's late," Digger concluded. "Go home. Get some rest. We'll continue this conversation tomorrow."

Kate's thoughts were still whirling, and she almost missed his next words. "We have another intel briefing tomorrow and I don't think we're going to like what we'll hear. This deployment is going to be tough. It's going to require every ounce of your talent and creativity to hold the team together, but I have faith in you."

Great, Kate thought as she left Digger's office. *Digger may have faith in me, but what about the rest of the team? After today will they still have faith in me? And what do I say to him about Spud?*

Chapter 11

"Fall out, you scum!" Schimmelhorn, the German sergeant who had enlisted Merlyn, bellowed. "Ten minutes rest. Drink some water and then it's back to drill for you."

In a clatter of equipment, men dropped to the trampled grass. They had spent the afternoon practicing the nine-step musket-loading drill under the warm April sun. Merlyn shot a glance at George, sitting in the grass next to him. George's face was red, blotchy from the heat. He removed his kepi and wiped his face with a bandana that had probably been clean a week ago but was now gray with grime. Merlyn pulled the cork from his canteen, took a sip of the brackish water, and offered it to George.

He had not found it hard to get close to the younger man. As the regiment formed, men coalesced into natural groups. Those from one neighborhood or township drew together, friends who had joined together sticking together, brothers, cousins making their groups. Most were farmers, shopkeepers, laborers—even a few vagrants seeking pay and regular meals. The youngest was sixteen. Merlyn guessed the oldest to be approaching sixty. They were the raw material of war.

Among this mass of men, George stuck out like a sore thumb. He was better dressed, better mannered, and better spoken. Obviously from a different class. If the men did not actively shun him, they avoided him. They had little in common with this outsider who had landed in their midst. That made it easy for Merlyn to approach him, to offer companionship to an isolated young man in need of a friend.

Surprisingly, George had an aptitude for military life. He mastered drill quickly and grew impatient when others struggled with it. He had a quick and inquisitive mind. Not content to follow rote, he constantly wanted to know the why behind what he was being asked to do.

As was his habit, he filled the downtime with a question. "Why do we have to do the musket loading drill over and over and over?" From others it would have been a complaint; from George it was an honest question.

Merlyn shot a glance at the men crowding close to hear his answer. Some were genuinely interested. Others seeking to fill a moment of boredom. His eye lit on an older man in his forties. Another misfit, different from the younger men flocking to answer their country's call. He said little and observed much, all the while puffing contentedly on a battered clay pipe. Hermann Johanns, another German, farmer, father of four. He might make another good officer when elections came. Merlyn dismissed the stray thought and focused instead on George.

"We drill so we can perform automatically under fire. When the first minié ball whistles past your head, your guts are going to turn to water and you're going to lose your ability to think. You still need to be able to load and fire when every instinct is telling you to turn and run."

George looked uncomfortable. "That's cowardice," he exclaimed.

"Not cowardice, reality," Merlyn declared. "And you need to be prepared for it."

He looked around him and felt a surge of grief. How many of these men could he keep alive in the months to come? How was he going to keep George alive?

Movement at the corner of his eye caught his attention. He turned to see Schimmelhorn striding up. "On your feet, Professor," he bellowed. "Colonel wants to see you."

Merlyn climbed to his feet and grabbed his musket. He followed the sergeant as the small group of onlookers hooted and jeered.

"You're in for it now!"

"What did you do to get the old man riled up?"

Since seeing him at the recruiting post days before, this was Merlyn's first opportunity to examine his commanding officer up close. Colonel Amos Fothergill sat at his desk in a dimly lit, airless tent, working his way through a stack of papers. A partially smoked cigar lay in an ashtray, sending up lazy tendrils of smoke. Merlyn blinked rapidly trying to ease the burning in his eyes from the acrid gray miasma that pervaded the tent.

Several moments passed before Fothergill looked up at Merlyn standing at attention before him. His hair, worn over his ears, was black, but his neatly trimmed beard was beginning to streak with gray. His face was stern, proud, but also fleshy, florid, ravaged by too much good food and an abundance of drink. Rumor among the men had it that he'd been a politician before volunteering to raise a regiment. Merlyn had watched him frequently lose his temper as his fledgling troops bungled a command or took too long during loading and firing drills. At those times his face had become alarmingly red, and Merlyn wondered idly how Fothergill could possibly survive the rigors of an army in the field.

"The men call you the Professor." It was more a question than a statement.

At Merlyn's nod he continued, "You've caused me to lose a lot of sleep these last couple of nights." He raised an eyebrow and looked at Merlyn as if expecting a reply.

"Sir?" Merlyn kept his face impassive.

"I've been watching you and I can't make you out. You present yourself as a common soldier, but you're not. You have experience and the men sense it. They flock to you. They look to you for leadership. Who are you and why are you here?"

Merlyn had known the question would come at some point and had rehearsed an answer he hoped would not sound too hollow. "I'm just a man who wants to serve his country." It bothered him to utter the lie.

Fothergill stared intently at him as if to measure the truth of his answer. Merlyn stared at a point slightly above his head, not meeting his eyes.

Fothergill seemed satisfied. He abruptly changed the subject. "This undisciplined rabble is taking too long to whip into shape. We move south in two weeks, and I fear the men will not be ready."

Merlyn's ears perked up. That was news he had not heard, although the rumor mill had them moving out in anywhere from a week to a month.

"All attempts to instill the most rudimentary discipline are wasted on them. Election of officers is to take place tomorrow. The captains, lieutenants, and sergeants are to be selected by the men, but I am concerned whom they will elect. The men I brought with me to make lieutenant colonel and major lack military experience. I find myself in a quandary."

Merlyn offered no comment. His counsel was not being sought.

Fothergill leaned forward and gave Merlyn a penetrating stare.

"I gather you have military experience?"

Merlyn nodded.

"Officer?"

Merlyn nodded again.

"Have you led men in battle?"

"I have."

"You appear too young for Mexico. Where did you do it?"

"In Europe and other places." It was the truth, but Merlyn hoped this line of questioning would not force him to lie again. Fortunately, Fothergill did not press the point.

"What do you see as the problem with the men?"

Merlyn weighed his answer for a moment. "The problem is not the men. They have high spirits and are spoiling for a fight. What they need is a firm hand and discipline. Your sergeants are lax. They may have regular army experience, but I doubt they have battle experience. We need leaders who know how to fight." He took a deep breath before continuing. "May I speak candidly?"

Fothergill nodded.

"I mean brutally candidly?"

Fothergill's eyes narrowed, but he nodded again.

"The second problem is you. I have no doubt at all you are committed to this regiment, but you the lack experience to lead it. You have leadership ability, but you have not led in this type of environment. You will rapidly gain the skills you need, but perhaps not rapidly enough to prepare the men fully in time for battle."

He fell silent and surveyed the man seated before him. He could see in Fothergill's face that he did not like his answer, but his eyes conceded the point.

"What would you recommend we do?" Fothergill's voice was edgy, angry, not accustomed to challenge.

"First, put the fear of God into the sergeants. Second, focus on the basics. The men are not ready for regimental drill. Hammer home individual and company drill. Only when they have that down, work on the regimental drill. Third, the men need firmer discipline. They are brash and boastful, but they lack discipline and consequently the confidence that will prevent them from breaking and running when they hear the first shot fired. Fourth, and this is going to sound contradictory, institute a system of rewards. Encourage competition between the companies. Reward performance and accomplishment. That will build morale and *esprit de corps*."

He paused. "Fifth, delay electing officers. The regiment is not ready for that. Watch the men closely. Rotate those with apparent talent through the sergeant and officer positions. That will give you a chance to assess them. It will also give the men a chance to assess them. When the time comes, appoint officers instead of holding elections. The men will support the choices you make."

He could have offered more but stopped there. Fothergill did not give an immediate reply. He stared past Merlyn's shoulder for a few moments, deep in thought. Merlyn watched him as he appeared to struggle with a decision. But no decision came, and after an uncomfortable pause, his eyes snapped back to Merlyn's. He nodded.

"Thank you for your opinion, private. That will be all."

Merlyn came to attention, saluted, and did a smart about-face. His back straight, he strode through the open tent flap and set off to find his company.

Chapter 12

Kate sat in her darkened living room rubbing her fingers along the seam of the bloodied towel, carefully avoiding the brownish stain in the middle. The handful of memories from her dream played over and over in her mind like a song on endless replay.

"Who are you?" she whispered aloud. *Is your blood really on this towel along with mine, or is my imagination just working overtime?* There was no answer, but then she hadn't really expected one.

I just got my dream job, the next step on my career ladder. I should be over the moon. Why do I feel so bad? The answer was evident. Too much was coming at her at once. The accident. Her new job. Spud. The squadron coming apart. She felt like a pressure cooker with a plugged valve. Add to all that, the dream.

She needed help, but no matter how often she had resolved to talk to Lisa, she couldn't bring herself to do it. As logical as Lisa was, she would never understand. There was only one other person she could talk to. Mom. Mom wouldn't judge her. Wouldn't try to fix her. Would just listen and love her. She needed that more than anything else in the world right now.

Kate dropped the towel in her lap and reached for her iPhone. It would be an hour later back home in Wyoming, but Mom normally stayed up praying until the early hours of the morning. Would Dad still be up? Would he be the one to answer? The thought was enough to make her snatch her fingers back. Gritting her teeth, she forced herself to pick up the phone.

She breathed a silent prayer of gratitude as Mom answered on the second ring.

"Hi, Mom. It's me."

"Hi, sweetie," there was a note of delight in Becky Trenary's voice that made Kate realize with a pang she should call more often.

"Mom, is Dad there?"

"No, hon, he's out with the horses. Do you want me to get him for you?"

"No," Kate said sharply as she stifled a surge of panic. "It's you I need to talk to. I just don't want Dad around when I do. You know what he's like."

The silence on the line confirmed Mom did.

"I had a dream a couple of weeks ago," Kate started hesitantly, feeling foolish. "An incredibly vivid dream, but I can't remember much of it."

Once started, she picked up speed until her words gushed out in a torrent.

"I fell in love with someone in the dream. I can see his face. I know his name. It feels more real, more intense than anything I ever felt with Nick." She felt vulnerable uttering the words. What was Mom, let alone Dad, going to think if she couldn't separate dream from reality?

"I'm not sure I can even communicate what I'm feeling, but this dream has grabbed me so hard it's turned my emotions upside down. I can't let it go. It keeps coming back over and over."

There was silence on the line.

"Are you there, Mom?" Kate asked.

"I'm here, honey. Just letting you speak."

Looking down at the towel in her lap, Kate realized she needed answers. She was going to have to confide in Lisa, ask her to find a lab and send the towel off for DNA testing.

"I have a cut on my hand that I can't remember getting, and a scar on my arm that the only memory I have of it is in the dream. It's driving me nuts." She lapsed into miserable silence. A moment passed, then she asked quietly, embarrassed at the plaintive tone in her voice, "Am I going crazy, Mom?"

"Honey, I don't know what to say." Her mom's voice was weak, shaken, but then strengthened with sudden urgency. "Listen, sweetie, your dad just came in. He wants to talk to you."

Kate felt a surge of panic. "Did he hear anything?"

"No, I don't think so." Her mom's voice was hesitant.

"Don't tell him anything, please," Kate pleaded as she heard her dad's voice barking in the background. "Give me the phone, Beck. I'll take this in the study."

Kate heard heavy footsteps on bare wood floors as her dad walked quickly from the living room to his private sanctum. She recreated the image of it in her mind, burned there by hours of watching him sitting at his desk working his way through the ranch's precarious finances. Log walls, windows positioned to catch and magnify the light. A threadbare oriental carpet covering worn floorboards. The battered oak desk positioned so Dad could look out of the floor-to-ceiling windows facing out across the valley. On the wall, a framed print of a Tomcat landing on a carrier, the mat signed by the flight crews in the air wing he had commanded. She felt a sudden pang of homesickness that made her eyes prick.

"What's going on, sweetheart?" Max Trenary's voice was deep, gravelly, laced with concern, but was it concern for her or his dreams for her that had him worried? She hated herself for feeling the doubt.

Praying he had heard none of what she shared with Mom, she gave him a quick, highly edited summary of her conversation with Digger and her concerns about Spud.

If he seemed elated at her sudden change of job, his excitement was overshadowed by concern about the situation with Spud.

"You've just taken an important step up the career ladder," he declared. "Ops Officer is a critical job. You know as well as I do you have to succeed at it if you're gonna make skipper. You've worked hard to get where you are. Don't let this nugget ruin it for you. Can him fast before he kills someone and takes you down with him."

Kate screamed inwardly with frustration. *This is not a conversation I want to be having right now!*

"I have a question," she asked through gritted teeth.

"What's that?"

"Just to get a sense of what's going on with him, I looked through his records this evening. I was surprised at what I saw. He did well all through training, never busted a check ride. He did okay with us at first too. It was only after workups started getting hot and heavy that he started having trouble."

"Doesn't matter," Dad replied with an edge in his voice. "Either he's cutting it or he's not. Fix him or get rid of him."

"But, Dad . . ." She got no further.

"Dammit, Kate," he interjected angrily. "Don't go all soft on me. I thought I trained you better than that."

Holding her phone well away from her ear, Kate hunkered down to weather Dad's barrage of advice. Only half listening to his rant, she had a sudden flash of insight. Dad and Animal were two peas in a pod.

And that was the problem, she realized, her stomach doing a slow flip-flop. Animal. The pilots had looked up to him for his brash, take-no-prisoners approach, but he could be a bully in his efforts to get newbies to toughen up and fly better. Had Spud simply shut down in the face of Animal's pressure?

Ultimately it didn't really matter why it had happened. It was ancient history. As of now, Spud was her responsibility. But what to do about it?

I can't stand the guy, Kate admitted to herself. *Nor can the rest of the squadron. Is there any point in trying to salvage him?*

She wanted to give voice to the question but said nothing. There was no opportunity to say anything. Spirits crashing, she sat quietly, waiting for a break in Dad's tirade.

An image, soft as a feather, bubbled to the surface of her mind from the maelstrom of dream-memories constantly churning within her.

Morgan sat across the table from her, a finished meal between them, his soft brown eyes intense, compelling. He held his hand in hers, her heart thrilling at the touch. "Every human being has value," he said. "They are the product of their choices and the environment that shaped them. God loves them just as they are, and we need to do likewise. Nobody ever deserves to be written off."

He was talking about me, she thought. *He didn't write me off after the fencing accident, and there is no way he would abandon Spud. He would take him under his wing just as he did me.*

The gauntlet was thrown, the challenge made. Could she do no less?

But I'm not you, every fiber of her being protested, and then, *what about the risk?* Without conscious thought, her mind rejected the challenge. This was reality, not a dream. Dad was right. She had to make the tough choices. Lives hung in the balance. The squadron did not need a weak newbie holding it back. She now knew what she had to do.

***

24 February
NAS Lemoore, CA

Heart pounding with trepidation, Kate raised her hand to knock at Digger's door. She dropped it and started to turn away when she realized Digger was not alone. Torch was with him. She steeled herself. While this was a conversation she wanted to have with Digger alone, Torch was going to know the substance of it soon enough.

She took a deep breath, tried to calm her racing heart, and rapped sharply on the doorjamb.

A smile creased Digger's face as he looked away from the earnest conversation he was having with Torch. "Am I interrupting?" Kate asked as Digger wordlessly waved her in.

"No, we were just wrapping up," Digger said, motioning to the empty chair before his desk. Kate flopped into it and shot a glance at Torch. Everything about him, from the rigidity of his posture to the set of his jaw, communicated frustration.

Kate tensed. Was this really the right time? But she was here. She had to do what she had come to do.

"Boss, I hate to say it, but I agree with Animal—Spud needs to go." As she blurted out the opening words of her carefully rehearsed speech, she felt an uncomfortable tickle deep in her spirit. This felt wrong somehow, but she steeled herself and pushed on, ignoring the sudden narrowing in Digger's eyes. "I know I said earlier he's a nugget making nugget mistakes, but he really is weak. His mission the other day was a disaster. If we go to war, I don't think he's going to be able to hack it."

Digger continued to stare at her. She shot a glance at Torch, but his face, masked by his habitual scowl, revealed nothing.

"Perhaps we just leave him behind," she backtracked. "Let him fly with one of the other squadrons while we're gone. Build his skills . . ." She let her voice trail off. From the darkening of Digger's face, she realized she'd just made a monumental mistake.

Digger's next words confirmed it. "Elsa, I'd expected better from you." His voice had an edge to it that made her feel like a child about to get her knuckles rapped. Her throat tightened as she realized he wasn't as much angry as he was disappointed in her.

Great, she thought. *I just get the job I've been preparing for my whole career, and I've blown it royally.*

"Like Animal," Digger continued, his voice flat, "I don't need you telling me how to run my squadron or what to do with my pilots. Right now, I need to rebuild a team that Animal and some of the hardcore younger pilots have almost torn apart. I need Torch, I need Trojan, but above all, I need you to make it happen.

"What you don't know is that I had any number of conversations with Animal about his divisive approach and was on the verge of removing him. You were probably going to make this cruise as OPSO in any case."

Torch shifted in his seat beside her, and Kate shot a glance his way. She saw a flicker of something in his eyes quickly masked. *He wasn't happy about that decision,* Kate thought, and then her pulse quickened as another thought hit her: *Perhaps he's not happy about me getting the job.*

"A squadron is a team." Digger's words came out like pistol shots. "If you have a bunch of pilots out there all trying individually to be aces like Animal did, the squadron is going to fail at its mission. Your job is to teach them to fly and fight as a team. Never ever forget it."

He paused, his eyes boring into Kate with an intensity that made her want to shrink in her seat. "I expect you to take Spud under your wing. Help him to succeed. More importantly, I expect you to work with the other pilots, undo the damage Animal has done. Help me rebuild the team. Integrate Spud. I'm holding you accountable for making it happen. Do I make myself perfectly clear?"

Not trusting herself to keep her voice steady, Kate did the only thing she could and nodded.

As she fled Digger's office, everything about Torch, from the slump of his body to the set of his eyes, communicated he was as unhappy with the situation as she was. She knew exactly what she had done, but what on earth was eating at him? Whatever it was, she had a sinking feeling in her gut it did not bode well for her.

Chapter 13

The past two days had not been pretty. Merlyn could see Fothergill had tried to take his advice, but the ineptitude of the sergeants and the two men he would have made his senior subordinates had made every effort a disaster. The men were not ready for battle and would not be ready if things kept up like this. He batted aside the twinge of concern that was threatening to grow into a serious worry. Right now, he had something more important to focus on—George.

In the deepening twilight, the men had been given a few moments to relax. Merlyn and George sat together in the grass outside the dog tent that provided them a modicum of shelter from the elements. Merlyn sipped from a canteen and prayed he would not succumb to the dysentery that had already claimed several of the recruits. The rough wool tunic he had been issued itched abominably, and he scratched absently under its collar.

George surprised him with an out-of-the-blue question. "How old are you, Merlyn? You seem older than you look."

Merlyn shot a surprised look back, not expecting that depth of perception in someone so young. "I'm thirty-one," he replied, giving the age he was when called to this mission, not the innumerable years he had lived since then.

"They will make you an officer, you know. Is that why you joined? To become an officer?"

"No," Merlyn replied slowly. "I joined to make a difference and will serve in any capacity I can do that." He shot a glance at the young man beside him. George's eyes were fixed downward on a piece of hardtack he turned over and over in his fingers. "Why did you enlist?"

George took a bite of hardtack and chewed thoughtfully.

"It's a long story," George said slowly. In his ill-fitting uniform, he looked impossibly young—far too young to be engaged in this bloody business. "I was a difficult youngest child. My father is a banker. I have two older brothers. One is a businessman and the other is a lawyer. I have two sisters, both married to up-and-coming young men. I don't fit the family pattern. I have no interest in business. I don't want to be a lawyer or a politician or a doctor. I went to Harvard because it was expected of me, but my heart was not in it. I was sent home because I was failing all my classes. I was drinking too much and was deemed to be of poor moral character."

George's face reflected the pain this memory brought to him. "Father was furious. Mother took to her bed for a week. For months I just drifted. I had no job. Finally, I grew tired of Father yelling at me to make something of myself. I knew if I didn't do something to change my circumstances, I was going to end up in the gutter."

He gave a wry laugh. "If I couldn't make something of myself, then perhaps the army could. I got good and drunk one morning to bolster my courage and went down to city hall and enlisted. I've never seen my father so angry as when I told him what I had done. When I left home, neither he nor Mother were speaking to me."

Although he sensed that George was not seeking comfort, Merlyn tried to offer it anyway. "I'm sorry. I can tell how much it hurts you. I'm sure they will come around eventually." The words sounded lame to him.

"You don't know Father. When he gets something in his head, he will never let it go. I've never measured up, never been good enough for him, and he never passes up an opportunity to tell me so." George's voice shook with suppressed emotion. "I don't understand much of what we're doing here, but I'm going to make something of myself, or die trying." The words were spoken with quiet determination.

Merlyn felt a small surge of recognition. In the callow young man sitting beside him, he sensed the first beginnings of the iron resolve he had seen in Kate. George was going to do just fine—if he survived the hell that was to come.

Merlyn was exhausted but sleep would not come. The bugle had sounded lights out an hour earlier. George snored softly beside him. Through the small opening at the end of the tent, he could see light seeping through chinks in Fothergill's tent. Apparently, the colonel was having another sleepless night too.

Lord, why have you brought me here? Is it to keep George alive so Kate will be born? The thought caused a surge of terror to rise up within him. The resemblance between George and Kate was too strong. He had to be an ancestor or closely related to one of her ancestors. If Kate was a direct descendant of George, then he had to keep George alive at all costs. But how was he going to do that if he and George were simply cannon fodder?

The sound of footsteps walking though the camp snapped him out of his reverie. They were coming nearer, approaching the tent where he lay. He stole a glance. Yellow light from a lantern bobbed closer. A foot kicked his. "Professor," a voice hissed. It was the German sergeant. "*Raus mit dir.* The colonel wants to see you again."

Merlyn wiggled out of the tent, trying not to disturb George, who groaned and rolled over. He pulled on his jacket and boots and followed the pool of light through the camp.

Fothergill was seated at his desk. It was as if he had not moved since their previous interview. His eyes were red-rimmed, his face haggard with fatigue. There was an open bottle on the desk and an empty glass beside it. Merlyn felt a momentary twinge of alarm. Was Fothergill one of those men who sought courage from the contents of a bottle?

Fothergill looked up as Merlyn approached the desk and saluted.

Fothergill returned his salute, poured himself a half glass from the bottle, lifted it to his nose, inhaled deeply, but did not raise the glass to his lips. "Can I offer you a drink?" he asked.

Merlyn's response was automatic. "Thank you, sir, but no."

"Good," Fothergill responded.

He poured the glass out on the ground beside him. Placed it back beside the bottle. "Haven't touched the stuff in years myself. Too hard on the digestion. Keep a bottle around just to test my willpower. Have a seat, Professor," he said and motioned to a stool by the desk.

Merlyn sat, feeling as if he had just passed a test. Compassion for this man washed over him. He was obviously out of his element in an army camp, but he had heart and was determined to succeed. It was just that he did not know how. Good officers and NCOs could make him a success, but he did not have them. He had the raw materials but nobody to help him fashion them into the tools of war.

"I spent the past two days watching you, and the better part of this evening on my face before the Almighty, praying for guidance," Fothergill said slowly. "I don't know that he answered me, but I could not stop seeing your face in my mind. You say that you have military experience. Can you help me whip this regiment into shape and make it an effective fighting force?"

Merlyn rapidly considered the pros and cons of what he knew in his heart Fothergill was about to offer. The commission would certainly affect his growing friendship with George. It was a responsibility he did not particularly want. But, by serving the greater good, he might be able to keep some of these men and, all importantly, George, alive.

Merlyn kept his voice level, trying not to let his reluctance show. "I believe I can, sir."

"Will you support me to the absolute best of your ability, and not undermine me in any way because of your superior experience?"

"I will."

Fothergill took a deep breath. "I don't know you, but somehow, I trust you. I had a rather unpleasant conversation with the governor this afternoon, but I persuaded him of the rightness of my position. He had his heart set on his nephew being lieutenant colonel, but he will be satisfied with his being made major. Will you honor me by serving as lieutenant colonel of this regiment and helping me ready it for war?"

Merlyn breathed a quick prayer for guidance. There was no answer, only the thought that it was the best way he could serve George and, in a way, Kate. Throat tight, he said quietly, "I will."

No sooner had he spoken than he had a sudden, incongruous thought—perhaps he had been too quick to dismiss Midnight.

***

May 6th, 1862
Albany, NY

"Are the men assembled?" Fothergill asked Major Summerfield. If Summerfield resented the diminishment of his expectations, he did not let it show. Mid-thirties, tall, his face constantly radiating good humor, Merlyn found he liked the man.

"Yessir."

Outside the tent, the men were gathered in ranks—eight companies of a hundred. Fothergill's recruiters had done well, Merlyn mused. The regiment was almost full strength. *Now we get to see the quality of the men they have found.*

The late-afternoon sun glinted off bayonets, buttons, belt buckles. Fothergill had spared no expense in outfitting his regiment. The color guard stood facing the men, flags dancing in the light breeze.

Ramrod straight, with Merlyn trailing, Fothergill marched forward to stand before the color guard and snapped to attention.

Off to the side stood the regimental staff—Lieutenant Ambrose, the quartermaster. Captain McElroy, the surgeon. Lieutenant James, his assistant. Rounding out their number, the chaplain, Nehemiah Barings. Tall, scarecrow thin, with his beaked nose and iron-colored beard, he looked like a prophet of old in his ill-fitting black uniform frock coat.

Fothergill raised his hand from the hilt of his sword. "Men," he began in a low tone that somehow managed to carry even to the soldiers in the farthest ranks. "We are assembled here to build a regiment, the 172nd New York Volunteer Infantry. *We* are the 172nd." He took a breath and paused to allow his words to sink in.

"Today we appoint officers and sergeants," Fothergill continued.

"Adjutant, Lieutenant Billy Keys, report," Fothergill ordered, his voice stern. This was the one part of the ceremony that had been pre-scripted. Although the men did not know it, Keys did.

There was a stir in the ranks, and a slight figure half ran to stand before the colonel. "Sir, Lieutenant Keys reporting as ordered." He saluted as he spoke. Fothergill delayed a moment before returning it. "Take your place."

Keys did a smart about-face and took up station halfway between Fothergill and the assembled companies. He turned and saluted again. "Regiment is all present and accounted for, sir," he shouted, his voice carrying over the wind.

Fothergill returned the salute. "Give the regiment parade rest!" he bellowed.

Keys turned. "Parade." He drew the word out then paused to allow the preparatory command to be heard. "Rest!" he shouted, barking out the word in a sharp command.

In unison, eight hundred men relaxed slightly.

"Officers!" Fothergill shouted, and there was no doubt in Merlyn's mind even the back ranks could hear him easily. "When I call your name, come forward, hand your musket to the detail." He nodded to a small band of soldiers standing off to the side of the assembled troops. "They will give you your sword, then take your place in front of your company. Am I understood?"

"Yes, sir!" eight hundred voices bellowed in unison.

Fothergill paused for dramatic effect. "Company A. Captain Johanns, come forward and take command of your company." The ranks parted as Johanns, a surprised look on his face, stepped forward. He handed his musket to the detail of soldiers, accepted his sword, and buckled it around his waist. He strode confidently to take his place before his men.

One by one Fothergill called out the remaining officers and the sergeants who also came forward to take their place before the company.

He repeated the process for Company B and Company C. The sun was noticeably dipping toward the horizon as Fothergill started on Company D.

"Captain Maxwell, take command of your company." Merlyn watched George's face as he came forward. If he was surprised or overwhelmed by the responsibilities he was assuming, he did not let it show.

The light was fading as Fothergill finished with Company H, but he was not done.

"Call the Regiment to attention!" he bellowed.

Orders were shouted and echoed, and the men turned as one. The band struck up a martial air and the regiment began to move. As the last light of the setting sun gleamed on bayonets held high, the regiment marched slowly past, ranks perfectly aligned. Each captain saluted Fothergill with his sword as he led his company past where the colonel stood. When Company D came to the front, George saluted as the officers before him had done, but while his sword motioned toward Fothergill, his eyes met Merlyn's.

Dear God, Merlyn breathed. *Help me keep safe this man you've entrusted to me. Help me keep them all safe.* Yet, despite the overwhelming sense of dread in his heart, he felt a small glimmer of pride that would not allow itself to be extinguished.

Chapter 14

Kate sat in her unaccustomed seat in the front row of the Outlaws' ready room and sipped her coffee. She grimaced. It was not Starbucks, but something lighter, astringent, and acidic. Not good, but she needed it

The USS *Theodore Roosevelt* thrummed about her like a living organism. For the first time since they had taken up station off the coast of South Korea three weeks ago, she felt she was beginning to understand the nuances of her new job. Training and scheduling were her primary responsibilities, but Operations went so much deeper. At its most basic, it was all about maintaining the combat readiness of her squadron and its pilots. It was an all-encompassing, all-consuming job, and she found her days aboard the ship were even longer than those she had experienced as a junior officer.

Overall, she was pleased with her performance. The mock air battles with Air Force F-16s stationed at Osan and Kunsan Air Bases had gone off without a hitch. Bombing scores from the trips to the range were high, both indicators of a squadron at peak readiness.

But, she grimly reminded herself, there was one area in which she was failing. A quick glance at the greenie board—the visual record of the squadron's landing grades, posted prominently on the ready room wall—caused her stomach to tighten. One month into the deployment, Spud was not off to a good start. The board was largely green and yellow dots, representing acceptable performance, but Spud's row at the bottom was mostly yellow with too many browns and one red indicating an unsafe pass. At this rate, he was going to lose his wings, or worse, have a ramp strike before the cruise was over. Even Jethro, one row above him on the board, was doing much better.

How she wished Lisa were here to talk to. But Lisa was home, not here to offer the support and no-nonsense practicality Kate needed. With the communications blackout imposed to counter Russian and Chinese cybersecurity concerns, ship's email was out of the question. There was no way of communicating, other than by letter or by waiting in line for an opportunity to use one of the satellite phones provided for the crew to call home.

Kate heard footsteps on the deck, firm, heavy, and turned. She rose in an automatic gesture of respect when she saw Digger entering from the passageway where the skippers of the flying squadrons had their staterooms. He stifled a yawn with the back of his hand, poured himself a cup of coffee, took a sip, and grimaced. "Only one thing worse than army coffee, and that's navy coffee," he said ruefully as he came up to stand beside Kate.

As if reading her mind, his gaze latched onto the bottom row of the greenie board. "Not going too well there, is it?" he commented wryly, his words a mastery of understatement.

"No, sir," Kate replied.

"We need to figure something out," Digger said, his tone indicating that there was no "we" about it. "As we all know," he continued, his eyes fixing Kate's with a penetrating stare, "we're on the hook to redeploy to the Middle East if things continue to go sideways with Iran. The other pilots see Spud as a hindrance to the squadron and want me to do something and do it now. They're blaming you for my decision to keep him around."

Kate felt her throat tighten as adrenaline surged through her system. If the squadron was fracturing because of the impossible situation Digger had put her in, how was it going to reflect on her? If they were heading for war, they didn't need a junior pilot holding them back. Spud was dead weight, not worth the time and effort to keep trying to bring him up to speed. Why couldn't Digger see it?

No sooner had the thought crossed her mind than something deep within her rebelled, a thought quiet in its assurance, unlike the turmoil roiling within her mind: *No. That's not right. He's a human being of infinite value. He does not deserve to be written off as you would so easily do.*

Kate felt a surge of confusion. Where did that come from?

She felt Digger's eyes on her, probing, speculative.

"What went through your mind just then?" he asked.

She was tempted to provide only a half-truth but threw caution to the wind and shared the thought that had so unexpectedly flitted across her mind.

"Good. You see it. I wasn't sure you did. The Outlaws have a rather unique dog-eat-dog culture." A grimace twisted his mouth as he spoke. "More like a frat house than a professional organization. We can't keep operating that way, but being new, I'm an outsider and finding it difficult to get the attention and respect of Animal's crowd. I could do it by breaking heads, but that's not the way I like to operate." His eyes remained locked on Kate's in a direct, unblinking stare. "We need to stay the course. I'll keep working with the squadron and tamp down some of the grumbling. You concentrate on Spud. Find a way to get through to him."

There it was again, that unpleasant feeling deep inside of being compelled to do something she did not want to do. Her mouth suddenly dry, she forced her eyes to meet Digger's, although she wanted to look away. "I'll try," she said reluctantly. "Maybe there's something happening on the home front we don't know about. Perhaps you could have a word with him as well—something kind, fatherly. I don't know . . ." She let her voice trail off.

He turned to go but paused. "A word of advice, Elsa. I'm one of your biggest fans, but remember, leadership is all about people."

As Digger headed back to get himself another cup of coffee, Kate stared helplessly after him, the knot in her stomach solidifying. *What do I do?* she thought. *Everything I've worked so hard for is now on the line. Spud had better be worth it.*

Chapter 15

"Tomorrow the army attacks," Fothergill declared enthusiastically to his company commanders while pointing at the hand-drawn map spread out on a makeshift table. It lay illuminated in a pool of light from a lantern hanging from a tree branch. Troop dispositions were drawn in, the entire army arrayed to the northeast of the Confederate capital.

"General McClellan's intent is to defeat the Rebel army defending Richmond and bring the war to a speedy conclusion. Although the 3rd Brigade is to be held in reserve, I have no doubt we will be called on soon and I expect you and your men to do your duty in the days to come."

Upon completion of its initial training, the 172nd New York Volunteer Regiment had traveled south from New York, landing at the foot of the Virginia Peninsula, where it had joined the newly formed 3rd Brigade, commanded by Brigadier General Eades. Consisting of two Pennsylvania regiments, a regiment from Ohio and the 172nd New York, the brigade had marched northwest over barely passable roads and two weeks ago had joined the Army of the Potomac, encamped on the outskirts of Richmond.

Merlyn let Fothergill's words wash over him, had heard it all many times before—a nervous commander trying to give his subordinates a pep talk. He glanced over the officers crowded around the map, George among them, face red, intense, concentrating. All were new to combat, uncertain of what was to come in the morning, unsure whether they and their men would stand or flee. Merlyn felt a sudden surge of pity for them and the men they led.

"All right, gentlemen," Fothergill concluded. "I'm counting on you. Do you have any questions before I let you see to your men and try to get some rest?"

There was a moment of silence. As Fothergill opened his mouth to dismiss his officers, Captain Jameson, C Company commander, interjected, "Sir, what do you hear about the Rebs' new commander?"

"Lee?" Fothergill turned down the corners of his mouth. "Word among the generals is he's a smart man, but slow and deliberate. They don't think we'll have any trouble with him."

Merlyn had been staring down at the map still unrolled on the table. As Fothergill's words registered, his eyes snapped up to fix him with an incredulous stare. He cursed himself at the error and hastily composed his features into what he hoped would be perceived as an expression of bland neutrality, but it was too late. Fothergill had noticed the reaction.

"You disagree, Colonel?" Fothergill asked, a note of ice creeping into his voice. "Do you know something the rest of us do not?"

"No, sir," Merlyn lied. "Just scuttlebutt among some of the other officers."

His answer seemed to mollify Fothergill, who briefly scanned the faces of his audience. "If there are no other questions, dismissed."

The officers saluted before turning away into the darkness. In the dim light, Merlyn felt a stab of concern as he saw Fothergill wince and clutch his fist to his chest.

"Colonel, are you all right?" Merlyn asked quietly so that none of the other departing commanders could hear.

He saw a flash of irritation pass over Fothergill's features. "I'm fine," he growled. "This damnable army food disagrees with me. It's nothing but a touch of dyspepsia. See to the men and don't worry about me."

But Merlyn did worry about him. He could see the signs of high blood pressure and coronary artery disease. Fothergill was a man who had lived well—too well—and was now paying the price for his indiscretions.

As Merlyn settled into his tent, he wished there was some way he could seek out George. The opportunities to speak to the younger man had been few and far between, the chasm of differing rank putting a stop to their growing friendship. Merlyn had eight captains under his charge, as well as the staff. He could treat George no differently than the others or it would be perceived as favoritism. He ground his teeth in frustration. How could he witness to the man when there was no time alone?

He knew with awful certainty what the following days would bring. How could he keep George alive through what was coming? A stab of fear chilled him to the bone. If George did not survive, what were the implications? Would time rearrange itself around the loss and Kate would no longer be? *No*, he forced the thought away. To worry about this now was madness.

Merlyn redirected his mind, trying to find refuge in a more pleasant thought. Kate. How long was it now? He tallied the weeks, a knot forming in his stomach. Two and a half months.

Do you remember me, sweetheart? he thought sadly. *Or am I just a fading dream to you, a distant memory?* Had his plan worked, or was it all for naught? The frustration of not knowing was driving him mad.

In his loneliness, he cast back to pull up a pleasant memory, but it didn't come. Instead, another memory surfaced.

It was a Saturday. Kate and he were working out together. She wore a pink top that left her midriff bare, and black biker shorts that came to midthigh. She was all curves and long, shapely legs. Her hair was damp with sweat, and a rivulet of moisture trickled down her chest toward the hint of cleavage revealed by her tank top. The memory caused a surge of adrenaline that set his heart to racing.

His hand rested under the bar as she struggled to complete another bench press, ready to take the weight if her strength gave out. Her arms trembled with effort as they fully extended against the weight.

"One more," he demanded.

She groaned and slowly lowered the bar to her chest, gasping in a lungful of air as she did so. Her progress upward was infinitesimal, her arms shaking so violently, he almost took the weight. But with a herculean effort, she fully extended them.

"Great job," he said, as he started to guide the bar back to their supports. She shook her head and started to lower the bar again. He felt a surge of pride as the bar came up once more and then she went for yet another rep. Finally, exhausted, face flushed, she returned the bar to its cradle.

She lithely rolled off the bench and stood to face him. "Your turn," she demanded. The challenge was good-natured, taunting, daring him to best her.

His shoulder was almost healed but still twinged when he overdid it. This was not going to be fun.

"This is not some macho thing," she said. "You don't need to try to outdo me. Clear?"

He nodded as he added weights to the bar. He rolled onto the bench, took two deep breaths and slowly, concentrating on form, cranked out two sets.

"How's your shoulder?" she asked as he paused to rest.

"A little sore but holding." That was not quite true. It hurt like heck.

"How do you heal so quickly?" she asked, a puzzled look on her face. "After the wound I gave you, I wouldn't think you would be lifting any weight at all."

"I heal fast," he replied, choosing not to elaborate. "In a year or two, I won't even have a scar left."

"Supernaturally fast," she commented drily. "Wish I could say the same about the rest of us mere mortals."

Girl, you don't know the half of it. Time to change the subject yet again. "You don't talk much about your family, about growing up." There, the words were out. He'd asked the question that had been burning in the back of his mind for weeks now. What experience had led her to become so remote, so detached?

Her smoky eyes hooded as she brushed a strand of hair from her face. What memory had he intruded on? His breath caught in his throat as he waited.

"I grew up on a horse ranch in Wyoming," she said slowly, hesitantly. "Dad was a hard-charging naval aviator. A real go-getter by all accounts. On track to make admiral. Mom was a dutiful navy wife. I have three older brothers. I was a late addition to the family just before dad made O-6. Not a lot of captains running around with infants at home."

Her eyes were vacant, unfocused, lost in a memory as she absently took a sip from her water bottle.

"I was three when Dad suddenly retired and moved us to Wyoming. He said it was to take over the ranch from Mom's parents, who could no longer handle the load. I always wondered if that was the real reason, but Dad never said."

Her eyes locked on his, fixing him with a penetrating gaze. "There you have it. My two oldest brothers were already in college; Sam was there for only a year before he left home too. Then it was just me and Mom and Dad and the ranch hands and the families from the surrounding ranches. Mom homeschooled me. I grew up on horseback. In the winter I skied. We had an old Beechcraft Dad used to get around. I learned to fly as a kid. When they lifted the combat exclusion, it was a given I would follow in Dad's footsteps. And here I am."

There was a finality to her words. The wall was back up again, but he at least had to make the attempt to get behind it.

"Must have been kind of lonely growing up," he said softly.

A flicker of pain flashed across those extraordinary eyes. She was silent for a moment. "It was." Her voice was little more than a whisper and that distant look was back as her eyes focused on something a million miles beyond his shoulder. He wanted to reach out, take her hand, pull her into his arms, but it was too early—the rift between them only beginning to heal.

Her eyes suddenly snapped into focus and latched onto his. Her mouth eased into a smile, revealing even, white teeth. "It was lonely, but I didn't know any different. I was happy. Our valley was

96

remote, untouched, unspoiled. One of the most beautiful places in God's creation, and I love it there.

"My parents are polar opposites. Dad is brash and forceful. Mom is quiet and nurturing. She has to be to weather Dad's storms." Morgan watched her eyes closely, but they were hooded again, and he sensed there were unspoken encyclopedias behind those simple words.

Morgan saw it all too clearly. The isolation, her overbearing father, her passive if loving mother, had all served to drive her into herself.

"How would you like to meet my horse tomorrow after church?" The words were out of his mouth before he consciously formed the thought, and he instantly wished he could retract the invitation.

Her face brightened and she gave him another one of her dazzling smiles that made his heart stop. "I'd love to. I didn't know you had a horse. What kind is he?"

"He's of rather indeterminate lineage, but I think you'll like him anyway."

"Can I ride him?"

This was rapidly going into very unsafe territory. Morgan mentally kicked himself for opening his mouth. "He can be a handful, so let's see how he is tomorrow. Come on, let's get something to eat."

He put his arm around her shoulder. He intended it as a gesture of friendship, but it was obviously much more. She stiffened momentarily, relaxed, then moved closer to him, accepting his embrace. Together they walked out of the gym and back to their cars. As they walked, a thought settled into his mind. He wanted her beside him, always.

Merlyn tried to tamp down the wave of regret welling up inside him. *You could have used the accident to distance yourself, but you didn't. You used it instead to draw closer. What on earth were you thinking?* Thoughts churning, he slept little that night.

Chapter 16

The ready room was almost deserted, most of the pilots catching a quick bite before the evening's movie would be shown on the big screen. It would be another action flick, she knew. Trojan would see to that.

"Spud, can I have a moment?" Kate walked over to where Spud sat alone, immersed in one of the binders containing the volumes of reference material an aviator had to know cold. No one had asked him to join them as they left for dinner, nor had he made any effort to tag along.

She felt her nails digging into her palms as she stared into Spud's impassive blue eyes. They met hers for only a moment before looking away. *Odd,* she thought, *he's as uncomfortable in my presence as I am in his.*

She racked her brain for a way to open the conversation, to find some way to connect. *Lord, give me the words,* she prayed. Animal would have launched right into it, a direct, brutal head-on assault. She dismissed the thought. There had to be a better way. But what? Finding no answers, she decided to keep it neutral, safe. "How are you adjusting to life aboard ship?" she asked.

"No problems, but I can't say I'm enjoying sharing a stateroom with five of my closest friends."

Tamping down her visceral reaction to his grating voice, she forced a laugh. "I had a hard time at first too. I never had to share a room growing up, so I've always valued my privacy. Sleeping in a rack took some getting used to. How's your wife handling the separation? What's her name? Kim, isn't it?"

He nodded, his expression shifting so imperceptibly Kate almost missed it. *There's something happening on the home front*, she thought. *I must remember to talk to Digger about having the wives rally around her.*

"Is she plugged into the spouse's club?"

"She's gone back to spend the deployment with her folks."

Scratch that idea.

"I don't know that I've ever seen a picture of your child." His guarded expression dropped for a moment and an involuntary smile flashed across his face. Just as quickly as it came, it was gone, and the mask came back up. He fished in his wallet and handed her a small image, obviously a studio shot. A toddler dressed in blue denim overalls and striped T-shirt smiled toothily at the camera. She felt her heart go out to the child.

"He's beautiful," she remarked sincerely, handing the picture back.

Spud replaced it in his wallet.

"How old is he?"

"About two."

"I bet you miss him."

The mask shifted again. "I miss him a lot. To make matters worse, Kim is pregnant and due early summer."

Her first thought was to congratulate him, but she sensed this was what was eating at him. Was he homesick for his family and couldn't pull himself out of his misery?

Her frustration continuing to grow, she tried a different tack and changed the subject. Motioning to the binder beside him, she asked, "What are you reading?"

He showed her the cover. It was the tactics manual. Good on him for being in the books, but he didn't need to be studying tactics. He needed to be studying the flight manual, focusing on the basics of flying the Super Hornet. However, what he needed most was not going to come out of a book. He was going to have to find it deep within himself.

She took a deep breath and tried to marshal her thoughts. "Spud, I'm concerned about you. I look at the greenie board and your string of traps stands out like a sore thumb compared to the other pilots. In carrier quals you did just fine. What's going on?"

He looked at her again, his wide face expressionless. It took him a moment to answer. "I dunno. Things just don't seem to be coming together."

"Is it crosscheck? Are you overcorrecting? Are you not listening to the LSO?"

He looked down at his lap. "I'm not sure. Things happen so fast I feel like I'm a couple hundred yards behind the jet."

That concerned her. It was the confession of a newbie, someone still struggling to master the basic skills of flying a jet that could cut through the air at almost twice the speed of sound and land on a postage stamp at a speed most people would never consider driving.

"I'm not in your head, so I can't pinpoint your problem. You know how to do this. You just need to find that space inside of you that you had before. I have confidence in you."

Lord, forgive me for the lie.

Again, there was no expression, no emotion. There was much more she wanted to say, but she stopped herself. *Let's focus on one problem at a time, and right now the biggest is getting safely back aboard the ship.*

She climbed to her feet. "You'll be okay, Spud. I'm here for you."

Great job, Kate, she thought sarcastically as she walked away. *Lord, why do I find it so difficult to talk to this man, and why do I find it so hard to like him?*

She hadn't expected an answer and was not surprised when she didn't get one.

Kate stared in frustration at the rows of words on her computer screen. Her conversation with Spud had unsettled her, ruining her concentration. She rubbed at her burning eyes and tried to make sense of the words parading across her screen, but her eyes refused to focus. Even though she'd seen the movie before, the sounds of battle as US Army Rangers stormed ashore on Omaha Beach were a constant distraction.

Her fingers wandered to the small scar on her forearm, but she snatched them away. *Don't go there. No time for daydreaming.* She forced herself to stare at the computer screen but groaned as she felt the familiar tickle at the back of her mind. *Not again.*

She tried to force the memory back, but it was no use. Images began to unfold in her mind just like the video unfolding on the screen at the front of the ready room.

"Why didn't you tell me you had a horse?" Kate demanded as Morgan's truck downshifted. She had been expecting him to stop at a stable, but instead, he was taking them up a steep dirt road leading deep into the Sierra foothills.

He shrugged and offered a wry smile. "It didn't cross my mind." The response was lame, and she wanted to take him to task for it, but the warm sun beating down from a cobalt sky made her feel lazy, relaxed, companionable. She let the non-answer go.

Morgan pulled off the road into a large meadow ringed by trees, mountains rising steeply beyond.

"Eat first, or horse first?" he asked casually.

"Horse," she replied, perplexed. There was no pasture, no fence, no stable. Why on earth would he keep a horse out here?

"Horse it is," he said with a smile.

He whistled loudly. At first there was nothing. Pines sighed softly in a gentle breeze. A bird called. She turned to him, an impatient question on her lips, but relaxed as she saw him staring intently into the trees across the meadow. Her eyes followed his but saw nothing but an unbroken expanse of green.

She heard it first, the drumming of hooves echoing across the meadow, and a moment later, saw movement among the trees.

A large black creature, unlike any horse she had ever seen, cantered out into the meadow. Her breath caught in her throat as impressions piled one on top of another. Large like a warmblood. Long mane and tail streaming. Blacker than night, he didn't glisten but almost appeared to absorb light. He was not handsome like a

101

thoroughbred but more a creature of raw, elemental power. Sensing danger, she drew closer to Morgan and grasped his arm.

The horse came to a stop about fifty feet from them and snorted loudly, tossing his head. "Wait here," Morgan commanded. She was glad to hold back while he approached the magnificent creature. She expected the horse to rear up, but instead he lowered his massive head and nuzzled Morgan's chest. Morgan stroked one side of the creature's face and the horse seemed to take pleasure from it, a deep rumble emanating from his chest.

Morgan motioned her closer. Wild eyes rolled as she approached, and the animal shifted but quieted at Morgan's soft whisper. Midnight shivered at her first, tentative touch, but calmed as Morgan continued to whisper softly to him. Shoulder to shoulder with Morgan, she rubbed the horse's face and felt the tension gradually ease from the massive animal.

Morgan smiled. "Thought you would like him."

"I do. He's . . . magnificent." It was the only word she could think of. "What's his name?"

"Midnight."

"It fits. Can I get a picture of you two together?"

Morgan posed obligingly while she shot half a dozen pictures with her iPhone. "You're too stiff," she chided him. "Loosen up. Do something funny."

He placed his hands on both sides of Midnight's muzzle and made as if to kiss him. Midnight puckered his lips in return and gave Morgan a slobbery kiss that practically enveloped his whole face.

Kate held the shutter release down, taking a whole burst of pictures.

"Yuck," he exclaimed, wiping his face while Kate dissolved in peals of laughter.

He took her hand. "Come on. Let's go get something to eat."

He spread a blanket on the ground and fetched an ice chest from the truck. She expected sandwiches or KFC. Instead, he pulled out roasted Cornish game hens, potato salad, and strawberries dipped in dark chocolate.

"You must have been up half the night fixing this," she commented while her stomach rumbled its anticipation of the feast.

"I was." His smile made her heart flutter.

"You sure know how to impress a girl."

He smiled shyly in return. It was surprisingly vulnerable, an unusual break in his wall of self-assurance.

"Where did you learn to cook like this?" she asked around a mouthful of potato salad.

"I like to eat well. When I was younger, eating in restaurants all the time was not an option. Couldn't afford it, so I taught myself to cook."

Suddenly she wanted to know more about this enigmatic man sitting on the blanket with her.

"So tell me something else about you that I don't know," she demanded.

The corners of his mouth lifted in a self-deprecating smile. "Not much to tell, really. What you see is what you get. Nothing remarkable about my upbringing. Only kid. Christian parents. Both gone. Auto accident when I was at the academy. Went off to flight school. A few assignments and here I am."

"So, what's your favorite assignment?"

He looked uncomfortable, hesitated for a moment, then said, "This one, of course."

She blushed and shot him a glance. He was concentrating on a piece of chicken, studiously avoiding her eyes.

He changed the subject, obviously retreating to safer ground. "Tell me more about growing up in Wyoming."

After he had cleaned away the remains of the picnic, they lay side by side on the blanket. She looked drowsily at Midnight, grazing nearby.

The sky was impossibly blue. It was hot but not unbearable. A hawk shrilled overhead. Her eyelids grew heavy. She shifted to get comfortable. Her hand brushed his, grasped it. Fingers intertwined, she drifted off to sleep.

She slowly came awake, feeling deliciously lazy. Her hand felt small in his. A shadow crossed her closed eyelids. A cloud, she thought. Hot breath brushed her cheek. She opened her eyes. Midnight stood over her. He delicately touched her cheek with his velvety muzzle. She caressed his face with her free hand. He blew out another breath, raised his head, and walked slowly away brushing her with a strand of his tail as he turned.

She turned to Morgan, who, propped up on one elbow, was watching her with a broad smile on his face.

"I think he likes you," he said.

"I like him too. He's amazing. How long have I been out?"

"About forty minutes or so. You know you sleep with your mouth open?"

She slapped at him and started to utter an indignant, "I do not!" but he was laughing. She laughed with him.

He grasped her hand and hauled her to her feet. "It's getting late. We need to get you back to the base. You have an early go tomorrow."

She didn't want to leave but understood the necessity. "Can we say goodbye to him?"

"Of course."

Hand in hand they walked over to where Midnight slowly cropped the grass. She hugged his neck and he whickered softly in return. After a moment, Morgan slapped his rump and the horse turned and gave him what Kate could only interpret as an indignant look. Morgan slapped him again and the horse bolted into a full gallop, covering the distance to the trees in mere seconds. Kate gasped at the astonishing burst of speed. "Have you ever considered racing him?"

Morgan's eyes twinkled. "I've done it a time or two. It wasn't pretty."

"For him or the competition?"

"What do you think? Come on, sleepyhead. Let's go. We have a long drive ahead of us."

As her computer screen slowly swam back into focus and the sounds of battle resumed, Kate's mind whirled with confusion. How could something so real be just a dream? How could something so illogical be real? Yet the emotions, the sensations, the substance of it all felt sharp and focused, like something that had happened yesterday.

She felt a pang of loss. Morgan, so attentive, so unlike Nick. He saw to her core and found a way to nestle in beside it. She'd behaved so badly toward him, yet somehow their relationship had morphed into this comfortable easiness she had felt.

Where on earth was that DNA test? Lisa should have received it by now and forwarded it on. Was Morgan's blood actually on that towel or just hers?

Another thought exploded into her mind like a gunshot. *Morgan, you looked past all my ugliness toward you and found something to love. How do I find a way to look past Spud's?*

Chapter 17

"Colonel, why are we retreating?" George's question was not rhetorical. It was one that had burned in Merlyn's mind for days now. The Army of the Potomac, after its failed initial attack on Richmond, had withstood the various counterattacks the Confederates threw against it, held strong ground, inflicted heavy casualties, and yet it retreated from Richmond to make a stand by the James River, hostage to its commander's fears.

Merlyn lifted his feet from the clinging mud left by the previous night's rainfall and glanced back at the column of blue-clad men following them, rifles at shoulder, dejected, demoralized. They too shared George's question. They were still unblooded, had not participated in the last several days' fighting, but had heard the stories of Porter's V Corps holding strong, shattering and routing the Confederate regiments thrown against it. They had longed to join the fight while at the same time fearing it. They were leaner now, fitter than when they had left Albany. Their numbers were also fewer, illness and infirmity having weeded out the weak, the lame, the unable.

He loosely held Midnight's reins, the black horse plodding behind him, its hooves making a gentle sucking sound with each step it took. Hot sun blazed overhead, and he fished out a bandana to wipe a trickle of sweat from his forehead.

Merlyn had been making his way back down the long column, pausing briefly to chat with each company commander. Many of them had asked similar questions. Now it was George's turn. As with the other officers, Merlyn had no answer for him, at least not one he could share. He knew vaguely of McClellan's legacy from the history books. But that knowledge was for the future, not for the here and now.

If he seemed bothered by Merlyn's lack of response, George did not show it. Instead, he asked, "Will we ever get a chance to fight, or are we damned to this never-ending marching through this hellish countryside? If I never have to see another marsh or thicket, it will be too soon." He spat in the mud to emphasize his point.

Merlyn had seen the dogged determination in the young man, but had not realized the depth of his passion, had not expected this fiery outburst. Again, he knew the answer to this question as well. George would soon get what he was hoping for, in spades.

"Be patient, George," he said quietly. "We'll get our chance before too long. There's more than enough work for us to do. Your men ready?"

"Spoiling for a fight," George replied. "They're as ready as they will ever be."

A dull rumble sounded behind them, distant, muffled, and George flinched reflexively. Merlyn looked back at the column of men. A shiver rippled down it as some looked nervously in the direction of the guns. Others stoically kept their eyes on the mud. He could only guess which ones would stand and face the storm of lead that would soon come their way and which ones would break and run.

George lapsed into silence and the two men walked companionably shoulder to shoulder under a canopy of verdant green.

Merlyn welcomed the opportunity presented by a few moments alone with George. It allowed him to ask the question that had been burning inside him for weeks.

"I've noticed how you and the chaplain seem to avoid each other. Do you have a history?"

107

George kept his eyes fixed on the road and for a long moment, Merlyn did not think he would answer.

He kicked at a rock as his face twisted into a grimace. "Growing up, our family attended his church. He was all judgment and damnation. Whenever I misbehaved, he would accuse me of having a devil. He was very much cut of the same cloth as my father. Nothing I could ever do was good enough and they wasted no opportunity to let me know it." George's face tightened. "I don't share their faith," he said, his voice tight with barely suppressed emotion. "I don't need God. I get along just fine in life without him looking over my shoulder judging me. I get plenty of that from my father. And Barings is a hypocrite. He spews fire and brimstone against the enemy, but a less godly man I've yet to see. He doesn't have an ounce of human compassion and cares nothing for the men he's supposed to serve. Why should I listen to such a man?"

Reeling from the vehemence of George's reply, Merlyn considered his next words carefully. The door was open to plant a seed.

"God is a God of love," Merlyn answered. "Of peace, of joy. He doesn't want compliance from you; he wants your heart."

George turned to him, looking puzzled. "You have a rather strange view of religion, Colonel. You don't believe that God damns the unjust, the sinners, the fornicators? The people like me who have turned their backs on him?"

"I don't believe that God has any desire to damn anyone," Merlyn replied. "Life is not about measuring up, dos and don'ts, or following rules. I believe his heart's desire is that all men turn to him and enter into relationship with him. His hand is always outstretched, and the door to the kingdom always open. All we have to do is accept it. No matter what you think you have done, he is willing to wash it all away and make you right with him. You just have to ask."

George turned away, looking at the wall of green through which they were marching. "If only it were that easy," he said softly.

Merlyn saw the pain on his face, the regret, but also the stony set of his eyes fastened on the company before him. God was going to have his work cut out for him to soften this young man's heart. Merlyn would plant the seeds. God would see to the harvest. He hoped it would not be too long in coming.

***

July 1st, 1862
North of the James River, Virginia

"Here they come, boys!" Merlyn could not hear who shouted the words, thought it was one of the lieutenants. The voice was high-pitched, nervous.

After weeks of marching, it all comes down to this, Merlyn thought. The entire Union Army making a stand on this isolated hill in the Virginia countryside. The battle had raged for the better part of the afternoon before the 3rd Brigade had been thrown into the line during a lull in the fighting.

His men crouched behind a thrown-together jumble of logs and rocks, a slight depression hollowed out behind it. The late afternoon sun beat down on them. A trickle of sweat made its way down his back. His stomach knotted with dread at what was to come; he could see it all too clearly. The Union position atop the hill was strong, too strong for the Confederate regiments assaulting it. Cannon ringed the edge of the plateau, commanding an open field sweeping up to them from the north and west. They would massacre the Confederate soldiers marching up it.

The field was already dotted with fallen gray forms, some lying singly, some in ranks. A Rebel force had struggled its way up the hill and was now pinned down in a shallow ravine, safe from the cannon fire and the muskets of the blue-clad men waiting nervously behind their defenses.

Merlyn stared out across the field, where he could see more men in gray emerging from the woods, massing in ranks before stepping out into a hail of death and destruction. He took a quick glance to his left, saw Fothergill standing erect behind the center of the 172nd's line, flag-bearer at his side. Merlyn too was on foot,

109

Midnight safely to the rear. This was no place for mounted officers. He glanced at George, who was staring intently out over the field, and wondered what was going through his mind as he prepared to come under fire for the first time.

A few men shifted nervously as drums sounded and the Confederate ranks started toward them. With a roar, the cannon massed along the Union front opened up on the advancing soldiers with deadly accuracy. Merlyn looked up and down his line and breathed a quick prayer. *Lord, bless and protect these men today. Protect George and help him come through this in one piece.* He took his place by Fothergill and watched tragedy unfold before him.

The gray-clad lines advanced, the Federal artillery blowing huge gaps in them. Men fell, ranks closed, and still they came. He could see his own men tensing as the enemy drew closer. Some peered over the protective works, some bowed their heads, refusing to look. He saw one young soldier, a boy really, head down, lips moving in fervent prayer, the hands gripping his rifle trembling as with fever.

The Rebel advance faltered for a moment, then they were marching again, quicker, into the guns and into the waiting soldiers in blue. More fell. Passing the ravine where the other Confederates had taken shelter, some took advantage of the natural cover; most continued forward. A command echoed up and down the Union line. Soldiers rose, muskets pointed. Another command and muskets crashed, belching smoke and lead. The smoke obscured the field and caused his eyes to burn.

Men feverishly reloaded, preparing for another devastating volley, but it was not needed. As the smoke cleared, Merlyn saw to his horror that the neat lines of soldiers were gone, replaced by a carpet of bodies, some writhing, some stilled by death. A few enemy troops were left standing, but they were falling back, some leveling their muskets to fire, but most seeking the safety of the depression they had passed only a few moments before.

Merlyn scanned his own line. A few bodies testified to the accuracy of the Confederates' fire—some slumped forward over the log barrier; others huddled at its base. Many of the living stared out in fascination at the tableau of horror; others averted their eyes. One dropped his rifle and vomited violently into the grass.

"They're coming again!" The call was high-pitched, shrill. Around him, men stiffened their grips on their muskets. Many looked out over the defensive works at the oncoming enemy, their posture surer, less tentative than it had been earlier. They were becoming veterans.

Again, the Rebels threw their strength against the massed Union Army. Again, cannon and musket fire shattered their ranks. A pall of smoke hung in the air, thick, burning, choking. The sun dipped toward the horizon, blood red in its fiery intensity, appropriate for such a terrible day. He wondered at the pigheadedness of the commanders who would continue sending flesh and blood against massed iron and lead, and marveled at the courage of the men who would willingly march into such an onslaught of death.

But the battle had not been all one-sided. The last charge had almost reached the Federal line. More blue-clad bodies lay in the grass. Schimmelhorn lay on his back beside the flag, a massive, sodden hole in his chest, eyes staring sightlessly into the darkening sky. A young soldier, his arm almost severed above his elbow, cried softly for his mother as a companion wrapped a tourniquet above the wound. The sound wrenched at Merlyn's heart, as did the cries of the rest of the wounded up and down the line.

Cannon roared again, heralding another Rebel advance. *How long are you going to keep doing this?* Merlyn wondered.

Fothergill returned to the flag after having made a quick tour up and down the line. "Ammunition is starting to run a little low," he commented drily. "We'll beat these bastards yet." His face was red, slick with sweat. His jaw was firm, jutting forward. He had lost his hat earlier in the fighting, and his hair was wild, giving him the appearance of a berserker from an earlier age.

He gestured with his sword toward the advancing gray-clad ranks. "Magnificent courage. Got to hand it to these Rebs. They put on a good show."

If you only knew. If you only knew what is yet to come.

The advancing Confederates were thicker, more numerous, the ones who had been hiding in the depression rising to join their

111

ranks. Fothergill gave the order to fire. Again, smoke obscured the battlefield. When it cleared, the gray ranks were still coming. They stopped to fire a volley. This time it was their smoke that hid their lines. Something buzzed past Merlyn's head. Men grunted and collapsed as lead met flesh and bone. Balls smashed into timber, sending splinters flying.

There was movement in the blue line as several men dropped their muskets and backed away from the defenses. Sergeants hurled them back into line.

He approached Jameson, their company commander. "Keep a better hold of your men, Captain," he barked. "Your line almost broke there. We can't have that, not with this battle almost decided."

Jameson nodded grimly, his face streaked with soot, his kepi awry. "Sorry, sir. Devilish business this."

"It is that," Merlyn replied, forcing himself not to drop for cover as another volley buzzed past.

He looked up and down the line. The other companies were holding. Then he saw a sight that made him shudder with fear. In the midst of Company D, George stood atop the log barricade exhorting his men, pointing with his revolver toward an advancing regimental flag. He fired almost point-blank at the standard-bearer. The gray-clad man fell. Another Rebel soldier picked up the flag, and George shot him down as well. His men fired another volley, and the mass of enemy soldiers was gone, their flag toppling slowly to the ground. George darted out from the cover of the lines, snatched it up, and waved it back and forth, taunting the retreating men. A shot rang out and Merlyn's heart leapt into his throat as he waited for George to fall. The shot was wide, and George, walking slowly, dared the fleeing enemy to pause and shoot again.

Merlyn tried to calm his racing heart as he strode back to his place on the right. He glanced up to where Fothergill was standing still by the flag. He was breathing hard, fiery triumph in his eyes as he looked up and down his line. There were more bodies around him, those who had defended the flag with their lives. There was a tattered rip in the flag. *No doubt the first of many to come,* he thought grimly.

Cannon flashed orange in the gathering gloom. Then silence fell, punctuated only by the occasional musket shot and by the pitiful cries of the wounded.

Merlyn and Fothergill looked at each other. Fothergill extended his hand. "Thanks to you, Colonel, these men and I are now soldiers. I owe you an eternal debt of gratitude." Merlyn reluctantly took it, feeling only revulsion at his role in this butchery. He found no words to speak.

He was rescued by approaching hoofbeats. It was Eades and a couple of staff riders.

His face soot-streaked and grim, Eades leaned down out of the saddle to address them. "Well done, gentlemen. You held the line against the worst the enemy had to throw at you. We have new orders now."

Merlyn's stomach roiled, sensing what was coming. More caution. Opportunity thrown away. Victory turned into defeat. "Our brigade has been ordered to cover the army's withdrawal. We will remain along the crest of the hill and screen the army's movement. When they are clear we will get our orders to move out."

Fothergill was incredulous. "We've held off the entire Confederate army all day here. Why on earth would we retreat? We should go after the enemy, whip him soundly."

Merlyn was aware of shapes drifting in, listening to the exchange, the company commanders looking for orders.

Eades did not try to sugarcoat it. "Little Napoleon is concerned we're vulnerable here and is pulling the army back to Harrison's Landing. Several divisions are already on the road. As I said, we are the rear guard covering the withdrawal."

Fothergill spat again. "What safer ground is there than this magnificent hill? If McClellan has no stomach for a fight, why are we even out in the field rather than parading around some garrison like strutting popinjays?"

"That's enough, Colonel." Eades' voice was sharp. "You have your orders. Carry them out." He wheeled his horse, but before he could urge him forward, a voice spoke out of the darkness.

"General, a question before you go." It came out of the cluster of men behind Fothergill. It was too dark to see their faces, but Merlyn recognized George's voice. A tingle of dread worked its way down his spine. Was the brash young man going to make the situation even worse with some inane comment?

"Yes, what is it?" Eades' voice was tight with impatience.

"What is the name of this place my men spilled so much blood defending today?"

Eades' voice was incredulous. "They didn't tell you?"

"No, sir. We just marched up here and fell into line. Nobody told us much of anything other than to begin killing Rebs."

"This place is called Malvern Hill. Remember it," Eades said grimly. With that, he spurred his horse off into the night.

***

July 2ⁿᵈ, 1862
Harrison's Landing, Virginia

Exhausted, Merlyn sat outside his tent in the warm, sticky evening air. The scattered campfires were dying down, and around him the men were bedding down for the night.

The sight of George and Jameson walking together captured his attention, and he strained his ears to pick up what he could of their conversation.

"I have to hand it to you, Captain," Jameson said, "you displayed magnificent courage yesterday. Well done. If we keep this up, the war will be over by Christmas."

Merlyn saw George flush with pleasure at the praise.

"A moment, gentlemen," Merlyn called after them, pulling himself to his feet.

George and Jameson turned, expectation on their faces. "Captain, if you please, I need to speak with Captain Maxwell alone for a moment," Merlyn said softly but firmly to Jameson.

"As you wish, Colonel," Jameson replied, a note of relief in his voice.

"Walk with me." Merlyn motioned George away from the camp.

He turned as he walked, shot a glance at those familiar blue eyes in that familiar face, stern with determination, obviously sensing a dressing down. He felt another stab of fear. His being sent to a man was no guarantee of that man's safety. He had lost subjects before and still felt their losses as keenly as the day they had died. But this one was different. The very existence of the woman he loved more than life itself depended on the survival of this man.

"That was a very brave thing you did yesterday," he said softly. "But consider the risk to your men. Had that bullet struck you, you would have left the men leaderless when they needed you most. That flag would still have been lying there on the ground after the battle for you to retrieve at no risk to yourself and your men."

He lurched slightly as his boot snagged a root. George's hand shot out to steady him, and Merlyn was grateful for the contact.

George took a breath and Merlyn could see him gathering himself to argue. "George, a dead hero is no good to anyone."

"What do you mean?" George expostulated. "Can there be no greater thing than giving your life for a glorious cause?"

"You've been reading too much Horace," Merlyn replied softly. "Bravery is a good thing, but it is not an end in and of itself. The purpose of battle is to obtain an objective. It's to hold or take ground. It's to destroy an enemy's ability to make war. It's not to seek individual glory. Glory comes from a job well done, from achieving the objective."

George's face was a study in puzzlement. "Men will die in pursuit of the objective," Merlyn continued, "but don't throw their lives away on a foolish act. Don't throw your life away trying to be a hero. If you must die, then die doing your job.

"You might think that dying a glorious death on the battlefield will vindicate you in the eyes of your family, but it won't. All it will get you is dead, and then you're of no further use to the men you lead."

George was silent for a long moment, the only sound the muted noise of the army all around them. From the expressions crossing his face, he was struggling with Merlyn's words, not knowing what to make of them. Finally, he spoke.

"Thank you, Colonel. You've given me something to think about. I'm grateful."

The humility surprised Merlyn. But the matter was not over, not by a long shot. Three more years of war stretched before them. Hopefully George would take his words to heart, become the soldier he had the promise of becoming, become the man God called him to be. Then Merlyn's job would be done, and he could leave this awful place.

Chapter 18

Kate's head shot up at the sudden intake of breath in the Dirty Shirt wardroom. She knew instantly what it was, didn't need to ask, nor did anyone else in the compartment other than the greenest of nuggets. Someone was in the barrel. Her lungs tightened in involuntary sympathy as she remembered the night during her first deployment it had been her turn. The driving rain. The unstable air that tossed her jet around like a cork. The pitching deck and the meatball that refused to stay centered. Two wave-offs and the steadily illuminated "Fuel Low" light. One final chance to get her Hornet down or go for a swim. She'd done it, but reliving the terror of the moment made sweat bead on her forehead.

"Who is it?" she asked Trojan, sitting next to her, plowing his way through his second hamburger.

"Friggin' Spud," he replied, his voice tight with anger. "If he bends my jet, he'll wish he'd died in a ramp strike instead."

Kate swallowed hard against the bile rising in her throat and pushed her chair back. "Clean up for me, Trojan, please. I gotta go."

She had to get back to the ready room. *But why?* Being in the ready room might give her some false illusion of control, but there was nothing she could do for Spud. There was nothing anyone could do. The only person alive who could land his jet was sitting all alone in the dark above an empty expanse of ocean. It was him against his fears.

The ready room was quiet with tension, the LSO camera projected on the big screen, the radio communications playing over the speakers.

"You've got this, son," the LSO said as Spud began his turn to base, his voice a deep, calming southern drawl. "You've done this dozens of times before. You can do it tonight. Fly the ball and not the deck. Keep your corrections small. Wiggle your toes. Get rid of some of that tension."

Kate felt a momentary stab of sympathy but quickly squelched it. He had to man up, focus, get this right, or he was en route to another wave-off, or worse, a ramp strike. All naval aviators had seen the video loops, the succession of airplanes from F-4 Phantoms to F/A-18 Hornets—too low on their approaches and too far back on the power curve for the sudden application of afterburner to rescue them—plow into the back of the boat in spectacular explosions of flame and smoke. Never, ever be low approaching the carrier.

Spud was on final now, the LSO's voice on the radio calm and reassuring, keeping up a constant stream of chatter. "Two-six-one, three quarters of a mile. Call the ball."

"Two-six-one, ball, three point eight." In contrast to the LSO's, Spud's voice was tight, thrumming with tension like a cable on the verge of snapping.

"You know how to do this. Keep your corrections small. Fly the ball."

There was nothing to be seen on the screen but the glow of Spud's landing light against the blackness of the night. Kate bit her lip at the slight lurch that vibrated through her feet as the TR rolled with a swell. It wasn't much in the bowels of the ship, but to Spud alone in the dark, the deck movement would appear significant, magnified by the adrenaline coursing through his veins.

To cover the three quarters of a mile to the ship, it would take a little over twenty seconds, but they could be the longest, most terror-filled seconds of an aviator's life. "You're drifting right;

come slightly left." The LSO's voice continued to project authoritative reassurance.

Kate couldn't see the landing light move. The required correction was too small. "You're a little high. Bring her down."

There was an edge to the LSO's next command as Spud overcorrected. "Bring her up. You're dropping low."

The landing light was growing in the screen as Spud approached the stern of the TR. "Power. Power. Power." The LSO's voice conveyed in no uncertain terms the seriousness of the situation, and Kate felt her breath catch as she visualized the ball flashing red, directing Spud to abort his landing. "Wave off. Wave off. Wave off."

Her heart in her throat, Kate watched the landing light seemingly hang in midair. Thoughts cascaded through her mind. The remembered flash of fire as a Hornet crashed into the ramp. An image of Spud with his son.

She released her breath as vertical separation began to grow between the landing light and the stern of the ship. She thought she could hear the roar of engines as Spud rocketed over the ship for what would be his last pass before he ignominiously diverted to the Korean mainland and an expanse of stationary concrete that would pose no challenge to his compromised flying skills.

"Lord, please be with him." She breathed a silent prayer, surprised at the depth of her emotion. "Help him in his time of need."

Minutes ticked by as the tension in the room grew. Spud may not have been one of the boys, but everyone had been in his shoes. Everyone except Jethro, that is. He leaned over to make what Kate took to be a snide comment in Nemo's ear and received a sharp "not now" in reply.

Kate's throat tightened as Spud began his turn to final. "Give me one good pass, son." The LSO said calmly, as if he were out for a walk in the park. "You've got plenty of gas. No pressure at all."

A light appeared on the darkness of the screen as Spud's wings leveled. "Two-six-one, ball, three point three."

Her heart in her throat, she watched the light on the screen grow steadily larger. Strangely there were no words from the LSO, no course corrections, no drawling encouragement; just silence.

Spud's jet slammed onto the deck, decelerated rapidly to a stop, and the ballet of the deck crew began as he was disconnected from the wire and marshaled to his parking spot.

Kate turned away from the screen, the tension rushing from her body. Somehow Spud had dug deep inside himself and found what he was lacking.

The movie the squadron had been watching resumed on the screen as if nothing in the world had happened. Something about car chases and revving engines and highly improbable stunts and crashes.

Thirty minutes later, when Spud came back into the ready room, no head popped up from the banks of chairs to acknowledge his presence. Kate turned to see Digger, arm around Spud, lean close and whisper something into his ear. Even from a distance, Kate could see the slight smile blossom on Spud's face. Digger clapped him on the back and disappeared up the companionway toward his stateroom.

Hot and grimy from her afternoon flight, Kate carried her tray across the half-full Dirty Shirt wardroom. She grimaced at the contents of her plate. Salad with vinaigrette dressing, hamburger, no bun, a couple of slices of pickles. Her stomach growled for more, but finding the time to exercise was tough, and she didn't need to be packing on the pounds. However, her discontent over her meager dinner could do nothing to dispel the warm glow in her heart. Spud's row on the greenie board now sported a pair of greens since the red dot marking his turn in the barrel a couple days ago.

Banger, Toad, and Jethro sat together, and she angled that way to join them, but movement out of the corner of her eye caught her attention. She paused. A female aviator, one she didn't know, sat alone at a table in the far corner of the compartment, uneaten meal pushed aside, a letter spread out on the table before her. She looked furtively around her before dabbing at red, swollen eyes.

Kate looked away, not wanting to invade the woman's privacy, and resumed her progress to join her flight. Jethro threw his head back, his loud bray of laughter cutting across the quiet hum of conversation filling the compartment.

Before she could form a conscious thought, she found herself turning, making her way toward the solitary figure. As she approached, she gave the woman a quick once-over—tanned, slender, with the exception of her close-cropped blonde hair, the spitting image of any number of young women who hung out on Southern California beaches. Kate scanned her patches. Her name tag read "Heather Lawson." Railroad tracks on the shoulder of her flight suit proclaimed her to be a lieutenant. Pilot's wings. Black and silver death's head patch and scythe with the logo "Reapers."

One of the EA-18G Growler pilots who had joined them from NAS Whidbey Island, Kate realized. She had the greatest admiration for the crews who flew the suppression of enemy air defenses mission. Their job was to hang it all out and duel with the SAMs and AAA surrounding a target so the strikers could do their job. It was dangerous work. Over the years many had not come home.

Her footsteps faltered as she approached the table. *Why am I doing this? I don't know her.* But before she could turn away, she found herself depositing her tray on the table and sliding onto the bench.

"Hi, I'm Elsa," she said, holding out her hand.

The woman looked up, startled, and reflexively reached out to take the proffered hand. "Sparkle," she replied, and quickly added a rueful, "Don't ask," to Kate's raised eyebrow. "Just a little buffoonery that's going to stay with me my whole career."

"I'm sorry for intruding," Kate stammered, her voice betraying her nervousness. "I don't normally do this, but you look like you could use some company right now. Anything I can do to help?"

Sparkle's red-rimmed eyes widened with surprise, but Kate saw the set of her shoulders relaxing a tad as her words sank in.

"If you want to be alone I understand," Kate interjected quickly.

121

"No, it's okay," she responded. "There's nobody in my squadron I can talk to. The other two women are married, and the guys won't understand. They'd just tell me to suck it up."

"Bad news?" Kate asked, nodding to the letter that Heather had hurriedly tucked under her tray.

Heather's eyes started to shimmer again, and she angrily brushed her hand across them. "Fiancé dumped me," she said, her voice trembling with barely suppressed anger and hurt. "He doesn't like that I'm gone all the time and didn't have the guts to tell me to my face. He came to Whidbey to see me off and then dropped this in the mail that afternoon. Coward."

Kate felt her anger rising in response as her own memories of her final conversation with Nick came flooding back. She opened her mouth to respond, to add her own tale of woe, but a small nudge in her spirit stopped her cold. This was not the time to start in on a session of male bashing.

"At least mine had the decency to tell me to my face," Kate said slowly. "I had the opportunity to tell him exactly what I thought of him. But it didn't make it any easier," she hastened to add as she saw Heather's mouth firm into a thin line.

"How did you deal with it?" Heather asked. "My emotions are going crazy right now. I want to find a quiet corner, to curl up and cry, but there's no privacy in my stateroom. At the same time, I want to get angry, break something, just get it out of my system. I feel like I'm coming unglued."

"I felt the same," Kate replied. "I threw myself into my work and used it as an anesthetic. In time the hurt went away. Or maybe I just buried it," she added reflectively, wondering why she was opening up so much to this stranger.

"But you got over it?" Heather asked, her chin quivering slightly.

Kate thought a moment before answering. "Yes and no," she said slowly. "Work gave me something to focus on, but the hurt never really went away until I replaced it with something else."

Heather's eyes narrowed quizzically. "How do you mean?"

Kate took a deep breath. "It only went away when I opened myself back up and chose to love again. In effect, I replaced hurt with love and that made all the difference." *Why am I telling her this? Yeah, love overcame hurt, but that love is a dream. It's not real.*

Heather's eyes met hers, probing, searching as if to gauge the truth of her words. Finally, she seemed to find what she wanted and nodded her head in silent satisfaction. "Thank you, Elsa. That helps. Or, should I call you Kate now that we're going to be friends?"

Kate bristled slightly at the presumption, but truth be told, Lisa's absence had left a hole in her life. With the way this deployment was going, it would be good to have someone outside the squadron to talk to. "I'm Kate to my friends, Heather," Kate replied. "Elsa's for the squadron. Let's leave it at that, shall we?"

With a fullness in her heart, she watched Heather pick up her fork and take a first, tentative bite of her meal.

Chapter 19

"Get away from him, you ghoul." Merlyn bore down on the figure that was bent over a blood-soaked body sprawled against a shattered tree stump. The camera sitting on its tripod, the donkey cart nearby, clearly told what was happening. His rage increased. Gruesome as the scene was, it was a postage stamp-sized tableau of horror set against a much larger tapestry, the wreckage of human and animal life covering the ground as far as the eye could see.

He picked up his pace, almost running, as George struggled to keep up.

The photographer looked up, startled, revealing the dead man.

Sickened, Merlyn recognized Jameson's face. His rage continued to grow. The thought of this brave man's mangled body memorialized for all time in black and white caused his stomach to heave.

The photographer uttered a profanity but quickly quieted as Merlyn's hand went for his pistol. Grumbling, he gathered up his equipment and put it into the back of his cart.

"Damnable business, George," Merlyn said, wiping his face with a bandana. He looked down at the body. Jameson had died from a single bullet wound to the chest. He had not died instantly or easily. Instead, he had bled out from the massive trauma of a one-ounce lead minié ball ripping its way through flesh and bone.

He beckoned to the small group of his men who hovered nearby. "Collect his body and have it prepared for shipment home," he ordered.

He looked out over the field. Bodies were strewn everywhere, some individual, some in clusters. Some wore blue, some gray. A few yards away a half-dozen Company C men lay shoulder to shoulder, felled by a single volley. He knew them each by name, knew of their families and their hopes and dreams, now forever unattainable. He felt bile rise in his throat and quickly looked away.

Just beyond them, a twelve-pounder Napoleon lay, carriage shattered, muzzle buried in the ground, its crew dead around it. Beyond it . . . *No*, he thought, forcing his eyes to look away. *Concentrate on the task at hand,* he ordered himself impatiently.

Months of marching and countermarching had all come down to this. The Army of the Potomac and the Army of Northern Virginia had collided two days ago outside the sleepy Maryland town of Sharpsburg in the single bloodiest day in American history. Merlyn had known of it from the history books, but the reality of the slaughter had been far beyond anything he could possibly have conjured up in his feeble imaginings.

All around them groups of men collected the wounded and laid out the dead for burial. The afternoon sun was sweltering, the bodies starting to bloat. The odor of death permeated the warm and sticky air. His stomach contracted painfully, and he fought the almost overwhelming urge to empty it onto the ground.

When he had forced his stomach into submission, he began to mentally trace the regiment's progress across the battlefield, trying to pinpoint where Fothergill had fallen.

Not far from them, Merlyn noticed a scarecrow-like black figure walking slowly among the dead. Barings, giving solace in his fashion to the dying.

"Mother," a weak voice came from somewhere nearby.

Merlyn grasped George's arm. "Stop. Listen," he hissed.

The voice came again from off to their right.

Merlyn started that way.

"Mother, please . . ." The voice was barely a whisper.

"Over here, sir." George motioned Merlyn to a huddled butternut-clad figure, abdomen black with blood, entrails spilling out of a gash in his shirt.

George turned away and emptied his stomach onto the grass.

"Chaplain, over here," Merlyn called to Barings.

Barings turned and walked slowly over to them. He looked down at the wounded soldier and spat. "He's a rebel," he declared, his face pinching in disdain.

"I don't care if he's a rebel," Merlyn spat out the words, his anger burning white-hot. "He's a human being."

Barings turned away with a dismissive snort. "Our own men need me." He walked off with a bobbing gait that reminded Merlyn of a vulture in search of carrion.

Fighting the urge to shout after Barings, Merlyn dropped to his knees. The rebel soldier was little more than a boy—maybe sixteen, possibly younger. He took the boy's hand. It was calloused, hard. The boy's head turned slowly, glazed, unfocused eyes seeking his. His chest rose as he struggled for breath.

"Mother?" The word was barely more than a soft expulsion of breath.

Merlyn felt tears prickling his eyes. He was dimly aware of George kneeling to the boy's other side. "Dear Jesus," he whispered. "Show this child your love. Give him grace. Accept him into your kingdom."

With his other hand, Merlyn gently cupped the boy's face. A tear fell from his eye onto it, and he brushed it gently away with his thumb. The boy's chest rose once more, fell, and then was still.

Merlyn closed the staring eyes and rose to his feet, his knees creaking painfully. George stood beside him white-faced, eyes shimmering. Wordlessly, they resumed their search.

They found Fothergill's body after another half hour of searching. He lay in a crumpled heap where he had fallen, eyes open, unseeing, teeth clenched as if in pain.

Merlyn rolled Fothergill on his back. There was no blood on his tunic or anywhere on his body. A wave of sadness rolled over him.

"I think his heart gave out, George," Merlyn said softly. "I knew he wasn't healthy, but he drove himself until his body just couldn't handle it anymore."

Despite Fothergill's brusque, arrogant manner, Merlyn had liked the man. He had cared deeply for his men and had led them as best as he was able. Now he was gone, and it was up to someone else to lead the regiment.

He climbed wearily back to his feet. "George, make arrangements to get him home to his family. Since Summerfield's wounded, you're acting major."

He paused. There were so many things to tend to. Burial details, recording the names of the dead and wounded. Appointment of new officers to replace the fallen. Barings' insubordination. He began barking orders which George absorbed, a dazed look on his face.

He's going to have to step up to the responsibility being forced on him, Merlyn thought grimly. I just hope he's ready.

"I'm going to visit Major Summerfield," Merlyn concluded. "The wound on his leg was bad and I'm thinking he's going lose it."

Clutching his bandana across his nose and mouth in a vain attempt to shield himself from the miasma of death that pervaded the hot, humid September air, he strode back across the battlefield.

That evening, Merlyn stood before his tent surveying the grim, haggard faces of the surviving officers, arrayed in a semicircle before him. They were exhausted, but the resolve flowing from them was almost palpable.

"You and your men fought magnificently," Merlyn declared, allowing his pride to reflect in his voice. "The nation will always remember what you did here. You dealt Lee and his army a blow they will never forget. You have shown the enemy they are not invincible. Whatever our critics may say, we are in possession of the field today, and Lee is slinking back home licking his wounds— wounds you gave him."

The words felt hollow to him, but they were words these young officers needed to hear. Still reeling from the horror of the battle, they needed affirmation and hope.

"I'm proud of you. Your country is proud of you. You have proven yourselves to be true warriors. We've lost a lot of officers and men. We need to rebuild so we can fight another day. Many of you are going to be in acting command of your companies and platoons until we can confirm you on paper. Don't let that formality stand in the way of your exercising leadership of your men."

"Colonel, a question?" Johanns interrupted.

"Yes, Captain," Merlyn responded.

"Does this mean you're colonel now that Colonel Fothergill is dead?"

It was the last thing Merlyn wanted. "No," he replied. "I'm leading only until General Eades appoints another colonel. However, we need to get the 172nd New York back into fighting condition, and we can't wait for the army to appoint another commander before we do so."

Johanns nodded somberly.

"You and your men did as well as any regiment on the field of battle," he said quietly. "Historians for centuries will examine what took place here. They will come to many different conclusions about who won and who lost or who made this mistake or that mistake. That's unimportant. They were not here. You were."

As the officers drifted back to their companies, George hung back, clearly wanting to talk. "What's on your mind, George?" Merlyn asked gently.

"Did we really do well or are you just saying that?" George asked. "We lost so many men, and for what? The enemy is gone, and here we sit doing nothing. Why?"

Merlyn had no good answer for him. It was the question of the day, one which drove to the heart of McClellan's legacy. He looked at George and let his silence speak for itself.

When George saw he would get no answer, he turned away, spat out a profanity, and strode off into the camp.

The sun dipping below the horizon painted the sky a tapestry of brilliant reds, golds, and oranges as Merlyn sank onto a camp stool. A blanket of moist, steaming air hung over the camp, making him long for the days, still far in the future, of air conditioners and light, loose-fitting clothing.

The sound of horses approaching pulled him out of his reverie. He recognized Eades and Captain Saunders, his aide. Merlyn rose and saluted. Eades' face was gray and haggard, lines of strain etched into it. A blood-soaked bandage wrapped his right hand.

"Good evening, Colonel. Pardon me if I remain mounted. I can only stay for a moment. How are your men?"

"Spoiling for a fight."

"They'll get their chance, I'm sure. Please assemble your officers."

Merlyn turned to Keys, who was hovering within earshot, arm in a sling, a bandage around his head. "Lieutenant, have the bugler sound 'Officer's Call.'"

The bugle's clear notes rang out across the camp, and the handful of surviving officers quickly assembled behind Merlyn.

"Gentlemen, I can only stay for a moment," Eades announced to the group standing expectantly before him. "You and your men fought fiercely in the great battle that took place here. General Munro and I observed how valiantly you charged the enemy's position and how bravely you held your position when the enemy counterattacked. You are a credit to your state and to your country."

He paused and looked each officer in the face. Merlyn could feel them stiffen with pride.

"I lament the loss of your brave colonel. He was a great man on and off the field of battle. But this is war, and the fight must continue. Therefore, I am appointing Lieutenant Colonel Michaelson, colonel of the 172nd New York."

His officers' spontaneous cheer interrupted Eades' speech. Eades smiled down at Merlyn. "I see that I have your men's approval. Well done, colonel." With that, he wheeled his horse and rode off into the gathering dusk.

The following morning found Merlyn in a quandary. He stared down at the two papers on the field desk before him. One would fill the lieutenant colonel position he had vacated; the other would replace Summerfield as major. All that remained was for the names to be added.

The air in the tent was stifling. With every breath it seemed as if he were taking in as much water as air. Exhausted, he wanted nothing more than to flop on the cot behind him and immerse himself in a pleasant memory of Kate, use it as a balm to purge the horror of the battle just fought. But rest would have to wait. This had to be done first, and then the appointment of the other officers.

The choices were clear. While all officers had done their jobs well through the summer of campaigning, two had risen to the top. Steady, reliable Johanns. With his practical common sense and his rock-solid steadiness, he would make an outstanding second. The men respected him and would follow him anywhere.

George deserved the job as much as did Johanns, but for different reasons. Where Johanns was practical and steady, George was imaginative and full of vigor. In a pinch, Johanns would stay and slug it out. George would find a way out. The men liked them both, would accept either choice.

Merlyn wiped his bandana over his face and forced himself to think, but it was as if his mind were working through wet concrete. The choice should be clear, easily made, but in his fatigued state it just wouldn't come. Johanns or George? Steady or brilliant?

All in all, he leaned toward George—courage and passion counted for much. So did dependability, his mind argued back. During the battle, George and his men had performed well. There was no sign of the recklessness he had shown at Malvern Hill.

But there was another reason to make George lieutenant colonel, one that had nothing to do with courage, dependability, or skill in battle. This one was entirely personal. Making George his number two would put them together more, give him more opportunities to do what he had been sent to this time to do. The sooner he could lead George to faith, the sooner he could get back to Kate.

He made his choice. Only after he had filled the names into the two orders did the thought cross his mind—*why on earth had he not thought to pray through the decision?*

His stomach tightened as another thought crossed his mind. *What day was it?* They all blurred together. September nineteenth? No, the twentieth. Just under three months until the next major battle and that damnable wall that caused the Union Army so much grief. Three months to get George ready for what was to come, but how do you get anyone ready for something like that? Even more importantly, how do you keep him alive?

Chapter 20

K ate sensed the charged atmosphere in the ready room the moment she stepped inside. Her muscles ached from the constant gs she'd pulled with Jethro, and she had an incipient headache, the result of never drinking enough water, given the primitive sanitary arrangements in the Super Hornet. *Why couldn't this be a normal deployment with normal pilots without this never-ending drama?* She stifled a groan.

She scanned the ready room, knowing instinctively the source of the tension. Spud. He sat in his seat, to all appearances engrossed in his NATOPS binder. She could tell by the set of his shoulders and the flush suffusing the back of his neck that something was eating at him. She glanced at the greenie board. Mercifully another green, so that wasn't it.

A loud guffaw sounded from where Bags, Toad, and Jasper had just been joined by Jethro, who had preceded her into the ready room. All eyes were directed at Spud, who almost imperceptibly hunched deeper into his seat.

She heaved a sigh. It would be so easy to ignore the incident. She was tired, her headache was settling in with a vengeance, and she still had to debrief with Jethro who had done at best an average job at BFM that afternoon. However, her sense of injustice was truly piqued.

"Knock it off," she ordered the group who were still chortling at the back of the ready room. With resentful glares they fell silent.

"Jethro, have a seat. I'll be with you in a minute." She gave a meaningful glare to Bags and Toad, who suddenly realized they had other work to do.

She scanned the compartment. Of the squadron leadership, only Trojan, head buried in a report, occupied the front row of seats.

"What the heck is going on?" Kate demanded, striding up to him. Trojan looked up, gave her a bland stare, and then glanced back at Spud.

Trojan shrugged. "Oh, nothing. Just some good-natured ribbing." His mouth twitched. "Spud got his ass handed to him by a viper chick out of Kunsan this morning." His voice rose in falsetto mimicry. "Tracking kill Hornet right-hand turn."

Kate felt her cheeks flame. "Trojan, you know better than that. Knock the gender stuff off," she snarled. "I can hand any of you your asses on any given day."

Trojan bristled but kept his voice calm. "The difference is, Elsa, you've earned your place. You're good and everyone knows it. It's not about you. It's about him. He's weak, not pulling his weight."

After a brief, silent debate, Kate decided to allow him to dodge the real issue. Right now, the focus had to be on Spud.

"Trojan, I need your help," she said, tamping down her anger. "Today Jethro couldn't find his ass with both hands. They're nuggets. They make mistakes. You guys accept Jethro because he's a party animal and tries to be part of the crowd. Spud has an awkward personality, and you're pushing him away because of it. If I were a nugget and you treated me the way you treat him, I'd shut down too. Cut him some slack."

She paused and glared intently at Trojan, refusing to release his eyes. Seconds ticked by and finally he nodded and looked back at the tablet on his lap. "Thank you," Kate said more harshly than she intended. "You do your part, and I'll get him to meet the rest of us halfway."

The earnestness in her voice must have carried some weight because he visibly relaxed, his mouth curling into a humorless smile. "You got it, Elsa. Sorry for the comment earlier. It was inappropriate. I'll talk to the guys, but you gotta get through to him. It's not going to work unless he makes an effort."

An hour later, debriefing finished, Kate glanced at her watch. It was late. The evening movie was about to start, and she'd not had dinner. Still, she had unfinished business. She made her way to where Spud was seated. He'd closed the NATOPS manual and was staring blankly at the screen at the front of the ready room, his face a frozen mask. "Hey, Spud. I haven't eaten yet. Join me for a snack?"

He jerked, startled at the sound of her voice. "I'm not hungry." The reply was automatic.

"I figured you'd already eaten, but you've seen this movie before. I have something I want to talk to you about."

Astute enough to tell the difference between an order and a request, Spud rose to his feet.

In the Dirty Shirt, Kate took only a couple bites of her burger before pushing it aside. She took a deep breath. *Here goes nothing,* she thought. *Just lay it out straight, the way it is.*

"Spud, we have a problem." Despite her soft, conversational tone he visibly stiffened. *So much for the direct approach. Now he's on the defensive.*

"I want you to know I'm on your side," she plowed on. "You have the makings of a good pilot. You're doing as well as any other nugget on the boat. In the air, you're doing okay. You fixed your landings. You're in a much better place than when we talked a couple of weeks ago.

"The problem seems to be something else, something that's holding you back from committing to the squadron, becoming part of it. Animal was rough on you, but he's gone. The rest of the guys are willing to make you part of the team, but you have to meet them halfway." She paused, offering him the chance to respond, but he looked down at the table and remained stubbornly silent.

"Spud," Kate said, suddenly frustrated. "You may not believe this, but I'm trying to help. I care about you."

Spud's head snapped up, his eyes narrowing with disbelief. "Really?" he snorted. "I would have thought you only cared about yourself."

I'm done with this. Kate started to push away from the table but stopped herself. *He really believes that.* The realization crashed over her, stunning her to immobility. *That's the way Morgan saw me too.*

Spud stared defiantly at her, undoubtedly expecting a dressing-down for his temerity.

Her cheeks burned with shame. *I've been going about this all wrong.* Was there anything she could say that wouldn't make an already bad situation worse? Had she lost him irrevocably or was there still some way to win him over?

She drew a deep, shuddering breath as she tried to collect her thoughts. "I'm sorry you feel that way," she said slowly. "I can see why you'd think I've been riding you. It wasn't my intent and I apologize. I have been trying to help. You worked hard to become a naval aviator. Don't throw it away because the squadron got crosswise with you. Try to join them. If you make the effort, I'll do everything in my power to see to it that they let you in."

Spud remained silent, a rock of isolation. Kate felt a sharp pang of sympathy as she climbed to her feet. How awful it must be to be alone and friendless in an environment where everyone lives and breathes as a member of a close-knit team.

"Spud, I'm truly sorry." Kate tried to project every ounce of sincerity into her voice and was surprised to find she meant it. Her vision shimmered and Spud must have seen the moisture welling in her eyes because his face softened.

As Kate walked away, she wondered if she heard or imagined the soft "okay" that followed her retreating back.

"What did you expect?" Heather demanded the next day. "The squadron has ostracized him. You approach him like a bull in a china shop. Of course he's going to be defensive."

As much as it hurt, Kate had to admit the truth of Heather's words.

Kate's hair whipped in the breeze caused by the TR plowing through the ocean at more than twenty knots. Normally frequented by non-flying types, vulture's row high on the island gave them a panoramic view of the flight deck. Kate liked to escape up here for a glimpse of daylight and a breath of fresh air. The morning go had launched and recovery operations had not yet started, so there was a lull in the noise that normally engulfed the flight deck. For just a brief moment conversation was possible.

"But what should I do? My attempt to talk to him last night was a disaster. He shuts down whenever I'm around him. He's almost worse with me than he is with the rest of the squadron."

Heather's eyes fixed on Kate's, her brow furrowing. "We haven't known each other very long," she said with a slight hesitation in her voice. "Can I speak plainly with you?"

Kate's throat tightened. *On top of all the issues with the squadron, with Spud, now what?* Reluctantly she nodded.

Heather took a deep breath, fear replacing anxiety in her eyes. The sight caused Kate's heart to miss a beat. *Why is she afraid of me?* Mouth suddenly dry, she dreaded the words to come.

"I don't know if you're aware, but you can be intimidating as hell," Heather blurted out and stopped, anxiously scanning Kate's face for any sign of disapproval. Kate tried to keep her face bland, encouraging, stifling her immediate defensive reaction. *Roll with it. Don't shut her down. She's trying to help.*

"You're not a bitch who throws her weight around, uses her gender to get what she wants. I wouldn't be your friend if you were like that, but you're aloof, distant. I know you don't like your call sign, but Elsa kind of fits you."

Heather stopped, anxiously biting her lip, obviously wondering if she had gone too far. Kate looked away from her out over the fantail at the green and white wake churning behind the carrier. *Like my emotions right now,* she thought ironically. Everything within her screamed, *Shut this down. Get out of here. She doesn't know you. Oh, but she does,* a small, rational voice deep inside of her spoke softly. *She has you pegged.*

Kate turned back to Heather, who was still worrying her lip, looking as if she wanted to flee. "It's all right," Kate said, trying to muster what little reassurance she could find. "I need to hear this."

Relief flooded Heather's features. "It's not that you're doing anything wrong," she said breathlessly. "You're so together, so competent, so in control. You never let anyone see the real you.

You don't really reach out to people, and they don't see you as approachable. They respect you but also give you plenty of space. That's why none of the other girls in the wing are connecting with you."

That hurt. In her dream, the man she'd loved had told her something similar. "You connected with me," she stammered. "Why are you different?"

"I'm not," Heather replied. "You reached out to me. Remember?"

Kate nodded as Heather continued. "You let me behind your wall and showed me that you really are a caring, sensitive person. You approached me to find out what was wrong and didn't tell me how to fix it. You allowed me to connect with you. That makes all the difference.

"And that's your problem with your nugget. You've been telling him he's broken. You're trying to fix him. He's hunkered down behind his own wall. You're trying to batter it down when you should be trying to connect with him as a person."

Kate felt a slight shudder in the deck beneath her feet as the TR began its slow, ponderous turn into the wind to begin recovery operations. Soon this peaceful window would close as the scream of jet engines would make further conversation impossible.

Kate let out a long, sighing breath. "Thanks for that," she said softly. "It hurt to hear, but I needed it. We should head below."

As she made her way back to the Outlaws' ready room, one thought played over and over in Kate's mind: *You're going to have a real hard time overcoming past damage with Spud. Problem is, with the news out of Iran getting worse every day, you're not going to have a whole lot of time to do it.*

137

Chapter 21

"Ugh, I can't eat this mess." George pushed his plate away after having taken only a couple of bites of the congealing stew. "If it were possible, this food's gotten worse since the battle."

Merlyn pushed his stool back from his desk, which was serving as a makeshift table. "Follow me," he demanded, making only a half-hearted attempt to tamp down the anger surging up inside him.

He found Lieutenant Guthrie, the commissary officer, sitting on a barrel, reclining against a tree, crossed legs resting on a keg of salt. He had wisely positioned himself upwind of the three cauldrons suspended from a stout log over a firepit. Two soldiers had been detailed to cook, but with them was another man—this one a civilian.

He was raggedly dressed, close-cropped hair, his skin the color of coffee. A contraband, an escaped slave who had been dragooned into performing manual labor for the army, Merlyn guessed.

Guthrie was a slovenly, heavyset man. His sack coat was unbuttoned, the calico shirt under grease-stained. Indeterminate items of food matted his thick, curly beard. His eyes barely registered Merlyn's approach as he absently chewed on a piece of hardtack.

Anger surging, Merlyn kicked the keg out from under Guthrie's feet. "When a senior officer approaches, you stand. Show some respect."

Thrown off balance, Guthrie almost fell but struggled to his feet. Merlyn nearly gagged at the reek of body odor mixed with cheap alcohol emanating from the man.

"The next time I see you," Merlyn said through clenched teeth, "you will be wearing a clean uniform, properly buttoned, and you will render the appropriate military courtesies. Do I make myself clear?"

Guthrie's face blanched as he uttered a strangled, "Yessir."

"Follow me," Merlyn barked as he turned toward the cooking pit. He didn't check to ensure George and Guthrie were following him.

"What's your name?" Merlyn demanded of the black man who stood by one of the pots, a wooden paddle dripping with grease hanging by his side.

"Moses, sir." The voice was cultured. He stood straight, his eyes confidently meeting Merlyn's.

"Escaped slave?" Merlyn's throat tightened at this new injustice feeding the anger already roiling inside of him.

"Yessir." Moses offered nothing more.

The man didn't look or sound like a field hand—probably a house slave, Merlyn concluded. There was a whole history there he would have loved to have unpacked, but now was not the time. "What went into those pots?" he demanded.

Moses shifted uncomfortably, his eyes flickering toward Guthrie and then back to Merlyn's.

His temper at a breaking point, Merlyn spun to face Guthrie. "The army pays you well to feed my men," he hissed, making no attempt to suppress the tension in his voice. "If I even begin to suspect you are selling supplies meant for them, I will break you. It will be you stirring those pots. Do you understand me?"

Guthrie mumbled something incomprehensible that could have passed for assent.

"I said, do you understand me?" Merlyn allowed his anger to boil over.

Guthrie's eyes widened. "Yessir. I do, sir." His head bobbed nervously.

Merlyn turned to go but spun back to Guthrie. Pointing to Moses, he said, "Treat that man well. He's been through hell. Don't even think of taking this out on him."

"You know what bothers me most about this, George?" he asked as they made their way back to his tent and the roiling inside him began to subside.

"No, what?"

"It's the fact of that piece of damn paper circulating through the camps—the one that supposedly sets the black man free is not going to make slightest bit of difference."

"What do you mean?" George asked. "I thought you were against slavery."

"Oh, I am, all right. I hate it with every fiber of my being, but a piece of paper is not going to change how men think. Do you for one moment think that the attitude that caused the enslavement of an entire race will vanish when this war is over, and this document becomes the law of the land?"

He felt rage beginning to boil in him again and paused to draw breath, but George jumped in to fill the gap before he could continue.

"But won't the black man be better off when he is free than when he is a slave?"

Merlyn thought of the poverty, the injustice, the overt and subtle discrimination he had seen growing up in a society that professed itself to be colorblind. "George," he replied, his voice sharper than he had intended, "do you think that because the black man is suddenly free, he is going to be accepted? Do you think that he will be welcome to attend your church? To come to dinner with you and your family? Do you think your family would be comfortable with your sister marrying one?"

"That will never happen," George expostulated angrily. "My sister would never entertain such a thought. Father will never allow it. How can you say such a thing?"

Merlyn smiled sadly. "You just made my point, George. This proclamation is absolutely the right thing to do, but just because the black man is free does not mean that society will accept him on equal footing. We will have spilled an ocean of blood purchasing his freedom, but following this war, I am afraid that our society is just going to forge for him a different kind of chain, a chain of hatred, bigotry, and intolerance. A chain that is going to make him and his children every bit as much a slave as he is today." He shook his head sadly. "No, George, the black man does not have an easy road ahead of him, but if through the light of charity we can, in our hearts, see him as equal, as another one of God's precious children deserving of the same love and mercy we offer each other, then perhaps he has a chance."

***

November 8th, 1862
Near Warrenton, Virginia

"What do you think of our new commander?" George asked Merlyn around a mouthful of hardtack. They sat at a folding table outside Merlyn's tent, picking at the remains of a chicken one of the foraging parties had brought in. It was evening and around them the regiment was winding up its daily activities and settling in for the night.

Following a month of inactivity, McClellan had finally moved his army across the Potomac on November 1st. But it was too late for the laggardly commander. Frustrated with his lack of progress, Lincoln relieved him on November 7th.

"Burnside?" Merlyn answered slowly, trying to dredge up a fact or two from his scanty knowledge of the time. He found his memory maddeningly blank—he knew only that the man would last a few months in the job and that he was the engineer of the disaster that would befall the army in just a few short weeks. The thought turned the food in his mouth to ashes.

"Don't know much about him," Merlyn dissembled. "I guess the president has confidence in him, even though he moved slowly at Antietam. Only time will tell." *Yes, it will tell,* he thought resentfully to himself. How many more of his men were going to die before the army could finally find a man who could lead it to victory? Meade would hold the field at Gettysburg, but before then, the army had to endure both Burnside and Hooker.

"Why was McClellan relieved?" George asked.

"It's not mine to say, George," Merlyn replied knowing the non-answer would only fan the flames of George's frustration.

As George let his emotions boil over, Merlyn studied the younger man's face. His reddish hair was growing long. Traces of a beard now clung to his chin. His eyes were sunken with fatigue but burned with bright intensity. The question was not idle gossip. It was a question being asked around a thousand campfires by an army that, if not demoralized, was increasingly perplexed by its inability to achieve victory.

Merlyn sat back feeling a glow of contentment the bitter anticipation of future battles could not dampen. Given George's elevation to the lieutenant colonelcy, he could spend time with the younger man and not give rise to resentment or speculation. With time came the opportunity for conversation and mentorship.

But Merlyn's anticipation of accomplishing his task quickly and moving on was rapidly diminishing. Despite his many attempts to witness to him over their time together, George's faith was proving a tough nut to crack, which did nothing to ease Merlyn's nagging sense of urgency. His return to his own time, if and when that were ever going to happen, was going to be delayed, as was any possibility of a reunion with Kate.

He tamped down his irritation. *Concentrate on the moment,* he reminded himself. *Do what you were sent here for.* After all, with every conversation there was always the opportunity to plant and water a seed or two.

Later that night, lying sleepless atop his cot, he allowed his mind to drift back to another conversation, a conversation enfolded within a delicious memory of forbidden love starting to bloom.

The wound Kate had given him was healing. Winter had given way to spring. Kate was becoming more comfortable in his presence, less quick to flare, more ready to listen, to learn.

"Do you ski?" she asked out of the blue at the end of a long debriefing, catching him by surprise at the sudden turn of her thoughts.

He hesitated before answering. "I used to, but it's been a long, long time. I doubt I could keep up with you."

"Mammoth is a little under three hours' drive away. I've been to the Tahoe ski areas many times, but never Mammoth. Let's go this weekend. I need to get away. Get into the mountains. Unwind for a bit. You game?"

He wasn't. Knew he shouldn't be, but before he could stop himself, he was nodding his assent. "I'm game, but go easy on me."

How long had it been since he was on skis? He couldn't count the years. But he found the thought attractive, appealing. Perhaps allowing her to be better than him at something would take another rough edge off their relationship.

He had found skiing to be like riding a bike—once you know how, you never forget. He surprised himself by how quickly he picked it up, but there was no keeping up with her. She moved with a grace, style, and absolute fearlessness that left him breathless with admiration.

They stood at the top of Chair 23 looking down the impossibly steep terrain of the chutes cutting their way through the cliff at their feet. "You up for that?" she asked, nodding downward. His common sense screamed, *No way!* but she quickly reversed herself. "Let's give it a pass. You're doing great, but no sense in tempting fate."

He found himself amused at the sudden reversal of roles. Up until now, he had been the leader, the decider, the driver in their relationship. A part of him had wondered if she would use the exercise to dominate, assert power, but she seemed solicitous of his abilities, not pushing him further than she thought he could go. Now he found it fun observing her, just being along for the ride. She pointed her skis down, parallel to the bowl, and found an easier way down. "You still have to drop into this one, but you have lots of room to maneuver. You can do it in your sleep."

He hoped she was right, and after a couple of turns he found that his legs and body quickly reattuned to the rhythm of constant turning, and he allowed himself to relax a little.

Kate chose Italian for dinner. After the exertion that day, he had expected her to wolf down a full meal, but she toyed with her food, eating little more than a half-plate of lasagna and a slice of garlic toast. "Come on, eat," he chided her. "You need the carbs to replenish."

She shook her head and pushed away her plate. There was something on her mind and he wondered if she would feel comfortable enough to broach it with him.

She took a sip of wine, put the glass down. Her eyes, while looking toward him, were focused some distance beyond. She took a deep breath. "We talked about legacy a couple of weeks ago. I've been doing a lot of thinking about what I want mine to be. I want my life to matter. You said it's not necessarily what we do, but the lives we touch. I don't know that I've touched that many lives so far, and I keep asking myself why. What is it about me that I don't really connect with people?"

He could see she did not want an answer, and he did not offer one. She looked suddenly shy, vulnerable; not the self-confident, assertive person he had come to know and love. "I want to be a force for good, for Christ, in the people around me. But in order to do that, I can see that I have to change, be less focused on doing and more focused on listening, on being, on other people rather than the job."

He wanted to interject, give her his perspective, but knew she needed to talk, say the words that were troubling her spirit. He toyed with his wine glass, not wanting to break the moment.

Her eyes suddenly snapped back to his, and he found himself drowning in those pools of liquid blue.

He couldn't remember much of the rest of that conversation, but the next memory from that trip was burned into his mind like a blowtorch etching wood.

He lay awake in his hotel room, sheets thrown back, unable to sleep, thoughts racing, acutely, dangerously aware of the woman that was becoming his all-consuming passion, sleeping next door.

What would happen if he knocked on the door connecting their rooms? The thought blossomed into his mind, causing his heart to race harder.

No! Don't go there. He barked the mental order to himself. *Lord, help me stop this obsession. I am violating everything you have called me to, just by being here with Kate.*

He rolled out of bed, dropped to his knees, and rested his head on folded hands. *Lord, help me to release her back to you. Deliver me from my lust and desire. I want to be right with you, obedient to you, faithful to you.*

The last came out as a tortured, silent cry, but still, heaven remained silent. There was no release to the turmoil that twisted his insides into knots.

He prayed until his knees hurt, and his eyes became gritty with fatigue, but still he could find no peace. He glanced at the clock, its red numerals bathing the wall in infernal light. 3:08 a.m. He knew there would be no sleep that night and climbed back into bed, feeling suddenly cold as he pulled the covers over him.

Snapping back to the present, Merlyn pulled his coat around him. There was a bite in the air that heralded the onset of winter. He lay within the confines of his darkened tent. Around him were the sounds of an army at night. The crackle of a fire. Footfalls of a man making his way to the privy. The jingle of metal as a sentry shifted his position.

He allowed his mind to play over the conversation with George once more. Like the younger man, he found the inactivity maddening. While McClellan and now Burnside dithered, Lee was back in Virginia, regrouping, waiting. He would not offer the Army of the Potomac another opportunity like the one they had just squandered.

Merlyn turned his thoughts to what he knew was coming. Fredericksburg and the open field in front of that awful, indomitable stone wall. Marching men across that field into the face of a withering enemy fire was almost as insane as ordering cavalry to charge machine guns as the generals would do fifty years in the future. In his heart he knew the 172nd would be ordered

145

across that field, would stand up in front of that wall. Many of his men would die, and there was not a thing he could do to prevent it.

Chapter 22

Not again. Kate groaned inwardly as she looked up at the LSO camera now being projected on the ready room screen. Digger stood beside her, phone glued to his ear.

"You sure he shouldn't be diverting to the mainland?" Digger asked, his tone clearly conveying his unhappiness with the Air Boss's decision. Kate strained to hear the reply but only made out a couple of unintelligible words at a pitch that indicated the Air Boss did not like having his decisions questioned.

Digger replaced the handset and looked up at the screen. A low, shuddering vibration rocked the TR as it plowed through heavy seas, the remnants of a storm that had passed through a couple of days previously.

"What's going on?" Kate asked anxiously.

"Spud blew an engine. Air Boss is bringing him in now."

Kate felt her palms grow sweaty as she thought about the scattered squalls in the area, the layered clouds, the pitching deck. Spud was going to have his hands full bringing in a crippled jet. At least it was light out. Thank goodness for that small mercy.

"The Air Boss is clearing the deck for an out-of-cycle recovery? Must be serious."

Digger nodded. "He had a fire light but it's out now. His jet's still trailing smoke, though. He made the decision to land on the boat and not divert."

Kate's eyes wandered involuntarily to the greenie board. The string of greens since his night in the barrel was unbroken. Perhaps she should not be worrying quite so much. The Super Hornet was perfectly flyable on a single engine.

Torch came into the ready room and came up to stand beside Digger. "I heard," he said.

He stared for a moment at the screen, scudding clouds standing out in white contrast against the gray of the overcast, and shook his head. "Not a good idea. He doesn't have it. He should be going somewhere safe, not trying to trap a crippled jet in marginal conditions."

Digger didn't speak for a long moment. Finally, he said, "He's the pilot in command. At some point we're going to have to trust him."

Torch shot him an incredulous look. "Trust him? He's a screwup."

Digger's eyes narrowed as he met Torch's glare. "Is he?"

Torch looked away, and Kate felt herself relax at the crisis averted but feared there could be a greater one unfolding in the air. Mesmerized, she watched a dot appear on the screen and steadily grow larger. She worried her lip as, perfectly on glide path, it snagged the third wire and vanished out of the field of view of the camera.

Kate exhaled with a whoosh. As she turned away from the screen to begin preparing for her afternoon mission, she heard Digger say in a barely audible but no less firm voice, "Back off and cut the kid some slack, Torch."

Trojan met Spud when he came into the ready room, sweat-drenched, hair plastered to his head. "Nice job, man. Thanks for the save. We're gonna need that jet when we redeploy."

Spud froze. "Redeploy?" he asked, a slight tremble in his voice.

"Yeah. With Iran now threatening to lob rockets into Israel you can bet on it," Trojan replied airily. "It's just a matter of time."

Spud's face turned white. He stood rooted until Nemo grabbed his arm. "Come on, let's get a bite to eat." With that, Spud allowed himself to be led out of the ready room.

What was that all about? Kate mused. As she watched Spud's retreating back, she couldn't shake the uncomfortable feeling she was missing something important.

Later that night, as the movie wrapped up and the pilots drifted off to their racks, Kate looked up from her computer to the greenie board feeling a small glow of satisfaction. The day's grades had been posted. Spud had earned a rare "5" on his landing. *That should silence his critics for a while,* she thought.

Stifling a yawn, she stared down at her computer and groaned. It was going to be another late night. But try as she might, she couldn't focus. Too many thoughts swirled in her mind. Thoughts of war. Thoughts of the squadron. Thoughts of Spud.

Finally she admitted defeat, tidied her space, and began to make her way through the warren of passageways to her stateroom.

For weeks now, she had been so focused on flying and on her job that she had thought of little else. But as her mind began to decompress, thoughts of that magical dream of Fallon came tumbling in. With a pang in her heart, she realized she'd been so consumed with work she had given her recently surfaced memories scarcely a second thought. Now with fatigue threatening to crush her, she found herself vulnerable, almost afraid.

Lord, what are you doing to me? Why are these things coming into my mind—false memories of a time that never was?

Or was it?

The thought was hard-hitting, almost stopping her in her tracks. While struggling with the implications, she brushed past a sailor who flattened himself against the wall to allow her to pass. It was a dream, nothing more. How could it be anything else? She started back toward her stateroom again, her mind whirling.

The gray-painted passageway with its maze of pipes and endless sequence of bulkheads faded as another memory crashed over her.

She had no intention of going to the formal ball hosted by the Naval Aviation Warfare Development Center, TOPGUN's parent organization. She would be out of place, a solitary student amongst a host of permanent party officers and enlisted. But when Morgan mentioned it would be a good idea for her to attend, her resolve crumbled.

She arrived shortly after the start of the cocktail hour and scanned the gathering crowd. Not seeing him, she made her way to the bar and ordered a club soda. As she looked around at the mass of uniforms, she was surprised to see most people ordering soft drinks and the occasional glass of wine. No one ordered anything stronger. At most navy functions involving aviators, alcohol flowed freely and even this early in the evening, many would already be showing its effects, but here that was not the case.

She sensed rather than saw Morgan enter the ballroom and turned to greet him. Her heart lurched. Tall and erect, his mess dress fit him like a glove. His medals gleamed softly. His eyes were riveted on her and there was a broad smile on his face. "I'm so glad you came," was all he said.

They sat together at one of the group of tables set aside for TOPGUN staff. The skipper and his wife and two other instructors and their wives completed their table.

Dinner passed at a leisurely pace, the food was good, the conversation lively. Morgan was quiet mostly, and she often caught him looking at her, an unfathomable expression in his eyes.

When the plates had been cleared, the coffee poured, and the speeches made, it was time for dancing. Kate planned to leave after a decent interval, when her departure would not seem too rushed. She half hoped, half dreaded Morgan asking her to dance. It was not something she was good at or comfortable with. She stiffened when he stood, but it was the skipper's wife he asked to dance, not her. The skipper stood and extended his hand to Kate. She was trapped. Mortified, she allowed herself to be led to the dance floor.

She tried to move her body to the beat of the music as the others on the floor were doing but suddenly caught sight of Morgan and his partner. Ramrod straight, he was holding her in a classic stance, gliding across the floor in a series of steps that were both elegant and beautiful. She found herself envying the other woman's ability to move so smoothly with the music.

When the music ended, she returned to the table and sat down thankfully. Morgan returned his partner and sat down again beside

Kate. She leaned over to him. "Where did you learn to dance like that?"

He smiled sheepishly. "I've lived among a couple of cultures where knowing how to dance is a survival skill."

She wanted to ask him which ones, but he deflected her question before she could ask it.

"You want to try?"

Her mind said no, but before she could speak the word, her head shyly nodded its assent.

"Let's wait this one out. The beat's not right."

They sat together quietly, watching the others dance. On the third number, he nodded to her. "This one's perfect."

As he took her hand to lead her to the dance floor, it seemed like a bolt of electricity ran up from her fingertips straight to her heart. She was acutely aware of her hand in his. It felt right somehow.

On the floor, he put his left arm around her waist and took her hand in his. "Relax and follow me," he said. His movements were simple, and she tried to anticipate them. To her chagrin, she stumbled a time or two. He bent and whispered in her ear. "Only one of us can lead," he said gently. "Let go and feel the music."

She surrendered to him and concentrated on the feeling of his body close to hers. She felt his muscles through his uniform and the surprising smoothness of his hand. As she got the hang of moving with him, his steps increased in speed and complexity. The feeling was magical, and she gave herself up to it totally.

All too soon, the music ended, and she found herself hoping he would ask her to stay on the floor with him. Instead, he led her back to the table. He danced with a couple of the other wives before asking her to dance again. From that moment on, he was her constant partner.

Long before she was ready for the night to end, the DJ announced the final song. With a start, she realized it was well after midnight. There were only about a dozen couples remaining. She had never stayed until the end of a ball before. It was a novel feeling. A slow Peter Gabriel number flowed over the dance floor. She instantly recognized the opening notes of "The Book of

Love. " It was a strange choice, but it seemed somehow appropriate for what had been a magical evening.

Morgan put his arms around her and held her close. She placed her head against his chest. It felt right, like she belonged. She sang the words to herself as their bodies swayed together, wishing the song would go on forever. At the final lines, she had a startling realization. This was a man to whom she could give herself, a man whose ring she could wear, would gladly wear. The sudden revelation made her knees feel weak.

As they left the dance floor, she kept her eyes averted from his so as not to betray the depth of her feelings.

He walked her back to her room in the visiting officer's quarters. The night was still warm. Stars blazed overhead. He did not reach for her hand, nor did he speak during the short walk. Outside her building, she turned to face him. His eyes were luminous, pain filled. She wanted him to take her in his arms. He clearly wanted to do so but something held him back. He leaned forward. She tilted her head so his lips could meet hers, but they brushed her forehead instead. "When this is over, we need to talk." His voice was husky with pent-up emotion. He grasped her hand, clearly wanting to stay, but he let her fingers slide away as he turned and strode off into the night. She wished he had said more, but his eyes had said all that needed to be said.

The memory faded, and she was back in the long passageway again. Disorientation washed over her, and she clutched at a bulkhead for support.

"You all right, ma'am?" a sailor asked, concern on his face.

She fought to clear her head, reading his collar insignia. "I'm fine, chief," she replied impatiently, immediately regretting her tone, while frustrated at her weakness.

Wordlessly, he brushed past her. She turned to look at his retreating back, wanted to call an apology after him but couldn't make the words come.

Back in her stateroom, she collapsed on her rack without even bothering to take her boots off, pulled the curtain closed, and lay there in the half darkness, her mind whirling. This wasn't a reprise of the dance memory from so long ago when she had woken up from that first dream. This was a different memory, but just as shattering.

She laced her fingers behind her head and cast her mind back, reliving every moment searching for every detail, imprinting it and the emotions it contained indelibly in her mind. This memory was too important. She couldn't afford to lose it. She pulled out her laptop and began to type, adding another memory to the growing list.

As she typed, an idea began to coalesce in her mind. This was not just a dream, but something real. The thought frightened her. How could it be real? It was impossible. But the thought refused to go away. *If this is somehow real,* she thought, *that means, dream guy, you're real too. And I think I'm beginning to like you. Where on earth is that DNA test?*

Chapter 23

"Boil two pots of water, George," Merlyn ordered. "I have a clean shirt among my things. Find it and tear it into strips for bandages."

The wound on his arm was not serious, but it was deep and required care. The makeshift bandage on it was gray and blood had soaked through.

"I still don't understand why you won't let McElroy take care of it," George stated. "He deals with this sort of thing every day."

"Humor me, George. McElroy is competent as surgeons go, but he has his hands full with the more seriously wounded. We can handle this. I'll talk you through it."

The truth was, Merlyn was concerned about infection. McElroy, like his peers, had no knowledge of the causes of infection and how to prevent it. Should the gash become septic, it could cause him to lose his arm, or worse, prove fatal. He was not going to take a chance of that happening by putting himself in McElroy's hands.

As he and George waited for the water to boil, images of the previous day assaulted him like a battering ram. No matter how hard he tried to barricade his mind against them, it was no use. There was no keeping anything like that at bay.

December 13th had been another day of unimaginable slaughter—unimaginable, that is, to anyone who had not seen the sheets of fire and the bodies lying thick across the battlefield. Merlyn seethed at the incompetence of the commanding general who had hurled his troops over an open field, against a stone wall lined with ranks of heavily armed Confederates. It proved the adage that insanity is doing the same thing repeatedly and expecting a different result. Burnside had done the same thing fourteen times that day, and each time the result was the same— shattered regiments and more blue-clad bodies littering the ground in front of Marye's Heights.

The 3rd Brigade and its four regiments had gone in late in the afternoon. Like the other brigades thrown piecemeal into the fray, it had been unable to stand before the withering fire from the massed Confederates secure behind their stone wall. Now many of his men were gone, still lying frozen on that vast killing ground. He could picture their faces, men who had traveled south from Albany that spring, filled with bravado. Over the course of the long summer, they had become hardened veterans. Now they lay silent, slaughtered by Burnside's arrogance.

"The water is ready." George's softly spoken words forced Merlyn back to the present and the task that had to be endured. He sat down at his camp table and surveyed the assembled gear on the tray in front of him. Brandy. Curved needles and forceps he had accumulated over the past months. Soap. Clean cloth. He was no doctor, but he knew what needed to be done. Of primary importance was making sure everything that touched his wound was sterile or as close to sterile as he could possibly make it.

"Start by washing your hands thoroughly with soap and water, as hot as you can stand," he directed George. "Then scrub down the tray with soap and boiling water. Make sure it's totally clean. Boil the instruments, cloth, and thread for at least ten minutes, then lay out what we will need on the tray." He curved his lips into a smile. "The brandy is for the wound, not for you and me to drink, but by the time you're finished, we're both probably going to want some."

George's face was white. "I really think you should let McElroy take care of this," he said, his voice shaking slightly.

Merlyn's voice brooked no argument. "No, George. He's set in his ways and will not listen to what I tell him. We're going to do this, and if you don't help me, I'm doing it alone."

His face and body radiating unhappiness, George set about following Merlyn's instructions.

An hour later the task was done. Merlyn had come close to passing out when George scrubbed out the wound, and again when he sutured it. His arm throbbed. He looked down at the wound and grimaced.

"George, you're never going to be a seamstress," he declared ruefully. "Bandage it up with the strips from the clean shirt and we'll pray infection does not set in."

"I still don't see the point of all this. Why not just let the surgeons do their work and care for the wounded as they are supposed to do? Why do their work for them?"

Merlyn carefully considered his answer. He had been interfering with history and George had caught him red-handed. Lister was only now conducting his groundbreaking experiments on antiseptic surgery, and his methods would not be adopted for another twenty years.

"It's something I picked up on my travels," he said. "There is an idea that dirt may cause infection. If by cleaning the wound and the surgical instruments you can prevent dirt from entering, you have a greater chance of preventing infection. It's a very new idea, and our doctors—including McElroy, who's a good surgeon by the way—are not open to it."

A wave of pain washed over him and Merlyn gritted his teeth against it. The wound would heal, and the scar would eventually disappear as others had over the years. He needed to change the subject.

"Let's see to the men, George." He rose to his feet and clutched the table for support as the tent spun around him. George grasped his good arm to steady him. The dizziness passed.

"Help me with my coat," Merlyn demanded. "We've got work to do."

Darkness came early as the solstice approached. Merlyn and George dined in Merlyn's tent on hardtack and stew. It had an unidentified protein source that Merlyn thought was either horse or mule but was better by far than what they had been eating that summer. George ate in silence, Merlyn's attempts to draw him into conversation met with monosyllabic replies or silence.

Merlyn wiped his bowl clean and pushed back his chair. George was playing with his half-eaten food, his eyes staring, unfocused, obviously seeing something Merlyn could not see.

He felt a twinge of concern. These people had not yet come to terms with post-traumatic stress disorder—shell shock, as the term would be coined fifty years from now. What would finally be known as PTSD was seen as cowardice and dealt with as such, often harshly. Was George starting to exhibit early symptoms? How could he not be, after the horrors he had seen over the past several months? How could any of his men not be?

"Talk to me, George," Merlyn demanded. "Your mind is obviously miles away from here. What are you thinking about?"

George looked up and lay down his spoon. "Many things are going through my mind." He met Merlyn's eyes, and Merlyn was relieved to see determination in them. "I'm wondering when we're going to get a general who can lead us to victory. McClellan wouldn't fight. After what we saw yesterday, I'm afraid Burnside will just continue throwing men's lives away because he can't think of anything else to do. We can beat this enemy, Merlyn. We have the resolve. Our cause is just. If we just had the leadership, we could have ended this war by now."

It was not the answer Merlyn had expected. The young man he had met on the church steps was becoming a warrior.

"If we had men like you at the head of this army, we would be camped on the heights above Fredericksburg, and the enemy would be dining on swill in Richmond tonight. But that's not what truly bothers me. Where is God in all this? Why does he allow our men to be needlessly slaughtered when we are obviously on the side of right?"

George forestalled Merlyn's reply by abruptly rising to his feet and picking up his bowl. "I know you're concerned for me, Merlyn, and I'm grateful. I'll be all right. I'm just fatigued, and my mind is running with too many thoughts. A good night's sleep and I'll be all right. With your permission . . ." He saluted, about-faced, and left the tent.

Merlyn fully understood. Like George, too many things were churning in his own mind. But they were different things. Standing before the wall, he had felt an almost overpowering fear. It was not fear for himself, but for George and for Kate. It had taken a Herculean effort of will not to throw himself on George, to shield him from the incoming hail of minié balls. For seconds that seemed like an eternity, he wrestled with the fear before forcing it back and concentrating on steeling his men. The memory of it caused his palms to grow clammy.

As an orderly cleared the table, Merlyn's mood mirrored George's. He could not go out among the men feeling like this. They needed him to show them confidence and optimism. More than that, they needed him to show them hope. They needed to know that everything would be all right, that victory would follow defeat. It was not something he could promise them. A long winter stretched before them and then, the horrors of Chancellorsville and Gettysburg. After that, two more years of war and countless battles before Appomattox. And somewhere out there lay the horror of Cold Harbor. A chill ran down his spine at the knowledge coalescing in his mind. That battle would mark the end of his time here.

For the thousandth time, he wished he were ignorant of what was coming. He wished he could face the future with his men's blind optimism. They believed in the righteousness of the cause and were confident that one day the Union would prevail. Merlyn knew the outcome, but he also knew the tragedy and suffering these men would endure before their final victory. He wondered how many of them would be left alive to savor it.

He took out his journal with the all-too sporadic letters to Kate. Although she was never far from his mind, he was busy from dawn until well into the night, and the time was just not there to pour his heart out onto paper.

He laid his drawing on the table, gently smoothed the folds, and stared once again into her eyes. His heart ached with an intensity that was almost physical. "My sweetheart," he said softly. "Will I ever see you again? Will I hold you in my arms once more?" He felt like weeping, but the tears would not come.

He stared down at the open journal, now half-filled with letters scribbled down in the few moments of spare time he could muster. He knew he should write another, but the words would not come.

He wrote the date at the top of the first blank sheet. December 19th. Six days until Christmas. He had been in this hellish place for eight months. The thought caused his heart to chill, and he fought off a wave of panic. He did a quick mental calculation. Kate had been nearing the end of pre-deployment workups. Say, a month to go before she deployed. Eight months of deployment. Nine months total. In a month she would be home. His heart told him he was going to be here a lot longer than that. The thought caused a resurgence of panic. She would be coming home, and he would not be there to meet her. He would break the promise he had so rashly made in those last moments together.

Lord, please release me from this call on my life. It was a prayer of purest anguish. *I can't handle the constant suffering and loss anymore. I just want to go back to Kate.*

A question washed over his mind, cutting off his thoughts. *What is your heart's true desire? Is it to seek My will for your life, or your own?*

It stopped him in his tracks. He paused for a moment to think, to evaluate his feelings. They were such a jumble he could not say with clarity which he wanted. He had served God for so many years with no thought of himself, but now there was something he wanted more than life itself. The answer should be obvious, require no thought, but it was not so simple, was it? He took a deep breath while fighting to calm to his roiling emotions.

Lord, I just can't take the death and the dying anymore. I don't want to be part of it. I've seen too much pain and suffering.

Have I not always been your very present help in time of trouble?

Merlyn stopped to consider. If he were truly honest, he could come up with dozens of examples in which God had been there alongside him, had given him strength, had helped him through his pain, had given him words to speak. Yes, his life had been difficult, but it had also been rich and full.

It was as if the Lord ran with his thought. *How many assignments have I carried you through?*

Merlyn thought for a moment. *I don't recall exactly. Two dozen? Three?*

Have you lacked anything on any of those assignments?

The first thing that popped into Merlyn's mind was the privation he had experienced. But then a host of other memories, good memories, followed. Time spent close with God and with people he loved flooded his mind, a balm soothing the recollection of harsher times.

And have I not healed your body and emotions when needed?

Merlyn had to concede that point too. *Lord, I've done everything you asked of me, gladly, and you've given me great joy as a result. I've loved the people you've sent me to, but I've never fallen in love before. It changes everything.*

Does it?

Merlyn considered. *I think it does. Because of it, I chose to disobey you. I sought my will and not yours.*

Where does that leave us?

You're Lord and I want with all my heart to serve you, to be right with you once more. At the same time, I want with all my heart to be with Kate, to settle down with her, to experience what the life you have called me to has denied me.

What if I have other plans for Kate?

The thought was pure anguish, piercing his soul like a sword cut.

You made my point. That's the crux of the matter. I ask you again, what is the true desire of your heart? Is it to pursue your own will for your life or is it to pursue Me?

Merlyn could not answer through the misery crashing over him.

Another thought flowed into his mind. *You're so fixated on time. What is time? What is an hour? A week? A year? Has time ever hindered Me before?*

Before Merlyn could form an answer to the question, a memory broke into his mind like a star shell of a Christmas years ago, spent in a shell crater in the Flanders mud. He had fashioned a cross from barbed wire, given it to the wounded Lieutenant Morcombe lying beside him. God had brought the cross back to him at another low point in his life, a symbol of his love and affirmation.

How many years had it been for Morcombe when you saw him again?
Merlyn did the math. *Almost thirty.*
And how much time was it for you?
Merlyn tried to count the intervening assignments. *I'm not sure exactly. Fifteen or so, I guess.*

The implications of what the Lord was telling him flooded his mind. Time really did not matter. When he finally went home—if he went home, his mind amended—he would very likely go back to his own time the moment he had left it. He pictured his home on the outskirts of Anchorage. What would it be like to go back? To pick up exactly where he had left off all those years ago?

He felt his blood turn to ice and his mouth go dry as a new thought crossed his mind. What conflict had he prepared Kate for? A memory surged, insubstantial in mists of time. A conflict fought. The world on the brink of nuclear war. Staggering losses on both sides. That had happened just before the Lord had called him to this life. Was it that, or was there another, more deadly conflict on the horizon? Why had he not thought to ask Kate more about her own time?

Merlyn impatiently pushed the thought from his mind. He couldn't allow his thoughts to keep spinning like this all night. He had to do something, anything productive that would keep his mind occupied.

He took a deep, shuddering breath, stood, buttoned his coat, and prepared to go out into the cold. It was time to summon his officers and make preparations for Christmas. The men were far from home and family. What they most needed now was hope and cheer. Although these were the furthest things from his heart, he would do his best to make sure they got them.

Chapter 24

Kate pushed away the small bowl of ice cream she had allowed to accompany her dinner and fixed her eyes on Heather, seated across the table from her.

"I don't see any way we're going to avoid war," she replied to Heather's question, her pulse quickening as she uttered the words. "The Iranian government seems to be doing everything in their power to provoke us. They're not going to back down until we relax sanctions and allow them to have the nuclear weapons they've been after for decades. That's something we're just not going to do. We're going to have to fight."

Heather's face went pale. "I hope you're wrong," she said, twirling the uneaten spaghetti on her plate with her fork. "I don't think any of us want that. I certainly don't."

"I don't think any of us do, if we're honest with ourselves," Kate said. "I know some of the guys are talking a big storm, but deep down, unless there's something wrong with them, they're as nervous as the rest of us."

Heather looked up and fixed Kate with a speculative stare. "So how's your problem child holding up? Is he going to be able to cut it when things get ugly?"

"I honestly don't know." Kate carefully weighed the pros and cons in her mind. "He has the basic flying skills. He seems to be trying to connect a little more but isn't doing it very effectively. Digger is doing what he can, but Torch isn't a fan, and most of the other pilots aren't either . . ." She allowed her voice to trail off, reflecting her frustration.

Kate watched Heather's head snap up and a calculating expression cross her face. "Speak of the devil," she announced with a gleeful tone that made Kate feel decidedly uncomfortable. Kate followed Heather's gaze and spied Spud, tray in hand, navigating the crowded compartment toward an empty table in the far corner.

"Hey, lieutenant," Heather called, raising her voice to project above the din of a dozen aviators engaged in various levels of boisterous conversation. Spud looked her direction and seemed inclined to ignore the invitation, but Heather impatiently waved him over. Spud's eyes landed on Kate, and she realized, *He's waiting for me to offer the invitation. He won't accept unless I say it's okay, nor will he refuse without some sign from me.* She waved him over.

A wary look on his face, Spud placed his tray on the table and sat heavily. Kate made the introductions.

"Sorry for waving you over," Heather said airily, projecting an aura of insincere innocence that Kate could have cheerfully throttled her for. "Nobody should be alone at a time like this."

Spud muttered something incoherent, but Heather latched onto it with the intensity of a terrier worrying a bone. "Is that a North Carolina accent I hear—or Virginia? I'm from Georgia, so that makes us practically neighbors."

She paused, leaving Spud no choice but to fill the void. "North Carolina. My folks have a farm not far from Asheville."

Kate was surprised he'd volunteered so much, more than he'd ever told her. She listened in amazed envy as Heather deftly drew him into conversation and, in short order, despite his reticence, elicited from him that he was the eldest of six kids, had grown up on a farm, played football in high school and college, had married his childhood sweetheart, and that flying had always been his dream.

"Wow, it seems like you two have a lot in common, both growing up on a farm and all that." Heather sat back and shot Kate a calculating look as if to say, *Your turn now.*

"Actually, I grew up on a ranch," Kate said, feeling awkward at being drawn into the obviously contrived conversation. She shot an apologetic glance at Spud and was surprised at what she saw on his face. Gone was the habitual scowl and in its place was a shy, embarrassed smile. It transformed his features, and Kate felt a pang of sympathy for him that caused her irritation toward Heather to soften.

She took a deep breath and decided to play along. "My folks raised horses and some cattle in a pretty remote part of Wyoming. What did you guys raise?"

"Apples," Spud declared, his face beaming with pride. "We have one of the largest orchards in the state, and my folks have turned it into a destination with a shop, tours, stuff like that."

With Heather facilitating, Kate was surprised how easy it was to maintain a conversation with Spud. They had something in common beyond a love of flying—several things, if she stopped to think about it. Time flew by, and long before Kate was ready to stop, Heather pushed her chair back. "I'll leave you two to it. I've still got some work to wrap up, and I know my squadron is probably halfway through another mindless action thriller by now."

Kate's eyes met Spud's. She could read the moment was over, but the ice was broken. She no longer saw him as an object needing to be fixed, and hopefully he no longer saw her as an ogre that was persecuting him.

"Thanks for being a good sport, Spud," she said as they made their way out of the wardroom. "It was good to finally start getting to know you. I'm sorry it has taken me so long to do it."

Spud's mouth curled as he inclined his head in acknowledgment. There was nothing more that needed to be said.

***

22 May
USS Theodore Roosevelt, Sea of Japan

Breathless from her dash back to the ready room, Kate slid into her seat. She had cut it close, but so had many of the other pilots. She glanced back and felt a small glow of satisfaction as Spud laughed briefly at something Jasper had said. It was a small sign of the thaw occurring between him and the rest of the pilots.

The wing had stood down for the day. Except for a single air patrol flown by the Chiefs, all pilots were in their ready rooms to hear the words their skippers had gotten from Captain Somers, the TR's air wing commander, that morning.

A hush settled over the ready room as the seconds ticked down toward 1300. Precisely on cue, Digger strode into the ready room and stood before the squadron, hands clasped behind his back.

"Okay, folks, I'll give it to you straight, no sugar-coating it." His voice was calm, no hint of the magnitude of the news he was about to convey.

"Iran announced yesterday that they have enriched enough uranium to assemble an unspecified number of nuclear weapons. They also claim to have mated warheads to Ghadr-110 medium range ballistic missiles. Our intelligence believes their claim to be accurate."

Kate felt her stomach tighten painfully at the news. Although she had fully expected something bad when the wing stand-down was announced, this was far worse than anything she could have anticipated.

"Here's the bad news," he continued. "Iran has stated that if we, the UN, or anyone else interferes with their weapons-development program, they will use those missiles to wipe Israel off the map. Worse, they claim to have developed a missile that can now reach Western Europe." He paused, and Kate clearly heard the sound of several pilots shifting uncomfortably in their seats. She swallowed hard, trying to muster saliva in her suddenly dry mouth.

"As you all know," Digger continued, "Russia has declared its unconditional support of the Iranian regime. For the last thirty years they've been watching how we operate and are going to try to take away our primary advantage, our airpower. They've learned from their mistakes in Ukraine and are going to put those lessons to the test. Also, it's no secret they've been beefing up Iranian airborne and surface assets as a reward for their help in Ukraine. Iran now has some of Russia's very latest toys. We have to assume the Russians are teaching them how to use them, so we cannot dismiss Iran as an ineffective foe."

Digger paused and looked around the room before continuing.

"The Air Force is deploying assets into Iraq, Saudi Arabia, Bahrain, and the UAE. Stennis is already on station in the Indian Ocean. Chuckie V is on its way there. NATO is not on board yet but probably will be soon. We're sailing into a massive stare down and are going to have our work cut out for us."

He paused and took a deep breath. *Here it comes,* Kate thought.

"This is going to come as no surprise to you. We've known it would be a possibility since before we deployed, but tomorrow, we're making all speed for the Persian Gulf."

There was a collective groan as Digger finished his announcement. While the news came as no surprise, all had been anticipating the five-day port call at the US naval base at Yokosuka, Japan scheduled for the end of the month. Kate and Heather had a whirlwind itinerary planned that included climbing Mt. Fuji, a sightseeing tour of Tokyo, and a day shopping before rushing back to the TR. Their highly anticipated break had just gone up in smoke.

She turned around and scanned the faces of the other pilots. They were universally grim. Besides the loss of the port call, the redeployment to the Middle East potentially meant months more at sea and longer separations from their families, to say nothing of the increasing probability of war.

Spud's face had taken on a greenish cast, and she felt a stab of concern. What was going on inside his head? How was this news going to affect his gradually thawing relationship with the rest of the squadron, and more importantly, with her?

"Everybody's dismissed. Department head meeting now," Digger ordered, bringing the briefing to a close. "My stateroom."

The four department heads obediently trailed Digger and Torch to Digger's stateroom.

Wasting no time, Digger turned to Trojan. "Give me a rundown on the jets."

Trojan went through the list of the squadron's assigned aircraft from memory, ticking off the issues with each one. "Overall, they're in great shape," he summarized, "but are showing the normal stresses and strains of deployment. However, if we get extended, we are going to see more and more issues cropping up. Even so, we can handle an increased flying schedule."

"Thanks, Trojan." Digger turned to Kate. "Elsa, operations."

Kate thought for a moment. "Pilots are ready, but I'm concerned about experience levels." She ticked off her concerns, concluding, "The nuggets and junior pilots are okay, but again, inexperienced. When we begin combat operations, it's going to be—"

"Whoa, whoa," Digger interrupted. "It's a little bit early to be thinking about combat operations. We're just moving into the AOR; we're not launching strikes into Iran any time soon."

Kate levelly met his gaze. "Boss, you pay me to think ahead. You said it yourself—the world cannot live with a nuclear-armed Iran. The president has been taking a hard line publicly in the lead-up to today's news. I believe in my heart of hearts we are going to end up going into Iran. However, it isn't just the Iranians we'll be fighting . . ." she let her voice trail off.

Digger looked thoughtful. Torch cut in to fill the silence. "You're thinking too far ahead, Elsa. War, if it comes, is going to be months or even years from now. We may very well be home by then and another ship replacing us. Let's look near term. Do we have any pilots who will have serious problems with the extension to our deployment?"

"The only one I'm truly concerned about is Spud," Kate replied. "He hasn't said, but I get the idea things are rocky on the home front. That may be partially to blame for some of his performance issues. His wife is probably close to term, and I would bet he was hoping to get home in time for the birth. I think he's going to take this extension really hard."

Her eyes shifted from Digger to Torch. His eyes locked onto hers, his face expressionless. Kate shifted her weight uncomfortably, not liking the vibe she was picking up.

"I think you're doing fine with him. Just keep doing what you're doing. He'll be okay," Digger said. He turned to Torch. "Elsa's right. There's every indication things are going to get interesting.

We need to be prepared. I'll start setting the expectation that this may turn into a combat deployment."

Kate felt a surge of gratification. It helped to know she was not the only one who expected the worst to happen.

168

Chapter 25

"Let's review the facts, gentlemen," Eades declared after the prisoner had been marched out of the schoolroom that served as a temporary court. Eades was a balding man in his midforties. Lean, spare, nervously energetic, he reminded Merlyn of a sparrow bobbing in search of food. Merlyn found him to be gentle, soft-spoken, surprisingly likable. "Captain Saunders?"

His aide, who had served as prosecutor, stepped forward with a sheet of paper in his hands. "The accused, Private Wiltz, was reported absent without leave on January 18th. He was apprehended two weeks ago stealing from a farmhouse north of Lancaster, Pennsylvania. He had no answer to the charge of desertion."

Merlyn shifted uncomfortably as the word was spoken, could see exactly where this was going. The army had little tolerance for those who would not stand and fight.

"Colonel." Eades turned to Merlyn, who was sitting on his right. "What sort of man is he?"

Merlyn looked down at the scarred surface of the table at which the three men sat, marred by generations of use.

"The worst kind," he replied. "Azariah Wiltz is a shirker, a lecher, a thief, and a coward. He tried to run at Malvern Hill, and again at Antietam. He was too ill to take the field at Fredericksburg. In camp he lies, gambles, and sneaks away often to visit the women who follow the army. Frankly, I can find nothing in him that is redeemable."

Eades turned to George. "Colonel, do you have anything to add?"

Merlyn could clearly see the contempt in George's eyes. "We're better off without him," he declared.

"It seems cut and dried to me," Eades said slowly, his face tightening. "We have a single charge—desertion. Do we need to discuss it further?"

Merlyn shook his head sadly. "No," he whispered.

"Then how vote you, colonel?" He turned to George.

"Guilty."

"And you, colonel?"

"Guilty," Merlyn replied, feeling as if his heart were breaking.

"And I vote guilty as well," Eades declared. "Captain, record the verdict."

"Now, as to the penalty. The articles of war allow for some discretion, but the penalty for desertion is death."

"It would free us of a troublemaker," George muttered.

"What was that, colonel?" Eades asked.

"If that is the penalty," George replied, "then that's what we must do."

"Is there nothing in the man that speaks in his favor?"

George chewed on that for a moment. "No. We would be much better off without him."

Merlyn felt a niggling disquiet at the easily passed judgment. *No, don't interrupt,* he thought. *See where George takes it.*

George took a deep breath and launched into Wiltz's history, laying it out in all its lurid detail.

Eades' face darkened as George spoke. Finally, he interrupted the litany of wrongdoing. "Enough," he declared. "I do not need to hear more."

He turned to Merlyn. "You've been very quiet, colonel. What say you?"

Merlyn pushed back his chair and turned it so he could face the two men. "I would have us not be so hasty on this matter. What would you have us do? Shoot everyone who has no stomach for a fight and slinks away home? We're burying enough of our men as it is from disease and the enemy. Public support for this war is shaky enough. What do you think is going to happen to it if we start shooting our own in droves?"

Eades' eyes narrowed at the comment but let Merlyn continue.

"We have many options. Shooting is just the harshest penalty. We could choose branding or imprisonment, or something Wiltz will find truly galling: permanent extra duty around the camp."

George was clearly unhappy with Merlyn's words. The frustration in his voice was palpable. "So you would just let him go free, no consequences, no penalty for his actions, for letting down his comrades?"

"Oh, there will be consequences. The men deal with and discipline their own. In another regiment, the bad apples could contaminate the whole barrel. I have enough faith in our men that they will not allow that to happen here."

"Yes, but," George protested, "there will be nothing public, nothing visible to shame him?"

Merlyn chuckled drily. "He is plenty shamed in the eyes of the men, although he probably won't feel it much. I don't think he has much shame in him. All in all, though, I'd rather it be a Reb bullet that does him in than one of ours."

The debate continued long into the afternoon.

Finally, Eades looked from George to Merlyn and back to George again. "What is your recommendation now, colonel?" he asked gently.

George's face was pinched, his eyes troubled. "I defer to Colonel Michaelson."

"No, colonel," Eades replied. "You must choose."

George shifted uncomfortably in his seat. "My head tells me to shoot him and be done with it. I understand, though, what Colonel Michaelson is saying. With great reluctance, I say we take on the task of rehabilitation."

Merlyn released the breath he had been holding. "I vote the same way."

"There you have it," Eades concluded. "I was going to lead the discussion that way after hearing your points of view, but you did it for me. This is not the time to be imposing the harshest discipline for infractions. Desertion in the face of the enemy is one thing; running away from camp is something else."

He turned toward Merlyn, his face suddenly stern. "Make sure he is never given the opportunity to run again, or I will impose a harsher sentence next time."

"You're a strange man, colonel," George said as they walked back to the 172nd encampment. "You're one of the fiercest and most courageous men I've seen in battle, yet you're one of the gentlest commanders to the men. You're showing Wiltz leniency far beyond anything he deserves. I don't understand you." He lapsed into silence.

Merlyn understood George's frustration and was strangely fascinated at his own reluctance to deal harshly with the deserter. "George, I cling to the hope that Wiltz can make something of himself, despite his many flaws. That's why I argued for grace."

George's head jerked up. His eyes narrowed. "You mean grace, like you say the good Lord offers us?"

Merlyn chuckled. "I wouldn't go that far, George. I'm not the good Lord and don't pretend to be. But you make a point. We offered grace in hopes that Wiltz will reform. He doesn't deserve it. Deserves quite the opposite. Perhaps God is a little like that. We're deserving of death, yet wretched as we are, he loves us so much he offers us grace. All we have to do is accept that gift and allow him to make us right with him."

George screwed up his face, testing the thought, finding it disagreeable. "It can't be that easy, Merlyn. Surely God demands more of us than that."

"Not really, George. It's pretty simple. All he asks of us is to act justly, love mercy, and walk humbly with him. He makes it possible through his grace. The magnificent thing is, it's free. Unmerited. Unearned. Lovingly offered with no strings attached."

George pulled his coat tighter around him at the evening chill. "Merlyn, why is it that almost every conversation we have comes back to God and faith?"

"Because God is the center of who I am. To talk about me is to talk about what God is to me and what he is doing in me. God is everything to me. I live to do his will. I go where he leads and try my best to honor him and please him in everything I do. I cannot talk about myself or anything that is dear to me without talking about God."

He looked at George, gauging the impact of his words.

George scratched behind his ear, swatted something away. "Why would God bring you here into the midst of this hell?" he asked.

It was a reasonable question, Merlyn thought. He knew the answer but could not speak it. "I trust that God has a purpose in everything he leads me to do. He has called me to be salt and light wherever he plants me. Perhaps his purpose is for me to be salt and light to the men of this regiment. Perhaps it is to be salt and light to you."

George started at that. "Why on earth would he do that?"

"Because he loves you with an undying love, George, and wants you to choose to be reconciled with him. If I can help that process in some way, then I am serving his purpose for me."

George looked unhappy, screwed up his face as he tried to wrestle with what Merlyn had just said. "Why would God put you through all this just to try to influence me? It hardly seems fair to you."

"It's not a matter of fairness. I choose to follow Jesus. I go where he leads me. I do what I believe he places in my heart to do. I am blessed no matter what circumstances I find myself in or what suffering I could go through."

"But you could be killed, maimed."

Merlyn considered for a moment. "Of course I could. But I gladly lay down my life for him who gave everything to me."

George looked startled. "What you're saying then is that you would lay down your life for me?"

"I didn't quite say that, but that is the implication. I could end up giving my life in the process of God drawing you back to him."

"And that is all right with you?" George's face wore an incredulous look.

Merlyn smiled at him. "If that's what God calls me to do, then I am all right with it. Of course, I have dreams. Dreams of what I will do after this war, but I will sacrifice them to follow God's will for my life because I know that in all things, his will is what is ultimately the best for me."

George exhaled in a long rush. "Merlyn, our conversations are never dull. You always keep me thinking. You make it sound so attractive. I wish I could have the kind of faith you have."

"You can," Merlyn said quietly. "All you have to do is ask God into your heart."

George walked beside him in silence, his face a study in thoughtfulness. Merlyn's heart was in his throat. Was this the time? Would George make the decision he had been wrestling with for the past year? Would Merlyn finally be able to leave this awful place? He held his tongue, afraid that the slightest word could shift the conversation in the wrong direction.

George opened his mouth to say something, and Merlyn's chest tightened in anticipation. Was this the moment?

George visibly deflated and kicked at a pebble. "I want to believe like you do, but I need to digest what you've just said. It's too much for me right now."

"George, don't put off the decision," Merlyn said, wishing he could tell this young man what was ahead of him, the awful chance he took, but he had said too much already.

Later that evening Merlyn pushed back his chair from his desk and surveyed the half-tent, half-cabin that had been his home for the winter. It was not much different from those occupied by the men. A little larger, a little better built. Shake roof instead of canvas. One cot instead of four. A desk. A chair. A trunk for uniforms that doubled as another seat.

Rain beat with a dull roar on the shingles overhead. He shivered and pulled his coat tighter around him. He should sleep but wasn't sleepy. He pulled the drawing from the pocket next to his heart and propped it against a stack of papers on his desk.

He opened the journal in front of him. He had a letter to write, but his thoughts were a jumble, repeatedly coming back to the conversation with George.

Grace. Was that what he had offered Kate after the fencing accident? He didn't think so, but that was how she saw it. Was that really what it was? He leaned back in his chair and laced his hands behind his neck. He closed his eyes and in an instant was back in Fallon.

"You did great out there," he said, wrapping up the debriefing. His shoulder twinged slightly as he pulled out a chair and sat across the table from Kate.

Kate's hair was plastered to her head from the close-fitting helmet. Her flight suit still showed damp spots from drying perspiration. She leaned forward, her elbows on the table, chin resting on her clasped hands. Her gaze was penetrating, direct, and he felt his heart lurch as he stared into the impossible depth of those extraordinary blue eyes.

"How can you possibly forgive me after what I did to you? You should hate me, or at the very least want nothing to do with me." The question was characteristically direct, no whining, no self-pity, just a sincere desire for understanding.

How could he be honest about his thoughts and emotions? He couldn't. He couldn't bare his heart to her, no matter how much he wanted to.

He ran his fingers through his own still-damp hair, slicking it back from his eyes, buying time to answer her question. "I take full responsibility for what happened," he said slowly. "It was too dangerous fencing without protection. I should never have suggested it."

"There you go again," she said, her voice raising sharply. "You're taking responsibility for my actions. This was my fault, not yours. The issue of safety is not the point. I hated you, and I've never hated anyone in my life before. I wanted to beat you, to humiliate you no matter the cost, and you forgive me. Why?"

How could he tell her the truth that she was no doubt coming to suspect? I love you completely, totally, that I would sacrifice anything for you, including my own life.

"I goaded you, nursed your anger," he said slowly. "Therefore I have to take some responsibility for what happened."

"But why?" she asked, genuine bewilderment on her face, and then he saw the sudden flush of comprehension. He expected

175

disgust and repudiation to follow but was surprised at the sudden faint blush and shy smile, quickly controlled. She reached across the table and lightly brushed her fingers across the back of his hand. Once more that bolt of electricity surged through his hand and up his arm. He wanted to pull it back but couldn't. He was trapped, drowning in those luminescent eyes that searched his face so intently.

His heart raced, the still-sane part of him hoping that she would say something to repudiate him, but nothing came. Instead, she pulled her hand back and stood. "Sorry, gotta go. I have class in five minutes. See you at the gym afterward?" She flashed him another smile—kind, inviting, all hint of challenge gone.

He nodded miserably and watched her glide out of the classroom. At that moment, the awful certainty hit him with the force of an out-of-control bus: he was totally, irrevocably lost.

Chapter 26

Mind shifting into high gear, whirling with possibilities, anticipating the change in operations tempo, Kate returned to the ready room. The TR had already turned southward. Everyone on the ship had felt the change in direction.

The low buzz of conversation as pilots clustered into groups added to the tension that hung palpably in the air. Kate drew up short as her eyes fell on Spud.

He had not joined in any of the conversations taking place — instead, he sat alone in his seat in the back row of the ready room.

What on earth?

Seaman Garcia came up to her. "Ma'am."

Concentration broken, Kate looked away from Spud.

"Yes, what is it?" Her tone was harsher than she intended.

"Planning meeting in CVIC at 1330."

Kate glanced at her watch. She had an hour, just enough time to collect her thoughts and grab a quick bite.

Her eyes fell on Spud again. Hunched in his seat, red-rimmed eyes staring down at his hands clasped in his lap, he was the picture of isolation.

I don't have time for this. Kate made her way to the front of the ready room but stopped short as another memory crashed into her mind with all the subtlety of a battering ram.

Kate pushed her chair back. As always, the club did a magnificent job with Sunday brunch. Morgan had eaten sparingly, as had she. She felt a pleasant sense of lassitude claiming her. It was a beautiful day outside. Flying had gone well that week. It felt good to sit in the club with other officers and simply unwind. She sipped at a glass of orange juice and gazed at Morgan sitting across from her, drinking in his hazel eyes and rugged good looks.

Somehow the conversation had turned to art. It was probably in response to her question about where he had learned to dance. He intrigued her. He was master of so many things and had such varied interests.

"I think art is how we translate what we see with our hearts into our medium of choice," he said. "Some feel music deeply and translate it into movement. Some see a beautiful shape captured in a block of marble and chip away to set it free. Some see a tale that must be told, and it becomes a book. I think all of us have an innate God-given desire to create."

"I don't agree," she had protested. "I think to be an artist you have to have a certain temperament. I don't have that desire to create. I enjoy living in God's creation and doing something worthwhile with my life, but I'm not artistic."

He smiled at her. "I disagree. There's artistry in what you do with a jet. Some people can fly it mechanically very well, but you have a unique grasp of spatial relationships, of things moving very rapidly in three dimensions, that you're able to do things others can only wish they could do. But on a simpler level, I've seen what you can do with a camera. You have a good eye and the ability to compose and capture an image that shows me you do have that creative ability you deny having."

His eyes sparkled with humor. She felt as if she were drowning in his gaze. It was time to take the focus off her. "So, you dance well. What other artistic talents do you have?" She winced inwardly. She hadn't meant it to sound so much like a challenge.

He thought for a moment. "Do you have a pencil?"

She rummaged in her bag and produced one. "It's not very sharp," she said apologetically.

"We can fix that." He pulled a small knife from his boot and used it to sharpen the pencil, depositing shavings onto his plate.

He grimaced and looked around at the other diners. "Hopefully I'm not mortally offending some admiral's wife's sense of propriety."

She giggled.

"Look at me and hold still for a few minutes."

She did as she was told. He took an unused paper napkin and began attacking it with the pencil, making bold, broad strokes at first. He looked up from his work every so often and stared at her as if reading her face. She tried to see what he was drawing.

"No cheating," he ordered. "Look at me, not the drawing." She did as she was told. As she watched him work, she began to notice things she had not seen before. There were small flecks of gray appearing in his close-cropped brown hair. There were crow's feet at the corners of his eyes. Laughter marks, she decided, rather than too much time spent staring into the sun. His lips were full, almost sensuous, and she found herself wondering what it would be like to kiss them.

He looked up at her and smiled. "What are you thinking?" he asked.

Embarrassment flooded over her. "I'm not thinking anything," she lied. "Just looking, like you told me to."

"You're blushing."

"I am not."

"Yes you are." He laughed, and she found it impossible to be irritated with him.

He turned the napkin around and she stared in astonishment at what he had created. "Is that me?" she whispered.

"It's how I see you."

"She's beautiful. I'm not like that," she protested.

"Look at the drawing and tell me what you see." She examined the drawing. The pencil strokes were bold yet sparing. It was definitely her face yet it was not her. It was something idealized, almost a fantasy. She tried to find the words to describe what she was seeing. "I see a fairy-tale princess," she said haltingly. "She's strong. She's bold. She's sensuous. Yet at the same time, she's very vulnerable, almost fragile. Is that how you see me?"

He turned down the corners of his mouth. "You're not a princess and you're not fragile. I tried to put strength and boldness into the drawing, and just a hint of vulnerability because I don't want you to get too puffed up with pride."

He pushed the drawing over to her. "Keep it. It's yours."

As she took the drawing her hand trembled. She had seen one more thing in it that she had not mentioned and neither had he. Love.

Like everything else, the drawing had not made the translation from dream to reality, and she felt a sudden pang at its loss.

"God is the ultimate artist," he continued. "Look around you. You can see the hand of the Master in a beautiful sunset. You can see it in the mountains at dawn. You can see it in a mother with her child. You can see it in the people around you. We are God's masterpiece, and to the degree that we surrender to his hand, he uses the stuff of life—the good, the bad, and the ugly, to make us into something sublimely beautiful." It was spoken naturally, from the heart. She wished she could be as genuine in her faith as he was in his, to just believe, go with the flow, to simply be what she was called to be.

But what was she called to be? What was happening in her mind? She looked back at the string of coalescing memories. There were still more gaps than concrete memories, but they were starting to give her a picture of a concrete whole. Of a TOPGUN experience vastly different from the one she had completed years before—an experience full of inconsistencies and impossibilities. An experience that had changed her, had made her see life differently. Had made her see people differently.

The ready room snapped back into focus, and before she could form a conscious thought, she spun and strode to where Spud was sitting alone, a picture of frozen isolation.

She touched his shoulder lightly. "Hey, Bud. Let's go find somewhere to talk."

He stiffened at her touch but unfolded out of his seat, not challenging her as he would have a couple weeks previously.

Where to go to find a little privacy where hopefully she could get him to open up to her? The ready room was full. The Dirty Shirt would likewise be full of officers grabbing an early dinner. Inspiration struck.

The ship's chapel was a small compartment, sparsely furnished, little more than panels on the wall simulating stained glass, a few rows of seats, and an altar. But it offered a modicum of privacy.

She nodded at Father Matthew, the Catholic chaplain, who was engaged in hushed conversation with a sailor in the front row, and led Spud to a pair of seats in the back.

"I saw how you reacted when Digger announced the redeployment," she said when they were seated, trying to put every iota of concern she could muster into her voice. "What's going on?"

Spud looked away, his body rigid, almost trembling. His lower lip quivered. He took a deep breath, fighting for control. When he turned back to her, his eyes shimmered.

"Take your time," Kate said gently.

He nodded and took another deep breath, and an aura of calm descended on him. The old Spud was back—a mountain, inviolate. Kate half expected him to rise and leave, but he surprised her.

"Things have been really bad at home." His voice was flat, calm, belying the raging emotions she had seen in him just moments before.

"Kim and I were high school sweethearts," he went on. A spasm of pain crossed his face as he spoke the words. "We married while we were at college. Tyler was born a year later. We have a little girl due in a couple months, and I'm not going to be there when she's born.

"Although I tried to explain it to her, I don't think Kim ever bought into navy life. She didn't realize the amount of time I'd be gone. The long hours at flight school took their toll. We had our good times, but that's when we began arguing. And when I joined the Outlaws, Animal and the rest of the squadron made my life a living hell. I took it home, and that's when things started to get really bad.

"Making it worse," he continued, his eyes staring past her shoulder, unblinking, "we were facing an eight-month separation. Kim was pressuring me to find some way of getting out of the deployment. We were fighting almost every night, and I was bringing that to work. A couple days before deployment, I was almost ready to march into the skipper's office and hand him my wings."

His voice quivered and he brushed angrily at his eyes. "Yokosuka was my last hope. Kim and I were going to meet there for one final try to patch things up. See if we could save our marriage. Now that's not going to happen." He bit his lip and looked away, a tear trickling down his cheek.

He gathered himself with a deep, shuddering breath. His eyes met Kate's and she was startled at the depth of emotion revealed in them.

"I'm not a quitter." His mouth twitched then settled into a firm line of determination. "My dad taught me that. It was tough on the farm growing up, but he never bent." His voice hardened. "I may never fit in, but I'm not going to give up. It may cost me my family, everything else—maybe even my life—but I am not giving up."

He deflated and stared at her as she searched for words to reply. "There you have it. There's the mess that's Spud." The words were hard, defiant, but there was a subtle plaintiveness to them that Kate could not help but recognize as plea for help. She blinked hard at the sudden prickling in her eyes. There it was. He'd bared his heart, laid everything out in black and white. She felt an answering flood of sympathy. Slowly, hesitantly, she reached out and lightly touched the back of his hand. She was mildly surprised when he didn't jerk it back.

"Thank you for sharing with me," she said, pacing her words to give herself time to think. What could she say? What could she do? For ultimately, the battle was his and his alone. "I had no idea."

"Thank you for listening," Spud said as he rose. She was surprised at the lack of anger in his voice. "I don't need you to fix me. All I want is a chance—a fair shake to make or break." His eyes met hers in a moment of silent entreaty before he pushed past her and strode out of the compartment.

As Kate watched his retreating back, she felt a sudden surge of sympathy for this lonely, unlikable man.

Thoughts swirling in her mind, she made her way back to the ready room. One thing was crystal clear. Spud didn't need her lecturing him. He needed her to come alongside him, help him lift himself out of the sewer. He was a man in distress, and he deserved no less than her best to help him through this lowest point in his life. She straightened her shoulders and felt a sudden bounce in her step as she resolved to give it to him.

Chapter 27

"Thank you, Moses. Dinner was excellent tonight."

The ex-slave's face beamed with delight. Over the winter he had acquired cast-off uniform items and was now dressed in a pair of raggedy light-blue trousers and a sack coat equally tattered and worn. His gray shirt had probably been white at one time, but he wore the items with pride.

After Moses had cleaned away the remnants of the meal, Merlyn pushed back his chair and surveyed his staff. George sat to his right, Johanns to his left. Farther down the table Lieutenant Ambrose sat next to the new adjutant, Lieutenant Harrison, recently promoted from the ranks to fill behind Lieutenant Keys, who was now commanding a company. Barings sat across from them, face dark, disapproving, seemingly uncomfortable with any form of conviviality.

Rounding out the number, McElroy sat at the foot of the table. He fished out his watch and gave it a quick glance. "Apologies, colonel. I need to see to the sick soldiers. Thank you for a fine meal."

Ambrose and Harrison took their cue and left as well. Merlyn hoped Barings would do likewise, but the chaplain seemed uninclined to move.

Moses appeared again, bearing a coffeepot and a half-dozen mismatched China cups. "Where on earth did you find these?"

Merlyn asked in amazement, as Moses filled them with steaming black liquid.

"Here and there," the black man replied. "T'ain't fittin' the colonel should drink out of a tin."

"He seems to like the uniform," Dutchy mused at Moses's retreating back. He scraped ash from the bowl of his pipe and banged it against his boot.

"He does at that," Merlyn agreed. "You think he'd want to be a soldier?"

"I heard they're forming a regiment of negro soldiers up north," George commented. "It's a long way for him to go, but he could join them if he wants to."

Merlyn stifled a tickle of amusement. "What about enlisting him right here?"

George's head jerked up, and Dutchy paused filling his pipe.

"You cannot be serious, colonel," Barings expostulated. "He's a negro."

"So, what's your point, chaplain?" Merlyn replied. "He's a human being just like you and me. Do you think because of the color of his skin he is unfit to serve?"

If Barings heard the anger in Merlyn's voice, he chose to ignore it. "It's a long way from the plantation to the army. What makes you think that he's remotely capable of performing drills, following orders?"

"Chaplain, I wish you could hear yourself." Merlyn's rage was white-hot now, and he fought to keep his voice steady. "That man you are demeaning is no less a child of God than you or I. He is every bit as capable of shouldering a musket, fixing a bayonet, and charging the enemy as any one of our men. If you think he lacks courage, think of what he went through to make his way here. He has every making of a good soldier, but your prejudice won't let you see it."

Barings rose to his feet, banging the table, causing coffee to slosh over the rims of the cups. "Sir, I will not be abused in this way. May I have your permission to withdraw?"

"Please do," Merlyn replied, ice hanging from every word.

"Why do you hang onto that insufferable man?" George said as he watched Barings' stiffly retreating back. "A less godly man I have yet to see."

"I wish it were that easy, George," Merlyn lamented. "I find his form of Christianity abhorrent, but that is not reason to sack the man. Besides, I would have to find another chaplain, and that would be hard to do. But let's not talk about him. What about my earlier question?"

"You make an interesting point, Colonel." Johanns had his pipe going and exhaled a cloud of blue smoke. "The men like him. He's an excellent cook. They might just accept him into the ranks."

George's brow furrowed. "Assuming he would want to enlist, how would you do it? He is a negro, after all."

Merlyn heaved an exasperated sigh. "You're looking at this all wrong. Moses is not a negro. He is a human being, a child of God, who has dark skin. He deserves to be treated equally, like any other human being. If he wants to be a soldier, you enlist him like you would anyone else who wants to serve. There should be no distinction because of the color of his skin."

"It's not that easy, colonel," Dutchy interjected. "In God's eyes, all men may be equal, but in man's eyes they are anything but. Most of the men would accept him, but someone will object and make a fuss."

Merlyn conceded the point. "Yes, but we should never allow what somebody may say to stop us from doing what is right. We must have the courage of our convictions."

Later that evening after George and Dutchy had gone about their business, Merlyn leaned back in his chair and closed his eyes.

A tune started playing in the back of his mind—a tune from a different time, so different in style from the music heard everywhere in the camps, the homesick melodies played by the soldiers and martial tunes blaring from the regimental bands. He brought it forward, heard Brandi Carlile's raspy, plaintive voice once more. Kate had introduced him to the song and had played it often. He let the words flow though his mind, caressing it, deepening his sense of longing and bringing forth another memory.

Morgan drove as Kate sat curled up in the passenger seat watching the miles tick by. The previous evening, she had declared she was growing weary of the brown, featureless desert around Fallon and needed green and water. Lake Tahoe was just the place to dispel her mood. Morgan had happily embraced the opportunity to spend more time with her and had consented to drive.

Kate's favorite playlist streamed softly over the car stereo. She fiddled with her phone, selecting another song. With the opening bar, he recognized it. "The Story." Again.

He lost himself in the words, letting them speak to him, draw out his emotions, his sense of loss, his guilt. Their time was coming to end. Graduation was a few weeks away. Another assignment loomed and she was going back to the world she knew. The very thought of parting was agony in his heart. He knew with crushing certainty, and she was blissfully unaware, thinking their time together would go on forever.

Yes, I've broken all the rules, he thought as the song faded, crossed all the lines. *This mess we're in is my fault, and I see no way out. Now we're both going to get hurt, badly hurt, and there's nothing I can do to stop it.*

He felt a hand on his knee and shot her a sideways glance. She was staring intently at him, a look of amusement on her face.

"Hey, where did you go just then? You were a million miles away."

She was getting to know him too well, could read the ins and outs of his moods, knew when he was present or when his mind was wrestling with something.

"Just thinking about the words," he said slowly, his voice weighed down by the heaviness in his heart. "We've all got a story to tell, whether or not it leaves lines on our faces."

"So, what's your story? What's left those lines around your eyes that crinkle every time you smile?"

Girl, if only you knew, he thought, and was wildly tempted to tell her, tell it all. Come clean in a massive purging. Rock her world.

See where it led from there. But reality set in just as quickly. *Can't go there. Can't speak the words I long to speak.*

"Too many hours staring into the sun," he said, avoiding the truth of his past. "Occupational hazard of a fighter pilot."

Time to change the subject. He was getting pretty good at that—too good. "You listen to this song a lot. I get the sense it speaks deeply to you. Who are you thinking of when you hear it?"

She didn't answer right away. He shot another glance at her. She was staring forward, eyes unfocused, obviously seeing something different than the road ahead. "I think about both Mom and Dad and the lives they've led—Dad mostly, though—when I hear this song. Not all the song, though; just the part about lines and stories and being made for each other."

She lapsed into silence, and he was acutely aware of her hand still resting on his knee. "As difficult as Dad can be, he's an amazing man," she continued. "Sacrificed everything for his family.

"Mom's the quiet, steady type. A prayer warrior. She's the warm, gentle breeze to Dad's hurricane. They complement each other so well, playing to each other's strengths, and filling the gaps left by their weaknesses. They're wonderful people. And I believe with all my heart God made them for each other. I hope and pray that there's at least some of what makes them great in me."

She fell silent again. He took her hand, laced his fingers with hers, and drove one-handed. As brown desert sped by, he felt a firm resolve form in his heart. He could not let Kate go. There had to be a way out of this.

He had found a way, given it his best shot, but sitting in his rough cabin in the deepening twilight, a continent and several lifetimes away from Fallon, he had no way of knowing whether it had worked. When she made her transition, her arm and hand could have been wiped clean, just as her memories could be altered.

No scar on her arm, no cut on her hand, no comingled blood. Apart forever. He had been fooling himself that such a childish stratagem would work. How could it work? The God who made

188

him what he was could easily undo his pathetic attempt to influence his plan. The thought was staggering, crushing. What had he been thinking? How could he have been so presumptuous as to challenge his very creator?

A bugle sounded in the distance, and he felt a chill run down his spine as he listened to the new call that had started in Butterfield's brigade the previous year and was being adopted by more and more brigades across the Army. Now it was simply "Lights Out." Future generations would know it as "Taps." The mournful notes tugged at his heartstrings, and he impatiently brushed away the tear that shimmered in the corner of his eye.

Chapter 28

K ate watched disinterestedly as Seaman Garcia, surrounded by pilots, prepared to slide the day's mail delivery into the distribution cubicles at the back of the ready room. In this connected world, mail was not normally a big deal, but given the blackout of ship's email, letters had become a vital connection to the outside world. No sooner did Garcia's hand approach a cubicle than the envelope it contained was snatched from her grasp.

"Ma'am, here's one for you," Garcia called to Kate.

Her heart missed a beat as she looked at the return address. Fingers shaking, she tore it open. She scanned the opening lines and forced back the surge of disappointment that crashed over her. No test results. Two sentences said it all: "I mailed off the lab report at the end of March. I don't know why you haven't received it. I tried calling the lab, but they won't give me another copy without your say so."

As Kate scanned the rest of Lisa's letter, she became aware of Spud hanging back slightly from the press of bodies. Finally, Garcia was down to one envelope. Instead of sliding it into a cubicle, she proffered it to Spud. His face blanched as he took it and his body recoiled as if struck. Heart in her throat, Kate watched him gingerly turn the envelope over and over in his hands. Finally, he stuffed it unopened into his flight suit and fled the ready room.

Later that evening, Kate found him alone in a corner of the Dirty Shirt. Pilots from the various squadrons formed noisy groups. She spotted Heather laughing gaily amongst a contingent of Growler aircrew. At another table, a half-dozen Outlaws were engaged in an intense conversation, hands recreating another air battle. She automatically started to move in that direction but stopped, arrested by the solitary figure in the far corner of the compartment.

She embraced the pang of sympathy that welled up in her and steered her feet in that direction. Spud had pushed aside his largely uneaten meal and sat staring at a typewritten letter on the table in front of him. He looked up as she approached, eyes red-rimmed, face ashen, then looked back down at the letter. Kate slid into the bench opposite.

Long moments later, he looked up, his normally bland face unable to contain the emotions raging beneath the surface.

"Bad news?" Kate asked gently.

Spud appeared to struggle with himself for a moment, then pushed the letter across the table to her. Kate turned it, scanned the logo boldly emblazoned across the first page, and began to read. Two sentences into the curt legalese, she felt her eyes tearing up. There was no reason to read any further.

She looked up and met Spud's eyes. "I'm sorry," she said, sincerely meaning it.

"I didn't see this coming," Spud said shakily. "I thought we were going to try to patch things up at Yokosuka, but I see now she wasn't planning to go." He worried his lower lip for a moment. "She wants an amicable divorce. Shared custody. She doesn't hate me, just can't handle navy life and me being gone all the time."

Kate said nothing. Spud needed a sympathetic ear, not a pep talk.

For almost half an hour, Spud poured his heart out, laying his feelings bare. Much of it was a repeat of what he'd shared a couple of days before, but Kate listened quietly, her heart slowly breaking as she listened to his narrative of lost dreams and inner struggles.

"I don't know if the divorce can proceed without me, but when I get home, I'm going to fight for my marriage," he said flatly, all emotion gone from his voice as if sucked out by a giant vacuum cleaner.

Kate struggled to find words, but there was nothing she could say that would even begin to help fix Spud's situation. She could see it clearly now, the view from the other side, and felt a growing feeling of shame for how easily she had judged him, had participated in what had begun as the Outlaws' customary hazing of a new squadron member but had become something much deeper, more malevolent.

Shaken, she took a slow breath. "Spud, from my heart, I'm sorry for how this has all played out, how we've treated you." There. It was said. But she was alone in her point of view. Now it was up to her to help how the rest of the squadron saw him. But that was for the future, not now. Instead, she had to focus on the problem at hand.

"Take a day or two off the schedule. We can spare you. Get your head together. When you're ready, I'll put you back up in the air." It was all the help she could offer.

Spud shook his head. "No. I need to fly. I need something to focus on. I'll get through this."

As they continued to talk, a knot began to form in Kate's stomach. She was nowhere near as confident as he that this was going to have a happy ending.

***

24 May
USS Theodore Roosevelt, Indian Ocean

Kate dabbed at a trickle of sweat on her neck as her lungs fought to extract every atom of oxygen from the ready room's stifling, moisture-laden air. The southern tip of India lay a couple hundred miles north of where the TR was plowing through moderate seas. She stood with Digger under the air conditioning vent at the back of the ready room. Little more than a trickle of cool air emerged from it, the TR's cooling capacity being dedicated to the functioning of its vast array of electronics rather than the comfort of its pilots and crew.

Digger's face gleamed with a sheen of perspiration, and sweat turned the pits of his flight suit black. An aura of tension hung over the pilots engaged in their various activities. Two days from now they would enter the AOR and take up station off the coast of Iran.

"So how's our boy doing?" Digger asked, nodding to where Trojan and Spud were wrapping up a debriefing.

"I think okay," Kate replied cautiously, while stifling a yawn. Planning for increased operations once they hit the Gulf of Oman had consumed every waking minute and many of the ones she should have spent sleeping. "The divorce papers yesterday hit him hard, but he seems to be taking it in stride. I offered him a couple of down days, but he didn't take me up on it. Underneath that quiet exterior, he's pretty tough."

"Things are going to get interesting soon," Digger said in a mastery of understatement. "You and I have a lot invested in him. I hope he has what it takes."

The hint of uncertainty in his voice caused a ripple of consternation to flow through her and set her nerves jangling. Was Digger having second thoughts after all this time? Despite her recent connection with Spud, she'd never stopped having them.

As Digger made his way back toward his stateroom, Kate could not force herself to move from under the meager downdraft of cool air. She rubbed at her eyes, which felt gritty and irritated. She wanted another cup of coffee, but her nerves were already jangling. Trojan and Spud drifted out of the ready room, undoubtedly on their way to an early lunch, but the thought of food caused an unpleasant growl from her already unsettled stomach.

She watched curiously as Banger posted the morning's landing grades on the greenie board. A string of green dots gave her a small sense of satisfaction that was quickly dispelled by a surge of irritation as the last grade went up. A brown dot—a no grade—on the bottom row.

"Looks like your boy dropped another turd." The words softly whispered just beside her ear caused her to jump almost out of her skin. She whirled, but there was no mistaking that deep voice. Torch.

Did he do that on purpose? she wondered, not putting it past him to deliberately startle her, put her on edge, before finding something new to criticize.

"Today's an anomaly," she replied, irritated at the defensive tone that crept into her voice.

"It's not just his flying," Torch declared, an edge in his voice. "The other pilots can't stand him. The only reason they tolerate him is because you keep shielding him."

Torch's inky black eyes fixed Kate's with a penetrating stare. "You're putting the skipper at risk 'cause you don't have the guts to do what needs to be done."

Kate felt frustration rising up like a wave within her. This was so unfair and so wrong. She opened her mouth to speak.

"The skipper's not going to ground Spud," Torch continued, cutting her off, "unless you recommend it. I know he shot you down before, but because this is turning into a combat deployment, he's starting to waver. You need to support him by doing the right thing."

He paused and drew a deep breath, his eyes continuing to bore their way into Kate. "Spud may be doing okay in the air, but he's just not cutting it as a member of this squadron. You're going to get the boss fired if Spud kills himself or someone else, plowing into the back of the boat. Don't do that to him. Our job is to protect him, make him successful, not put his job at risk, which is what you're doing by your inability to lead and make the right decision."

Kate stifled the urge to lash out at the unfairness of the accusation. "I have no intention of putting the skipper at risk," she said, her voice trembling under the strain of suppressed emotion. "I'm trying to do the right thing by everyone, and that includes Spud. We have an obligation to him to—"

"We have absolutely no obligation to him," Torch replied harshly, cutting her off midsentence. "He's a nugget—the only obligation is his to us."

Kate opened her mouth to reply, but Torch drove relentlessly on without giving her a chance to speak. "I told the skipper you were too soft for the job."

Kate felt an icy chill run down her spine as she fought back the surge of shock and panic rising up within her. *This can't be happening,* she thought, her mind struggling to grapple with the magnitude of

Torch's accusation. *He's just like Animal. Heartless, abusive.* With just a few words, he'd cut away the ground under her and she found herself suddenly in freefall.

Her tongue felt glued to the roof of her mouth as she struggled vainly to find words to reply.

"You heard the news this morning?" Torch continued.

Still reeling from her shock, the sudden change of direction left Kate off-balance. She mutely shook her head.

A grim smile of satisfaction lit Torch's face. "Iran conducted another missile test today. Another long-range shot down into the Indian Ocean. They now have the capability to not only hit Israel, but they can hit Europe as well. All it takes is for them to mate warheads to missiles and they have true nuclear capability.

"If we're going to war, it's going make all our wars in the past thirty years look like a walk in the park. It's going to be downright ugly. There's not a man in the squadron who's going to want Spud on his wing going into a fight like that."

Kate bit back the harsh words that rose to her lips and forced herself to meet Torch's gaze.

"Do. The. Right. Thing," Torch said, punctuating each word like a pistol shot. Feeling as if her carefully constructed world was crashing down around her, she helplessly watched Torch's back as he strode from the ready room.

Chapter 29

Muscles aching, eyes gritty, and stomach sour from an all-night forced march, Merlyn trudged amidst the seemingly endless line of blue snaking northward. The rising sun, already warm, caused a trickle of sweat to run down his back despite the earliness of the hour.

George had fallen silent hours ago, leaving Merlyn to his thoughts. He probed the recesses of memory, trying to dredge up what little he could remember of the battlefield, but could find little there other than a vague recollection of monuments scattered as far as the eye could see, each memorializing the individual patches of ground that men in blue and gray had fought and died over. An idle thought crossed his mind: *What monument would someday mark the ground on which the 172nd would stand and die? Would he be one of the ones laying down his life? Would George?*

The ground began to fall into a valley between two ridgelines. He saw a white building with a red cupola off to the right on the one opposite. A line of trees sat before them a few hundred yards away. He looked back and felt his stomach clench. Soldiers, small like ants, lined a stone wall on the ridge from which they were descending. His mind screamed in protest. If the army was taking a stand on the high ground, why was Eades leading them down and away from the safety of the main Union line, so far out front where they were unsupported? They would be chewed up piecemeal by the attacking Confederates. What was Eades thinking? But it wasn't just Eades, he corrected himself. There were other units out here. At least a division, perhaps the entire corps. The Confederate army was going to roll right over them. A whole lot of his men were going to die today.

Morning was rapidly passing. There was yet no sound of battle. Where were the enemy? Eades was there suddenly, mounted on a gray horse. His face was tight, drawn with fatigue.

"Colonel," he said urgently. "Get your men into line aside the Ohioans, along that road there."

He pointed with his sword. "Quickly. The rebels will be coming out of those trees at any moment now." He rode off to continue the work of transforming his brigade from column into line.

Orderlies led the horses to the rear as Merlyn barked commands, his troops spreading out into ranks, each man knowing his part perfectly. He stood beside the colors, the United States flag, and the dark-blue flag of the 172nd New York, sun-faded and torn beside it. He looked up and down the line at his men standing nervously. Some fidgeted, some stood still. But all instinctively knew the hell that was to come. *How few there were of them now. How many fewer would it be tonight?* He banished the thought.

He scanned the thin line of blue. To his left were Smith's Ohioans and Harkness' Pennsylvanians. To his right were Parker's Pennsylvanians. Beyond them were other regiments. Sun glinted off the steel of thousands of musket barrels. Flags hung limply in the still air. A fly buzzed his ear and he swatted at it.

Minutes dragged by like hours. The waiting was always the hardest. The agonizing anticipation of what was to come. The fear so palpable it could be smelled. Each man knew what was coming, what he must do in the drama that was about to unfold. But none of them knew what the outcome would be. The outcome for them personally, the outcome for the army. So they waited, each man alone with his thoughts.

The sun dipped past the horizon as morning turned to afternoon. Merlyn glanced over at Eades. The brigade headquarters was behind the seam where Merlyn's line connected with Smith's Ohioans. Eades and his staff were still on their horses. He fought the urge to shout at the general, tell him to dismount, to not present so inviting a target to the Confederate sharpshooters waiting in the trees.

He turned back to the tree line, scanned it, looking for any sign of movement. Nothing. He wiped his face with his bandana. It was devilishly hot. Why were they not coming? Why was Lee delaying so long? He looked back at the stone wall along the ridgeline and wished with every fiber of his being that his men were up there rather than here. He scanned the tree line again. The enemy were massing there—he knew it beyond a shadow of a doubt. He knew also that just behind that wall of green, artillery sat, waiting to pour its maelstrom of shot, shell, and canister at his exposed troops.

He glanced back at Eades, sitting erect on his horse like a statue, a monument to this awful place. His brain scrambled to process what came next. The slap of bullet against flesh. Blood spurting. Eades spinning in his saddle. His horse spinning with him as Eades yanked on the reins. The distant retort of a rifleshot. Eades falling to the ground.

Merlyn broke into a run, grasping his sword to prevent it tangling with his feet. "Take command!" he shouted over his shoulder at George who was staring in shock at the crumpled form on the grass just yards away.

Captain Saunders had already dismounted, was kneeling beside the fallen general with a couple of orderlies. Smith was sprinting in from beyond Eades. Merlyn shouldered Saunders aside and was only dimly aware of the roar of cannon fire beginning.

Kneeling beside Eades, he quickly took stock. The bloody stain was spreading from the wreck of his shoulder. The man's face grimacing. Smith forced his way into the crowd surrounding Eades.

"General, how badly are you hurt?" His voice was solicitous, the question inane. At best he would lose an arm, at worst . . .

Eades turned his face to Merlyn. Merlyn lowered his head to catch the injured man's words. "Colonel, I am done for," Eades gasped. "You take command of the brigade."

Smith protested. "Parker is senior, General."

Eades turned his head, gasping at the pain the movement caused him. "No, Colonel. Michaelson takes command today. Saunders, write down the order. Sort it out after the battle." He turned back to Merlyn. "Godspeed, Colonel. Give those rebels hell."

His head lolled back on the grass and Merlyn saw blood at his mouth. Merlyn stood.

"Saunders, get General Eades back to a hospital. Let the other commanders know what's happened." There was probably little doubt in their minds. The brigade was barely stronger than a regiment, the line impossibly short—they had seen it all. "Colonel Smith, get back to your men."

He mounted Eades' horse, aware of the target he made, and spurred it toward the 172nd.

George put a hand on the horse's rein to steady him, his face pinched.

"George," Merlyn kept his voice low, firm, under control. "Today you're in command here. No heroics. Do you understand?"

The boy's eyes grew flinty with resolve. He nodded. Merlyn leaned down, gripped his shoulder. "God bless you and be with you, my friend."

George nodded solemnly and turned back to his men. Merlyn wheeled and rode back to the men surrounding the brigade flag still hanging limply under the blazing sun. He saw movement in front of the trees and there it was, a solid wall of men in butternut and gray. Ragged, but every bit as determined as the men in blue standing before them. Sunlight glinted off a forest of bayonets.

"Dear Lord," Merlyn breathed, "protect George and all these men who stand here today. Be with us and help us defend the cause of freedom—"

He was unable to finish his brief prayer before his world dissolved into an earth-shattering storm of shot and shell.

Chapter 30

Kate squirmed, trying to get comfortable. After three hours in the air, her tailbone and glutes were starting to ache from the hard ejection seat. The Super Hornet's cockpit was like an oven as the air conditioning system struggled to keep up with the sun baking through the canopy. She watched the data link symbols march down her radar display. Flankers. Not good.

Who was piloting the two jets coming at her at near supersonic speed? Iran or Russia? She had to assume the worst.

The words from the intelligence briefing several days ago flashed through her mind. "With Russian and Chinese help, the Iranian Air Force has undertaken a complete modernization of its air and surface-to-air forces. It has procured Su-35 Flanker-E and other aircraft from the Russians. We believe the Flanker variants sold to Iran include electronically scanned array radars with similar capabilities to those found on US fighters. It has also upgraded its air-to-air weapons inventory to include the latest variants of the AA-10 Alamo, AA-11 Archer, and AA-12 Adder. It has become a modern and capable force."

Kate fixated on the word *Flanker*. The Sukhoi Su-35, NATO codename Flanker-E, was the allied fighter pilot's worst nightmare. Big, highly maneuverable, and capable of carrying twelve air-to-air missiles, it was a formidable foe. It owned most of its potential adversaries throughout their flight envelopes, and only truly met its match in the US Air Force's F-22 Raptor.

Kate and Digger had exchanged a quick glance. Technology was one thing, but what really counted was the pilot in the cockpit. It took years to produce a capable fighter pilot, years of training and hard-earned experience. Novices climbed into a jet to fly; experienced fighter pilots strapped on a jet. There was a world of difference. The Russians could provide that difference.

The briefer's next words had caused a shiver to travel up her spine. "Since we are now in effect in a combat zone, you will be flying round the clock fleet defense missions. Expect Iran to probe and test. They will do everything they can do to provoke, to get you to fire and create an international incident or better still for them, catch one of you off guard and score political points by shooting you down."

And that's exactly what had been happening since the TR entered the AOR. A line in the sky had been drawn. Iranian or Russian fighters could not be allowed south of that line or the US carriers and their supporting battle groups operating in the Arabian sea would be within range of any anti-ship missiles they might be carrying. Today it was Kate and Spud's job, along with other pairs of fighters—all fully loaded with radar-guided AIM-120 Advanced Medium Range Air-to-Air Missiles, AMRAAMs, and heat-seeking AIM-9X Sidewinder missiles—to ensure no enemy aircraft posed a threat to the US fleet.

Air Force E-3 AWACS aircraft, Navy E-2D Hawkeyes, and other intelligence gathering platforms built a three-dimensional picture of what was happening in the airspace over and around Iran. Data link brought that picture into the cockpit of Kate's F/A-18E Super Hornet, granting her situational awareness.

She reached the end of the racetrack pattern she and Spud were flying. The data link symbol representing her adversaries was beyond her commit range, the distance at which she and Spud would start racing to intercept them well before they could threaten the fleet.

She dipped a wing away from Spud and waited for him to respond to her signal. A moment later his airplane rolled toward her. She rolled into a ninety-degree bank, eased her throttles forward, and pulled back on the stick in a moderate turn, g-forces pulling her down gently into the seat. She rolled out after 180 degrees and found Spud rolling out, two miles off her left wing, exactly where he was supposed to be.

She left her throttles up, allowing her speed to creep up from fuel-conserving to employment speed. She glanced at the display. Her adversaries, probably supersonic, were overtaking her.

They were approaching commit criteria. She opened her throttles and started a climb. She would need every knot of airspeed and every foot of altitude for the aerial ballet about to begin.

The calm voice of the Hawkeye controller came over the radio. "Anvil three groups, bandits. First group Bullseye one niner five for sixty-two, angels thirty, multiples. Second group one six seven for sixty-two, angels thirty-five. Third group one four five for seventy-five, angels thirty. All groups hot."

The terse communication gave the entire air picture. The Hawkeye was tracking three sets of enemy entities, spread out in a line, roughly thirty miles apart, sixty miles south of a reference point off the Iranian mainland. The three groups were at approximately 30,000 feet. The first group, her responsibility, had at least two aircraft in it, flying far enough apart that the narrow beam of the Hawkeye's radar could resolve them into separate tracks.

The Hawkeye's call was her cue. "Texaco 31, commit, commit." She turned in to Spud this time, pulling harder on the stick while simultaneously pushing her throttles forward into afterburner.

As she rolled out heading north, she did a quick scan of her instruments—climbing through 35,000 feet, airspeed approaching 500 knots, fuel: 8.1. All good.

Her feet tingled and her mouth went dry. *Come on, see these guys,* she willed her radar. She shot a glance at Spud flying off her right wing. His position was perfect.

Her RWR shrilled, causing her heart to lurch. She scanned her displays, noted the illuminated AI light and air-to-air threat symbology at twelve o'clock. They had been targeted.

"Texaco 32, spike 12, far." Spud's voice sounded tense on the radio.

"Texaco 31, same. Float." She tried to sound calm while anticipating the radar-guided missiles that could soon be coming their way. She turned slightly away from Spud and he from her, increasing their spacing, hoping that only one of them was targeted and the other could drift outside of their adversaries' radar beam. As the distance increased, the symbols vanished from her RWR. She was no longer being tracked.

"Texaco 31, naked."

"Texaco 32, still spiked."

She checked the range. Their adversaries were approaching launch range.

"Texaco 32, drag," she ordered and immediately saw Spud yank his jet around, turning away from the incoming Flankers.

She looked back at her radar. There they were—a pair of radar returns superimposed over the data link tracks. *Line abreast, close formation.*

She moved her radar's acquisition symbols over the closest return. Just as she was about to lock onto the nearest adversary, her RWR shrilled again. Another symbol on her display at twelve o'clock, but closer this time. She imagined the missile leaping off her adversary's wing and streaking toward her at several times the speed of sound.

She hit the chaff button and rolled into a hard, descending turn. "Texaco 31, spiked, notching east," she transmitted. After ninety degrees, she rolled out and checked to ensure that the symbol representing the incoming Flanker was exactly at her nine o'clock position.

"Texaco 32, naked, turning hot." Spud's transmission could not have come at a more opportune moment.

Sweat rolled down her face. Her feet continued to tingle. She scanned the horizon hoping for an early tally-ho, a visual pickup of the adversary. *Find him fast, buddy*, she willed Spud. *What's taking you so long?*

Her spike dropped. She slammed the throttles forward and pulled hard, back into the incoming Flankers. As they appeared on the screen just where she anticipated, she heard Spud's radio call, "Texaco 32, sorted eastern."

There they were, on her screen, just where she anticipated. She moved the acquisition symbols over the closest, easternmost target, and obtained a lock.

"Texaco 31, sorted western," she transmitted.

She heaved a brief sigh of relief. They were unspiked and each had radar lock on the appropriate adversary. The intercept was back on their terms. The incoming Flankers now had to be wondering if the American pilots had launched missiles or not.

The aspect angle of the incoming fighters broke. They were turning away. "Texaco 31, bandits dragging," she transmitted.

"Anvil, same." Her Hawkeye controller was seeing it too.

For several minutes, they pressed north, pushing the pair of Flankers away from the fleet. She pulled her power back and slowed, allowing their distance to increase. A smudge appeared on the horizon. The Iranian coastline. They were now approaching a different kind of threat—the enemy's surface-to-air defenses. Time to turn south.

She broke her radar lock and pulled a hard 180-degree turn. "Texaco 31, drop. Reset CAP." It was time to return to their preplanned orbit.

She flexed her fingers and tried to relax. This game of BVR chicken was fraying her nerves. She felt a small glow of satisfaction as Spud dropped into position off her right wing. Gone were the missteps and errors. He'd executed perfectly.

"How did it go up there today?" Heather asked as she mopped up a last bit of ketchup with a French fry.

Her eyes were red-rimmed, face haggard with fatigue.

That's how I must look, Kate mused, glancing around the Dirty Shirt. There were only a handful of aviators present at this late hour. She took a sip of Coke to wet her mouth. "Kind of like staring down the barrel of a gun wondering if the guy on the other end is going to pull the trigger." As her sweat-soaked flight suit testified, the stress was excruciating. "That's three in as many days," she continued. "Their tactics are always the same. Come at us. Spike us. Then drop and run at the last minute. They're building an expectation on our part, and then when they want to hurt us, they are going to do something entirely different and catch us off guard. If this keeps up, somebody is going to get hurt."

The tightening around Heather's mouth indicated her agreement. "Your guy handle it okay?"

"Did fine," Kate replied, wondering why she felt a niggle of discomfort as she spoke the words.

"How did he handle the news about the ultimatum this afternoon?"

"Pretty much like the other guys. Took it in stride. We all knew it was coming. Nobody has any doubt Iran is not going to give up its nuclear arsenal and completely dismantle its nuclear program. We're going to war in two weeks when it expires." Giving voice to the thought caused her heart to miss a beat.

As Heather pushed her tray aside, Kate could not miss the slight shaking in her friend's fingers.

"I know. Me too," Kate said softly. "I don't have a good feeling about this. It's going to make OIF look like a walk in the park, and I have a squadron that's barely holding together."

"I thought with Spud doing okay that was fixed."

"Not really. Spud may be doing okay, but the guys still barely tolerate him. Torch is the worst. He's leaning hard on me to convince Digger to take his wings. As angry as I get at Torch, I don't think he's being malicious—just doing what he thinks is in the squadron's best interest. The way he does it makes me doubt myself. It's driving me nuts."

She took a deep breath to calm her fluttering nerves. "I feel for Spud and the agony he's going through. Yet despite it, he's hanging in there and flying well. Grounding him would be a monstrous injustice."

Heather took a hesitant breath. "You're in a tough spot. Would you mind if I prayed for you right now?"

Kate's heart skipped a beat. She'd been meaning to speak of faith to her newfound friend. Heather had just confirmed what she had been coming to suspect.

"Please," she replied. "I need all the help I can get."

"You have a good head on your shoulders. Just listen to the Lord and you'll do the right thing."

Kate felt herself begin to unwind as Heather's calm, assured tone began to bring a semblance of peace to her racing thoughts.

"Dear Jesus, we love you and we thank you for every blessing you give us. We thank you for your presence in our hearts and in our lives. Our heartfelt desire is to be closer to you. Bless and guide Kate as she struggles with the tough decisions before her. Give her your wisdom and insight and help her to do the right thing. We trust you to keep her safe through the work you are doing in her life. Give her the desires of her heart and the peace and joy that comes from knowing you. Amen."

"Amen," Kate echoed softly. "Thanks, Heather. I needed the reminder I'm not alone in this."

Feeling a sudden lightness in her spirit, she began to pray for her friend.

Chapter 31

"Steady boys, steady," Merlyn called in a firm voice. Still astride Eades' horse, he sat behind Smith's shattered regiment to steady it. The surviving Ohioans stood in a ragged line facing the small draw out of which the rebel hoards had emerged in screaming waves three times so far that afternoon. The horse shivered under him, and he rubbed a hand down his neck to calm him. It came away red. A minor wound, he hoped, but there was no time to spend in compassion for the animal that had served him well. He only hoped it would stay up through the remainder of the day. There was no time to find another.

He quickly checked his lines. To his right, the New Yorkers and Parker's Pennsylvanians still stood firm. Glancing left he felt a surge of anger at furtive movement where the Ohioans butted against Harkness' Pennsylvanians. Men were starting to drift back. Were it to continue, the line would crumble, quickly becoming a rout.

"Captain, dress your lines," he said urgently to a young officer standing shakily by the regimental colors, a pile of bodies at his feet, among them Colonel Smith. He pointed with his sword to where the line was beginning to crumble.

The captain bellowed an order and sergeants hurled the men back into line and stood behind them to steady them.

Bodies carpeted the ground so thickly in front of his thin, ragged lines it was almost impossible to distinguish friend from foe.

A keening wail echoing from thousands of throats rose from the trees lining the other side of the field and a wall of gray burst into the open. The horse flinched at the sound and Merlyn felt something tug gently at his arm, leaving a burning sensation in its wake. The horse's movement had just saved his life.

Despite the roar of muskets and cannon all around, the field seemed to grow deathly quiet as the rebel force approached. "Wait for it." He drew the words out under his breath, holding his sword high as the distance closed.

"Fire," he yelled, dropping his arm. A thousand muskets erupted in smoke and flame and the front row of Confederates melted away. He choked on the thick haze of smoke now covering the field obscuring the approaching rebel lines. Men reloaded feverishly, and as the smoke settled, he saw the enemy line come to a halt, a seemingly impenetrable wall of gray standing against his own thin, ragged line. Time seemed to freeze to a standstill as the enemy raised their muskets to the ready.

Merlyn shot a glance to his right. George stood grim-faced by the New Yorker's flag, as did the captain of the Ohioans before him. Merlyn saw the eruption of fire and the billow of smoke from the densely packed enemy line long before he heard the roar.

Bullets zipped past his ear or met flesh with a loud slap. All around him, men fell. Merlyn felt a stab of fear as, out of the corner of his eye, he saw George fall backward, his hand flying to his head. *No!*—he choked off the anguished scream before it could leave his mouth and stifled the urge to spur the horse to his friend's aid. Johanns would assume control of the New Yorkers. The Ohioans needed him here. The young captain was gone, as was the sergeant holding the flag. It stood tottering, riddled with holes, but with no hands to steady it. In a moment it would fall. Merlyn spurred forward, grasped it firmly, holding it high, but rough hands grabbed it from him. He looked down into the weathered, gray-bearded face of a sergeant whose eyes glittered determinedly. "I've got it, sir," he said, and stepped forward bracing the pole at his side.

Another volley roared out from his lines, thinner than the first, but still deadly, as more Confederates tumbled to the ground.

"Sir, sir." A runner had approached from the left, was clamoring for his attention.

Merlyn leaned over as another volley roared past. "What is it, son?"

The runner, little more than a boy, face white with fear, was gasping for breath, unable to form the words he needed to say.

"Slow down," Merlyn said gently. "Take a deep breath."

The boy did as he was told, and a little of the fear left his face. "Sir, Colonel Harkness sent me to tell you the 2nd Brigade is falling back. He can't stay where he is or he'll be flanked."

The firing thinned and settled down to a dull roar as both sides commenced firing at will.

Merlyn captured the situation in an instant. Saw the danger facing his lines. "Tell the New Yorkers and Parker to fall back to the fence line behind us," Merlyn ordered Saunders. "We'll make a stand there."

At his order, the Ohioans began to fall back, as did Harkness' men, but his heart stopped as he looked down the right of his line. Beyond the New Yorkers, Parker was falling back, but the New Yorkers were stubbornly holding their ground, firing into a wall of gray that was slowly advancing upon them.

His heart lurched as he saw George, blood streaming from the side of his face, defiantly standing by the flag in the face of heavy rebel fire. Merlyn saw the awful inevitableness of it in his mind's eye. His men tumbling to the ground at the next rebel volley, the survivors overrun, falling to a field of bayonets.

He fought back the surge of anger that threatened to overwhelm him. The boy from Parker's regiment was still beside him. "Go," Merlyn screamed at him, extending his arm toward the New Yorkers' flag. "Tell that fool colonel to fall back now or he will cause the entire line to collapse. Go as fast as you can."

The boy took off at a run, dodging around huddled mounds of blue and gray, tripping over one, falling to his hands and knees only to rise again and continue his dash. He reached George, tugged hard at his sleeve.

George looked back to where Merlyn sat atop Eades' bay and shook his head. The boy expostulated to him and Merlyn turned the horse in George's direction. Gray was already starting to lap at the ends of his line, and then Merlyn saw George shout something inaudible over the roar of gunfire, and the thin New Yorker line began to fall back in good order.

"Cover them," Merlyn yelled to the bearded sergeant who seemed to be all that was left to lead the Ohio regiment. The sergeant barked an order and muskets barked their fire into the wave of gray swirling around George's left. Farther down the line he saw Parker's men doing the same.

Merlyn allowed himself to relax slightly. The New Yorkers would make it back to the line, but at what cost? How many men had died because of George's foolishness?

As the rebel attack faltered against the strengthened Union line, Merlyn spurred Eades' horse over to where George stood. He had only a moment, he knew. The rebels would be back sooner than he would like.

George's hat was gone. Blood streamed down his face from a gash on his temple. What wasn't covered in blood was stained gray from gunpowder smoke. His eyes flashed wildly, the blue accentuated by the darkness of his face. He smiled grimly at Merlyn's approach, teeth flashing white.

"Reckon we can hold them right here, Merlyn," he said with grim satisfaction.

Merlyn ignored the stupidity of the comment. There was no holding rebels here. The entire corps was nothing but a speedbump in the path of the rebel juggernaut. They were going to roll over his lines no matter what. All they could do was buy time for the main Union line to strengthen along the ridge behind them.

Merlyn leaned over the horse's neck, rage tightening his throat. "George, if you ever pull a stunt like that again, I'll break you so fast it will make your head spin," he growled, his anger making his voice shake. "Your job is to stay in line and follow orders, not engage in stupid heroics. Do I make myself perfectly clear?"

George's face tightened in shock, and his hand fell away from the horse's bridle. His mouth opened and closed as he struggled to find words.

"I said, colonel, do I make myself clear?" Merlyn demanded.

"Yes, sir." George's face rearranged itself into an expressionless mask. "Perfectly clear, sir."

Without waiting for a salute, Merlyn wheeled the horse and spurred it back to where the Pennsylvanians waited.

Already the keening wail was rising from across the field. The rebels were moving. He only hoped his shattered brigade could hold long enough to give the forces on the ridge the time they needed. Even so, he knew, it was going to be a very close thing.

Chapter 32

Kate's heart hammered as she stared down at the thick envelope Seaman Garcia had just handed her. It was battered and stained. Cancellation marks almost obscured the postage stamps. But her address on the front and Lisa's return address in the corner could still be clearly read. After all these months chasing her around the world, the DNA test had finally caught up with her.

It wouldn't tell her anything about a naval aviator named Morgan Michaelson, but at least it would reveal if his blood was on the towel along with hers. She was surprised to find herself strangely reluctant to tear the envelope open. What were the implications if her hopes were quashed, the dream nothing more than a pleasant fantasy? She released her breath in a rush.

Digger, standing close by, heard her sigh. He looked at her, concern etched into his face. "You okay, Elsa?"

She tried to look nonchalant. "Fine, Skipper. Just been waiting for this letter for a while." She stuffed the envelope into the calf pocket of her flight suit.

"Everything okay back home?" He wasn't giving up.

She smiled brightly back at him. "Everything's fine. Mom and Dad are fine. I thought this letter had been lost."

He looked at her speculatively. "Elsa, I know you well enough to know there's something going on. You're wound tighter than a two-dollar watch. Besides getting us ready for war, I know you're worried about Spud. Do I need to be worried about you?" His gaze was direct, assessing, and she felt an irrational fear he could somehow read her heart.

It was the last thing she wanted, but her mouth betrayed her. Before she could stop herself, she had blurted out a heavily edited version of her story, telling Digger little more than she had fallen in love with a man who was now deployed. As she wrapped up, she angrily brushed away the tears that sprang to her eyes.

His gaze softened. "I'm sorry, Elsa, I really am. I can imagine how tough it is for you. I'm happy you've found someone. But I've got to say this—this isn't the time for romantic daydreams. I need you as focused as you've ever been in your life. Don't let us down."

His tone was kindly. She stared into his eyes and saw something she was not expecting. Compassion. *He really is worried for me*, she realized. *Not for the job I need to do, but worried for me as a person.* She smiled weakly at him.

"Skipper, I'm pretty good at compartmentalizing. I'll give you all I've got and then some." It was the truth. She hoped he believed her.

He turned to leave. "I'm looking forward to meeting this guy. He must be special if he's able to meet your high standards."

Kate sat alone in the back corner of the Dirty Shirt and took another bite from her sandwich. Emotions whirling, she read again the test report laid out on the table before her. Two people's blood on the towel. Hers and someone else's. Someone male. Something from the dream had actually translated into reality. It was a game-changer. Morgan's blood was on that towel. He had said he was going to give her an anchor. He had. She only wished it had come sooner, had not been lost in the mail. But even if it had, would it have made the last few months any easier?

213

She turned her attention to Lisa's brief note:

Here's the lab report you asked me to get. I didn't open it. I'm assuming it has something to do with that Michaelson guy you told me about. I did some asking around.

She stifled a slight surge of irritation. She hadn't asked Lisa to pry.

Nobody knows anything about a naval aviator named Morgan Michaelson. I did an intensive online search to see what I could come up with. Whoever he is, he's kept a very low online profile. No social media account. No mentions in other people's social media posts. The guy's a ghost, but I did find one hit. Apparently, an air force captain named Michaelson did an exchange tour with the navy and attended Tailhook several years ago. That's all I could find. Sorry I couldn't be more helpful.

She cast her mind back, sorting through the now almost complete set of memories from that time in Nevada. So much still seemed dreamlike. So many inconsistencies she had not thought to question at the time. Why a tailored TOPGUN course? Why would an air force guy be teaching it? Had Morgan been wearing an air force uniform? Why in her dream had she never thought to call her mom? The list went on and on.

Later that night Kate lay in her rack staring up at the tracery of pipes in her tiny stateroom's ceiling. A flurry of thoughts churned through her mind, driving away any hope of sleep. In just three days the ultimatum would expire, and all aboard this floating island knew what that meant.

She rolled over, glanced at her clock, and groaned. 0133. She would be a basket case in the morning. What could she do to force herself to sleep? Could she extract some new memory from the dream and use it to relax? With an effort, she tried to calm her raging thoughts, make her mind go blank, see if something would percolate to the surface. To her delight it did, and she gave herself over to it fully.

Kate looked around the living room of Morgan's tiny home. It was hardly bigger than an apartment. Kitchen, breakfast bar, two bedrooms, and a living room. Spartan in its simplicity.

She had asked about it on an earlier visit. His reply had been cryptic. "I keep things pretty basic. No point in accumulating stuff when you're just passing through." She had wanted to explore the point with him, but the conversation had taken a different turn and she had soon forgotten the comment, only to have it reappear now.

Her eyes were drawn to the one piece of individuality in the room. It hung on the wall by the TV. It too was simple, basic, a stark statement, and she wondered what it meant. Weathered wood framed a small expanse of black velvet. Mounted on the velvet was a cross, fashioned of rusted barbed wire, about four inches tall by three wide. A pair of barbs, one on the upright, another on the crosspiece, reached out to snag the unwary passerby. She had asked him about it. Like so many of her questions, he had deflected it. "It's a long story, complicated. I'll tell it to you someday. Let's just say I got it from a man on a train." Looking at the cross, she resolved that one day soon she would get the story out of him.

She turned her attention back to the TV. Closing credits scrolled across the screen as a commercial started to play. She looked over at Morgan sitting in the chair, gazing at her, amusement written on his face.

"What?" she demanded.

"It looks like you clocked out on me there. The movie that boring?"

"Not boring," she replied. "Predictable. High-powered female business exec consumed by her job finds herself stuck in a small town. Has conflict with a local blue-collar guy. She learns there's more to life than her job. They fall in love. Fight. Reconcile. The end.

"All the movies this channel plays follow the same formula. Why do you enjoy watching them rather than the other stuff that's on TV?" She rattled off a list of programs that were more to her taste.

His face took on a thoughtful look. "I don't mind the occasional action movie or whodunnit, but I don't think it's a good idea to have a constant diet of the stuff. These movies we've been watching are light and fluffy, but after the stress we experience every day, why would we want to add more through the things we watch?"

She conceded the point and found herself relaxing to a degree she would never have thought possible just a few months earlier. She was comfortable with Morgan in a way she had never been with Nick or the other guys she had dated before. They were edgy, always trying to impress, full of their self-importance. Unlike them, Morgan was comfortable in his skin, had nothing to prove, and was genuine in his solicitousness for her.

The fact that he was sitting in the chair and she on the sofa was just one example. He didn't push the bounds of their relationship, never made her feel uncomfortable, was careful to maintain distance and not put them into a position in which a random spark might become a forest fire. She was grateful for it and was content with where the relationship was heading, sensing a growing permanence. With graduation only a couple months away, though, the nagging question was starting to nibble at the edges of her mind as it undoubtedly was with his. What was next?

"These movies always have a special place, a place away from the bustle of the world. What's yours?" he asked.

There was no hesitation in her answer. "Home. It's my very favorite place in the whole world. Mountains, trees, fields. It's so peaceful and quiet, like a slice of heaven here on earth."

"I'd like to see it some time."

She resolved to take him there. "So, what's yours?"

His face took on a faraway look. "It's a place that's very dear to me. It's called Thalassa. Picture a Mediterranean village built into the side of cliff. White houses, steep, narrow streets, red roofs. Sun-baked but not too hot. A small harbor with water an impossible shade of blue, so clear you would think you could see through it for miles. Fishing boats go out each morning with the tide and come back at nightfall. You can almost believe they have been doing it for all eternity.

"There are no cars. No trucks. No stereos blaring. Just people laughing, talking, and doing the stuff of everyday life. It's like time and the world have passed the place by. I've been there twice and did nothing but just soak in the peace of the place. It's a wonderful way to draw close to God." He paused, appearing to bask in the memory for a moment. "What do you want out of life?" he asked, surprising her with the change of direction. "Are you like the exec, comfortable in her position and the busyness of her life, or are you searching for more?"

There he was again, that maddening way of his, turning a conversation around, taking the spotlight off himself and putting it back on her. She wanted to deflect the question, turn it back to him, but she found herself considering, digging deep for the answer. She was surprised at the words that came from the depth of her heart.

"I guess I do have something in common with these movies. I was happy with my life, consumed by flying, career, the constant thrill seeking. Now I'm not so sure. I think you're a bad influence on me. You've got me thinking there should be more to life than flying and the navy."

His eyes twinkled. "You ever think of marrying, raising a family? I think you'd make a fabulous mom."

She found herself blushing. "Why? Are you asking me?" she asked shyly.

He smiled. "No. Not yet, but I must admit that I find the idea fascinating and tempting. Life with you would be an adventure and a dream come true."

She was surprised at the surge of disappointment that welled up inside her. *Come off it, Kate. It's much too soon for that,* she chided herself. *You barely know the guy.*

That's not true, she corrected herself. You know him better than you've known any other man in your life.

"I think God is doing something in your life, Kate," he said gently. "I think he has a special plan for you—something that will challenge you but also bless you beyond measure. Please be open to it."

"Does that plan include you?" she asked, suddenly feeling sleepy.

A flash of pain almost imperceptible crossed his features. "I think that's entirely up to him," he said hollowly. "I hope it does."

In that dreamlike space between sleep and wakefulness, she found herself hoping with every fiber of her being it did too. Yet, despite the fullness in her heart, she felt the slightest niggle of worry. What was stopping him from asking the question she so wanted him to ask?

Chapter 33

Merlyn sat against a tree, physically and emotionally exhausted. Around him his staff slept where they had dropped. No one had suggested pitching a tent. No one had suggested making a fire. Pickets had been sent out. Sentries had been posted. The three days of purest hell at Gettysburg, followed by the weeklong chase of the escaping rebel army had sapped the strength of every man in the brigade, including himself.

As tired as he was, Merlyn couldn't sleep. Heartsickness gripped him like a physical malady. The image of his shattered regiments breaking and streaming back to the relative safety of the thin Union line, ringing the high ground, played over and over in his mind. The next day hunkering down against the massive artillery barrage, and then holding the line against what seemed like an ocean of gray advancing toward them, breaking against the wall of blue, then retreating, leaving a wake of bodies like foam on a beach.

And now, the enemy had escaped across the Potomac. The ever-cautious Meade had allowed it to happen and there was nothing Merlyn could do about it. Though Gettysburg had been a decisive Union victory, the carnage, the waste of lives, the missed opportunities dragged his spirits down until he thought they could go no lower. Two more years of fighting loomed before him. Two more years of separation from Kate. The thought was unendurable.

The night was still and warm. Stars peeked through gaps in the blanket of clouds overhead. Cicadas sang in the woods around him. Exhaustion turned his stomach sour and dampness soaked through his trousers, but he didn't care. Sleep started to claim him. His head drooped until it rested on his knees. His last conscious thought was a memory of holding Kate in his arms, softly swaying on the dance floor, her body pressed into his, her head resting against his chest.

The challenge of a sentry caused him to wake with a start. A rider was approaching. A lantern was lit and held high. The rider drew up his horse and dismounted. George. The bandage around his head gleamed softly in the lamplight.

He gave Merlyn a crisp salute. Still groggy from his few moments of sleep, Merlyn returned it with a half-hearted wave.

"I hope I didn't wake you, general," George said, concern in his voice.

"It's still colonel, George," Merlyn answered wearily. "I only have the brigade until they assign a permanent commander." He patted the ground beside him. "Come sit for a spell. The ground's a little damp, but you've endured worse."

George lowered himself with a groan and rested his head against the rough bark. "How are the men holding up?" Merlyn asked. Before the battle they had been his men. Now, at least temporarily, they were George's, but Merlyn still felt paternal toward them.

"They miss you, sir."

"Would you stop with the 'sir,' George?"

"How do you do it, Merlyn? I've been watching you this last week. It's almost like you knew the enemy was going to get away. You've been trying to get the generals to move faster, but they will not listen."

Merlyn leaned his head back against the tree and looked at his friend, a mere shadow in the darkness. "George, as I told you before, good generals win battles. Great generals exploit victories and win campaigns. We could have ended the war now, had we been more aggressive in following up our victory." He was talking too much, but he didn't care. "Because we lacked the vision and courage to seize the opportunity presented us, we're going to have to do it again and again and again until there is no more enemy left."

"Was it really a victory? So many men died on both sides. How can we call it a victory when it cost us so much to secure it?"

As in so many of these conversations, Merlyn had the answer and couldn't speak it. "I think, George, when we're both old and gray, we'll be able to look back at this and see it clearly for what it was. Time will reveal the answer."

"You speak to me like you're convinced I'll see that day. Had that bullet been an inch to the left, I would be lying in a shallow grave back there on that field like so many of our men. I saw my life pass before my eyes too many times those three days to ever believe I will survive this war."

"As I've told you many times before," Merlyn said patiently, "with God, all things are possible. He has a plan for your life, and if that plan has you surviving this war, then you will survive it. Have faith."

"How can you talk to me about faith?" George interjected angrily. "How can the loving and just God you speak so much about allow such slaughter as we've witnessed these past days? Answer me that, Merlyn."

Surprised at the uncharacteristic rage in the younger man's voice, Merlyn battled to dispel the fog clouding his mind.

"You don't need to say anything," George said, the anger draining from his voice to be replaced by a note of defeat. "I value your friendship, truly I do, but speak to me no more of God and his loving-kindness. I want nothing to do with a God who allows death and destruction on such a scale, or who allows this."

He dropped a letter into Merlyn's lap. Merlyn picked it up but was unable to read the writing in the dim moonlight. "I can't read it without light. What does it say?" he asked, handing it back.

"It's from Mother—the only letter I've received from home since I joined the army. She wrote to inform me that my brother, William, died in an accident. The carriage in which he was riding tipped over, crushing him."

George fell silent again as he visibly deflated, all anger spent.

221

"I'm so sorry, George," Merlyn said. Compassion welled up in him, but he recognized the total inadequacy of words to assuage his friend's grief.

After a moment, George spoke again, the words coming in a rush. "I don't understand. We have lived through so much death and destruction. Why is he gone and I am here? I have been near death a dozen times, none so close as this most recent, and yet I live. He has never in his life come close to death, and yet a foolish accident claims his life.

"Merlyn, I'm tired and I'm heartsick. I was not close to William, but I loved him for the brother he was. Those I hold dear have turned their backs on me. I've lost my brother. I've almost lost my own life, and I have been forced to confront my own mortality in the most graphic way imaginable. It's almost as if God is stripping away everything from my life and reducing me to the most basic and elemental thing that is me." He lapsed into silence, and Merlyn could feel his pain. George abruptly heaved himself to his feet. "I'm sorry. I shouldn't have intruded on your rest. I just needed someone to talk to."

After George left, Merlyn sighed deeply and leaned back against the tree. Like his last assignment, this one was all going so horribly wrong. His stomach churned with exhaustion, yet the conversation with George had driven all thought of sleep from his mind.

His young charge was so different from Kate. When Merlyn met her, she already had faith, was comfortable in it, had thought through a lot of the difficult issues. God's call was on George's life, just as strong as it was on Kate's, but George resisted the call. Kate had said there was a strong legacy of faith in her family. Did that come from George, or another ancestor?

Kate. Like George, she was a warrior and had seen the elephant—only hers was of a different variety. Instead of dealing with death up close and personal, the fighter pilot seldom saw the direct impacts of her actions: the mangled bodies, the screams of the wounded, the awful smells of the battlefield. Her war was sterile, self-contained, yet no less deadly.

He had spoken of it a couple of times to Kate, the last on that fateful trip to Lake Tahoe.

Morgan and Kate sat out on the deck over the remains of a late lunch, water lapping rhythmically against the pilings. Music played softly in the background. Only a handful of diners braved the hot afternoon sun, so they had their corner of the deck to themselves.

"Dad made sure I thought it through before I went to the academy," she replied to his question. She looked pensive, unsure, as she flicked back a strand of hair that strayed toward her eyes. "As always, he was having my back and wanted me to know exactly what I was getting into. People think of the world of the fighter pilot as being all glamor and fun. But he made sure I understood this was not a game. That I was signing up to fly and fight. That it's a deadly serious business in which the slightest mistake can have disastrous consequences, and you have to get it right every time."

Her eyes dropped to her plate, refusing to meet his. With her fork she slowly rearranged her uneaten food.

"What's wrong?" he asked, reaching across the table to take her hand. It was limp, unresponsive.

For long moments, he didn't think she was going to answer. When she finally spoke, her voice was little more than a whisper. "I don't want this to end."

She looked up at last, and he was surprised at the depth of emotion in her eyes—fear, grief, confusion. He felt a surge of guilt. His interfering had caused this pain in her and there was no way he could fix it. He didn't want to fix it. He wanted what she wanted. But there was no way he could avoid the awful inevitability of their parting.

He took her other hand, laced his fingers with hers. "I don't either," he said softly.

He should break the relationship now. The pain he caused would be temporary. She would get over it. Her heartbreak almost certainly would not transition with her back to the real world. But he couldn't do it. He was in over his head, drowning, with no way out.

He lifted her hand to his lips, kissed it. "Kate, in you I've found something infinitely precious, special. I love you with all my heart."

There it was. What had only been hinted at was now out in the open. No going back. It was the ultimate betrayal of his calling, of his master. Misery rose up inside him, but he ruthlessly pushed it aside.

"I love you too." Her words were hesitant—again little more than a whisper.

Morgan rose, came around the table, and lifted her to her feet. He wrapped his arms around her, pulling her to him in a fierce embrace. Shocked at the depth of emotion washing over and through him, he bent his face to hers, kissing her hard, passionately. Her lips were warm against his, parting slightly. Her body melted against his.

He was dimly aware of music playing over the speakers, their bodies swaying to its gentle rhythm. It was a moment he wished would go on forever.

A bugle sounded, jolting Merlyn out of his reverie. A tree root dug into his backside. Agony surged inside of him. He had made promises he had no way of keeping. He had given her hope of a life together when he had no right to do so. Then he had brutally crushed it.

***

Two days later, Merlyn was summoned to division headquarters.

"Congratulations, colonel," Major General Munro said, as he tapped his pipe on his desk, dislodging a small cascade of ash. "The 3rd Brigade is yours. You've earned it. I just wish it were under better circumstances. General Eades was a good man."

Tall and slender but stooped by the burden of his duties, Munro looked every bit the regular army officer he'd been when the war started.

"You did a fine job handling his brigade in terrible circumstances," he continued as he used his index finger to scrape more tobacco from a worn leather pouch into the charred and darkened bowl of his pipe. "I don't know that anyone could have done any better. Don't worry about Parker. I spoke with him last night and he will support you with everything he has. He did not want the promotion. He'd rather stay with his men."

As would I, Merlyn thought. But even though this new command would pull him further from George, making his already difficult job even harder, he sensed a rightness to it.

"If you have any reservations about Maxwell leading your New Yorkers, I need to know it by this evening. We'll be moving out in the morning, and I need to finalize our command structure."

Merlyn nodded his assent. He'd already thought it through. It was tempting. George's rashness on the battlefield was cause for removal. It would give him a place of relative safety on division staff, but it would end Merlyn's relationship with the younger man. George would never forgive him. *But it could very well save his life,* a part of him argued back. *If George lives, so does Kate.*

"I value initiative and bravery," the general continued. "Maxwell has both. Please don't saddle me with an officer I need to goad to move. Make the right decision."

"I will, sir," Merlyn replied, raising his hand in salute.

Munro returned it with a negligent wave of his hand.

Merlyn stepped out of the farmhouse that had been pressed into service as divisional headquarters and felt his eyes contract painfully against the glare of the midafternoon sun. He had a couple of hours to make his decision. He knew what he wanted to do, but it was what he *must* do that caused a tingle of unease to run down his spine.

He took Midnight's reins from a waiting orderly and hefted himself into the saddle. His mind a riot of thoughts, he rode slowly back to the 3rd Brigade encampment. All around him men struck tents, loaded wagons, preparing for the morning's move.

Merlyn's mood could not have been any blacker. Kate's ancestor was clearly the reason he had been sent to this time, but he now also had a responsibility to all the men of the 3rd Brigade.

Where best could his responsibility to George be discharged? As commander of a regiment under Merlyn's command or as a member of the division staff? Merlyn swore under his breath, angry at the younger man for forcing this decision on him.

He led Midnight a circuitous route back to camp, buying himself time to think. Thoughts tumbled through his mind like dry sagebrush in a breeze, none of them sticking. Logic told him to remove the boy, but something in the deepest recesses of his heart rebelled. Yes, George had made a mistake, but Munro was right. He had fight and the army needed fighters.

Back in camp, he summoned George. "Walk with me, colonel," he ordered. Around them, smoke from dozens of campfires climbed lazily into the air and then, seemingly out of energy, collapsed into a blanket of haze, adding weight to the fetid humidity clinging in the warm evening air.

Merlyn sensed the tension in the boy walking next to him. *No, not tension,* he corrected himself. *He knows he messed up and is afraid of what I might do. Don't keep him in suspense. Get to the point. Lay it out for him.*

"Munro is drafting up the order giving me command of the brigade. I have a decision to make about who leads the 172nd." George's sudden intake of breath was slight, but Merlyn heard it clearly over the sounds of the camp.

"I need a colonel I can trust to take care of his men. One who will fight in concert with the rest of the brigade and with the division, for that matter. One who will obey orders and not go off chasing his own personal glory."

George's eyes locked onto his, afraid but unflinching, his face white and pinched despite the suffocating warmth.

"George," Merlyn softened his tone, "you've done a fine job with the regiment. With the one exception, you did a fine job at Gettysburg." He stopped in the shade of a spreading elm and turned to face the younger man.

A vein pulsed by the corner of George's eye; otherwise his features were immobile, as if chiseled from granite.

"I need to know," Merlyn said, putting an edge of steel into his voice. "What happened out there?" The question gave George an opportunity to provide an excuse, and in the excuse, he could take the measure of the man.

George's eyes flicked down and then unblinking back to Merlyn's. "No excuse, sir." He said, his voice tight. He stood ramrod straight, his body almost vibrating with tension.

Merlyn stared into George's eyes for a long moment. Counter to his expectation, he did not find defiance there, rather a softening, a faint misting as if the boy were holding back a tear. That would do.

He held out his hand. "Congratulations, colonel. The regiment is yours."

As they walked in silence back to the camp, one thought played over and over in Merlyn's mind: *Lord, I hope I'm doing the right thing.*

Chapter 34

"Folks, in a little over twelve hours, our ultimatum will expire, and the stuff's going to hit the fan." Digger paused for dramatic effect and let his eyes sweep over the assembled Outlaws in their seats in the ready room.

Trojan shifted uneasily next to Kate, subtly amplifying the tension in the room that crackled in the air like electricity. A thought flashed across her mind: *Morgan, how would you handle a moment like this?* The answer came just as quickly: *You strike me as a man who has come to grips with his fears. You'd do it with calm self-assurance just like Digger is trying to do, only you'd do it better.*

If she were honest with herself, she would have to admit to being a little afraid. After all, who wouldn't be, but the unwritten rule of the fighter community was never, ever show fear. The pilot who showed fear was weak, unreliable, not to be trusted to perform when things got rough.

Digger's face was somber, serious. "You've all seen the plans and know how this is going to play out," he continued. "We'll be fighting an air campaign with limited objectives. Our overarching goal is to eliminate the handful of nuclear weapons Iran has developed, thereby destroying its ability to threaten its neighbors. Furthermore, our intent is to eradicate its capability to produce more weapons. To attain this goal, the air campaign will achieve the following objectives: Decapitate the Iranian political and military leadership by taking out their ability to exercise command and control. Gain and maintain air superiority. Take out Iran's supply lines. Destroy their nuclear capability."

Digger paused his summary of what each pilot had already read in the operations order for the air campaign. He looked out over the tensely expectant ready room, and Kate felt her stomach tighten at what she knew was coming next. The words Digger had spoken were simple on the surface. In execution, they would be anything but.

"Most of you have seen combat over Iraq and Afghanistan. But this is going to be combat unlike anything we've experienced before. We're going up against a country that has upgraded its military with the latest toys. But our toys are every bit as good as theirs, and our training is a couple of orders of magnitude better. Still, this is not going to be a walk in the park. Unlike Desert Storm and Iraqi Freedom, we're essentially going this alone. As you all know, the Russians have publicly declared they will stand with Iran. Whether they follow through on that promise, only time will tell. If they do come into this, don't take for granted they're going to get their butts kicked like they did in Ukraine. Each and every one of us is going to have to dig deep and give them everything we've got. I'm going to turn it over to Elsa, who is going to walk you through the plan for the first twenty-four hours."

Wiping her palms on her flight suit, Kate stood. Digger extended his hand to her as he returned to his seat. His grip lingered as he whispered in her ear so low that even Torch and Trojan, sitting just feet away, could not hear: "Give it to them straight. Don't sugarcoat it but leave them with something they can hang onto when you're done."

Kate felt a surge of annoyance at the sudden trembling in her knee. She shifted her weight and straightened her leg, willing it to be gone. She shot a glance at Digger. *Man, I wish I could feel as calm as he seems to be,* she thought enviously. Torch seated next to him, arms folded across his chest, wore his customary frown. No help, no encouragement there.

Her eyes scanned over the other pilots, some outwardly calm, others exhibiting signs of tension. Mogas' jaw clenched tight. Gator's fingers drummed on the arm of his chair. Bags chewed absently at the corner of one of his fingernails. Japer squirmed uncomfortably in his seat.

Finally, her eyes came to rest on the nuggets—Jethro looking a little green around the gills, Spud motionless beside him, his eyes fixed expectantly on Kate.

Who's not going to be here tomorrow night? A week from now? The questions crossed Kate's mind, causing her stomach to tighten unpleasantly. *Will I be here?* She forced the thought from her mind, took a deep breath, trying to still her racing heart.

"H-hour is 0200 tomorrow morning," she began, gratified at the sense of calmness that descended on her as she spoke the words. "Allied forces will cross into Iran and strike command and control targets, critical infrastructure, and nuclear facilities across the country. The Outlaws will be first in, leading a strike package made up of squadrons from our wing and the Abe's deep into central Iran. Torch is strike lead; I will be leading the second Outlaws division."

As she spoke, Kate felt her confidence growing. *I have this. I've done it before and trained for it all my life.*

"When we land, our jets will quick turn and Digger will take our first daytime mission. Trojan will have the second, and then we turn to the second ATO period."

For the next two hours, Kate walked through the first twenty-four hours of the war in detail, outlining who would be flying with whom, what weapons loads they would be carrying, what targets they would strike, what threats they would be facing, explaining the rules of engagement for tackling air threats, walking through emergency procedures.

"There you have it, gentlemen," she concluded, utterly wiped, her flight suit soaked with perspiration. "Day one of the war."

She surveyed the assembled pilots once more. The atmosphere in the ready room was calmer. The Outlaws were professionals. They would rise to the occasion as she would. Her eyes caught Spud's. Would he?

Kate sealed the letter to her parents, the knot of tension in her stomach driving away sleep. As she lay in her rack, above her on the flight deck jets were being fueled, loaded, and prepared for war.

She wondered how many other pilots in the air wing—and the air wings on the other aircraft carriers—were finding sleep impossible. It wasn't that she was afraid of dying. She knew where she would go when that happened. It was that there was so much life left unlived. With deep regret, she suddenly had to admit the truth the dream had revealed to her. She had poured herself into her career while neglecting what was truly important. She had played and had fun but had not invested herself in the things that really mattered. Morgan had given her a taste of it, and she now realized she wanted it more than anything else in the world.

She absently rubbed the heel of her hand. The scar, the cut, the blood. All had served to tie her to him. Did they mean that, counter to all logic, there was a possibility he was real, that the dream was real? More importantly, she loved him deeply, passionately. He had said he had come to her for a purpose. This was it. She knew it in her heart. Something supernatural had touched her life, something she did not understand, but by faith she would trust there was a reason behind it all.

Dear Jesus, she prayed with vehemence, *I want to live. I want to live life as you want me to live it, embracing the things I've missed out on. I want the true fullness that comes from knowing and walking with you. Please protect me. Please protect Morgan wherever he is. Help us to both make it through this war and bring us together when it's over.*

She pulled out a pen and paper and began to write another letter. It took her the better part of an hour and two drafts before she found the words she wanted to say.

My Dearest Morgan,

When you receive this letter, you will know why I'm writing it. I don't believe in writing "to be opened in the event of my death" letters. Things that need to be said should be said in person now. Although my heart longs to speak to you face-to-face, it cannot be.

Tonight we go to war. I should have written this letter weeks ago, but I could not make myself do it—could not face the possibility of a permanent goodbye. Now the reality of it is staring me in the face and I cannot ignore it. I must deal with it and say the things I need to say.

I'm not afraid to die. I know Jesus, and I am totally confident when he calls me, I will go to spend eternity with him. Nothing can compare with that. I don't have many regrets. I've been blessed. I have a wonderful family, parents who love me. God has let me do the one thing I dreamed of since I was a little girl.

And I met you.

Yet I'm sad about a few experiences I may never have. I would have liked to have gotten to know you better. I would have liked to have held my baby in my arms. I would have loved to grow old beside you, enjoying warm summer evenings watching the sun play on the mountains, and looking back on a life well lived. These things may still happen, but I give them to God because I must focus on tomorrow.

I'm sorry for being maudlin, but when you're looking into eternity, you learn what is truly important in life—loving God, loving other people, and allowing them to love you. Thank you for coming into my life. Thank you for loving me. You mean the world to me. I just pray God allows us to have a future together.

I love you with all my heart!

Yours always,

Kate

P.S. If we see each other again, you're going to have a whole lot of explaining to do!!

She folded the pages, inserted them in an envelope, sealed the flap, and wrote his name on the front. She took another sheet of paper, scribbled down instructions to Mom and Dad, inserted it and Morgan's letter into another envelope. She would mail it before the flight. If something happened to her and if he came looking for her, then at least he would have some closure.

She turned off the light and lay in half-darkness once more. Two hours until her alarm would go off. She did not expect to sleep, but before she knew it, she was awakened by the soft chiming of her clock. Time to go to war.

Chapter 35

As summer passed into autumn, the Army of the Potomac and the Army of Northern Virginia marched and countermarched, colliding from time to time in an inconclusive skirmish before coming to an uneasy rest along the Rapidan River.

Merlyn's time with George was invariably spent in the company with the other regimental commanders. Since his dressing down at Gettysburg, George had conducted himself with punctilious politeness, no hostility or resentment in his demeanor, just a coolness that discouraged conversation.

Merlyn sighed heavily, his eyes refusing to focus on the latest strength report. The opportunity had never presented itself to heal the relationship. The rift festered deeper with each passing week it remained unaddressed.

"Sir, Colonel Maxwell asks to see you at your earliest convenience." Merlyn started. Lost in his thoughts, he had not heard Saunders enter the tent.

"Know what it's about?" he asked.

"The colonel didn't say, sir. He just asked for a moment of your time when it's convenient."

This might well be the opportunity. The numbers could wait. The thought of spending another moment in the closed confines of his tent on such a glorious fall day filled him with dread. Meeting

George on his turf might put the young colonel a little more at ease.

"Very well then," he said, pushing back his chair. "I'll go see what he wants."

"Sir," Saunders protested. "I can send a runner for him."

"No need," Merlyn replied. "I'd prefer to go see him."

Saunders glowered. "Very well, I'll have a groom saddle Midnight for you."

"I can walk." Merlyn fought back a slight feeling of irritation. What he wouldn't give for a few minutes alone, away from this teeming mass of men, a few moments to lose himself in his thoughts and memories. But it was not to be. He had a brigade to lead, a thousand minute details to resolve before the army was once more on the move in search of the elusive men in gray, led by a master of feint and deception.

"I wish you'd let me help you, sir."

"It's fine, captain. Truly." Merlyn patted Saunders' shoulder. "I'm low-maintenance."

His aide's brow wrinkled in confusion. "Sir?"

Merlyn mentally kicked himself for his lapse. "Sorry. Just a term I picked up somewhere. It means I don't need a lot of looking after."

He buttoned the sack coat that had served him well since the early days in Albany. It was faded, frayed, the sleeve roughly repaired from where the bullet had nicked him before the wall at Fredericksburg. He knew he should replace it with a new one but couldn't be bothered.

He pulled on his equally worn kepi, stepped out into the open, and inhaled deeply, the smell of manure, livestock, and men packed closely together assaulting his nostrils. Only a few short weeks until the army settled down into the grinding boredom of winter camp. And then . . . his stomach rolled unpleasantly at his line of thinking.

The 172nd New York was encamped on the other side of a copse of maples, and Merlyn chose to saunter through it rather than around. Leaves were already falling, turning the forest floor into a kaleidoscope of color that surged around his ankles and rustled under his feet. He found George and Johanns in quiet conversation by the edge of the trees, looking out over the mass of tents that housed the regiment.

The two men stiffened to attention and saluted at his approach. "Thank you, gentlemen," Merlyn said, acknowledging the salute.

"Congratulations, general." Johanns offered his hand.

"Thank you, major," Merlyn replied. He had submitted the paperwork requesting promotions for both George and Johanns, back in July, but the army had sat on its duff, content to move senior officer promotions while allowing field-grade promotions to languish.

"Major, would you give us a moment, please?" he asked, noting the fatigue in Johanns' face, his once-gray beard now almost completely white.

"George, you asked to see me," Merlyn said, as Johanns disappeared into the warren of tents.

A look of concern crossed the younger man's face. "I'm sorry, sir. I didn't mean for you to come to me. I was just hoping for some time this evening."

"It's all right," Merlyn replied. "I needed to get out and you gave me a chance. Is there a place we can get off our feet?"

George led him to a giant, spreading oak, two log rounds standing erect amongst a carpet of golden leaves. He motioned to the logs. "Dutchy and I come here if we need to get away for a private conversation. Will this do?"

"Perfect." Merlyn lowered himself to one of the logs, feeling the dampness quickly soak through his trousers.

"What is it you wanted to see me about?"

George looked down at his muddy boots for a moment. When he raised his head, there was a look of nervous embarrassment in his eyes, and spots of pink highlighted his cheekbones. "I want to apologize for the way I've been behaving," he said quietly. "I was foolhardy at Gettysburg, and you were right to chastise me. I also understand why you had reservations about me commanding the regiment. I'm sorry."

Those were the last words Merlyn had expected to hear. He fumbled to find a reply.

"No, don't say anything, general. You've been more than gracious with me. I just needed to say I'm sorry and assure you I will never take an unnecessary risk again."

He continued, the words coming out in a rush, "I have one more thing I'd like to discuss with you, if I might."

Merlyn inclined his head for him to continue.

"Do you remember Moses, the cook?"

"How could I forget?" Merlyn replied, his interest piqued.

"He wants to enlist." George's voice was hesitant, guarded. "What do you intend to do about it?"

"What would you recommend?"

The boy needed to make the decision, not be led into it. "What do you want to do?"

"Would you support me if I enlisted him?"

Merlyn tamped down a slight surge of irritation. "George, it's your regiment. As long as it's not illegal, immoral, or unethical, you have pretty broad discretion."

George chewed on his lip in that way Kate so often did when mulling over a problem, and Merlyn felt his heart miss a beat at the thought.

"I've talked it over with the other officers, and some of the men," George continued. "They support the decision."

Good, Merlyn thought. *He's beginning to grow into the position he finds himself in.* "I've learned, before making any big decision, to ask myself who will hate it and why. Have you done that?"

George's mouth turned down at the corners. "Why, Barings, of course, and some of the men will undoubtedly not like it."

"You have a plan for how to handle it?"

"I think so," he said, the words coming out slowly.

"Then do what you think is right and I will support you."

A look of gratitude suffused George's features. "I'll enlist him then." The words came out in a rush.

Well, that's something, Merlyn thought as he strode back to his headquarters. *George is progressing.* As he walked, he noticed a slight spring in his step that had been absent for a long while.

It was well past dark when Merlyn was able to find a moment to wolf down a quick meal of soup and hardtack. All around him the camp was quieting. Finally, a few moments of solitude. But then, he was never really alone. Kate was always with him, wrapped around his heart, a sense of oneness that time and distance could not break. In an instant, he was back at Fallon, reliving another memory, sweet in the experience, bitter in its aftermath.

"Pack an overnight bag," she said without warning, as they wrapped up the Friday afternoon debriefing. "Meet me outside the VOQ. I have a surprise for you."

They took his truck. She directed him north out of town but told him to turn off the highway as they passed the outskirts. His curiosity mounted as they approached Fallon's tiny municipal airport. She directed him to park in front of Desert Aviation. A sign on the building advertised flying lessons and aircraft rentals.

She nodded toward the restroom as they passed through the building. "I suggest you take advantage of that. We're going to be up for a long time."

Kate expertly handled the controls of the rented Cessna 182, leveling off at 7,500 feet on a northeasterly heading. As she set her course, he knew instantly where she was going. She was taking him to meet her parents.

It was the logical next step in their relationship, and he'd hinted enough at permanence that she was undoubtedly beginning to expect the proposal. Fallon was not that far from Lemoore. Just a six-hour drive. Sacramento was halfway between. A long-distance relationship was easily possible.

But he knew the truth. There would be no long-distance relationship. No future together, no matter how much his heart craved it. He needed to break this off, let her down gently. But he could not do it. He was hooked and enjoying the sensation, no matter where it happened to lead. But this was a new wrinkle. Her family was now being drawn in. *Lord, how are you going to work this out?* he wondered.

Kate didn't say much during the long flight. Morgan completely lost track of time, enjoying watching her quiet competence at the controls, her head on a swivel as she scanned the sky for traffic and periodically checked her map to back up her navigation.

He was almost sorry when, hours later, she started to descend toward a remote mountain valley. As far as the eye could see there were no towns, only dirt roads and scattered homesteads. She lined up on a grass landing strip. He saw paddocks, a barn, and a large house nearby.

She was disappointed to find her parents were not there. She had been unable to reach them before they left. "Phone service is iffy and there is no cell coverage," she explained. "I wanted you to meet them and was taking a chance they might not be here. But I also wanted you to see this." She gestured out over the horse paddocks, toward the mountains rising on the other side of the valley.

The house was large, plain, utilitarian, the furniture well-used, worn. It was a working ranch, not a rich person's abode. Kate led him to her father's study, where a lifetime of memorabilia and awards graced the walls.

"This is Dad's sanctum," she said. "I wish he was here so you could meet him and Mom. Maybe at graduation?"

"I hope so," he said, hoping she would not detect the uncertainty in his voice.

"You'll like them. Mom's a sweetheart, but as I've told you, Dad can be a little prickly at times. He was kind of rough on the guys I brought home, but he'll warm up to you quickly." There was something in the way she said it that made Morgan think she wasn't convinced that was going to happen.

She fixed him dinner. It was simple fare—a couple of steaks, potatoes, and green beans from the freezer. They ate sitting side-by-side on a wide porch overlooking the mountains.

"I love it here," she declared as they settled back into rocking chairs and watched the sky turn purple in the setting sun. "All my best memories growing up are tied to this place, learning to ride, flying, living in the outdoors. It gives me a sense of permanence, of grounding. In the hectic life we live, it's an oasis of peace and tranquility. I know heaven will be a wonderful place. I just hope it has some of this valley in it."

He understood her feelings perfectly.

He saw the tension ease from her body as she watched the sunset, the last of the sun's rays causing her hair to glow like a halo.

As he watched her, he realized how strong his love for her was growing. He reached over and took her hand. Fingers laced, her head resting on his shoulder, they sat silently together until the last vestige of red faded in the west and stars began to appear in the darkening sky.

And in that moment, he hatched the plan that would hopefully bind her to him and make a future together possible.

Chapter 36

I can't believe this is happening, Kate thought as she watched the clock tick the seconds down toward H-hour. Stars blazed overhead. A thin layer of scud obscured the ocean far below. No moon hung in the sky, the ultimatum timed to expire to provide maximum advantage to American forces who trained extensively to fight at night.

Hundreds of fighters marshaled just short of their push points. Tankers were stacked in orbits throughout the theater. Airborne early warning aircraft maintained a picture of the airspace over Iraq. Satellites watched airfields and missile sites for heat signatures. Special Forces teams had been on the ground for days now conducting reconnaissance of key targets. B-2 Spirit bombers and F-35 Lightning II fighters were already in enemy airspace, their bombs timed to impact their targets at exactly H-Hour. It was the largest massing of airpower since the opening night of Operation Desert Storm.

Iran had not blinked. Awaiting the massed strike packages of aircraft was a country on full war footing. Air defenses would be ready and waiting. Gunners would be watching their radars for the first blips of incoming aircraft and cruise missiles. Weapons would be ready to strike back at the fleet off the coast and at allied bases along the Persian Gulf and in Iraq. This was not going to be a cakewalk.

In the greenish glow of her night vision goggles, she scanned her displays. The route they would be flying was laid out on the MPCD. Her left DDI showed her weapons status. The right displayed the air picture. The Outlaws' callsign was Seahawks, the other navy squadrons that night also bearing the names of football teams. Torch's division orbited a couple miles to her left. To either side of them the TR's other squadrons waited at their marshaling points. Far to the right, the Abe's squadrons orbited.

The clock continued to tick down. Time for one more orbit. The Iranian long-range radars would be going down right about now, thanks to the work of Special Forces teams and cruise missiles. Her mouth was dry. She pulled out her water bottle as she began a gradual turn to the left, sipping just enough to wet her lips. She glanced at the MPCD. The rest of her division—Nemo, Toad, and Spud—were following her through the turn. Spud. Blue four. The novice aviator. It had all come down to this. She had staked everything on him. Would he perform?

She glanced once more at the time, tightened her turn slightly, and rolled out heading north. It was time to go to work. Fence in. She flipped up the master arm switch and knew that, with no command necessary, pilots in dozens of aircraft would be doing the same. Her jet was now hot, missiles and 2,000-pound JDAMs ready to release. She punched out the first of her towed decoys, her last-ditch protection against radar-guided missiles.

Time seemed to stand still as the coastline crept closer. Lights still shone brightly, washing out her NVGs. Bombs from the B-2 bombers would now be impacting their targets, taking down the air defense headquarters and decapitating the Iranian military command structure.

Her heart raced as she crossed the coastline. Feet dry. Over enemy territory. Her RWR was clear. No indication enemy radar was tracking them or SAMs were getting ready to fire.

Nothing on radar either, except for friendlies. Out in front of her, the Bulldogs, flying air-to-air-configured F/A-18Es provided air cover. The Reapers, in their Growlers, would take care of any surface threats with their impressive jamming suites and HARM missiles. In case anything survived the Growlers, she also had her internal jammer, chaff and flares dispenser, and towed decoy to help keep her alive.

Kate wiggled her toes, which were starting to ache from tension. There was a flash out front. The Growlers were doing their magic. One SAM site down. Although she kept her cockpit very cold, a trickle of sweat worked its way down her temple.

Miles of desert sped past as the strike package weaved its way north, threading gaps between SAM rings—the known SAM rings, that is. There was no telling what unlocated SAMs were along their flight route. The radio remained eerily silent, all pilots knowing their jobs, not highlighting their position by needless radio transmissions. The lights of a city far off to the right went dark— somebody else doing their job.

They were heading northwest now, into the more densely populated, and therefore more heavily defended part of the country. Her RWR chirped and her heart lurched in response. Somebody was looking at her. It was a single hit, but enough to cause her adrenaline to spike.

"Magnum, Magnum." It was an unnecessary call. Again, the Growlers were doing their work out in front. An AGM-88 HARM, high-speed, anti-radiation missile, was streaking toward an enemy SAM site. A flash far off to the left. A missile hitting its target or a bomb going off? She couldn't tell. *Not important right now,* she chided herself. *Concentrate!*

Far in front of them, lights. A city. As she drew closer, she could see large patches of darkness where the electricity was already out. More areas went dark as the inefficient power grid sought to correct the holes in its system.

The strike package was splitting now, the Abe's jets winging toward their targets northeast of her. The city suddenly erupted in a lightshow of tracers streaking up into the sky. Unguided fire. A panic reaction. She had seen the videos of the opening night of Desert Storm, but nothing prepared her for the reality of tens of thousands of rounds of AAA seeking a target, any target. They were flying well above it, but should any pilot be forced to react defensively to a SAM, they would drop down into it.

A flash and a trail of fire climbing into the sky. SAM launch. "Panther . . . defending SAM . . . south . . ." The call was broken, incomplete. Her head on a swivel, Kate scanned the ground for more launches, saw several, but none seemed to be guiding on her flight.

More large flashes on the ground. More defenses down. Her mouth was dry and the sour knot in her stomach refused to relax.

Working the ATFLIR, the advanced targeting forward-looking infrared pod, she found her target—a command and control facility on the far side of town. Even though it was still many miles away, the sensitive electronics of the pod allowed her to pick it out from the cluster of buildings surrounding it. As she got closer, she would refine the impact point to the exact spot on the building calculated by the CENTCOM targeteers to cause maximum damage.

She glanced at the MPCD. Five seconds to the next turn point. As she passed it, she checked thirty degrees to the right, heading directly to the IP, or Initial Point, from which the fighters would begin their attack. A quick glance at fuel—good. Torch's division would be splitting off to the left, their targets on the west side of the town. She checked her displays again for a quick situational awareness update. The other three aircraft of her division had followed her through the turn. The IP was twelve miles away. Less than two minutes at the speeds they were flying.

She was heads down in the cockpit now, taking quick glances outside and at her instruments to maintain situational awareness. The workload was intense. A quick check of radar—clean. Toad and Spud were splitting off now to their section's target.

"Seahawks, Chalice, hostiles bullseye 300 for 50." The AWACS controller's voice was calm, almost detached as she called out the enemy air threat.

Where did they come from? Kate wondered as she zeroed in on the single data link track still some distance away. One aircraft or multiples close aboard? Can't worry about that now. Need to focus on the target.

She reached the IP and turned ten degrees left to her attack heading. Heads down again, she refined the targeting cursor to her aimpoint, an air vent on the building's roof.

Her RWR chirped again. An air threat symbol appeared on the outer edge of the display. She was already amped on adrenaline; another surge caused her heart to beat painfully. Abort or press? The decision was instantaneous. Press. The incoming fighters would not be in missile range for another several seconds. She had time. She refined the cursor one final time. Checked symbology. In range. In parameters.

Kate mashed down the pickle button and held it until she felt a *thunk* as a two thousand-pound JDAM separated from her Hornet.

She snapped into a hard right turn while transmitting, "Seahawks 31 breaking right, spike eleven o'clock medium."

"Seahawks 32 breaking right, spiked."

Both she and Nemo were targeted. Not good. Her muscles were tense, her legs ached. Her heart pounded so hard she thought it would burst from her chest. She could hear the muffled rasping sound of her breathing through the oxygen mask. The spike hung on and she tried to keep it exactly at her nine o'clock. An inane thought crossed her mind: was she going to be the first woman fighter pilot to go down in combat?

Her NVGs flared slightly in response to a flash in the distance and a plume of fire streaking directly toward her. She deployed chaff and flares, jettisoned her external fuel tanks, and started a hard pull to put the missile off her wingtip. Its motor burned for only a few seconds, propelling it to over four times the speed of sound. Then the burn stopped. The missile streaking toward her was, for all intents and purposes, invisible. She pulled hard up and then down, trying to create angles for the missile, forcing it to bleed off speed. She gritted her teeth, awaiting the impact that could send her spiraling out of control. Nothing happened. She checked symbology for her towed decoy. It was gone, had done its job. She toggled out another.

The spike was gone too. She continued her turn and thumbed her radar into automatic acquisition mode. It found two targets heading directly at her. She mashed the IFF—identification friend

245

or foe—no friendly squawk. Targets hostile. She selected a slammer, tagged the first, and fired. Her missile came off the rail in a bright flash, washing out her NVGs. Thankful she had closed one eye to protect her night vision, she tagged the second and fired again. "Seahawks 31, Fox 3 2-ship." She transmitted the words simultaneously with her second depression of the pickle button. Just outside minimum range. Without waiting to see her missiles impact, she deployed chaff and turned hard to her egress heading.

Nemo. Where was he? She felt a momentary surge of panic when, at first, she couldn't find him, but calmed when she spotted him just aft of where he should have been, down her right wing line.

"Seahawks, Chalice. Picture clean. Splash two." The AWACS controller's voice showed a touch of excitement this time. Kate heaved a sigh of relief and felt her stomach muscles unclench slightly.

Time for the secondary target. This one was easier, a power plant to the southeast of town. She slewed the ATFLIR to the target's coordinates and began to look for her aimpoint.

AAA continued to spray up from the ground beneath her. She was high enough none could reach her, but there were a couple of explosions that seemed to be almost at her altitude. *Must be one of their Sa'irs,* she thought. RWR clean. Radar clean. Fuel good. A flash of light far to the west caught her attention. A trail of fire plummeting toward the ground. *Jesus, no!* The thought was instinctive. She forced her mind to calm. *Don't think about it. You still have a job to do.*

Three miles to IP. She found the smokestacks on the ATFLIR and followed the tracery of pipes to the generator building. Found her aimpoint. Before she knew it, she was at the IP. Slight adjustment to heading. A final check of RWR and radar. A final check of Nemo. In position. Head back down into the cockpit. Final adjustment to the aiming cursor. In range. In parameters. Mash down the pickle button. *Thunk.* Bombs away. Miller time.

But before it could be Miller time, she still had several hundred miles of enemy airspace to fight her way through. Her MPCD showed a splatter of data link tracks all heading in approximately the same direction, south toward Mom, the carriers from which they had launched.

Toad and Spud were several miles to the east but collapsing toward her to regain mutual support. She found Torch's data link symbol far off to her right. He had his division in tow. She turned slightly toward him, allowing the distance between them to gradually shrink.

She followed the line on the moving map display as it weaved its way through the SAM defenses back to the coast. The Growlers remained out front. She instinctively knew they had saved HARMs for the egress. The Iranian gunners wisely kept their radars down.

Kate didn't feel her muscles begin to relax until she crossed the coastline. The rest of the flight was automatic. Fence out, switches safe. Battle damage checks to make sure no golden BB had hit them. Take a sip of gas from the awaiting tankers. Find the TR. Land.

The sun was well above the horizon when her landing gear slammed into the deck and her tailhook snagged the third wire. Her mind in a fog, she followed the lighted marshaling wands to her parking space. She shut down, completed her postflight checks, pulled off her oxygen mask, and, absolutely drained, put her hands on the glare shield and rested her forehead on them. Mission complete.

The atmosphere in the ready room was somber. Torch and his division were already there huddled around Digger. Digger turned toward her as she approached the group.

"Nice job out there, Elsa." He extended his hand. "Congratulations. Outlaws' first air-to-air kills since 'Nam."

She looked at him in confusion. She had been so busy it had barely registered she had shot down two enemy aircraft. Then it struck her. She had just attained the goal every fighter pilot lives for—an air-to-air kill. "Thanks, Skipper." She had a more pressing concern, though. "I saw a fireball out to the west of town. One of ours?"

Digger nodded somberly. "The Knights got mauled pretty heavily."

"Did the pilot get out?"

"Don't know yet. Nobody saw a chute. They were pretty busy at the time." Digger's face was grim. "You can be darn sure if he got out and they catch him, they'll use him for propaganda purposes. It won't be pretty."

Kate's stomach rolled. If it weren't for the towed decoy, that could be her down there. Flying fighters was dangerous business and sometimes the good guys got hurt. She had a feeling before this was over, it was going to get a lot more dangerous.

Chapter 37

It was Merlyn's fourth stop of the day. He had saved the 172nd New York until last. Dusk was approaching. The unending rain had soaked him to the skin, and he fought to keep his teeth from chattering. Outside the cabin the 172nd was using as its headquarters, he dismounted and handed the reins to Saunders, newly promoted to major, who accompanied him on his rounds.

"Tie up the horses and come inside," he ordered. "There's sure to be something warm to drink and you can thaw out a little by the fire."

He rapped on the front door and entered. A wave of heat enfolded him in its welcome embrace. He took off his hat, shook the water from it, and ran his hands through his hair, trying to form it into some semblance of order.

Chairs scraped on rough planking as the officers recognized him and surged to their feet. A long table had been set up. The remains of a meal lay scattered across its surface, a ham bone with a few scraps of meat clinging to it, plates carrying vegetables nearly empty, a scattering of bottles. A stove glowed bright red against a rough brick hearth, providing welcome warmth.

"Merry Christmas, gentlemen," Merlyn said. "Please sit down. Don't let me interrupt your festivities." Hands clutched at his shoulders, helping him off with his slicker and hanging it, dripping, on a hook by the door.

George made a place for him at the head of the table. Someone placed a glass of brandy in his hand and an empty plate materialized in front of him. "I'm sorry, general, our meal is finished," George said apologetically. "But there's plenty of food left over. What may we offer you?"

Merlyn ruefully patted his stomach. "Thank you, but no. I've been making the rounds of the regiments and have been well fed already."

Saunders came through the door, soaked. "Well met, major." George greeted him heartily. "Please join us for a little bit of Christmas cheer."

"Don't mind if I do, sir," Saunders replied and squeezed in at the table.

Merlyn surveyed the 172nd New York's officers surrounding the remains of their Christmas feast. There were new faces mixed with old, men who had stood shoulder to shoulder with him through some of the worst the rebel army could throw at them. They were tough warriors, seasoned veterans, among the finest he had ever served with. He felt a lump forming in his throat at the horrors these men had yet to endure.

They looked at Merlyn, obviously expecting a speech. He had no lines rehearsed, so he just spoke from his heart. "Thank you for welcoming me back into your fold. You hold a very dear place in my heart, and I wanted to spend a few moments in fellowship with you as you celebrate this day. Let us not think of wars and battles but instead of the love of God who gave us the gift of his Son through whom we have eternal life."

There were nods and smiles around the table. He turned to George. "Colonel, this is your celebration. Please . . ."

George recognized his cue. "We were about to sing Christmas carols. Will you join us?"

Merlyn nodded and the men rose to their feet. George turned to a young officer Merlyn didn't recognize near the foot of the table. "Lieutenant Forbes, you have a good voice. Please lead us in 'O Come, All Ye Faithful.'"

Forbes sang in a clear baritone and led them through all three verses of the carol. He followed it with "It Came Upon a Midnight Clear" and "Joy to the World."

Merlyn fell silent just listening to the men singing around him. His heart was full. He loved them like brothers, especially the young colonel singing next to him. He never ceased to be amazed at how God could come into the squalor and ugliness of war and make his home in the hearts of those who loved him.

How different this Christmas was from the one a year ago. Then, the mood was somber, the memory of defeat and the killing field before the stone wall still fresh in the regiment's memory. Now the mood was joyful, upbeat, the hope of victory in sight.

A soft cough snapped him out of his reverie. The men had fallen silent, their eyes on him.

"Is there a song you would like us to sing, general?" George asked.

Merlyn thought for a moment. One came into his mind. He remembered his parents singing it when he was a boy. It had been one of his favorites. He didn't remember its history, but it felt right. He took a chance.

"This is a French carol," he said. "Hopefully you've heard the English words before." He took a deep breath and began to sing.

"O Holy night!
The stars are brightly shining . . ."

The men, who had looked quizzically at him at first, joined in as they recognized the melody. Soon the entire tent was singing. As they enthusiastically sang the final verse, he was struck by the appropriateness of the words.

"Truly He taught us to love one another;
His law is Love and His gospel is peace.
Chains shall He break, for the slave is our brother
And in His name, all oppression shall cease."

251

That was one of the reasons this army existed, why so many had given their lives during this terrible war. Jesus came to set the captives free; this army marched and fought to do the same. The words were not lost on the other officers. Their voices tapered off into silence. Merlyn knew they were lost in their thoughts—thoughts of home, of absent friends, of future battles. Soon the only sound in the tent was the ticking of the stove and a hollow cough from one of the officers.

Merlyn broke the silence. "Gentlemen, I have intruded on your festivities for long enough. Blessings to you all and Merry Christmas."

"Before you go, general," George said. "I'd like us all to thank the man responsible for our feast. Lieutenant Forbes?"

Forbes ducked out of the room and returned a moment later with a dark-skinned soldier in tow. He stood ramrod straight. His uniform was immaculate. His face was creased in a broad smile.

"Gentlemen, I give you Private Moses Addison. Private, thank you for your culinary prowess. You have done us proud."

Merlyn joined in with the thunderous applause.

Addison bowed, did a smart about-face, and disappeared back into the bowels of the house.

Saunders beat him to the door. George followed Merlyn outside onto the porch. Rain hissed down and their breath fogged in the chill.

"Addison?" Merlyn asked.

"He needed a last name for the enlistment papers. He took it from someone who helped him on his flight north."

Merlyn inclined his head. "It fits. I have something for you, George." He reached into his pocket and pulled out the piece of paper he had folded into a card. On the front, he had sketched a Madonna and child. The Madonna's face was Kate's. "This is something they are doing in Europe. It's a Christmas card. Just a few words to wish you the very best for this Christmas season. Who knows? Maybe they'll catch on here someday."

George looked surprised as he took the card. "I will treasure this always, Merlyn. Thank you."

Embarrassment colored his face, and he looked down for a moment before meeting Merlyn's eyes once more. "I have nothing for you, general. I'm sorry."

Merlyn reached out, squeezed George's shoulder. "That's all right, George. This may sound trite to you, but the baby whose birth we celebrate today is gift enough for me."

He turned to reach for Midnight's reins. George's hand on his forearm restrained him. "Stay a moment, Merlyn."

"George, it's pouring. You came outside with no coat."

"That's all right. I'll dry out by the fire afterwards. Thank you for coming by. It means a lot to the men in there." He nodded toward the room from which the sound of singing was emanating once more. "On days like this I can almost feel the truth of what you have been telling me about the Lord. It's the other days of the year I find it far more difficult. I particularly liked that last song and can see the parallel: the slave, the downtrodden is our brother. We lay our lives down for a cause. Jesus lays down his life for us."

Merlyn brushed away a rivulet of water trickling down his cheek and looked at his friend. He felt a surge of gladness. Maybe the chink in George's armor was widening. He wished he had something to say that would blow it wide open.

"That's what it's all about, George. The baby whose birth we celebrate today laid down his life to free us from our sins. Yet our faith is not about dying for a cause. It's what we do with the gift, investing in the lives of others."

"Like you have been doing with me," George said. His face softened and his eyes shimmered. He reached out and grasped Merlyn's hand. "Thank you. It means a lot to me. Maybe someday I'll be able to believe. I've kept you waiting in the rain too long. Godspeed, Merlyn, and Merry Christmas."

"God bless you, George," Merlyn replied as he swung onto Midnight's back. There was an ache in his heart that the season could not cure as he rode away from the men who were so dear to him.

Later that night, Merlyn pushed aside the stack of requisitions he had been working his way through. It was late. It was Christmas. He should be focusing on the Light of the World, not the pressing concerns of his brigade.

He looked around the cabin that had been his headquarters since fall, taking in the meager furnishings and his even more meager possessions. A premonition that had been lingering at the back of his mind solidified into certainty—his time here was running out. Soon he would be moving on again. Would there be time to lead George to faith?

He pushed back his chair from his desk, its legs catching on the rough-hewn floorboards, threatening to tip. Shivering, he pulled his coat tight against the pervading chill the fireplace seemed unable to dispel.

His mind churned with worry. Worry for George. Worry for the colonels of the other regiments, men who were becoming as dear to him as George. Worry for the men they led.

"Dear Lord, protect them," he breathed. "Keep them safe, but more importantly, help them to know you."

It was a brief prayer, but heartfelt. It was all he had the energy for. He dug back into his mind to find what was sapping his strength, pulling him down, robbing him of the joy he should be feeling on this most joyous of days.

It wasn't hard to find. Guilt, recrimination, regret. They had been his constant companions these past months, dragging down his spirits, sapping his strength.

The rich food he had eaten earlier that day congealed into an unpleasant lump in his belly. He pulled the drawing from his pocket, held it above him, stared at it in the dancing candlelight. Kate, my love, he whispered. "I miss you more than you can possibly know. I would gladly give my life right now just for the chance to spend one more hour with you, to try to make right what I did to you."

He reached for the journal. It was almost two-thirds full of letters, scribblings, and musings he hoped he would one day be able to share with Kate.

He pulled it open to a blank page, stared at the paper for a moment, and then attacked it with a pencil. In short order, he rendered an idealized view of her home and the surrounding valley. He then added a Christmas tree outside the house and a tiny F-18 in the sky overhead. The place was important to her and therefore important to him. He wished with all his heart he could be there right now instead of here. Home. It was something he had not experienced for a very long time, and he wanted to make one with Kate more than he had ever wanted anything before.

"Lord, you know the desire of my heart," he whispered softly. "I've served you faithfully more years than I can count. Please let me come home to her."

He sat at his desk for what seemed like hours, staring at the blank sheet in the notebook, searching for the right words. The lamp was burning low when, finally, they came and he started to write.

25 December 25th, 1863

Merry Christmas, Sweetheart:

Today we celebrate the birth of God's Son, our Lord Jesus Christ, the most precious gift ever given. There is nobody I want to share this day with more than with you. I spent today visiting the troops, but every moment, my mind was on you, wondering how you would be spending this special day. Hopefully the sun was bright, the sky blue, and your day was filled with laughter and good cheer.

Every moment I think of you, the sun breaks through the clouds in my heart and instantly all becomes joy and light. God is so good!

I thank God for the gift of his precious Son who brought light into this dark world, and long for the day we can celebrate a Christmas together.

In every waking moment I see your face in my mind's eye. I see your soft hair, your warm and loving eyes, your sweet lips I long to kiss once more. My heart longs for you with a yearning that brings tears to my eyes.

Fly safe, check six, and may God be the wind beneath your wings.

All my love

M

His heart aching, Merlyn reluctantly closed the journal and dimmed the lantern. It was Christmas, and he had never felt more alone.

Chapter 38

"Elsa, would you give this to my wife?" Exhausted, her mind consumed by the mission she would fly in just a couple hours, Kate started at the unexpected voice at her elbow. There was no mistaking it. Spud. She turned slowly, feeling a surge of irritation as she pushed the proffered envelope away.

"Give it to her yourself," she snapped, instantly regretting her tone of voice. Like her, most of the pilots had written such a letter, and she was surprised it had taken him this long to write his own.

"Sorry," she said, seeing the hurt flash across his face. "Give it to me. I'll return it to you when this is all over."

"What makes you so sure we'll make it through?" His voice was high, tight. He was battling his fears, as all of them were. Most of the other pilots were letting it out, though, through bravado, nervous joking, but he was not one of the crowd, had no such outlet. He kept his fear bottled up inside.

"We're starting day two," he continued. "And we're the only squadron in the wing that hasn't lost a jet. The Knights have lost two. When's it going to be our turn? I know how everyone feels about me. I don't want to be the one who makes a mistake, lets everyone down. Gets someone killed, like Animal kept saying I'd do."

Kate took a deep breath. The mission briefing would be starting in just a few minutes. This was the last conversation she wanted to be having. She pulled him into a corner of the ready room.

"Listen, Spud," she replied, "we're all afraid. We're afraid of what could happen to us. We're afraid of making a mistake. You did a great job last night—both targets destroyed. Get a couple more missions under your belt, gain a little confidence, and the fear will become manageable. You'll see."

She cast around for something else she could give him to ease his nerves. "We're meeting our objectives. We've done a lot of damage to their air defenses. We're a lot safer now than last night."

Spud looked dubious. "Yeah, but what about the Russians? They said they're not going to allow us to attack Iran unpunished."

Kate had to concede the point. Russia had not yet delivered on their promise to intervene. Their entry into the war would be a game-changer.

"What about the Russians?" she answered, trying to keep her voice light, but suspected she was failing miserably. "Yeah, they have great equipment, but they showed their lack of ability in Ukraine. The Iranians had the best of the best but didn't know how to use it. The Russians will be a lot better, but we still have the edge over them in training and proficiency."

His face looked as unconvinced as she felt. He shook his head. "Thanks for trying to make me feel better." His eyes met hers and she was gratified to see determination in them. "I'll do my job and won't let you down. I'd rather die than do that."

He nodded toward the letter Kate held by her side. "If something happens to me, I want Kim to have something that lets her know how much I love her, that tries to set things right. Give it to her in person. Tell her I was someone she can be proud of."

His eyes shimmered, and he impatiently brushed the back of his hand across them.

"Listen, you'll be fine. You're not going to let us down," she said with a confidence she did not feel.

Her stomach tightened as she checked the clock on the bulkhead. Five minutes until briefing. Were the skies over Iran going to be any safer than they were the night before or was she just fooling herself and lying to Spud?

***

From her vantage point at the back of the CVIC, the TR's intelligence center, Kate stared at the large screen at the front of the compartment, watching hundreds of tracks push into Iran from bases across the Middle East and from carriers in the Arabian Sea. It was an awe-inspiring sight, one that would have charged her with adrenaline had she not been so tired.

The mission she had just flown had gone well. Surface to air threats were greatly reduced. No enemy jets had lifted off the ground to challenge the allied formations. Despite his fears, Spud had done his job.

Now it was afternoon. She should be trying to catch some sleep before the next day's mission but could not force herself to look away from the battle unfolding before her.

As the strike packages pressed farther into Iran, someone in the compartment cursed softly. Tracks appeared near bases in Turkmenistan and southern Russia, moving southward toward Iran. A knot formed in the pit of her stomach. Russia had just entered the war.

She watched the developing air picture with a growing sense of dread. The bulk of the allied attack plan focused on the north and west of Iran, where the major cities and defense installations were located. The navy strike packages comprised the eastern flank of the attack. Air force F-22 Raptors and F-15 Eagles provided air cover to the strike forces. It was their job to sweep away the enemy fighters streaking southward to disrupt the attack.

Somebody had put the primary strike frequency on the loudspeaker. Until now it had been silent. She shot a glance around the room, noting people stiffening as AWACS broadcast the air picture.

She did the math. Although the Flankers and Fulcrums flown by the Russians would be at the edge of their combat radius, they would engage the strike packages just as they approached their targets. The timing could not have been worse.

She felt helpless, a fly on the wall watching a catastrophe unfold. Digger, Padres 11, leading the navy strike package with Jasper, Mogas, and Jethro on his wing, was going to have his hands full. She wished she were up there with him.

Spots on the desert floor flared red. A Defense Support Program reconnaissance satellite, scanning the earth with its infrared sensors, had detected missile launches. She waited, breathless, for the tracks to be displayed. Where were they headed? Israel, or the fleet? Computers did their work, but the processing load was intense. Finally tracks showed on the display. Three of them. "Oh, Lord, no," she breathed. They were heading toward Israel.

The minutes ticked by as the missiles streaked upward, reached their apogee, and then started down. She envisioned the people they were targeting. They had wanted no part of this war, had not started it, and were targets simply because of who they were.

More flares appeared on the display, this time from Israel, their Terminal High Altitude Area Defense system doing its job. Would it be enough? She held her breath until the three inbound tracks disappeared. A spontaneous cheer erupted in the CVIC. She released her breath and focused her attention on the impending air battle.

The Raptors were now pushing far in front of the strike packages they were escorting, their ability to cruise at supersonic speeds helping them close the distance to the incoming hostiles.

A cluster of tracks coming south from Turkmenistan was flanking the navy strike package, beyond the edge of their radars. She could see they were untargeted and wanted to scream a warning. Why was AWACS not directing Raptors in that direction? Digger should be able to see the data link tracks in his cockpit, had to know the Flanker radars would target him soon.

She turned her attention back to the air force jets now far in front of the allied formations. Incoming tracks lit up on the display, highlighting the enemy planes that were targeted. Moments later, they simply disappeared. But not all. A few turned tail and ran. A small handful of others continued to press toward the attacking force.

As minutes ticked by like hours, the untargeted tracks to the east resolved into a division of four Flankers, skirting outside Digger's radar coverage. As Digger approached his target, the enemy formation tipped in, heading directly toward him. *Why was nobody targeting it?* Kate felt her insides clench with frustration. The enemy fighters were still miles away, but they were nearing missile launch range. *Why was AWACS not calling out the threat? Why was Digger not reacting?*

AWACS finally came on the air. "Padres 11, Goliath. Hostiles BRAA 040 for 45, angels 20, hot." The switch from bullseye control to Bearing Range Altitude and Aspect conveyed the seriousness of the situation.

Kate knew what was going through Digger's mind. He would be making a lightning calculation of distances and angles and weapons parameters to determine if he could get a bomb off before having to react to the incoming fighters. She'd already calculated the odds and was anticipating his hard turn to react to the incoming threat.

Digger pressed the attack. The range between the formations decreased by a mile every four seconds. *Digger, break right,* she willed him. Missiles could already be in the air, and he was not reacting.

An eternity of seconds ticked by. Finally, attack completed, Digger began his defensive maneuvers. Kate knew exactly what he would be doing, saw him jettisoning his tanks and remaining JDAM. Her fingers moved with his to deploy chaff and flares. She could imagine him looking through the helmet-mounted sight as he scanned the sky for a tallyho on the incoming fighters.

She knew in a close-in fight, Digger would be the match of any pilot he went up against, but would he get the chance?

The Russians turned and ran. They had launched their missiles. By doctrine, they did not fire singles, they fired many to increase the probability of kill against the targets they were engaging. Digger and Nemo were going to have to jam and outmaneuver a wall of death streaking toward them.

Padres 13 and 14, several miles to Digger's left, turned tail to the threat and ran. Good move. Digger and Jasper turned hard into the notch. Her stomach lurched. No, they weren't. Digger was turning hot, into the incoming missiles. *Digger, what are you doing?* The question was rhetorical. He was hoping to get a quick shot off against the fleeing hostiles before going back into the notch. Ballsy move, but not smart. An awful feeling in her gut told her it would cost him dearly. Her heart in her throat, she counted down the seconds.

Digger's track disappeared from the display, while Jasper's turned southbound, rolling out about a dozen miles behind Padres 13 and 14.

Kate tasted bile in her throat as her stomach contracted painfully.

All friendly tracks were flowing south now, the few surviving Russian tracks flowing north. There were now only three in the formation that had claimed Digger. She was momentarily angry with him. *Digger, you knew better than that,* she thought. *Jasper survived. You could have too.*

Feeling as wretched as she ever had in her life, she quietly fled to wake Torch.

Chapter 39

Merlyn started at the soft rap on his cabin door. He had nodded off again, something that was happening more frequently given the grinding monotony of winter camp. Stifling a yawn, he looked up to see Saunders.

"Pardon me, general. Colonel Maxwell would like a moment of your time." His aide's tone was apologetic, embarrassed.

Merlyn stifled a sigh as he looked down at the paperwork strewn across his desk. Was there no end to it? "Very well, send him in."

Saunders looked down at his feet. "He and the other colonels would like to see you outside."

Merlyn stifled a slight surge of irritation, straightened his coat, and reached for the Hardee hat he had taken to wearing that winter, already dusty and showing wear.

Squinting through the bright afternoon sunlight, he spotted his colonels standing expectantly, a box on a tripod beside them, a photographer's wagon beyond. He groaned. How to dodge this one? The answer was: he couldn't. But he could play it out a little.

"Gentlemen, what can I do for you?"

Of the commanders who had taken the field at Gettysburg, only George and Parker remained. Major O'Halloran, recovered from his wounds, was the senior surviving Ohioan. Harkness was too ill to take the field and had been replaced by Rankin, his lieutenant colonel.

George stepped forward as spokesman. "General, we were hoping to have a photograph taken with you. Would you be so kind?"

Merlyn groaned inwardly but acquiesced. "How do you want to arrange things?"

"If you would sit here, general," George said as Saunders placed his camp chair before the cabin. "We will gather around you."

Merlyn did as he was told, and a few minutes later the deed was done. But George wasn't. "General, may I have a photograph with you, just the two of us?"

"Of course, George," he replied, touched by the affection in the younger man's voice.

Long, motionless moments later, the photographer's work was done.

Merlyn turned to bid his commanders farewell, but Parker had a question. "General, have you met our new general-in-chief yet? What's he like?"

Merlyn considered for a moment. Lincoln had elevated Grant to command of all Union armies a month prior, but Merlyn had only met him in passing and heard him speak just a couple of times. "He's shorter than I expected him to be. Quiet. Forceful. Determined. He's polite but direct and to the point. Bobby Lee is going to have his hands full."

"Have they said yet how the campaign is going to go?"

"I'm sure they are talking about it among the corps and division commanders, but they are not sharing down to the brigades yet. Still, it's not hard to imagine how it will unfold."

Parker wore a puzzled expression.

"It's pretty simple really," Merlyn continued. "We threaten Richmond, and Lee must come out to fight. Grant is going to cross the Rapidan and start moving south. At that point, all hell is going to break loose. Lee is going to come out swinging, and we're going to be in an all-out slugging match, which will end when only one army is left standing. Your men will be called on to fight like they have never fought before."

"They're ready," George said grimly. "Do you think this year will see the end of this bloody war?"

Merlyn considered, wishing he could tell his friend that a full year remained before the surrender at Appomattox. Once again, he was forced to feign ignorance. "I wish I could say I do. Lee has a lot of fight in him and a lot of tricks up his sleeve. If we can lure him into a decisive battle, that will end it. But I'm afraid instead, we're just going to have to grind him down until he has nothing left to fight with. It's going to cost a whole lot of lives—both his and ours. We've not seen the last of this, not by a long shot."

George's face hardened. "This year, next year, or the year after, we will finish this. We have sacrificed too much to let this end short of complete victory." It was the same iron will he had seen and loved in Kate.

Merlyn spent the afternoon dealing with disciplinary cases, the more serious ones that were beyond the authority of the regimental commanders. Bored men filled their time with mischief. Gambling, fighting, sneaking away to visit the women who followed the army, were all too prevalent. He could not escape the timeless constant that leadership was more to do with handling people than it was with getting things done.

The boredom of winter camp ground at him just like it ground at his men. He pulled his Bible to him and opened it randomly. He scanned the page, but his eyes refused to focus. He found his hand straying to the notebook of letters to Kate. It was almost full now. The mere thought of her name brought with it a surge of loneliness.

He reflected on the earlier conversation with his colonels. There was a place out there called Cold Harbor. Once more the thought of it filled him with a nameless dread. As clearly as if he were living the moment, he saw his men marching out onto a field, he at their head, only to be mowed down by the hundreds. He tried to cast his mind beyond that instant but found nothing. No hope. No expectation of life beyond that moment.

Panic tightened his throat, but it was not panic for himself, but panic for George. His friend had still not come to faith. What would happen to him on that killing field? What were the implications to Kate? His mouth went suddenly dry.

A thought crossed his mind—a thought that would have been unimaginable two years ago when he stood before the recruiting sergeant in far-off Albany. *Lord, I would like to stay and finish this thing. Even if it means another year of hell, I would like to stay with the men you have entrusted to me and see this through.* Just to think it sent a chill down his spine, but God did not have to speak to him for him to know the reply. It was not to be.

Lord, he prayed, *this young man you entrusted to me is in your hands. Please protect him and let him live through what is to come. I have been faithful, planted the seeds that will hopefully grow one day into great and fruitful faith. Draw him ever closer to you that he may know you and love you and come to enjoy a deep and abiding relationship with you.*

And please, he added, *whatever happens, let Kate be. And keep her safe through what it is you plan for her to do.*

He looked down and saw he had been drawing random figures on a piece of paper while he had been lost in thought. He crumpled it up and threw it toward the fireplace. Perhaps it was time to write another letter, to start wrapping things up, give Kate a sense of closure.

As he opened the journal, the first faint glimmerings of an idea began to form in his mind.

April 4th, 1864

My Dearest Kate:

For the thousandth time since we parted, I wish I had some way of knowing what is happening in your life. I can't help but shake the feeling you're in terrible danger and my heart recoils at the thought of it. But I comfort myself in the knowledge you're one of the most gifted pilots I have ever flown with. There is nothing out there you cannot handle.

Yet when we strap on a jet, we, in a very real way, commend ourselves to the Almighty. Even in peacetime there are no guarantees. We are hostage to an unimaginable blend of chance, circumstance, decisions, mechanics, and weather—I could go on and on. The combinations that could result in disaster are manifold. In combat, the ante goes up. Way up. With a knot in my stomach and fear in my heart, I try to smile at God and trust that he will preserve and keep you.

We never know what God has in store for us or for the ones we love. We take life as it comes. That does not mean we are fatalistic about it. God created us to love, to laugh, to enjoy life, but also to grieve, to sorrow, to feel compassion. To embrace an attitude that things will be as they will be, that there's nothing we can do about it, is to stifle life itself. I don't ever want to do that. What I want to do is fully live the life God has given me.

When I fell in love with you, fear became one of the consequences of my decision. Perhaps I'm selfish because I have not regretted it for one moment. Loving you and seeing your beautiful face in my mind's eye have made my years of wandering and sacrifice worthwhile. I would not trade our short moments together for any other reward.

I love you more than life itself.

M

A bead of sweat trickled down his back. He rose, crossed the room, and threw the window open. Campaign season was starting soon. A brigade lay camped just outside his door, a couple thousand men who depended on him for leadership. They weren't getting it while he was sitting here moping his long-lost love.

He bellowed loudly for Saunders. There was work to be done.

Chapter 40

"Go away," Kate mumbled, pushing away the hand shaking her shoulder.

"Ma'am, wake up. You're needed in the ready room." The voice in Kate's ear was urgent, insistent.

Slowly, like a bubble rising out of the depths of the ocean, consciousness returned. A bright light shone painfully into Kate's eyes as she struggled to bring her vision into focus. A face leaned over her. As her vision steadied, it resolved into Seaman Garcia.

Her stomach sour with lack of sleep, Kate swung her legs around and sat on the edge of her rack, trying to bring her thoughts into some semblance of coherency. Whatever it was, it must be urgent for her to be woken in the middle of crew rest.

"What's going on?" she croaked, her tongue seeming to stick to the roof of her mouth. She shook her head, trying to clear the fog clouding her mind.

"Mogas went down," Garcia replied, a look of almost panic on her face.

No. Not Mogas. Kate's mind rejected the thought.

"Commander, are you all right?" Garcia rested her hand on Kate's shoulder, looking urgently in her face. "Jethro's jet was badly damaged. We need you. Toad is awfully upset at Spud. I think they're going to fight."

Of course Toad would be upset. He and Mogas were close friends. Spud would be an easy target for Toad's grief.

Kate continued to struggle to bring her thoughts into focus. "Where's Commander Dennis? Can't he control them?"

"No, ma'am. He's in CVIC helping work a last-minute change to his mission. There's no one senior in the ready room."

"I'll be right there," Kate said, grasping the bulkhead for support as she lurched to her feet.

She dressed quickly, splashed water on her face, tugged her hair into some semblance of order and strode quickly to the ready room. Was this day four of the war or day five? She was so tired it was almost impossible to think. If Torch was flying and Spanky was planning, this had to be the end of day four. Where was Trojan? Then she remembered. The Knights had experienced heavy losses among their leadership. He had been reassigned as their XO. With Trojan gone, she was number two, the de facto executive officer. *Digger, why did you do it?* she thought, her throat tightening and tears forming at the corner of her eyes. *We need you now more than ever.*

The scene that greeted her in the ready room was utter pandemonium. Toad, struggling and yelling profanities, was being held back by Jasper and Bags. Spud, red-faced, was being likewise restrained by Banger and Nemo.

Kate pushed down the rage she felt bubbling up inside. "As you were!" she bellowed, putting every ounce of force she could muster into the words. The ready room fell silent, shocked faces turning her way.

"You, stand down and back off," she said, angrily advancing on Toad. "You! do the same," she shouted as she turned to Spud.

"Everyone, there's a war on outside, in case you hadn't noticed. Get back to fighting it instead of each other." She shot a menacing glare at the handful of pilots in the ready room. No one would meet her eyes.

"You two." Kate glared menacingly at Toad and Spud. "Over here." She motioned toward a quiet corner of the ready room.

"What's this all about?" she asked, allowing the edge of anger to remain in her voice.

"Mogas died hitting the target this scumbag missed yesterday." Toad started toward Spud again, tears welling in his eyes, but Kate interposed herself firmly between them, pushing him back, surprised at her own strength.

"Listen, Toad." She forced her voice to remain calm. She was aware of the other pilots furtively watching them. She had to de-escalate this at all costs.

"Spud did not miss the target. I've looked at his video. His aimpoint was dead on. Either the targeteers miscalculated the point needed to bring the building down, or his bomb didn't guide correctly. Spud did everything right. Besides, his is not the only target that's needed to be restruck. You can't pin this on him."

Her answer did nothing to defuse the hot fury on Toad's face. He opened his mouth to reply. She heaved a sigh. It had to be the hard way then. "That's enough, lieutenant," she cut him off roughly. "You're out of line. This is war. People die. Get over it. You're flying in a couple hours, so get your head straight or I'm taking you off the schedule. Got it?"

Toad shot a venomous glare at Spud and strode out of the ready room. She turned to Spud, whose face clearly communicated his unhappiness. "Same goes for you," she said, only slightly less roughly. "Keep your head in the game."

The chiming of the ready room phone caught everyone's attention. Kate felt dread rising inside of her as Nemo reached for it. The expression of shock and anger on his face confirmed her fears. Nemo slowly put the handset down. "Jethro didn't make it," he announced to the waiting pilots, his voice flat, his eyes riveted on Spud.

Kate's head throbbed as she sat in the TR's tiny chapel. *Lord, please help me through this. Help me keep the pilots together. Help me see what needs to be done and find the strength to do it.*

She rubbed at her burning eyes and looked down at her watch. Two hours until briefing time. She knew she should be in her rack but was so keyed up she knew she'd lie there sleeplessly, alone with her thoughts.

I need you like I've never needed you before. She continued to pray, reaching out, hoping to find peace, but it eluded her, driven away by the thoughts cascading through her mind, spinning, churning, crashing into each other. Thoughts of Animal, of Digger, of Torch, of Spud, of the rest of the pilots. And in the middle of the maelstrom sat one other, solid, unmovable: Morgan.

Gradually the storm subsided. The other pilots fell away and there was only he.

"What happened to you?" she whispered. "What happened to us?" It had been a week since she received the DNA results, but she'd been so busy, she'd not had time to process the implications. Had the dream ended with some definitive conclusion, or had it ended like most dreams did with her snapping awake, interrupting the dream mid-flow with no conclusion, no closure? She had no way of knowing.

But with a start, she realized she did know. He had taken her hand. While drowning in the intensity of his gaze, she had felt the sharp sting of his knife on the heel of her hand. She had looked down, had seen blood welling up . . .

No, I don't have time for this. I have to fly. Frantically she tried to push the memory away. Stuff it down. Bury it. Slam a manhole cover over it to prevent it from surfacing. But it was no use. The memory burst into her mind with the unstoppable force of an exploding star, and solidified there, dark, agonizing, a hammer-blow to her solar plexus that left her struggling, gasping for breath.

"I'm leaving on another assignment tonight," Morgan declared, his voice hollow, his face twisted with pain.

It was as if the bottom fell out of her world. Her heart lurched and her face tingled as the blood drained from it. Conscious thought fled, batted away by the sudden sense of shock and loss. She had to focus to catch his next words.

"I love you with all my heart and would give everything to be there for your graduation tomorrow, but I can't."

He stood against the desk in her BOQ room, his hands gripping an edge so tightly his knuckles turned white. She stood apart from him, arms clasped tightly across her chest as if hugging herself. Raw emotion warred on his face—love, sadness, and yes, even fear. His

271

voice caught as he continued, "Where I'm going, there will be no phones and no way I can write."

She stared mutely at him, her mind struggling to process his words. "You're deploying soon and we're going to be apart for a long time," he said. "I'm afraid to ask, but I'm going to. Will you wait for me?"

The appeal in his face was so strong that, hurt as she was, she wanted to throw herself into his arms. Prudence held her back. She had allowed herself to trust once more, and now her heart was being broken. Again. Not trusting herself to speak, she nodded.

She sensed his relief. "When you fly back to Lemoore," he continued, "I'll be waiting for you. If I'm not there, something has happened to me, and I won't be coming back—ever. Do you understand what I'm saying?"

Her throat constricted with fear. "Where you're going is dangerous?" She struggled to get the words out.

"In all likelihood. But trust me, I'm very good at what I do, and God has a plan for me just like he has for you. I will come back to you." He spoke confidently, but Kate detected a slight note of uncertainty in his voice.

She felt as if she were drowning in his hazel eyes as they stared hopefully into hers. "I'll wait for you," she promised. "And if you don't come back to me, I'll hunt you down and kill you myself." The feeble joke broke the spell. He laughed. She laughed too and cried and went into his arms.

He held her tightly. She felt the hardness of his muscles, smelled the distinctive odor of jet on his flight suit. He buried his face in her neck and squeezed her so hard she was afraid her ribs would break.

Reluctantly he pulled back and said, "I'm going to write you as often as I can, keep the letters, and give them to you when I get back, so you'll know I thought of you every single day we're apart. Will you do the same?"

She nodded, not trusting herself to speak.

He started to take her in his arms again but hesitated and said instead, "Kate, I'm so proud of you. I love you with all my heart. Tomorrow when you wake up, you must remember that this is real.

272

We are real. I'm going to give you something to help you hold onto that." She struggled to make sense of his words but couldn't.

His mannerisms were becoming increasingly urgent, as if he were bordering on panic. Reaching up, he brushed back her hair and cupped her face in his hands. He leaned close and stared intently into her eyes. "Kate. Sweetheart. I'm going to do something that will make no sense to you, but I promise it will later. I need to give you an anchor. Will you trust me?" The words were gentle and pleading, his eyes full of entreaty.

She had spent a year with this man. She had put her life in his hands and he in hers. She loved him. The answer could only be yes. She nodded mutely, wondering what he intended.

He strode rapidly into the kitchenette and returned with a clean dishtowel. She watched him, mesmerized, as he pulled a small knife from his flight boot and drew it across the heel of his left hand. Blood welled forth.

He gently took her hand. "I'm sorry, this is going to hurt a little."

She wanted to pull her hand back but couldn't bring herself to do it. As if from a distance, her rationality warring with her emotions, she watched him nick her palm. The knife felt icy cold yet burning hot as it sliced into her skin. She gasped slightly, and he pressed his bloody palm to hers. It was a ritual from another time and place, but she understood its binding significance.

"My blood, your blood, comingled, together forever." His words were gentle but urgent. "Now you say it."

She thought she would stumble over the words but as she spoke her voice strengthened. "My blood, your blood, comingled, together forever." The words rang in her ears like an incantation. While part of her wanted to scream at the irrationality of it, the greater part sensed oneness and rightness.

He gently wrapped the dish towel around her injured hand. "Our blood is on the towel. Whatever you do, don't take it off until morning. Leave it on your hand and sleep with it. Tomorrow things may seem different. Your mind is going to start playing tricks on you. It's going to make you try to doubt what has happened here. When it does, remember these three things."

He touched the scar on her arm he had inflicted months before. "Scar on arm."

He touched her bandaged hand. "Cut on hand. Your blood, my blood, comingled, together forever."

Tears sprang to her eyes. He was leaving her, and for some reason that she did not understand he was worried that she would not remember him.

"Now you say it."

She repeated the words, following his gestures. She could hardly get the words out so great was her grief.

He folded her into his arms again and held her so tightly she could hardly breathe. When he released her tears streamed down his cheeks. He kissed her hard and she could taste their saltiness.

"I have to go." His voice shook. "Remember this: I've loved you since I first set eyes on you. Whatever the future holds, I will always love you. When you come home, I will be waiting for you. Trust your heart and not your mind. Hold on to what you know is true." He kissed her once more and turned to the door.

He turned again, smiled at her, but the smile was sad, grief and loss etched on his features.

Mute, stricken, she watched the door close behind him. Her hand hurt. Her heart hurt much, much worse.

There it was, crystal clear in her mind, a dark, agonizing, recollection that left her struggling, gasping for breath. *No, it couldn't be. He had to know beforehand he'd be leaving. Why hadn't he told me? Had he been manipulating me, playing with my emotions?* As soon as her mind formed the thought, Kate rejected it. Every memory of him resonated with his decency and honor. It was unthinkable he would deliberately do anything to hurt her. *In that case,* her mind argued back, *how could he have treated me so terribly?*

She wanted to scream at the pain of it. Sobs wracked her body and tears streamed down her cheeks.

Lord, I can't take any more of this! Make it go away. But there was no answer. The doors of heaven remained closed in her face.

She didn't know how long she sat there, but gradually her sobs subsided and calm began to reassert itself. She looked at her watch. She had just enough time to catch a shower and change her flight suit before it was time to brief.

Three combat missions down and another tough one today. I need to be able to focus, Morgan. You couldn't have picked a worse time to drop this on me.

Chapter 41

Dry bones gleamed white in the rapidly fading daylight. Merlyn shivered as he walked through the tangled underbrush where, a year before, his men had fought and died. Rains and scavenging wild animals had unearthed many of the hasty burials that had followed the battle of Chancellorsville. Four skulls lay side by side, comrades buried together, the rest of their bones scattered.

It had been a long and difficult day. The march had begun before daybreak. Columns of men and horses and wagons had made their way over winding, barely solid roads down to the Rapidan and then up again on the southern side into enemy territory. Now they found themselves camped in dense woods not far from a place called Wilderness Tavern.

He dared not stray too far from the camp where his men lay curled in shelter halves or just blankets to protect them from the cold. A sentry could mistake him for an enemy, as had happened to the Confederate general Stonewall Jackson in these woods a year ago.

Something crunched behind him and he spun around. It was Saunders, ever watchful, ever protective. The man must have seen him leave and followed. There was a shadow behind him. Merlyn did not need to ask. It was George.

"Major, it's all right," he addressed Saunders. "I'm not straying far."

"General, you should not be out here. It is not safe." Saunders' voice was firm, insistent. "Please come back to the camp."

"Major, war is not safe. We are all right here. I promise I will go no farther. Colonel Maxwell and I will sit on that log and talk. I would prefer you go back to camp, but if it would make you feel better, you can stand nearby and keep watch."

Saunders opened his mouth to protest, but Merlyn raised a hand to silence him. He sat and motioned George to sit by him.

For several moments, neither man spoke, both content to stare off into the deepening gloom.

Merlyn finally broke the silence. "What's on your mind, George?"

"I came to bring you this." He passed Merlyn a small, framed daguerreotype. "The photographer's assistant brought it to me just as we were breaking camp.

Emotion constricted his throat, but he forced out, "George, thank you. I'll treasure it always as a memory of our time together." A thought struck him. "I want you to hang on to yours as well. Give it to your children to give their children and so on, as a memory of what you did to preserve the cause of freedom. Tell them your story so it will never be forgotten."

George was silent for a moment. He prodded with a stick at the dirt between his feet. "It's interesting you should say that. I never mentioned it to you, but not long after Fredericksburg I started keeping a journal. I never expected to survive this war, and I wanted my parents to have a sense of the man I have become, and perhaps find something in me to be proud of.

"You play a prominent part in my journal. My story is incomplete if it does not tell of the role you played in shaping me into who I now am. I don't know why you singled me out for friendship but thank you."

The silence between them lengthened as the darkness grew.

Finally, George spoke again. "What do you think is going to happen tomorrow?"

Merlyn wished he knew. "I have no idea. He gestured toward the last glimmer of light in the sky. "Bobby Lee is over yonder. I don't believe he is going to take kindly to our presence here. I think he is going to throw everything he has at us as we continue our march to the south. These woods are terrible ground for a fight. Tomorrow, whatever it may bring, is going to be ugly."

If Merlyn's words shook him, George did not show it. "If something happens to me, would you take my book home and give it to my father? Tell him I am a son he can be proud of." His voice was calm, almost defeatist.

Merlyn pushed away the image that rose in his mind of soldiers toppling like wheat before a scythe and took a breath to steady himself.

"George, neither of us has any guarantee we are going to come through this alive. I only have a couple of things to offer you for the days ahead."

George cocked his head.

"Put your faith in the Lord and he will give you eternal life. Second, be the man God made you to be. Don't allow yourself to be ruled by how your parents see you. When this war is finished, live your life to the fullest. Make a difference. Make the world a better place for your having been here."

He lapsed into silence, surprised by the vehemence in his voice. He envied George his future. If he lived, he would raise a family. Create a legacy that would live on for generations. Merlyn did not have that hope, only the certain knowledge that the next few days or weeks would see the end of his time here. Beyond that there was only uncertainty. Uncertainty for him. Uncertainty for Kate.

George put a hand on his arm. "And what of you, Merlyn? What are you going to do after the war?"

Merlyn thought for a moment before deciding to tell the truth. "I'm not going to survive this war, George. I don't know if it is going to be tomorrow, next week, or next month, but there's a bullet coming that has my name on it."

George started to protest but Merlyn silenced him. "You will have this brigade when I am gone, and you will lead our men to victory. It is going to be a hard road and will test every bit of your leadership, but you will succeed. I've done my job and I am being called home."

He sensed George tensing to argue and rose to his feet, forestalling further discussion. "Good night, George. Get some sleep. You'll need it for tomorrow."

Sticks cracking underfoot, they made their way across the clearing toward the waiting Major Saunders.

The following afternoon, Merlyn stared westward across a large clearing in the seemingly endless forest of twisted, tangled trees. The ground undulated softly, providing little cover. On the other side of the clearing, scouts had found Confederates waiting. The only question was, how many? Was it just skirmishers, or had Lee taken advantage of the darkness and brought up his entire army? Munro had been ordered to send his division into the woods to find out.

Merlyn's men stood in line of battle on the east side of the clearing. Midnight stirred under him. The black horse knew what was coming. He could sense it as well as the men could and his blood was up. Merlyn feared for him and wondered for the hundredth time whether he should not have called the horse back to serve him.

Bugles sounded and drums beat. He gave the signal to sound "Forward," and urged Midnight into a slow walk. The Pennsylvanians formed the left of the line, New Yorkers and Ohioans the right. Battle flags and pennants streamed, an attractive target to the waiting rebels. Beyond his flags were those of the division's other three brigades, fully eight-thousand men stepping out into the clearing.

He could hear the occasional zip of a bullet flying past. *Skirmishers.* The volleys would not come until the line was closer. Seated on Midnight, he knew the sights of the sharpshooters would naturally fall on him and wondered, when the impact came, if he would feel it. Would it be quick, merciful, or would he be one of the mortally wounded lying between the lines, his screams tormenting the men in blue who hunkered down awaiting the next order to charge the enemy's guns?

The line dipped down into a swale and up again on the other side. Sergeants goaded men forward. Lieutenants and captains kept the lines dressed. Gaps opened and closed as men flowed around the natural obstacles of the terrain.

Merlyn yelled at Saunders. "Get over there to Colonel Parker. His line is drifting left. Tell him to close up on the New Yorkers."

"Yessir." Saunders spurred his horse across the field.

The trees were much closer now. A sudden sheet of fire and billow of smoke erupted from the trees before them. Bullets buzzed like a swarm of angry wasps, many of them thudding into flesh. Men screamed or simply groaned, their huddled mounds left behind as the line continued forward. *Not too many. Must have been skirmishers, not a line of battle. Thank God there are no cannons.*

Time seemed to stand still. His senses focused, becoming razor sharp. His mind rapidly processed what was happening and instantly made decisions. He was in the groove, instinct to a large degree taking the place of conscious thought, just as if he were going into combat in a jet.

His lines entered the trees. Gray shapes flitted back through the underbrush—skirmishers falling back. A low-hanging branch slapped at his face. He brushed it aside. Couldn't see much of anything through the dense forest of thin, scraggly trees choked with underbrush.

Ahead, deeper in the forest, he spotted a jumble of dirt and logs piled waist-high. Flame and smoke erupted again. Once more, bullets thudded in flesh or smacked into trees with a harsh crack. More screams. A shower of leaves. Saplings falling, cut through by the hail of bullets, adding confusion to the lines. More huddled forms on the forest floor.

Another belch of fire. His men this time. Screams came from the Confederate breastworks. Men reloaded as the second rank fired, keeping up the pressure. Another exchange of volleys. The line surged forward. A final volley came from the men in gray before they ran, vanishing into the dense forest.

He spurred Midnight and, riding low in the saddle, made his way over to where he knew George would be. He pointed with his sword in the direction the rebels had vanished. "George, keep your regiment headed in that direction. You're the center of the line. Nobody can see anything in this cursed wilderness. The other regiments will guide on you. Keep moving in a straight line."

Without waiting for a reply, he rode off to his right, where the Ohioans were making heavy, going through tangled thickets. He hoped O'Halloran was still in contact with the 2nd Brigade. How could anyone maintain contact with anything in these blasted woods?

Saunders, fire in his eyes, rejoined him as he rode down the line. "Sir, Colonels Parker and Rankin report heavy casualties. Colonel Rankin has lost contact with the 1st Brigade. They are endeavoring to move forward."

"Get back and tell them to guide on Colonel Maxwell. They must press on."

O'Halloran, a heavily bearded whippet of a man, was striving valiantly to keep his lines together. Off to his right Merlyn could see more men in blue. The 2nd Brigade. O'Halloran was doing his job well.

In front of the line there was another heavy eruption of fire. Smoke billowed, obscuring its source. More men went down. Those still standing returned fire, shooting blindly into the smoke. Then the line surged. Before them came another ragged rattle of musket fire. Men staggered back, falling, screaming. The smoke parted, revealing another Confederate breastwork, this one higher, more solid, pouring fire into O'Halloran's ranks. His men stood, bravely firing, reloading, firing again, the roar of battle echoing off the trees.

A keening wail rose from the right. He wheeled Midnight in that direction. Confederates boiled from the woods like a swarm of angry hornets. The New Yorkers were thick in the fray. The Ohioans were the same, but farther to the right the picture was different. The 2nd Brigade was breaking, blue-clad soldiers fleeing, seeking safety in the trees, rebels shooting them down as they ran. There was a brief lull in the firing as the rebel attention shifted to their right where Union troops, his troops, still challenged their fortifications.

The situation was becoming dangerous. Even if his men could carry this section of the works, they would be vulnerable, unsupported on either the left or right. Gray soldiers were massing again, ready to punch into O'Halloran's exposed flank. O'Halloran saw it coming, pulled the men back, and refused his line so his position could not be flanked. The soldiers who had been pulled from the line sought cover behind trees, rocks, any deformation of the ground. Some piled stones in front of them, seeking any scant cover they could find.

The gray wave was coming now, the Ohioans held their fire, waiting to make it count. Merlyn sat astride Midnight, anchoring the refused line. O'Halloran screamed at him over the din to get back.

A sudden volley from the Union soldiers caused the front line of rebels to sink to the ground, but the second still came. Merlyn steeled himself. *We must hold or they will roll up our entire line.* His men fired again, but the gray hoard kept coming. Blue-clad figures rose from their cover, bayonets leveled, and rushed the oncoming rebels. A momentary pause, a shock as troops made contact. Hands grasped for his reins. Midnight reared, his hooves lashing out. A man fell, his head a bloody ruin. To his right, a rebel lunged at Midnight with a bayonet. Merlyn fired in his direction and saw the man fall, only to be replaced by another. Firing again, he saw that man falling as well. Two shots down, four left. Merlyn fired at an officer leveling a pistol at him. Three shots left. The gray mass fell back, regrouping for another go.

The position was untenable. They were isolated and taking heavy fire on both flanks. "Have the bugler sound 'Fall Back,'" he ordered Saunders. The words were bitter in his mouth.

Eight notes from the bugle started the men back. They fell back by ranks, move and fire, move and fire, the gray masses hesitant to follow. Back over ground that had been won at such high cost. Back over the bodies of men lost earlier in the day.

The woods gave way to the open field sooner than he expected. The firing was desultory now, bullets still zipping by. Occasionally one found its mark and a soldier would drop.

Back in the safety of the trees, his men sank down, finding cover, knowing the Confederates would soon be coming.

He stared back out over the clearing for a long moment. There was movement among the trees opposite. He turned to Saunders. "Pass the order to dig in. Throw up anything to give the men cover. The enemy is coming, and we are going to do to them as they did to us."

He felt cold fury. Fury at the generals who had dithered, allowing Lee to bring up his army and throw up fortifications. Fury at Munro, who had not committed his reserve. Fury at the brigade commanders who had allowed their men to break and flee the field. Fury at himself for not having pulled his men back sooner.

And suddenly the fury was gone, replaced by an infinite sadness. So many good men had died that afternoon, and for what? To temporarily hold a piece of line and then relinquish it?

His commanders were walking his way, seeking his orders, George leading the way. They had done well, and they had survived. But with the whole rebel army bearing down on them, for how long would that be?

Chapter 42

"No friggin way!" Toad's exclamation caused heads all around the ready room to pivot toward the source of the commotion. "I'm not flying with that worthless scumbag again. Put him with someone else."

Kate strode over to where Gator was trying to put the finishing touches on the schedule. The Outlaws' maintenance crews had pulled out all the stops and scraped together eight jets to contribute to the next day's strikes. Kate would be leading the midday mission.

"What's the problem?" she asked, allowing her irritation to show.

Gator looked up at her, wiping at the sheen of perspiration on his forehead. "We're all out of pilots. I was able to get eight with minimal rest, but Toad—"

"I told you. I'm not flying with him." Toad enunciated the words slowly, venom dripping from each one.

Kate did a quick inventory. The early morning go, led by Torch, would be taking off soon. They would land too late to be available for the midday go. Spud had to fly that mission. If not on Toad's wing, then someone else's. But whose? By rights, he should fly the fourth position in one of the two divisions. Bags was leading her second section. If anything, he hated Spud more than Toad did.

"Toad," she said, trying to keep her voice soft and conciliatory. "He needs to be on the schedule. There's nobody else."

"I don't care," Toad retorted angrily. "Borrow a pilot from another squadron. I'm not flying with him."

Kate bit back the angry retort that sprang to her lips. It would be easy to pull rank, force the issue, but Toad was close to self-destructing. Direct confrontation might force him over the edge, and she needed every pilot she could get.

She was aware of a presence standing by her side, and she turned her head. Spud. His face red, set, unhappy. *He doesn't deserve this.*

"Toad," she tried again. "Be reasonable. Spud is no better or no worse than any other nugget in the wing. You'd have no problem if it were one of them on your wing."

"Dammit, Elsa!" Toad exploded. "Everybody knows you're coddling him. He's a worthless turd not pulling his weight."

Kate felt movement at her side and grabbed Spud's arm, hard, using her nails. The last thing the squadron needed was another brouhaha that degenerated into fisticuffs. With Spud's bulk, she had no question how that one would turn out.

She glanced up at the schedule, and before she could think about it, the words were out of her mouth. "Gator, put him with me." She looked each of the hovering pilots in the face, her expression stern. "Spud is an Outlaw, and I expect you to treat him as such. Understand?"

Without waiting for a reply, she turned back to Toad. As much as she wanted to delay what needed to be done until tempers were cooler, it had to be now or it would never happen. "Follow me," she said quietly, trying to keep her voice steady under the rush of adrenaline coursing through her body.

She saw him gather himself up, open his mouth to protest. "Now." She put every ounce of authority she could muster into the word.

It worked. *Don't handle this as Animal would have done, with bluster and bravado.* She led Toad into the passageway just outside the ready room. *Do it quickly and surgically.*

As she turned to him, she saw that Toad had visibly deflated. A hint of anxiety hovered behind his eyes.

"Don't ever do that again," she said, rallying her rapidly vanishing anger. "You fly with whomever the scheduler tells you to fly with. I don't care what your personal feelings are, keep them to yourself. If I ever see another outburst like that, or if you ever disrespect Spud or anyone else again, you're going to wish you had never been born. Now get out of here and get back to work."

Wordlessly, back rigid, Toad strode back into the ready room. As he went, she sensed a presence behind her and whirled. Her heart sank as she saw Torch decked out in his flight gear. She thought he'd already stepped to his jet. Obviously, he hadn't.

"What on earth are you thinking?"

Kate jumped at his steel-edged whisper behind her. She spun to face him.

"You need an experienced pilot on your wing," he continued, his face twisted with fury. "Not some shit-for-brains nugget who doesn't know his ass from a hole in the ground."

Kate winced and felt her throat tighten at the unfair characterization. *This is it. The make-or-break moment.* "Boss, you pay me to make good decisions," she answered, trying to keep her voice level. Anger would not work in this situation. It was cold, hard logic or nothing. "You know the bind we're in. The pilots are exhausted, and we need everyone we have. You all want me to take a perfectly capable pilot off the schedule because you don't like him and, in your mind, he doesn't fit in. If I do it, I'm just going to be filling the hole with someone who's too tired to fly and could end up making a mistake that kills one of us. That what you want to happen, or would you rather I give us all a chance and put in a relatively fresh pilot?"

Torch opened his mouth to argue, but Kate rushed on, not giving him a chance to speak.

"Tell me one thing Spud has done wrong since the war started— one thing."

Torch's eyes narrowed and locked onto hers, his mouth compressed into a narrow line.

"You and the rest of the team are persecuting him because of his personality, not his abilities. Well, it stops here, and it stops now." Surprised at her own determination, Kate continued, "If the rest of you won't fly with him, I will."

She took a deep breath and tried to calm the butterflies doing a barn dance in her stomach. "I'm your operations officer. Either trust me to do my job or relieve me."

There, it was said. She watched Torch's face, only half caring which way he would decide. *I've given him all the ammunition he needs to can me. Either he sees it my way or I'm finished. Either way, I've done my job and been true to my integrity.*

She saw the slight relaxing of his shoulders and she released her breath.

His eyes remained locked on hers, a glint of satisfaction in them. They were in combat. Things happened. The risk was all hers—he could dodge responsibility if things went wrong.

"It's your choice and your responsibility. If this goes south, I'll ruin you."

Kate nodded, not trusting herself to speak. She forced down the bile rising in her throat and put everything she had into meeting Torch's angry gaze. His eyes were black, fathomless holes boring into her, making her want to shrink into herself. Abruptly, he strode down the passageway toward the flight deck.

Kate wiped a trembling hand on her flight suit and stepped back into the ready room. Gator was putting the finishing touches on the schedule, Spud still hovering anxiously over his shoulder. "You're on my wing this afternoon," she told him and reached out to give his beefy shoulder a reassuring touch. "We only have a few hours until we brief. Go get some rest."

CAG, the TR's air wing commander, stood ramrod straight before the assembled pilots of the afternoon strike. A small man, lean and trim, Captain Somers' face was etched with fatigue and the ravages of responsibility, but he still radiated an aura of quiet determination.

Twisting in her seat in the front of the Knights' ready room, Kate surveyed the cramped compartment and the thirty-two aviators Trojan would be leading over Iran in a couple hours. There should have been upwards of forty present, but losses had taken their toll, friends were gone, and the mission going out that afternoon would be much smaller than those that had launched off the carriers in the opening days of the war.

She wanted coffee, something, anything to drive away the fog of fatigue clouding her mind, but with a long flight stretching out before her, coffee was the last thing she needed.

She spotted Heather standing at the back of the compartment, face pinched, dark circles under her eyes. Not far from her, Spud stood hunched, drawn into himself, a picture of isolation.

"I've called you all together," CAG began without preamble, "because today is the most crucial day of the war so far, and I need to convey to you the seriousness of the situation. While we've been largely successful in destroying Iran's nuclear capability, it still has a handful of mobile launchers we've been unable to find. Iran has declared, and intelligence believes them, that they have married nuclear warheads to those missiles.

"Iran's supreme leader stated again last night that they will fight to the last man to defend their remaining nuclear capability and that they will use it at the time of their choosing to destroy Israel. Although the weapons they launched against Israel a few days ago carried non-nuclear warheads, all indications are that they will use nukes the next time they try."

Kate felt her mouth go dry as she listened.

"Israel has stated that if Iran attacks them with nuclear weapons, they will retaliate in kind. Russia has declared that if Israel resorts to nuclear weapons, it will strike with immediate, overwhelming force. Our president has stated that the United States will tolerate no further acts of aggression. While not specifically saying that we will resort to nuclear weapons, he has left that option open."

He paused and wiped the palms of his hands on his rumpled flight suit.

"International tensions are the highest they've been since the Cuban Missile Crisis. It is imperative we find and take out those last missile launchers. If we don't and they successfully launch at Israel, life as we know it is going to change significantly." One of the pilots tittered at the understatement, a high, nervous laugh giving voice to the tension permeating the compartment.

CAG glowered momentarily at the offender before continuing, "You know what's at stake. We have every asset scouring Iran for those launchers. Satellite, UASs, you name it. If we find them, expect all or part of your mission to be diverted."

He paused and allowed his gaze to wander over the men and women packed into the compartment.

"Given the situation on the ground, we're modifying weapons loads of the strikers to carry an extra JDAM."

Kate grimaced. Carrying an extra bomb would take up a weapons station reserved for an AMRAAM, leaving her only one. Still, she would have her two trusty AIM-9Xs for close-in work, should something get past the Chiefs, who would be providing air cover for the strikers.

"We cannot allow World War Three to begin," Somers continued. "If we take out Iran's remaining nuclear capability, the politicians will be scrambling over themselves to back down. If we don't . . ." He left the sentence unfinished. "Therefore, it is imperative we find and destroy the remaining launchers. No risk or cost is too great."

His eyes landed on Trojan's. "Do I make myself clear?" His carefully enunciated words sounded like gunshots echoing in a morgue.

Trojan nodded his understanding.

Somers drew himself up. "You brief in ten minutes. We'll make sure you get word if anything changes. Be flexible and don't necessarily expect to fly the mission you're fragged for."

As she rose to her feet, Kate fought back her growing sense of foreboding. Flexibility might be one of the keys to airpower, but winging it like this raised the risk exponentially.

Chapter 43

May 12th, 1864
Near Spottsylvania Courthouse, Virginia

Merlyn looked up in confusion at Saunders' dark form silhouetted against the lowering afternoon sky. The ringing in his ears reduced the sound of the battle raging all around them to a dull roar. Saunders' face wore a look of panic. He shook Merlyn's shoulder. "General, are you all right?"

Details began to come into focus. Saunders' kepi was gone. His face, already blackened with powder, was smudged with dirt. His hair was wild. Blood dripped slowly from a cut on his jaw. More blood covered his uniform.

"General, can you hear me? Are you all right?"

Merlyn stared at him in confusion. Why on earth was he asking that? He felt the grit of dirt in his mouth and turned his head to spit. A flare of pain racked him from head to toe.

He clenched his teeth and slowly, experimentally moved his right arm. It worked. He tried the other. It worked too. There were more shapes around him, more urgent subdued voices.

"General." Saunders' face bent lower until their foreheads almost touched. "Can you hear me?" He enunciated the words slowly. Merlyn felt a drop of something wet hit his chin. Then more drops. The clouds were beginning to let loose again.

"What happened?" Somebody elbowed his way through the press of crowding men. George. He dropped to his knees beside Saunders.

"General, how badly are you hurt?"

Merlyn tried to bring his face into focus, confusion still clouding his mind, the infernal ringing in his ears dulling George's words.

"A shell exploded right next to us," Saunders replied. "His leg looks bad. There are other wounds. I can't tell how serious."

"Major, you're covered in blood as well," George exclaimed.

"The blood's not mine," Saunders replied grimly. "The men next to us absorbed most of the blast."

Merlyn tried to follow the exchange, make sense of the words. He moved his left leg, gingerly rotating the foot. It moved. He tried the right, and white-hot pain seared through his body. He stifled the scream that rose in throat and gasped for breath.

Gradually, his surroundings came into focus. A pile of mud and debris. Logs strewn like toothpicks. A shattered tree. A dead horse nearby. Another just beyond it. Bodies, both blue-clad and gray piled all around him. His men in line firing doggedly through the haze of smoke that clung to every contour of the ground. The rain intensified, blurring what lay beyond in a sheet of gray.

His mind began to clear. "Major, help me to my feet." He grasped at Saunders' uniform.

George pushed him back. "No, general. You're not going anywhere. Your leg."

"Help me to my feet." Merlyn gasped the words through clenched teeth as another wave of pain racked him, collapsing his vision down to a small tunnel of light.

He gathered the cloth of George's jacket into his fist and tried to haul himself upward. This time the pain was worse, and he fell back, tasting the sharp, metallic tang of blood in his mouth from where he had bitten through his lip.

"You men, take him to the rear. Get him to Captain McElroy. Let no other surgeon touch him." George barked the words.

Merlyn grappled for George's jacket again, found purchase, and pulled the younger man to him. There was a roaring in his ears that was not the sound of battle, and his vision was tinged with red.

"Take charge, George." His mouth had trouble forming the words. "Continue the attack. Don't let the men falter."

The roaring was louder. His vision gone now. A bemused thought flashed through his mind. *Lord, I thought it was supposed to be*

Cold Harbor, not here. The raindrops on his face were like ice as rough hands rolled him onto a blanket and hoisted him in another sheet of white-hot pain. And then there was nothing.

***

May 20th, 1864
Near Spottsylvania Courthouse, Virginia

"Get me a crutch, George," Merlyn demanded.

"But, Merlyn," George protested. "You are in no shape to be moved. You must stay here with the other wounded and rest."

He swept his arm wide, encompassing the church that had been converted into a makeshift hospital. All around them, men lay on rows of cots. Some groaning with pain. Others lying quietly. Orderlies flitted among them. McElroy stood nearby, tending a soldier whose arm was gone.

"George," Merlyn said, putting an edge into his voice. "You told me the army is moving south to get between Lee and Richmond. I am moving with it. I am not leaving my command."

A look of confusion mixed with concern crossed George's face. "Merlyn, you can't be serious. You're badly wounded. You lost a lot of blood. Your leg is broken. McElroy was barely able to save it. You cannot march or ride."

Merlyn hoisted himself on one elbow. Gritting his teeth against the pain, with a supreme effort of will, he swung his legs around until he was sitting on the side of the cot. His head whirled dangerously, and he lowered it to his knees.

When the spinning subsided, he raised it again and took a ragged breath to steady himself. He looked down at his splinted leg. The bandage above his knee was red where blood had soaked through.

"Merlyn, you made my point. You're in no shape to be moved."

"If I can't walk and I can't ride, then I'll ride in one of the wagons. Better yet, commandeer me a carriage."

George opened his mouth to protest again, then closed it firmly. McElroy, white apron spotted with blood, hurried over. His face was gray with fatigue, his eyes rimmed red.

"General, what are you doing? Please get back in bed." There was urgency in the surgeon's voice. "You are too badly hurt. You'll open your wound."

"Both of you, listen to me." Merlyn tried to keep his voice calm against the panic rising within him. "I heal fast. I must go south with the army. I must be with my men."

The unhappy look on George's face deepened. "General, please rest. Trust me. Your men will be in good hands until you return. I will not do anything you would not do."

Merlyn felt desperation rising inside him. "George, this is not about you. I have every confidence in your leadership. Please understand, I must go with you."

A thought danced tantalizingly in his mind, seductive in its allure. *How easy it would be to stay here among the wounded. Let your worries and responsibilities go. Avoid the slaughter that is soon to come.*

No. Remember why you're here. You must see this through. You must find a way to be there. No matter the danger, you must be at Cold Harbor and try to keep George alive.

How are you going to do that if you can't even walk? his mind argued back.

You have no choice. Find a way. You must do it.

"George, I'm serious. Get me a crutch. Help me out of here." Merlyn kept his voice calm, steady, not allowing it to communicate his inner turmoil. He fixed George's blue eyes in a determined stare.

George met his gaze for a long moment then dropped his eyes. He turned to McElroy. "Doctor," he said, his voice resigned. "Do as the general says. Find him a crutch."

Chapter 44

Kate checked Spud's position. He was exactly where he should be, two miles out, line abreast. Without looking back, she knew Bags and Nemo were similarly spaced, two miles behind her. Her division, Buick 11, sped north in a mutually supporting, offset box formation, her second division a few miles back. Ahead of her, Trojan's divisions, Dodge 11 and 31 led the way toward the target area. Miles in front of them, Growlers and offensive counter-air sweepers, Packard 11 and Chevy 11 respectively, spread out in a wall of Super Hornets.

Kate dug deep inside, trying to find the surge of exhilaration she would have expected to feel being part of an air flotilla heading into combat, dozens of pilots flying one of the most sophisticated aircraft in the world, loaded for bear. But the sensation of invincibility she would normally have felt was gone, blown away by CAG's words.

The SAM rings on her MPCD were nowhere near as plentiful as they were on the first night of the war, testimony to the hard work done by those performing the suppression of enemy air defenses mission. Still, she kept an anxious eye on her RWR. Any number of highly lethal threats were still out there.

And of course, there were enemy fighters. While the Iranian Air Force no longer flew, the Russians still did, but they had modified their tactics as well. They no longer challenged the stealthy Raptors head-on, but relied on hit-and-run tactics, trying to get a pair of fighters in among the less stealthy F-16s and F-18s to disrupt an attack and earn a quick kill.

Kate checked her map. The target area was well north, twenty minutes flying time away. She grimaced and felt her stomach tighten as she spotted data link tracks appearing at the edge of her display. Russian fighters were airborne and the BVR dance of death would be beginning soon.

The radio came to life. "Buick 11, this is Centurion. Stand by for a CENTCOM time-sensitive tasking order."

Her stomach did a barrel roll. Centurion was the call sign of the air operations center in Qatar. CAG had anticipated correctly. All their careful planning had just gone out the window.

"Buick 11, ready to copy," Kate replied, while pulling a pen from the shoulder pocket of her flight suit.

"Buick 11 and 12 are retasked to the following high-priority target." Centurion followed with a string of numbers—the target coordinates. She jotted down the information on her kneeboard, a feeling of dread twisting at her insides. Only a serious threat warranted breaking the strike package's mutual support. Had one of the launchers been located?

"Target is entrance to a tunnel. Two JDAMs into the tunnel at a shallow release angle. Remaining ordnance is to be expended on support vehicles near the tunnel. Keep one JDAM each in reserve."

"Buick copies all."

"Buick 11, transmitting target information to you now," Centurion concluded.

"Roger, receiving," Kate replied. A full target portfolio could be sent in a matter of seconds via data link, a miracle of modern technology a pilot could only have dreamt of a few years earlier.

Now would come the helmet fire and map case explosion as she got out her maps and planned for her new mission literally on the fly. The target coordinates were well to the east and north of their original target. Rough calculations showed that she would have enough fuel for a brief loiter in the new target area and be able to make it back to Dubai on fumes, should they not be able to hit a tanker on egress.

She could not recall any threats in that area, but she and Spud would be significantly closer to the border with Turkmenistan and to the Russian bases there if the Russians wanted to come and play. It would be best that they not go alone; no point in making themselves easy pickings.

Trojan had come to a similar conclusion. "Packard 11, Chevy 11, you copy Centurion's tasking?"

"Packard 11, Ay-firm." The Growler lead's voice came over the air as a relaxed drawl.

"Chevy 11, Affirmative," was the air-to-air lead's clipped reply.

"Detach a section each to escort Buick."

Two zippers, double clicks of the mic button were the only response. Message received and understood. They would work out the details on their squadron-discreet frequencies.

"Buick 11, you're cleared off at your discretion."

Kate looked at her map and its hastily sketched route. "We'll push in five mikes."

The plan, such as it was, was put together, and she began to relax a little. She wiggled her toes to keep the blood flowing. For the dozenth time, she wished she had not been so quick to have Spud fly as her wingman. Instead of a nugget, she needed someone steady, reliable, experienced. Someone like Morgan. Still, it was done. Too late to change it.

She scanned the information Centurion had sent her, then brought up a picture of the target area. The tunnel lay in a valley surrounded by high hills. A narrow road wound toward it. Vehicles dotted a small, flat area outside.

Because of the contours of the valley, their attack would have to be on a narrow axis heading southeast. She scanned the picture for defenses but saw nothing. That did not mean they were not there. At a minimum, there would be MANPADs, SA-7, or SA-14 shoulder-fired missiles, and AAA. Her and Spud's attack profile would, of necessity, bring them down into their range, which in and of itself was dangerous enough, but if any of the newer, highly lethal SAMs were present it would up the ante exponentially.

She checked her map. Time to go her own way. "Dodge, Buick 11 pushing."

A zipper was the only reply.

She dipped her wing and turned twenty degrees to the right, the easternmost Packards and Chevys likewise detaching themselves from the mass of aircraft flowing northwest. Her smaller strike package was now on its own. As she watched her distance build from the mutual support of the larger formation they had just left, she felt very vulnerable and very alone.

Data link showed the hostile tracks she had noted earlier crossing the border into Iran. The number was indeterminate, but definitely multiples. The Chevys were going to have their hands full. She wished the Air Force F-22s had been fragged to sweep through the navy area of operations today, but the CENTCOM planners had believed they were needed in greater concentration to the west. Their stealth and BVR capabilities would have come in handy right about now.

Twenty minutes to go. A lot could happen in that time. Kate scanned her displays and instruments. All good. Fuel a little skosh, but okay. Head on a swivel, she kept scanning. Spud's six—clear. Her six—clear. Her escorts were several miles out in front, too far to see, but twelve was clear, nobody rolling out in between the formations. Back into the cockpit—radar clear.

Data link showed the hostiles inexorably marching down the display, but unless they turned, they would pass dozens of miles to the east of her small formation. If she did nothing, they could end up blocking her egress route. The Chevys saw it too and peeled off to push the adversaries away.

As Kate's small formation sped north, the featureless tan desert started to give way to low hills speckled with green.

Well to the west, Trojan's strike package entered its target area. The radio came alive. A break call followed by a Fox 3. Somebody being targeted and somebody shooting. A Mayday call as somebody was hit. A garbled call, "Defending SA-6."

She forced it out of her mind and continued her disciplined visual and radar search.

Forty miles. Five minutes to go. Time to find the target area on the ATFLIR. It showed hills that matched the profile of the image that had been sent to her. The tunnel mouth was hidden, wouldn't be visible until she was heading down the valley directly toward it.

Kate looped north around the target area, positioning herself for a quick run up the valley. The Growlers preceded them and set up a loose orbit. She checked the Chevys; they were far to the east, stiff-arming the Russian fighters. Good. One less thing to worry about.

What was in the tunnel? CAG's words replayed themselves in her mind. *It is imperative we find and destroy the remaining launchers. No risk or cost is too great.* Her jaw muscles tightened and her feet tingled. Were she and Spud winging their way into a death trap?

"Packard 33, Magnum." Her eyes skewed to their escort's location and saw nothing but a heavy trail of smoke. Too far away to see anything more.

Packard 33 came back on the radio a few seconds later. "Buick 11, orbit north of the target area. We have a little situation we need to take care of. There's an SA-15 on the ridgeline just east of the target giving us a little difficulty." The pilot's voice was casual, relaxed, his tone as matter of fact as if he were commenting on the weather.

Kate quickly pulled what she knew about the SA-15 out of her memory. Short-range air defense system. Medium altitude. Anti-missile capability. Highly lethal. Probably capable of knocking down a JDAM gliding toward the target. It was going to be tough to get past it. Her mouth, already dry, now seemed as if it had cotton wool in it, sucking up every drop of moisture.

She started a wide turn to preserve distance from the target and tried to imagine what was happening out there beyond her visual range.

"Magnum." The voice was Packard 33's.

"34, Magnum."

The two Growlers were undoubtedly attacking from different axes, complicating the radar solution of the missile operator.

"Packard 33, break right." Packard 34's call was urgent, directive. "Second launcher two miles south."

Kate held her breath. Things were getting ugly fast.

"Packard 33, Slapshot 150." The call was immediately followed by a terse "33's hit."

There were a few seconds of silence. Kate wanted to jump onto the radio to find out what was happening, but the last thing a pilot dealing with an emergency needed was an extraneous radio call to answer.

"Packard 33, you're passing through ten thousand, eject." Packard 34's voice was edged with panic.

"Negative. I've got this," was the clipped reply.

The two transmissions told Kate exactly what was happening. Packard 33's jet was out of control and had just passed through minimum ejection altitude. The pilot was going to try to hang on and save the jet rather than stepping over the side. That decision normally did not end well.

This time it did. A couple of seconds later Packard 33 transmitted, "33's missing part of our right wing. The jet's controllable. Bugging out south. 34, stay and help the Buicks."

"34, roger. Buick 11, 34's Winchester but we'll give you all the trons we've got. Let us know when you're starting your attack run."

Packard flight had expended all their HARMs. Not good. She and Spud would be relying solely on their own and Packard 34's jamming capabilities to keep the deadly SA-15s busy. She checked her MPCD and quickly oriented herself. "Buick, wilco. Pushing in twenty seconds."

Kate scanned the fuel gauge—only a few hundred pounds above bingo. Data link showed Spud's fuel to be slightly lower. She prayed it would be enough.

Thinking SA-15, she checked again to ensure her towed decoy was deployed and transmitted. "Spud, check dog."

Spud zippered in response.

"Buick's starting target run now." Her heart racing, Kate started a gradual descent. To get bombs into the mouth of the tunnel, she was going to have to plan on a shallow release angle. That was going to bring her down into AAA range. What truly worried her was the possibility of yet another, untargeted SA-15 in the area. She and Spud were coming down into the heart of its envelope. She pushed the thought out of her mind. *Focus, Kate,* she ordered herself and refined the targeting cursor a final time. Two JDAMS were going right into the mouth of the tunnel, just as Centurion had ordered. *Let's get this done and get out of here.*

As Kate dropped into the valley, the target came into view on her display. She refined the crosshairs onto the tunnel's dark opening and switched to infrared. Her screen blossomed. Something inside was generating heat. Back to optical. The target once more stood out like a crisp black-and-white photo. There was plenty of activity around it—trucks, men on the ground.

She followed the narrow valley with gentle dips of her wings. Brown hillsides flashed by in a blur. Refine aimpoint. Check Spud.

Suddenly the ground in front of her erupted with angry red flashes and streams of light. AAA. Normally she would jink to provide an unpredictable flight path and complicate the firing solution of the gunners, but she was on her final attack heading. *Hold it steady.* A fire hose of green tracer curved lazily toward her. Puffs of smoke filled with angry red detonated close to her aircraft. Heavy, aimed fire, she recognized. Symbology confirmed multiple AAA radars tracking her. She fought the almost overwhelming urge to move the jet, to get out of there, flee to safety, but instead forced herself to concentrate on her aimpoint.

Kate tensed for the chirping of the RWR that would indicate she had been targeted by an SA-15, but it remained mercifully silent. She concentrated on the mouth of the tunnel. AAA continued its barrage all around her, tongues of green fire snaking up off the ground.

She was approaching release range. Parameters good; aimpoint good. Her thumb hovering above the pickle button twitched slightly, longing for the mental command to fire. "Buick 11, Centurion. Abort, abort, abort. Snap east immediately. Launcher in the open."

Kate cursed as the panicked call interrupted her concentration. Operating as if time stood still, she yanked the stick to the right and dove for the ground, just as her RWR shrilled and the number 15 appeared on her display. "Buick 12, abort," she directed, stepping on Centurion's next transmission, while pumping out a salvo of chaff and flares.

Ground rushed by as she ducked into the neighboring valley and hugged a ridgeline she hoped would shield her from the missiles guarding the tunnel. The 15 was gone, as was the AAA. Good. She checked her DDI. Spud trailed her by a couple of miles.

She had a moment of breathing room. "Centurion, say again."

The radio remained silent. She cursed under her breath. She was below radio coverage. Every second that ticked by was time wasted. Gritting her teeth, she yanked the stick back and zoomed into a climb. By now she should have put enough distance between her and the short-range SA-15s guarding the tunnel.

"Centurion, Buick 11." Nothing.

Panic started to constrict her throat as she visualized a missile, erect on its launcher, heat blossoming around its base. "Centurion, Buick 11."

"Roger, Buick 11, Centurion. Did you copy my last?"

"Negative."

"New target bearing one zero five for thirty. Missile launcher deep in a valley. Target coordinates coming at you. Expedite. That missile cannot launch."

Kate felt a grim sense of determination settling over her as she transmitted a simple "Roger."

"Buick, belay that order." A new voice came on the radio, gravelly, older. "The tunnel is still a priority target. Split your flight. One aircraft on the launcher, one aircraft on the tunnel. We have other assets coming to help you, but they won't be there for another twenty minutes or so. We don't have that much time. We need both targets destroyed immediately. Do you understand?"

"Buick, roger," Kate snapped, feeling as if she would break under the pressure. She forced back an uncharitable and profane thought and replaced it with, *They must really be panicking at CENTCOM for them to put Spud and me in such an impossible situation. They've probably just killed us both, and now WWIII is going to start anyway.*

"Buick 12," she transmitted, trying to keep her voice calm. "Go back and hit the tunnel. Transmitting you my aimpoint." She sent the target coordinates via data link as she spoke. "Stay low and terrain mask your way in. Pop up at the last minute to acquire the target. Salvo two JDAMs into the mouth of the tunnel. Keep one for the launcher in case I don't make it. Got it?"

"Got it," was Spud's terse reply.

She glanced down at the target information now appearing on her display. Thirty miles. Three and a half minutes flying time. A lifetime. And nowhere near enough time to put together an attack that had a ghost of a chance of succeeding.

She glanced at Spud's data link symbol turning away from her. There was one more thing to do to help him. "Packard, stay and cover him."

"Lord, be with them both," she whispered. It was probably the most heartfelt prayer Kate had ever uttered in her life. *And with me,* she amended, equally heartfelt.

Chapter 45

"General, your brigade will march out onto that field tomorrow morning with or without you." General Munro drew himself up to full height, his eyes level with Merlyn's, who was standing rigidly at attention before him. Sweat beaded the division commander's forehead and his upper lip trembled with fury. "If you are too injured to lead your men, then Colonel Maxwell can do it. I will brook no further argument. General Meade has ordered the assault and this division will comply. Do I make myself perfectly clear?"

"Yes, sir. You do." Merlyn's vision swam red with anger. He could see what was coming all too clearly. At dawn, three corps of the Army of the Potomac would march out across unscouted terrain against Lee's entire army, which had been given twenty-four hours to prepare for the Union assault. Merlyn knew they had made every moment count.

"If I cannot walk tomorrow, I will ride. I will do my duty, as will my men. You can count on it." He made no attempt to disguise the bitterness in his voice.

The division commander's face did not soften. His tone was harsh. "I expect you to push against the enemy with every ounce of tenacity you have. If I even begin to suspect you are shirking your duty, there will be serious consequences."

Merlyn stared into flinty blue eyes. "I have never shirked my duty, sir." He spit the words. "Permission to see to my men, sir?"

Munro returned the salute, his face a granite mask. "Dismissed."

Adding to Merlyn's fury was his knowledge that his attempt to inject sanity into what was clearly a wrongheaded decision to attack had been perceived as cowardice. Was Munro blind to what was coming, or had he tried to head it off, only to be summarily dismissed as Merlyn had been?

Heart breaking, he allowed Saunders to help him up onto Midnight. The splint on his leg was gone, but it was still too stiff for him to mount unassisted.

He rode back to his men. Rather than preparing for battle, probing the enemy positions, the army had been ordered to make camp, while less than a mile away the enemy was feverishly digging trenches and erecting fortifications.

His mind focused laser like on a single question: What do you do when you know you have only a few hours left on this earth? The question distilled life down to remarkable simplicity. The answer was easy: Get right with God. Say goodbye to those you love. At this point, nothing else mattered.

Earlier that evening, without specifically saying the words, he'd said goodbye to his men, who had served him so faithfully. He did not need to tell them what was coming. They knew. Already they were sitting by their campfires, sewing their names into their uniforms so their bodies would not go unrecognized.

Sitting at his desk, Merlyn opened his journal for the last time, and for the last time, propped up his drawing of Kate by the lantern. He opened his watch. An hour before George was due to come. An hour to frame his final thoughts to the woman he loved more than life itself. He hoped the letter would be enough, but no mere words on paper could capture the depth of emotion burning in his heart—hope, despair, grief, fear. Wincing at the inadequacy of his words, he began to write.

June 2ⁿᵈ, 1864

My Dearest Love:

Goodbyes are always difficult, especially for people who love each other as much as we do. However, let us not think of this letter as goodbye, but rather a means of saying things that need to be said, just in case.

I cannot begin to tell you how proud I am of you and how blessed I have been to know you. Every hour of every day since we have been parted, I have thought of you, missed you, longed to hold you in my arms again. I have hardly dared to think of marriage, of a life together, but from the day we parted, that is all I have wanted. I want to live life to the full, with you by my side and enter the next big adventure God has for us. I pray with all my heart he allows it.

I am writing you on the eve of battle. I don't know what God has in store for me, for us, but I earnestly hope he allows me to live, to come home to your loving arms. And if that is not to be, then know that I go into eternity a better man for having loved you and having been loved by you.

Just as I was sent to you to train you, to prepare you for the job you had to do, I was sent to mentor and train another person—a man named George Maxwell. He has become a friend who is almost as dear to me as you.

I am entrusting this volume to him. I pray it will make its way to you somehow. If I am not there to meet you when you come back from deployment, what is written here will make all things clear to you.

Your family should have a picture of George. Look carefully at the man in the picture with him.

I must close now. I love you with all my heart.

Morgan "Merlyn" Michaelson

George would be here soon. He found a sheet of paper and hurriedly began to write instructions. When he was done, he bundled up his journal. He had a brief argument with himself about adding the daguerreotype George had given him but decided against it and put it instead in his pocket. He wrapped the journal in oilcloth and tied the parcel with a length of twine. He sealed his instructions inside another envelope and prayed the successive generations of Maxwells and Trenarys would honor the "do not open until" date he had printed in bold letters on the envelope. He had given it a lot of thought and hoped he had it right.

As he was folding the letter, Saunders cleared his throat outside the tent. "Yes, major, what is it?"

Saunders pushed aside the tent flap. "Sir, Colonel Maxwell is here to see you."

George strode into the tent, his face grim. Eschewing a greeting, Merlyn waved him to a camp stool. "Hold a moment, will you, George?"

Merlyn wrote George's name on an envelope, stuffed the second letter and instructions inside, and handed it and the parcel to him. "Hang onto this. Please keep it with your journal. Open your letter when you get home after the war. There are instructions for what to do with the parcel. I beg your solemn promise to do exactly what they say. There is a lot at stake."

George started to protest, but Merlyn held up his hand. "We all know what's going to happen tomorrow. I believe God has been preparing me for this. My time has come, and he is calling me home."

George cut in. "Merlyn, I wish you would reconsider. It's suicide for you to ride that horse onto that field tomorrow. I can take the brigade. Dutchy can handle our New Yorkers. Besides, what makes you think I will fare better than you?"

"Trust me, George. I don't know how he will do it, but I have faith that God is going to see you through this. Whatever you do, do not ride tomorrow, and march close to your men, not out in front of them."

George drew in a breath to protest. Merlyn raised a hand to cut him off.

"George, this is not about pride. A whole lot of men are going to die needlessly. You don't need to be among them. When the time comes and the attack falters, lie down. Find cover. Get your men down. Keep them alive and get them off that field."

Merlyn drew a deep breath. It was time to utter the words that needed to be spoken. "George, have you made peace with God? If the worst happens, are you prepared to stand before him? Can you say that Jesus' blood covers your sins and that the Holy Spirit lives in your heart?"

He stared at George intently, hoping that the answers to his questions would be yes. A knot of disappointment formed in his stomach as George dropped his eyes and shook his head.

"Merlyn," he said softly. "I wish I could believe what you have been telling me these past two years, but the evidence of my eyes wars against the call in my heart. I cannot do it. I do not wish to disappoint you, but I cannot surrender to a God who allows such evil to happen in the world."

Merlyn hauled himself to his feet and braced himself against his desk. "I will pray for you until I draw my last breath. God has a hold on your life. He is not going to let you go. But it is late; we must say goodbye."

George stared at him, stricken. Merlyn embraced him. The younger man's body felt thin, bony, frail, his arms hanging limply at his sides.

Merlyn stepped back, kept his hands on his shoulders. "Goodbye, my friend. It has been an honor and a privilege knowing you. God bless and keep you." He tried to smile through the tears welling in his eyes.

George bit his lip just as Merlyn had seen Kate do a hundred times before. Wordlessly, tears streaming down his face, he left Merlyn alone in the flickering lamplight.

Chapter 46

As Kate sped eastward, she called up the target information on her DDI. Just as Centurion had said, the launcher was in a deep valley surrounded by high peaks. What was worse, the valley curved, taking away any possibility of a straight run-in. A grainy photo showed a dirt road, what was clearly a launcher with missile in horizontal transport position, and a handful of support vehicles.

She could not assume the launcher was undefended. The tunnel had been surrounded by AAA and at least a couple of SA-15s. She could expect no less here. There was nothing good about this situation. She gritted her teeth in frustration. Centurion should have diverted the whole strike to take out these threats.

She took a deep breath as she formulated her plan. No sense driving straight into the valley as she and Spud had done earlier with the tunnel. That would be suicide. Just as she had instructed Spud, she would come in hugging the earth in an adjacent valley, pull up briefly to acquire the target, release two JDAMs, and dive for the relative safety of the ground, which she knew was not really safety at all.

A quick glance at the fuel gauge gave Kate a momentary twinge of unease. Her speed was rapidly eating into her margin of safety. She'd already spent too much time in the target area and would be on fumes when she hit the egress tanker.

She took another deep breath and felt a sense of calm descending on her. She could do this. She had to do this. If she failed . . . She forced the thought from her mind. She could not fail. Nor could Spud. Too much was at stake.

Seconds stretched out like hours as Kate made her run up the long valley next to the one in which the launcher sat. Twisting and turning, hugging the ground, she followed the contours of the terrain. Rocks sped past her wingtip as she took quick glances at the map to gauge her pull-up point. She wiggled her toes and tried to steady her breathing.

"Buick 12, bombs away." Spud's voice over the radio sounded tense, strained.

Action point. Kate willed him to safety as she pulled back on the stick. *God, I hope this works.* The ridge she was climbing would shield her for a few moments longer. But then she would pop up into the open, unmasked, while she acquired the target, designated it, released her weapons, and dove for safety. She'd only be exposed for a handful of seconds, but those seconds were an eon in digital time, as automated sensors found, tracked, and launched at her.

She popped up from behind the ridgeline and frantically began scanning the valley floor for her target. She relaxed slightly as she found a cluster of tan vehicles against a tan landscape. She rolled inverted, pulling her nose down as she slewed the ATFLIR to the launcher in the middle of the cluster. The missile was vertical. Not good.

AAA erupted all around her. A ping sounded close to her canopy, a *thock* farther away, like somebody had hit a sheet of titanium with a sledgehammer. She was hit! Her heart jolted. No time to assess the damage. She just hoped her jet would hold together long enough for her to release weapons.

She centered the aiming crosshairs on the missile launcher. Heat was flaring on the IR display. Her RWR screamed at her, but she didn't take the time to assess which threat was targeting her. All she needed was a second, maybe two, to get her bombs off, then she could be blown out of the sky. She'd have done her job.

She locked the launcher, mashed and held the pickle button.

"Buick 11, bombs away." She waited for the twin *thunks* indicating bomb release, rolled violently to the right, buried the stick in her lap, and dove for the ground, while at the same time dispensing a salvo of chaff and flares.

More tracers flashed past her canopy. "Buick 11, defending southwest, mud." Her heart pounding, she leveled out below 100 feet and pulled hard to the left. Shooting a downward glance, she saw a blur of faces looking up at her. She reversed her turn, making for the hills and rising up at the south side of the valley. They would be her safe haven from the maelstrom of fire trying to knock her out of the sky. Just a short distance and a lifetime to go. More AAA streamed up in front of her nose. She pulled obliquely up to the left to avoid it and then down to the right. More trucks, more tracer. The hills seemed a little closer.

Her RWR continued to shrill loudly, a pair of "15s" now highlighted on the display. Definitely not good. She dispensed chaff and flares and dropped lower until it seemed the vehicles were almost level with her canopy. Another hard turn and then the hills were right in front of her. She pulled up, hugging the contours of the rapidly rising terrain. The tracer was gone, but a single "15" remained. Rocks sped by in a tan blur. She turned again and dispensed more chaff to create problems for an incoming missile. The crest of the hill was before her, so she rolled inverted to lead the pull down to the back side and not highlight her jet against the sky. Rocks whizzed past less than fifty feet from the top of the canopy.

Don't do the gunners' job by smacking into one. She eased back on the stick. Then she was clear of the crest and pointing downhill. She rolled wings level and pointed down the next valley. The "15" was gone and so was the AAA. She allowed herself to breathe once more.

Kate quickly scanned her instruments. No signs of leaks or system failures. Craning her neck, she gave her jet a once-over. Nothing on the left side. Nothing on the right. She cycled her flight controls. The jet responded normally. She checked the decoy. It was gone. She deployed another.

311

Kate's breath caught in her throat as she spotted the hole in the canopy by her right shoulder. That had been close, but no point in dwelling on it. She was alive and her jet was still flying.

She turned southward and started a climb to the southwest, out of range of the missiles guarding the valley. She only hoped her bombs had hit before the missile had a chance to launch. She zoomed her ATFLIR into the valley and saw only a large crater and twisted metal. But what about the missile?

"Centurion, Buick 11," she transmitted, unable to dispel the feeling of dread causing her chest to tighten.

"Go ahead 11." It was the older voice, probably the flag officer running the air operations center.

"Target destroyed. Say status of missile."

"Negative launch. I repeat, negative launch."

The tension gripping her loosened slightly. Now what about the remaining jets in her charge? Had Spud survived? She wanted to shout her jubilation as she spotted his and his guardian Growler's data link tracks west of her, heading in her direction.

"Buick 12, status?"

"Two bombs into the mouth, as ordered." His voice conveyed quiet satisfaction.

"Are you hit?"

"Negative."

"Centurion, Buicks are one bomb each remaining, approaching bingo, standing by orders."

"Stand by Buick. Assessing targets now."

Moments stretched by as Centurion remained silent. Kate wondered idly which of the technologies available to the staff of the air operations center they were using. Satellite? Drone? Something new?

The radio came to life, causing her to flinch. "Buick 11, Centurion. Well done. Cleared RTB."

It was time for Kate to rebuild her situational awareness. She spotted Packard 33 on her radar and data link about fifty miles ahead of them. Well off to the east, the Chevys had pushed their adversaries north and had disengaged southward.

Kate's breathing began to steady as her muscles slowly uncoiled. Bombs delivered. Target destroyed. She had a few hundred pounds of gas as a safety margin and still had her air-to-air ordnance. She was alive and dangerous.

"Packard 34, cleared to rejoin 33. Buicks will cover your egress."

Two mic clicks were the only response. Nothing else needed to be said. They were still deep in enemy territory with a long way to go until the relative safety of the gulf.

Chapter 47

For the first time since his earliest days on the road, Merlyn felt truly afraid. Fear penetrated his gut, froze his heart, and clawed at his throat, threatening to paralyze him. It was not that he was afraid of dying. His faith in Jesus was unshakeable. He had absolute certainty about what would come after he breathed his final breath.

It was what the morning would bring that so filled his heart with dread. He pictured the annihilation of his regiments, the mountains of bodies, the thousands of young men cut down in their prime, and all for nothing—a futile charge against an army that had been given the gift of time to receive it. Would George be one of those left to rot in a shallow grave?

A parallel fear rose inside him, threatening to overwhelm the first. Kate. If George died on the battlefield, would she no longer exist? If somehow she did, how could the parcel make its way to her? She would never have closure, would live her life thinking of Merlyn as nothing more than a memory from a pleasant dream. The thought tore his heart.

Despite the numbing fatigue of the past month, a restless energy burned within him. Unable to sit still, he grabbed his crutch and began slowly and painfully to pace the floor of his tent. Four shuffling steps brought him against the canvas wall of the tent, turn. Another four steps. The opposite wall. Turn again. Four steps, turn. Sweat poured from his body. Four steps, turn. Four steps, turn.

Step by painful step he wrestled with his fear. When it came time to lead his men in the assault, he would be incapable. He would let them down. Many more would die because of it. That was unacceptable. He had to pull himself together.

When the pain in his thigh became too great, he spread a blanket on the ground and prostrated himself on it. Arms outstretched and feet together, he visualized himself lying at the foot of the cross before the savior, crucified for Merlyn and his sins. He emptied his mind and sought the presence of God. It was hard to find at first, given the turmoil in his heart, but as the clock ticked slowly toward midnight, a measure of calm welled up inside and his thoughts began to order themselves.

At last, he felt calm enough to pray. *Dear Lord, you say in your word that perfect love drives out fear. I give you my fear for the two people I love. You love them too and will keep them. They are in your hands. Keep them safe, bless them, and protect them. Turn George's heart to you and help him become a mighty man of faith. Kate loves you already. Help her grow in her faith.*

Peace began to flood over and through him. He felt himself in the presence of someone much greater than himself, kind and infinitely loving. No words flowed through his mind, but he felt a confidence he had long been lacking. God was in charge. George and Kate would be all right. He knew it, could have confidence in it, it would be so.

He felt a prompt deep in his heart. There was something else he needed to do.

Lord, Kate's your precious child and I love her with all my heart, but I release her to you. She's yours and you will provide the very best for her life.

As he formed the words in his mind, he felt as if a crushing weight had been lifted from him.

Lord, I also release to you all my desires for a future. Whether I live or die tomorrow, I surrender fully to you. If I die, I will be with you forever, and I am content. If I live, I will do whatever you call me to do. If you take me back to Kate, I will be overjoyed. If you take me to another assignment, I will be content. My life is yours and I do not want to live apart from you a moment longer. All my needs, all my desires are in your hands. I want your will for my life and not my own.

Peace continued to settle over him. The burden he carried was gone. His heart still ached to think of Kate, but she was the Lord's, not his. In time, the ache would heal. That is, if he lived through tomorrow.

Chapter 48

The sun beat down on Kate, the canopy of her jet concentrating heat like a greenhouse. Her flight suit was soaked but she hardly noticed the discomfort. She and Spud were on their way home. Besides the hole in her canopy, she had a golf ball–sized hole in her left aileron, a pair of holes in her right wing, and another hole in her right tail. Her jet was flyable, not leaking fuel, and no systems appeared to be damaged. That at least was a point in her favor.

As she climbed for a fuel-conserving altitude, she breathed a prayer of thanksgiving that the high bingo she had set gave them a margin of safety.

Far in front of them, Packard 33 limped his way toward home with Packard 34 in hot pursuit. Kate sent a silent prayer winging their way. The Chevys had pushed their adversaries well to the west and were now heading home. The fighters they had dueled with were northbound for their bases in Turkmenistan.

An idle thought flashed across her mind. This awful mission bore no resemblance to the easy victories of her dream TOPGUN missions. They had been clean, surgical, almost sterile. This had been confused and messy. *Morgan, how could you have possibly prepared me for this?* she mused.

Her RWR shrilled, shattering her reverie and causing her heart to miss a beat. Air threat, six o'clock close. She paddled off the limiter and snapped into a hard 9g turn to the left, praying her battered jet would stay controllable under the increased load. Straining to lift her arm against the g-forces, she punched off her external fuel tanks and remaining JDAM. "Buick 11, break left, spike six close." The words came out as a gasp as she forced them out against the crushing pressure compressing her chest.

Kate rolled out of the turn, putting the threat symbol at her nine o'clock, dispensed chaff, and stared down into the brown hills, trying hard to spot the incoming fighters. Where were they? They had to have snuck in low, terrain-masking through the mountains, otherwise AWACS would have called them out.

She spotted a flash and the corkscrew smoke trail of an air-to-air missile streaking up toward her out of the desert tan. Her heart lurched as she yanked hard on the stick while dispensing flares and pulling her throttles back. Energy bleeding off rapidly, her jet didn't have much to give. Its nose tracked infinitesimally across the horizon, giving the incoming missile a problem it could easily handle.

Kate paddled off another salvo of flares and braced for the inevitable explosion and the expanding pattern of shrapnel that would shred her jet, ignite its fuel, send it pitching out of control. Thoughts raced through her mind—Mom, Dad, Morgan. Joy. Regret.

The explosion didn't come. A fraction of a second before impact, the missile veered, passing well behind her, its seeker head driven off by the flares.

She saw a pair of tan-colored aircraft now, her eyes guided onto them by the missile's smoke trail. Flankers coming up at her, nose on, splitting, one going for her, the other for Spud.

"Buick 11, tally two Flankers, left nine low, splitting. Spud, keep your turn coming. Flares," she commanded.

Kate continued her turn, airspeed almost gone. Using her helmet-mounted sight, she snagged a radar lock on the Flanker pointed at her and thumbed back to select an AIM-9X. With no time to think or evaluate, she mashed the pickle button and observed the corkscrew trail of smoke leap out from her wingtip as a missile shot off its rail and bent hard toward her adversary. She slammed her throttles forward and followed it.

The smoke trail curled past the Flanker. The anticipated explosion and blossoming of fire didn't happen. Instead, her missile sped harmlessly past him. *Inside min range,* she thought while biting back a curse.

Kate pushed forward on the stick until she floated in her straps, trying to buy back a few knots of airspeed. *Man, that guy's big.* The Flanker flashed past her only a couple hundred feet away. Burners cooking, she yanked hard into him. A couple miles away, she spotted Spud defensive.

He'd turned right instead of left, handing his six o'clock to his adversary. It was about to cost him dearly. Her chest squeezed in panic as a missile came off his adversary's rail. "Spud, flares, keep your turn coming." She choked out the words, horror flooding her. Was she about to lose her wingman?

Spud's mistake, however, became his saving grace because it had opened the range between her and his adversary. Putting the reticle of the helmet-mounted sight over Spud's adversary, she locked, observed the firing solution, heard the proper tone, and mashed down the pickle button, sending an AIM-9X on its way. "Fox 2," she transmitted.

No time to watch her missile guide. Giving her full attention to her own adversary now, she continued her hard turn. The Flanker already had his nose on her but was too close for a shot. The little airspeed she had regained was already gone. *Can't keep this up. With those big motors of his and my heaters gone, he's going to own me. Need to take this into the phone booth, make it a close-in fight, pilot against pilot. Not a good place to be, though, if there are other hostiles in the area.*

She passed close aboard her adversary again, gauging the set of his wings, and reversed her turn to pull directly toward his high six o'clock. He took the bait, slowing rapidly, pulling hard back toward hers.

As they crossed again, Kate yanked her nose up, slowing forward motion. The Flanker pilot mirrored her move. Line abreast, noses pitched high, it was now a war of nerves. Who was going to run out of airspeed and fall off first? He had entered the fight faster and needed to bleed off energy, or risk squirting out front. She was slower. Could she keep her nose up long enough before her damaged jet stalled and fell out of the sky? Holding the stick back with every ounce of her strength, she willed her jet to keep flying.

She stared at her adversary a thousand feet off her right wing. He was sliding toward her, as she was sliding toward him, in a classic scissors maneuver. Sensing he was inching forward on her canopy, she maintained the back pressure on the stick. His forward motion increased. She was gaining the advantage.

She heard the roar of his engines as he passed under her nose and emerged on the other side, well out front now. With an infinitesimal wing dip, she turned back toward him.

Suddenly, the Flanker rolled inverted and pulled for the ground. *He's giving up!* Kate felt a surge of elation as she stomped hard on the rudder and pegged the stick to the side, rolling opposite and then pulling down hard, keeping her nose pointing well in front of his. *Keep pulling, let him fly up to the pipper.* As the Flanker's nose approached the aiming dot, she squeezed the trigger.

The Super Hornet's Vulcan cannon, capable of spitting out 6,000 rounds of twenty-millimeter semi–armor-piercing high-explosive incendiary per minute, held just over 400 rounds on board, which gave her about four seconds of gun. She held the trigger for two.

Flashes sparked just aft of her adversary's canopy. There was no explosion. That was Hollywood. Instead, fire rapidly engulfed the rear half of the Flanker as fuel tanks caught fire. It yawed right and a puff appeared at the front of the aircraft as the canopy came off and the ejection seat shot up and out.

Kate dove for the ground, burners cooking. She had to get her airspeed back, otherwise she was a strafe rag, an almost stationary target, waiting for her adversary's wingman to easily bag her. She tensed for an incoming missile or gun rounds as she strained her neck to clear her six. Nothing. Three and nine clear. Threat warning clear. She had her airspeed back. She pulled out of the dive and started searching for Spud.

A few miles away, she saw a column of smoke rising from the desert floor. Closer, a ball of fire plunged toward the ground. A parachute hung in the air behind her. Ivan had made it out.

"Buick 32, status." She checked data link before Spud could reply. He was southbound, five miles in front of her. The smoke had to be his adversary.

"Buick 32, blind, bugging out south." There was thinly disguised panic in his voice. "Right engine out. Partial hydraulics. Flight controls marginal."

"Copy. Keep south. I'll catch you."

Before she could work the problem, she needed to know what else was in the area that could threaten them. She called AWACS. "Darkstar, Buick 31, picture."

"Buick 31, Darkstar, closest hostiles BRAA zero three zero for fifty northbound."

Must be the ones Chevy was tangling with.

Only then did she become aware of the voice warning system urgently, repeatedly telling her, "Bingo Fuel." She checked the gauge and her stomach lurched. If her refueling system malfunctioned, she was going for a swim. She dialed the bug down to make the voice go away.

She checked Spud's fuel. It was a little higher than hers, but was he leaking fuel? Time to join and see what was going on with his jet.

Holes perforated the right rear of Spud's aircraft, making it look like Swiss cheese. A thin trail of smoke emanated from what remained of his right engine.

There was no sign of leaking fuel, but the Hornet's underside was red with leaking hydraulic fluid. Spud was going to have his hands full getting his bird home.

"Buick 31, Darkstar, hostiles BRAA zero three zero for seventy, turning southbound toward you."

She felt an icy tingle of fear. *What else could go wrong on this mission? Would this nightmare never end?*

Kate and Spud were operating at the extreme edge of their combat radius. The Flankers were well within theirs, giving them a comfortable fuel margin. Two questions burned in her mind. *How much afterburner had they used dueling with the Chevys? And how many and what kind of missiles did they have remaining?*

"Spud, push it up," she transmitted. They needed to preserve distance even if it meant sacrificing fuel.

She rapidly sifted through the variables. If the Flankers made a supersonic dash, they could quickly chase them down. If she and Spud tried to outrun their adversaries, they were going to run out of gas well within enemy territory. It was a no-win situation.

They had a few minutes until the Flankers could close the distance. Maybe their luck would hold and their adversaries would turn north. She watched their tracks anxiously, but they didn't turn. The distance was gradually closing. Fifty miles. Then forty.

Thirty miles. The coastline was hopelessly distant. It was time for the cavalry to come to the rescue, but there was no cavalry. It was just her and Spud in an empty, infinite sky.

There were no good options, only bad. She had one missile and a couple of seconds of gun left.

I'm sorry, Morgan, she thought as she snapped back toward their pursuers, determined to give Spud a chance to escape. She felt no fear, only a momentary feeling of regret. She quickly banished it and steeled herself to sell her life as dearly as she could.

Chapter 49

"It's time, Major. Help me up."

An orderly took Merlyn's weight as Saunders laced his fingers to provide a step for his good foot. Grunting at the pain that coursed through his leg, Merlyn grasped the pommel of his saddle and, half lying across Midnight's back, swung around until he was seated.

He sat upright for a moment, sweat beading his brow. The orderly maneuvered Merlyn's right foot into the stirrup as he felt for the left and settled his boot firmly.

He looked down at Saunders, who wore a distinctly unhappy look on his face. "General, you shouldn't do this. Stay behind, let one of the colonels take the brigade into battle. No one will think worse of you. At least let me ride with you."

Merlyn reached down and grasped his aide's shoulder. "No, captain. This is something I must do. You must walk. No sense making a bigger target for the rebels."

He swallowed against the lump growing in his throat. "Thank you for your faithfulness this past year. You have cared for me well, and I'm grateful. God bless and keep you."

Tears welled in Saunders' eyes as Merlyn turned away. *He knows as well as I do what's coming.*

To the east, the sky had not yet begun to lighten. The early morning fog prickled at his face, and he stifled a shiver as he moved Midnight toward the ranks of men standing quietly at ease, muskets by their sides.

Although he could not yet see him, Merlyn knew George was there at the front of his men to center right. Beyond him was O'Halloran and his Ohioans. To the left were the two Pennsylvania regiments, fading off into the darkness.

The fog seemed to reflect the attitude of the men. There was no false bravado. No exuberance. Just resignation and grim determination.

Somewhere in the darkness he knew Barings was walking the lines of the New Yorkers like a scarecrow, stopping here and there for anyone who wished to pray. *All the man needs is a scythe to complete the image.*

There was just enough light for him to see Wiltz standing near him at the far left of the New York line. Face white, eyes screwed shut, he mouthed something over and over again. Dawn must be approaching, for down the New York line he could now see the dim shapes of George and Dutchy gathered by the limply hanging colors.

Beside him, Saunders stood defiant. To his other side stood the color guard. He looked up and down his lines once more and breathed a silent prayer of protection over them.

He pulled out his watch, flipped open the case. It was time. His sword rang as he drew it from its scabbard and raised it high. A bugle sounded. *Father, into your hands I commit my spirit.* His lips moved as his mind formed the words. He straightened himself and let the sword drop as he spurred Midnight into a slow walk. They were off.

Midnight's hooves fell with dull thuds on the soft ground. Behind him he heard the shuffle of men and the clink of equipment. Someone coughed. There was no need to be stealthy. The rebels knew they were coming.

Seconds stretched out like hours as the Union line moved slowly forward. Every man knew what awaited them across the field. Merlyn could now see the green of the grass. Shapes were becoming apparent. A boulder here. A tree stump there. A flattened fence. A dip in the ground. His heart hammered painfully, and he bit his lip, anticipating the fury that would soon be unleashed on them.

A shot rang out and then a few more. Then nothing. The field was silent again, the fog muffling the tramping of 35,000 pairs of feet. *As soon as the skirmishers are back through their own lines, it begins.*

He didn't have long to wait. The fog blossomed red up and down the enemy lines as cannon opened fire, their sound muffled. Most of the shells passed overhead, but a few found their mark, blowing holes in his ranks. *Ranging shots. Then case, followed by canister as we get closer.*

More long moments stretched out. Someone in the Ohio line cursed and was quickly rebuked by a sergeant.

Lightning flashed in the fog again, this time brighter, a progressive ripple traveling from left to right. His eyes barely had time to register the sight before it was followed by booming thunder so loud it seemed as if the very sky were being ripped asunder. All around him men fell. Some individually, more in clumps, leaving ragged gaps in his lines.

Sergeants bellowed. The ranks closed and continued their inexorable trudge into the guns. He could hear musket fire now. Not volley fire but individual, the dug-in confederates firing as fast as they could load. There was the wet slap of bullet hitting flesh and one of the color guard went down. The rest did not falter, keeping pace with Midnight's slow walk.

The cannons fired a third time. He heard something roar past. All around him men fell, blown backward by the hot metal poured into them by the Confederate gunners. He shot a glance to his right and froze, icy claws of fear sinking into his insides. The center of the New York line was gone in its entirety. No Union flag. No regimental banner. No men left standing. Those of the New York line left untouched were sinking to the ground as if to become one with it, hiding behind the slightest scrap of cover. Beyond them, the surviving Ohioans did the same.

No. The word blossomed in his mind and trailed off in a silent scream.

"Down! Get down!" he yelled furiously at Saunders who was miraculously still standing, a dazed look on his face.

Merlyn turned to yell at the flag bearers to his right. "You too!"

"But, sir. The flag," the Sergeant expostulated, his face tight with fear.

"Forget the flag! Get down!" Merlyn bellowed, his mind automatically counting down the time until the next fusillade.

Merlyn did not wait to see if the man obeyed but spurred Midnight in the direction George had been.

His eyes were greeted by a scene of utter carnage. Men and pieces of men were strewn everywhere. The color guard lay together, a pool of red seeping into the soil. Before them, huddled on his side, Dutchy lay moaning. Beyond him, Merlyn saw a flash of orange against the green of grass. George. He lay motionless on his back, blood on his face, his kepi lying beside him. On his chest, a deepening stain, black against the blue of his sack coat.

Merlyn felt a rush of blind panic as he began to slide off Midnight's back. But at that moment, the world dissolved around him in an inferno of light and sound.

Chapter 50

K ate took inventory of her assets. A handful of flares, a few chaff bundles, one slammer, and a couple seconds of gun. Not enough. Not nearly enough. She had no expectation of repeating her success against the Flankers that had ambushed her and Spud as they fled the target area. Her only thought was to tie these two up long enough to allow Spud to escape.

Every muscle tensed, praying that her internal countermeasures suite would do its job against the missiles that had to be winging her way, Kate adjusted her flightpath just enough to keep the RWR symbology of the fighters targeting her exactly at her nine o'clock.

Eyes straining, she tried to dig them out of the haze that hung persistently over the desert floor.

She spotted them several miles away, mere dots a finger-width above horizon, the wingman staggered several thousand feet down his lead's wing line.

The seconds ticked down as the two jets grew larger. At any moment she expected to see a flash and plume of smoke as a missile launched, but nothing happened. Were they low on ordnance too?

Kate felt a powerful surge of relief when she merged with the lead Flanker. She had survived thus far, had a fighting chance, however slim, to survive. He had a clear energy and positional advantage, was already turning hard to bring his close-in weapons, his heat-seeking missiles and gun to bear, while she was still maneuvering defensively against his wingman.

Her mouth bone-dry, she watched his nose tracking toward her. She tensed, anticipating the smoke trail leaping off his wing, but there was nothing she could do to prevent it without exposing her vulnerable six o'clock to his wingman. She was trapped between them, a sitting duck, helpless.

The trailer closed on her. Finally, she was inside his missile range. She slammed her throttles forward and pulled hard for the lead, depleting her remaining energy.

Her turn did little more than deny him the opportunity for a missile shot, but he remained well behind her 3-9 line, offensive, in the driver's seat.

Splitting her attention between her two attackers, she knew she was in for the fight of her life. One Super Hornet against two well-flown Flankers. The outcome was certain unless she could pull a miracle out of her bag of tricks.

The lead Flanker was camped out behind her, too close for missiles, aligning his flight path with hers for a gun shot. At less than three thousand feet and closing rapidly, he had the range. Therefore, all she had left was to deny him lead and plane of motion if she was going to survive this close-in fight. She continued her hard turn, jamming him, trying to force an overshoot.

His nose pulled to point in front of hers, establishing lead. She was an instant away from dying. Anticipating his finger tightening on the trigger, sending a stream of cannon shells through the piece of sky she would occupy a second and a half from now, her only option was to jink and do it fast.

Pushing the stick forward, she unloaded, rolled 135 degrees, then buried the stick in her lap. Her flight controls felt mushy, unresponsive, but she had a new plane of motion her adversary would have to match, his previous tracking solution having been spoiled.

He hung behind her like a huge bird of prey toying with its victim. He matched her roll, closing slightly, and started to settle for another tracking attempt. She jinked again and saw tracers flash past her canopy as her jet changed flight path.

Left that one a little too late. She felt icy detachment, surprised at her lack of fear.

Time lost all meaning as the game of cat and mouse played out. Her adversary matched her move for move. Soon she was out of airspeed and ideas. She was dimly aware of her adversary's wingman hawking the fight a couple of miles away, unable to get off a missile shot due to the proximity of his flight lead.

She was heading straight down now, her altimeter unwinding at an alarming rate, the ground rushing up to meet her. More tracers flashed past her canopy as she changed direction yet again. She was aware she needed to pull out of the dive, but to do so would provide her adversary a stable target he could easily track. She jinked again and rolled her head to keep sight of him as his jet appeared on the other side of her canopy.

The physical demands of her fight to stay alive sucked every ounce of energy from her body. Her neck ached from the constant swiveling under the few gs her jet was still capable of pulling. Her arms trembled with fatigue; her feet ached.

Desert filled her vision from horizon to horizon. Way too low. If she didn't do something now, she was going to do her adversary's job for him by smacking into the ground, but at least she would take him with her. She held her turn for just an instant and jinked once more. As she did so, she stole a glance at her altimeter, the needle moving so fast it was a blur. Survival instinct took over. Her final jink was a desperate pull back on the stick, away from the ground, a forlorn attempt to pull out of the dive. But her jet would not respond. She was too slow, her flight controls unresponsive.

Her adversary was still camped behind her. Her last turn had jammed him, and he was trying to get his nose back in front of hers. She shot a look out the front of her canopy. While her nose was pulling above the horizon, her jet was still falling from the sky like a brick. She clearly saw scrub and definition on the rocks below. She was half a second from hitting the ground. She felt no fear, just the incongruous thought, *At least I killed myself and didn't allow him to kill me.* The ground rushed up and she braced herself for impact. Her Hornet would shatter into a million pieces so fast she would feel nothing.

But it didn't happen. Her flight controls finally grabbed enough air. Her downward vector slowed, then stopped, then imperceptibly turned into a climb as she braced for cannon shells to rip her jet apart. But they didn't come.

She broke the climb, started a slightly descending turn back toward where she thought her adversary would be. Staying as low as possible would give him a double problem. He would need to avoid the rocks while trying to get a shot on her. She looked back and was shocked when she didn't see him behind her. Then she spotted it—a fireball on the desert floor a couple of miles away, a plume of black smoke starting to rise into the afternoon sky.

One problem down, one to go. The wingman: where was he?

Her heart lurched as she found him a mile behind her, nose coming to bear, in almost perfect parameters for a missile shot. *The inevitable outcome of this uneven match.*

She tensed, anticipating the inevitable flash and the corkscrew trail of smoke streaking her way. But when the flash came, it was by the tail of his jet, not under the wing. She stared uncomprehendingly as the Flanker pitched up, yawed right, and lazily fell off to the right, its entire aft section engulfed in flames. *What on earth?*

"Buick 11, snap south. Visual is at your right five high for three miles." Spud's voice came authoritatively over the radio.

Obediently, Kate turned toward the coast, finally grasping what had just happened. Spud had come back for her. With a barely flyable jet and no gas to play with, he had stuck around and saved her bacon. The reality of it caused a surge of gratitude to well up in her heart, but it was instantly tempered by the knowledge that his action was almost certainly for nothing and could cost him his life as well.

She checked her dwindling store of fuel. The coast was still hundreds of miles away. She wasn't going to reach it and its awaiting tankers, not by a long shot. Spud hadn't spent the time in afterburner she had, might just be able to reach the gulf and bail out feet wet where friendly forces could easily pick him up.

Throat dry, she croaked on the radio, "Darkstar, Buick 11, point out to closest drogue-equipped tanker. I'm on fumes and need gas now." Sometimes plain English could communicate the urgency of the situation much better than standard terminology.

The controller's response was not promising. "Closest tanker is 170 for 450, angels 27."

Kate climbed into the upper thirties to preserve fuel and extend her range. She stared out at the miles of hostile territory stretching out in front of her. The gulf was somewhere out there, but it may as well be on the other side of the moon. She flexed her fingers and wiggled her toes, felt some of the tension in her arms and legs begin to diffuse.

She shot a glance at Spud, who had taken up position off her right wing. He shouldn't have come back for her. Now chances were that they were both going to die.

Newscasts had shown that a terrible fate awaited the allied pilots who had bailed out of crippled jets over Iran. Her left hand involuntarily strayed from the throttles to the pistol tucked into her survival vest. Would she have the courage to use it on herself to avoid capture, or would it be better to ride the jet in when it ran out of fuel?

Long, agonizing minutes ticked by. Her fuel gauge crept lower as the coastline inched closer. She was acutely aware of every sound, every vibration in her Hornet, as she awaited the cavitation of the fuel pumps, the sudden silence as her engines flamed out. Her mouth was dry. She licked her lips but there was no moisture on her tongue. She fished out her water bottle and took a sip of the tepid liquid, swishing it around in her mouth before swallowing.

The fuel gauge was barely reading. So many thoughts clawed at the back of her mind. Recriminations, regrets, a desire to say one last goodbye to the ones she loved. When her Super Hornet prepared to take its fatal glide toward the ground, she resolved she'd ask Darkstar to take down a message. Until then, all she could do was wait and pray.

Chapter 51

June 3rd, 1864
Old Cold Harbor Crossroads, Virginia

Fire blazed in Merlyn's side as a hammerblow knocked him sideways. He clutched at Midnight's mane for support, wrapping his fingers into the coarse hair, collapsing low over the horse's neck as his lungs struggled for air.

And then, Midnight began to run. Instead of running for safety, he ran in the opposite direction, into the maelstrom of fire pouring once again toward the Union lines. Merlyn tried to turn the horse, but he had the bit between his teeth and refused to respond.

The sound of battle faded as a tsunami of grief drove all else from Merlyn's mind. He had failed. George was gone. Kate would never be. He began to loosen his grip on Midnight's mane. How easy it would be to slide off the horse's back, to allow it all to end here, lying peacefully on the verdant grass as his life's blood ebbed slowly out.

He felt consciousness begin to slip away as he loosened his grip, but somehow his fingers remained stubbornly tangled in the horse's mane, the hair clinging to them like vines. Before him lay the rebel works, a mass of piled earth and jumbled tree trunks. Smoke from thousands of muskets billowed, and cannon roared, flashing dull, angry red as they discharged their hail of death and destruction through the gradually lifting fog.

As Midnight approached the line of guns, he launched himself forward and upward. Holding onto the mane for dear life, Merlyn had a brief impression of soot-smeared faces staring up at him as he soared over the rebel works. The big horse came down hard on the other side, stumbled slightly, and began to run for real.

Over the course of their many years together, Merlyn had learned to appreciate Midnight's almost supernatural speed. That morning he pulled out all the stops. At a velocity rivaling that of an express train, he tore through the enemy's rear, hooves churning up huge clumps of dirt and grass. Wind buffeted at Merlyn, and it took every ounce of his failing strength to stay in the saddle.

The sun was high in the sky before Midnight slowed. By then, Merlyn was barely conscious. Wetness ran from his side, down his leg, and into his boot. He had lost his hat; his sword was gone, dropped somewhere on that blood-soaked battlefield.

Moments later, the sun faded, obscured by darkening clouds, and snow began to swirl before them. The black horse entered the flurry at a walk and Merlyn, feeling the sudden bite of cold, pulled his coat around himself in a vain attempt to preserve precious body heat.

Minutes stretched by like hours and hours like days as Midnight carried a barely conscious Merlyn through a kaleidoscope of changing landscapes and seasons. Vague impressions came and went. The arc of the sun rising in the west and setting in the east in the span of a handful of painful breaths. Two moons—one small, one impossibly large—hanging in the evening sky. The impossible cold of an arctic desert. And then densely clinging fog once more. And still Midnight plodded doggedly forward.

He was in transition.

With time, the pain in Merlyn's side faded from a raging fire to a dull ache, but the occasional jolt as Midnight moved under him caused red-hot spears of agony to rip through him. He rolled with the pain as best he could, allowing the black horse to find his own way along the fog-shrouded path.

But it was pain of a different kind that threatened to overwhelm him—emotional pain, deeper, more intense, more all-consuming than the physical pain of his wound. He had failed. George was dead and all the agony, all the suffering of the past two years had been for naught. And because of his failure, the woman he loved would never be.

An eternity passed. Pain continued to jar him with Midnight's every step. The wetness on his side stopped spreading and his shirt began to crust as blood dried. An icy, biting wind cut through his coat, making him shiver uncontrollably. His breath came out in a white plume.

Transition. The thought brought no joy, no sense of anticipation, just numbness and grief. It would take no effort at all to release his grip on Midnight's mane, slip to the ground, surrender to the cold, let darkness blot out his all-consuming pain. But he could not do it. He could not give up. He had to hold firm to the knowledge that God was in charge, had a plan, and would somehow work some good from the disasters that had overtaken these last two assignments.

Barely hanging on to consciousness, Merlyn did not notice the point at which the path Midnight had been following changed to parallel tracks cutting through grass. As the fog began to lift, he had an impression of the ground leveling. He passed a stand of trees, white barked, their leaves fluorescent yellow as if in the first flush of autumn.

More time passed; he did not know how much, and then there were fences and a faint hint of wood smoke. A dog barked in the distance. And then there were corrals, horses, and a ranch house.

Hands grasped at him as he swayed in the saddle. "Easy now. Let me help you down." The voice was gravelly and deep. "Miguel, help me steady him."

His legs refused to support his weight. Rough hands steadied him, held him upright. He had an impression of shaggy gray hair topping a deeply weather-beaten face. Blue eyes measured him quickly and flared with concern.

"Miguel, take care of his horse. I'll get him inside. Becky, boil water. Quickly." The tone was commanding and decisive. Strong arms supported him and helped him up a short flight of steps and into the house. There was a chair. Something warm and sweet was pressed to his lips.

His jacket was pulled away. Then there was a searing flash of white-hot pain as his shirt was peeled back from the crusted blood on his side. He heard a sharp exclamation and then, "Get on the horn to Doc Swenson. Tell him we need him out here, now!"

"No hospital." The words were little more than an exhalation, but the gray-haired man nodded his understanding.

Merlyn rolled with the pain as a warm, wet cloth began to dab away the dried blood. His vision began to tunnel and then there was only darkness.

Chapter 52

Consciousness returned, slowly, laboriously like a bubble rising from the depths of the ocean. As the fog blanketing Morgan's mind began to release its grip, he became aware of soft sheets beneath him. A scented breeze wafted in through an open window. A pillow smelling faintly of lavender cradled his head. He sensed darkness around him, didn't bother to open his eyes, just lay there in the stillness and let sleep gradually reclaim him.

When he woke again, the fog had retreated but still hung at the edge of his mind, dulling his thoughts and making him yearn once more for the oblivion of sleep.

But sleep would not come, so instead, he opened bleary eyes and tried to take in his surroundings. The first sight that greeted him was a digital clock on the nightstand, its numbers glowing softly. A dresser and mirror sat against the wall opposite the bed. Through an open door he glimpsed a flash of white porcelain. A bathroom, he realized.

To his right, another door sat ajar and through it he glimpsed what looked like a hallway. To his left, chintz curtains framed floor-to-ceiling windows. Beside them, his uniform coat and pants lay neatly draped over a chair, still heavily caked with blood. He stared at them momentarily in confusion then back at the clock, his mind refusing to come to grips with the sight. How could things so separated in time coexist? It violated the very rules that had governed his life for so many years.

Something about the room seemed familiar, but in his befuddled state, he could not for the life of him think what it was.

His eyes registered other things spread out on the nightstand by the clock. The daguerreotype. His drawing of Kate, the bottom third obscured by a rust-colored stain. A wallet. Keys. A cell phone. He picked up the drawing and stared longingly at it, his heart breaking. Kate, who would never be.

He reached for the wallet, gasping at the sudden stab of pain in his side. He ran his fingers over the familiar grain of burgundy leather. It was the wallet he had used during his time with Kate. He opened it, examined the contents. A handful of bills. Credit cards. Driver's license. Military identification card. He stared at the plastic rectangle, drinking in the details, his mouth suddenly dry. His name. His rank: major. Air force. Active duty. And then, heart lurching painfully, he stared at the expiration date. His mind still befuddled by sleep, it took a moment for realization to sink in— he had finally come home to his own time.

He sank back against the pillow, an unbearable sense of loss making him want to curl into a ball and hunt for the refuge of sleep. But it wouldn't come. In his time with Kate, he'd played with fire. Then he'd failed with George and, as a consequence, there was no Kate.

A knock on the door snapped him out of his destructive spiral. An older, white-haired man came into the room. In his hand he carried a large leather bag.

"Good," he said cheerily. "You're awake, I see. How are you feeling?"

Without waiting for a reply, he fished in his bag and pulled out a stethoscope. A model of brusque efficiency, he helped Morgan into a sitting position. Reached under his pajama top and listened to his heart and lungs. Quickly examined his side and leg. Filled a syringe and jabbed it into Morgan's buttock.

Finished, he placed his things back into his bag and fixed Morgan with a stern glare. "You slept for about a day and a half. That's good. You weren't in great shape when I saw you the other night. I wasn't too happy just sewing you up, but Max was pretty adamant about not calling for an air ambulance. Gotta admit, though, you've done a remarkable job healing.

"That's quite a collection of injuries you have there," he continued drily. "You took a helluva risk not getting that wound in your side treated sooner. You're lucky that whatever it was hit you went clean through without hitting anything vital. How long has it been? Couple of weeks?"

"Something like that," Morgan said.

The doctor held his gaze for a moment before continuing. "You were lucky. Could have gotten infected and then you'd have been in a world of hurt. You really should get to a hospital and get it checked out. That was a broad-spectrum antibiotic I gave you on top of the one I gave you the other night. He fumbled in his pocket and laid a container of pills on the nightstand. These will hopefully kill any bugs until you make it to the hospital."

He turned down the corner of his mouth as he looked down at Morgan's leg. "You been through the wars or something? I can see this one's much older. Whoever sewed it up made a hash of it."

He fixed Morgan with a pointed stare. "Although it's largely healed, you should get yourself to a good orthopod, get it checked out. A plastic surgeon could do something about the scarring. Your call," he said, his shrug indicating his doubt of whether Morgan would take his advice. With that he turned for the door.

He paused with his hand on the knob and looked back over his shoulder. "I'll send the housekeeper to get you up." And then he was gone, the door closing behind him with a snick.

All thoughts of sleep gone, Morgan swung his legs around and sat on the edge of the bed. He lowered his head against a surge of dizziness, his mind still struggling to process what the doctor had said.

Max. The name rang a bell, but he couldn't recall where he'd heard it before.

There was a soft knock at the door. Morgan looked up to find a wiry, dark-skinned woman enter, followed by a tall, burly man in dusty jeans and faded denim shirt.

"Hello," the woman said in heavily accented English. "I'm Inez, Señora Becky's housekeeper. This is Manuel, our foreman. We'll take care of you until Señor Max and Señora Becky return."

They helped Morgan to the bathroom, Manuel staying silently with him as he gave himself a sponge bath and changed into fresh pajamas. Manuel handed Morgan a battered housecoat hanging from a hook on the back of the door.

His mind grappling with a powerful sense of déjà vu, Morgan shuffled out of the bedroom and down a hall, Manuel grasping his arm to offer support. So much about this place seemed familiar, but why?

The hall opened out into a high-ceilinged great room. The wall opposite contained a man-high fireplace constructed out of river rock. On each side floor-to-ceiling windows framed a view of mountains and trees.

Again, it all seemed so familiar. He'd been in this place before—but when? He glanced at the pictures lining the mantel. And then all at once, everything fell into place, and his mouth went dry.

In a couple of steps, heart racing painfully, he was by the mantel reaching out for the picture at the far right. His mind refusing to come to grips with the implications, he stared at a younger Kate. She was standing by a jet, foot on the bottom rung of the ladder, hand grasping the rail, her other clutching a helmet. Her eyes staring out of the image met his with a bolt of electricity that set his nerves jangling.

His knees buckled as an indescribable feeling of joy and relief crashed over him. Manuel's grip on his arm tightened and Morgan was glad of the support. A single thought burned in his mind with the intensity of a halogen spotlight: *Kate is.*

·

Chapter 53

Morgan stared out over green pastures at the mountains Kate loved so dearly, rising steeply a few miles away across the valley. The autumn sun hung high in the sky, bathing him with its soft glow, but that glow was nothing compared to the raging fire of elation that burned in his heart, eclipsing his despair.

Bees buzzed around hanging flower baskets that had been lovingly tended and nourished. Horses whickered contentedly. Midnight foraged peacefully nearby. *I'll have to send him home soon, but not yet.*

He sat in the same rocker he had sat in when Kate brought him here. A gentle breeze caused the tubular chimes hanging at the corner of the deck to sound, a pleasant, baritone ring that made him think of church bells. Kate had said she never felt closer to God than when she was in this valley. He understood why and opened his heart to it, allowing the peace of the place to enfold him in its embrace.

A thought intruded, bringing with it a tickle of irritation. He so wanted news of Kate, but the housekeeper and the foreman had been close-lipped. "You'll have to talk to Señor Max," had been the former's response to his query. Manuel's terse reply had been just as brief: "Max will fill you in." Their evasion was maddening, but Morgan did not sense this was a household in mourning. That was hope, but he wanted more. He wanted confirmation.

He picked up the letter Inez had given him and read it once more while marveling at the beauty of the neatly formed letters marching across the page.

Dear Morgan:

Welcome to our home. Max and I have gone for a ride to talk and pray. We will be back early afternoon. We have much to discuss. Your sudden appearance here presents many questions. You will undoubtedly have many of your own. We will try to answer yours as we hope you will answer ours.

Blessings,

Becky (Kate's mom)

Morgan sat back in the chair and considered. They knew his name and had seen his drawing of Kate. If Kate had any memory of him at all, she would certainly have spoken to them about him. The brief letter convinced him she had. The thought caused his throat to tighten and his eyes to mist. Kate remembered. She must have. His ill-conceived plan to give her an anchor had actually worked. *Thank you, Lord.* It was as heartfelt a prayer as any he had offered in a long time.

Midnight's rumble of warning snapped Morgan out of his reverie. Two figures on horseback, still some distance away, approached the house. He straightened in his chair, wincing at the bolt of fire that shot through his side.

A ranch hand appeared from around the barn to take the horses' reins as the riders alit. Morgan observed the pair as, hand in hand, they walked toward the house. He recognized the gray-haired man from when he arrived. *Must be Max, Kate's dad.* He turned his attention to the woman. Trim figure. Deeply tanned face. Long, silvery hair with just a few strands of blonde remaining. While

Kate's dad exuded weathered strength like a deeply rooted pine, he sensed a reservoir of peace and serenity in her mom.

Morgan tried to struggle to his feet, but Max motioned to him to stay seated and pulled a couple of chairs around to face him.

"Inez, be a dear and bring us the pitcher of iced tea in the fridge," Becky said to the housekeeper, who stood silently in the doorway.

Max flopped heavily in his chair. "Don't you want to go get it now?" Becky asked him.

"It'll keep." Max's voice was a low growl as he waved her toward the chair beside him.

She sat on the edge of her chair, appraising Morgan with the same frank stare he had seen so often in Kate.

Butterflies danced in his stomach. *Now the grilling begins.*

He expected Max to take the lead in the conversation, but Becky surprised him. "I'm sorry we were away for so long," she began. "When we need to pray through a difficult situation together, we normally go for a ride. Being out in God's creation has a way of bringing us closer to him and helping us to find clarity."

She turned to Max and grasped his hand while smiling sweetly at him. "This grizzly bear would have been all bluster and bravado if we left the conversation up to him."

The sternness in her eyes belied the smile on her lips, communicating an unmistakable message: *Behave.* She seemed completely undaunted by his answering scowl. Morgan sensed she was every bit as strong-willed as her husband, but unlike his strength, which was all concrete and rebar, hers was steel wrapped in velvet.

"We're dealing with something neither of us understands," Becky continued, turning back to Morgan. "I think we all know who each other is, but in any case, let's do the proper thing and introduce ourselves. I'm Becky Trenary, Kate's mom, and this is Max, Kate's dad."

She didn't give Morgan the chance to introduce himself. "You're Morgan, the man from Kate's dreams. Forgive us for going through your things. We were looking for a phone number, a family member to call, but when we realized who you were, we thought it best to leave things be."

Morgan relaxed slightly. So, Kate at least had some memory of their time together. That was cause for hope, for celebration.

Becky switched gears before he had a chance to reply.

"Max and I have been praying very hard since Kate told me about her dream and the effect it's had on her life. She asked me not to tell her dad, but with the war and everything, I had to. Although Kate has told us some strange things, our prayers have given us a sense of peace that God has been at work through this whole time. Your being here seems to confirm it. I know you probably have any number of questions about Kate, but could we first find out a little more about you?"

Morgan tamped down his impatience. He was going to have to play this exactly right or run the risk of losing them, and in the process, probably lose Kate as well.

Becky hesitated slightly, and he understood the tightrope she was walking. Given Max's bluster, she was as afraid as Morgan was of the conversation going sideways. He gave her what he hoped was a reassuring smile.

She gathered herself and asked, "So, who or what are you? I would gather from your injuries—" She stopped in midsentence. "I think I'll just leave it there."

"It's a fair question," Morgan replied. "Something apparently supernatural has happened to Kate, and you want to know if I'm its cause?"

Becky inclined her head.

Inez forestalled his need to answer. She deposited a tray with a pitcher of iced tea, the sides already beading with condensation, on the table beside Becky. She poured three ice-filled glasses, handed one to Becky, one to Max, who drank deeply from it, and put the third by Morgan's elbow.

"Thank you, Inez," Becky said, and Inez was gone as silently as she came.

Morgan took a sip of tea, placed the glass down on the table, and turned to Becky. "In answer to your question, I'm not the cause of what happened to Kate. I'm just an instrument. I'm as human as you and Max are."

He risked a quick glance at Max, saw the coiled tension in him, his eyes fixed on Morgan in an unwavering stare.

"As you've probably gathered, God uses me in a rather unique way, to lead people to faith or to help them on their spiritual journeys," Morgan continued. "It's obviously a lot more complicated than that, but that's the essence of it."

"So Kate was one of your assignments?" Max interjected. Becky laid her hand gently on his arm. No words passed between them, but Max sat back in his chair, his jaw clamped shut.

"Yes, sir, she was," Morgan replied.

"Max and I have walked with God all our lives," Becky continued. "But what's been happening to Kate these past several months is far beyond our experience. Was her dream real or not?"

There was only one way to win Kate's parents over: the whole truth and nothing but the truth. *Lord, I hope I'm doing the right thing, that I'm not causing more damage by saying what I shouldn't.*

"It was real," he said. "I don't know exactly how it was done, but for a year we were away from here in a different corner of creation." He briefly walked them through their time together. As he summarized, he felt a check in his spirit. He was leaving too much out. These were Kate's parents. They needed to hear it all—the facts, his feelings, his emotions, everything. He took a deep breath and, for the next half hour, bared his soul, laying it all out for them, the good, the bad, the ugly.

"I love her," he concluded, staring down at the rough deck boards. "I love her more than I ever thought it was possible to love another human being. I know I hurt her, and I hope with all my heart she'll forgive me."

He looked up, saw tears glistening in Becky's eyes, glanced at Max, who was studiously staring down at his dusty boots, most of the tension gone from his posture. After a moment, Max raised his head, fixing Morgan with a piercing stare.

"That's quite a story, young fellow," he said drily. "We've been able to piece some of it together from the little bits and pieces Kate told her mom. I don't get the how and why of it all, but I'm not sure it's important right now. If what you taught Kate kept her alive, then we owe you an eternal debt of gratitude."

Morgan's heart missed a beat as joy surged up inside him. Kate was alive! Not only that, her memories were intact. The anchors had held. *Thank you, Lord.* He wanted to scream the words but kept his elation in check.

Max read him, gave him a wry smile. "You had no idea how this was going to turn out, did you?"

Morgan felt a stab of pain as a more recent memory intruded. "No, in all my time on the road, I seldom get to see the end of the story. My time with Kate was to prepare her for something, not to see her through it. In the assignment I just came from, I ended up walking through the fire with the person I was sent to, and I lost him anyway. There was nothing I could say or do that could help God's love penetrate his heart."

An odd look flashed over Max's face for an instant and was gone. *What did I just say?* Morgan wondered.

"So why did all this happen? What was the purpose?" Max asked, his voice softer, less combative.

Morgan began to feel a flicker of hope. Perhaps his gentle approach was starting to win the man over. "I don't think I ever really know the true purpose of why God brings me into someone's life. I think that is between God and that person. My job is to mentor, to help them grow into what God wants them to be, for whatever purpose he wants them to serve."

Becky stared at him for a long moment with a wise, knowing look. She turned to Max, signaling something silently to him, then sat back in her chair, relaxing imperceptibly.

"I'm going to ask the jealous dad question," Max growled, leaning forward in his chair. "What are your plans for Kate now that you're back? Are you thinking of just picking up where you left off with no thought for the pain and heartache you caused?"

Morgan felt a stab of familiar guilt. "I've tortured myself for over two years with what I did and how I treated her. As to the future, I can only hope she finds it in her heart to forgive me. I love her more than life itself. Thoughts of her were about the only thing that kept me going through the worst two years of my life . . . ."

His voice trailed off. He saw sympathy in Becky's eyes, something unreadable in Max's.

Becky responded to his unasked question. "You're afraid to ask how she feels about you, aren't you?"

Morgan nodded, the lump in his throat preventing him from speaking.

"That's something you're going to have to work out with Kate," Becky replied gently. "She's been at sea for seven months. It's been a very difficult time for her emotionally. Although we've sent a few letters back and forth, I don't know if she's truly come to grips with her feelings and struggles."

She turned to Max. "Dear, why don't you tell him Kate's story?"

Morgan worried his lip, emotions rising and falling as Max launched into a lengthy narrative, describing Kate's challenges with her squadron, her emotional turmoil, and her wartime experiences.

"Given the impossible situation she was in," Max editorialized, fixing Morgan with a pointed glare, "she needed her entire focus to be on her flying, not on trying to straighten out her personal life."

Morgan hung his head. The implied accusation was entirely justified.

"At one point she almost died." Max paused, words failing him, and wiped at his eyes. "One of her missions went sideways. Her wingman got himself shot up pretty badly. Out of gas, they were being chased down by a pair of Flankers. Kate could have beat feet for safety but did what any of us would have done—turned back to take on the Flankers and give her wingman a chance to get back to safety. Then, with a damaged jet, he saved her bacon.

"They were over central Iran, way low on gas, hundreds of miles from feet wet, and were going to flame out long before they got onto a tanker. A tanker broke formation and came north to get them. Her wingman is a young pilot with a newborn baby he's never seen. They've made heroes out of them and it's going to be a helluva media event when she flies off the carrier."

Morgan felt his muscles begin to relax slightly, unaware they had tensed painfully all through Max's narrative.

"She's my little girl," Max said, his voice breaking. "I love her more than life itself. I'm prouder of her than I can possibly say, but it darn-near killed me to think of her out there in harm's way."

"Dear," Becky interrupted, "you can tell him the rest later."

She turned to Morgan. "Fly-off is four days from now. We're leaving for Lemoore the day after tomorrow to go and meet her. You're coming with us, of course, if you're well enough."

Four days! Morgan wanted to shout with joy. Only four days until he would see Kate again! He felt a surge of affection for this couple who had been so accepting of him. "You can count on it," he promised. "Thank you for opening your hearts to me."

"Isn't that what God calls us to do?" Becky replied. "Just because something has happened that we don't understand doesn't mean we have to hold you at arm's length. Besides, you've just played an important part in Kate's life, and we would have to deal with her if we treated you shabbily. She can be just as much a bear as her dad when she gets riled up about something."

"Don't I know it," Morgan said, laughing. "I have the scar to prove it."

He looked over at Max, saw the thoughtful look on his face.

"You have something else you want to ask me?"

Max hauled himself to his feet. "No, I have something I think you'll want to see. I'll be right back," he growled.

Morgan looked at Becky. She shrugged her shoulders in reply.

Max returned a moment later, placed a wooden box on the table, and handed Morgan a framed photograph. Morgan's stomach did a barrel roll as he recognized the image. What on earth? George was dead. How had this survived? Why would Max have it?

He almost missed Max's next words.

"That's the twin of the picture you had with you. The original is in New York with my mom."

Without giving Morgan a chance to reply, Max leaned forward and opened the box. Morgan looked down in shock at the faded, cracked oilcloth enshrouding the yellowed envelope with its "do not open until" date. He grappled for words but could not find them.

"I can see you recognize it," Max continued. "Although it says to open it this summer, we were waiting for Kate to come home so we could do it as a family."

"What makes you think you failed on your last assignment?" Max pivoted, surprising Morgan with the question.

Morgan looked at him in surprise. "What do you mean?"

"You said you'd failed. Why?"

"I'd think that was obvious," he replied slowly, reliving again the horrifying sight of George's dead eyes staring sightlessly at the sky. He pointed at the man beside him in the picture. "That's the man I was sent to minister to. He died unsaved on the battlefield at Cold Harbor."

Max reached out and took the picture from him, wiped away a fleck of dust with his shirt cuff.

"That's George Maxwell," he said gently. "He's my great-great-grandfather."

Morgan felt the blood drain from his face as he stared at Max, uncomprehending.

Max answered the unasked question. "He was badly wounded at Cold Harbor. He rejoined his regiment after he got out of the hospital, took over the Brigade in late 1864, and led it all the way to Appomattox. You didn't fail. He left a legacy of faith that's touched every generation of my family. I'm a believer. Kate's a believer because of him. If you're responsible for that legacy, then we all owe you an eternal debt of gratitude."

Morgan leaned back in his chair as a river of tension and despair flowed out of him. He breathed a silent prayer of thanks as tears began to roll down his cheeks.

Chapter 54

K ate sat in her seat at the front of the deserted ready room, her squadron mates either grabbing a late meal or doing their last-minute packing for tomorrow's fly-off. A riot of unprocessed thoughts ricocheted through her mind. Long months at sea. A war fought. A world war averted. Friends gone. Other friends unalterably changed. A romance found and lost.

She glanced at the greenie board. Digger's, Mogas', and Jethro's grades stopped short of those earned by the others, but Spud's continued, a string of unbroken green. Spud had lived; more than a dozen aviators across the air wing had not.

Despite her grief, she felt a small glow of satisfaction. She'd been right. In combat, Spud had performed as well as the other nuggets in the air wing, probably better. What's more, he'd come back for her, had braved almost certain death to save her. Would Toad have done the same? Would any of the other pilots?

"I miss him too." The unexpected voice at her elbow caused her to jump, jolting her out of her reverie.

Kate spun around, but there was no mistaking that voice. Spud. "You and he were the only ones who believed in me."

His eyes, focused on the name at the top of the board, shimmered slightly. "I was hoping to find you here," he said, his voice oddly tense. "I wanted to thank you, privately, for everything. You gave me a break, trusted me when no one else would." His voice vibrated with emotion. "I was self-destructing.

Both at work and at home. Even though I made it hard on you, you never gave up on me. You were my one lifeline when I thought my life was coming completely unglued. Thank you." It was simply said but heartfelt. He wasn't finished, though. "My kids will now grow up having a father. Now if I can just repair the damage I caused to Kim . . ."

Kate struggled to find something to say that wouldn't sound trite but couldn't find the words.

Turning back to the board, he drew himself up, and she was gratified to see calm confidence emanating from him. "We lost a lot of good friends over Iran."

Kate shuddered. It was bad enough. The losses were staggering. Thank God Heather wasn't one of them.

Spud was still speaking, and she struggled to catch up. "I'm glad everyone came to our senses and backed down. Bad as it was, it could have been a whole lot worse."

Kate's stomach clenched at the memory of streams of AAA fire surrounding the tunnel mouth and the launcher. Captain Somers had singled them out the day after the fateful mission. "Congratulations, Elsa and Spud. We've confirmed the missiles they took out yesterday had nuclear warheads. An air force jock took out the third in western Iran. Now perhaps everyone can go back to their corners and stand down."

They stood for a moment staring at the greenie board with its string of dots, both lost in their memories.

"I have a question for you," Spud said softly, hesitantly, breaking the comfortable silence.

Kate inclined her head.

"How do you do it?"

She stared at him in confusion. "Do what?"

His face reddened and he seemed to struggle with his words. "How do you deal with the stress of everything you've been through? You're totally different from Animal. You're quiet, self-assured. You're not loud and in-your-face like so many of the other senior pilots. There really is something different about you. I'd like to know what it is. What do you have that they don't?"

350

She took a moment to gather her thoughts. That question was the last thing she had expected from him. "Spud, I have faith, purpose in life, a greater power to lean on." In as few words as she could, she outlined the essence of what she believed.

Spud listened quietly, his face reflective, digesting her words. He did not interrupt her.

When she finished, she looked at him expectantly, her heart in her throat, awaiting his response. For several moments, he said nothing, but finally looked up and met her eyes. "I want what you have. I want peace in my heart. I want the confidence you have."

This was so unexpected. Her heart hammering, she said, "You can have it. All you have to do is ask."

He looked thoughtful, seemed to be struggling with something deep inside. She waited expectantly, hoping this was the moment his eternal future would change.

He relaxed visibly, an expression of peace transforming his face. "I will," he replied. "Would you pray with me?"

"Of course." Kate tentatively rested a hand on Spud's shoulder and began, "Dear Father—" But heavy footsteps on the deck caused her to whirl and see who it was at this late hour. Torch. His face was grim. He looked tired, almost haggard. The idle thought crossed her mind, *Probably how I look too.*

"Hey, Bud. Can you give Elsa and me a moment?" His voice sounded as tired as he looked.

"Sure, sir," Spud replied cheerfully. "Catch you tomorrow, Elsa."

"For sure, Spud. Let's finish this conversation over breakfast."

Torch waited until Spud left the ready room before speaking.

"I'll only keep you a moment. I have something I wanted to say to you before we get back to the crush of daily life."

Kate felt her chest tighten.

"Digger would have been real proud of you—all of you," Torch said. "You did a fabulous job, Elsa. Not just with the squadron, but with Spud as well. I just want you to hear that from me personally."

At a loss for words, "Thank you" was all she could find to say.

351

Torch inclined his head. "Digger put you in a tough spot. I wasn't sure you were ready for it, but you done good. Real good." His voice conveyed pride and affection, so different from the harsh judgmentalism he had exhibited toward her earlier in the cruise.

Despite her reservations about the man, Kate felt her heart swell.

"You and Digger were right about Spud," Torch continued. "Me and the rest of the guys were wrong. We made it real tough on the two of you. I don't feel good about that. Bad mistake on my part to let things get so out of hand. You handled it well, though, and stood up to me. That took courage on your part. Almost as much courage as you displayed in the air.

"You know media is going to be waiting," Torch said, rescuing Kate from the need to reply. "They're going to want a piece of you. Female pilot downs five enemy aircraft and destroys two nukes. That sort of thing. It's going to be a big deal."

A big deal was the last thing she wanted. All she wanted to do was go home, spend some time alone, and find some of the peace that had eluded her since that fateful morning when she woke up from her dream.

"They made a big deal about the couple of Raptor aces when they came home several weeks ago, so you can expect the same thing. I know you don't want to do it, but it's good PR.

"Before he died, Digger mentioned to me that he thought you had a guy waiting for you," Torch said, changing the subject. "Is he going to be there tomorrow? I look forward to meeting the man who could capture your affections. He must be quite something."

Kate bit her lip before answering. *I'm not going to think about it. I'm not going to get my hopes up. That chapter of my life is over, closed.* "There's a guy," she said, trying to keep her voice flat so as not to convey her swirling emotions and the pain in her heart. "I hope he'll be there, but I'm not sure. He's been deployed for longer than we have. I haven't heard from him for a long time. I'm not optimistic."

Torch touched her arm briefly. "I hope he's there. I want to see you happy." He turned to go. "I'm going to turn in now, Elsa. Try to get some sleep. Tomorrow this deployment is over. I just want to say it one last time, while we're still aboard the ship—I couldn't be more proud of you."

Packing done, Kate curled up in her rack with her laptop open. She desperately wanted sleep but knew her roiling emotions would make it impossible. *Tomorrow will see the end of this deployment, and then the healing process can begin.* A night at her place in Lemoore, a couple of weeks R & R in Wyoming. After that, start rebuilding her shattered life.

Hours seemed to pass before she felt grounded enough to start typing out her thoughts, putting a bookend on the string of rambling recollections and handful of letters that comprised her dream file.

Hey, Dream Guy, or should I say, Morgan. This is my last letter to you. I still don't know if you're flesh and blood, or the stuff of dreams. As I think back over the time we spent together and over the many months since we parted, I have to say thank you. You taught me a lot. You taught me about how to be a better fighter pilot and leader, but you also softened me, took some of my rough edges off. I owe you an eternal debt of gratitude. I can't say it in person, so I will say it in caps: THANK YOU!!

Even after all this time, part of me still loves you—loves you in a way I never thought possible. If you were real, I think I'd want to spend the rest of my days with you by my side, loving each other, enjoying each other, and becoming one.

I don't know what tomorrow holds. You promised you would be waiting for me when I came back from deployment. Are you going to be there? How can someone who's a dream become flesh and blood? I have no expectation I'll see you, only a desperate hope. Kind of pathetic, isn't it? Hoping Mr. Right will come riding out of a dream to snatch me up and carry me away.

She lay back against her pillow, imagined his eyes staring intently into hers, felt the memory of his lips on hers, his arms around her. Could something that intense, so deep, so intimate really be just a dream, just a piece of her overworked imagination?
She started once more to type.

A big part of me wants you to be real, to be there waiting for me, but I can't invest all my hopes and dreams in a fantasy. I don't expect in my wildest imagination you'll be there, but if you are, I really don't know what I'm going to do. My head says run away, but I don't know if that's the right thing to do. Instead, I'm going to let my heart decide.

I must close now. I need to get some sleep before tomorrow's fly-off. Whichever way it goes tomorrow, know I'm eternally grateful to you, and a part of me will always love you.

Kate

Chapter 55

"The Outlaws are ten minutes out." The blast of the loudspeaker echoed across the Lemoore flight line. Morgan's excitement was so great he could almost taste it. He felt giddy, buoyed up by an uncharacteristic sense of lightness that had been absent from his life for a long, long time. The Lord had redeemed his disobedience. More than redeemed it, he had shown him that the work he had been called to mattered, had shown him a legacy of faith that charted the course of generations. Best yet, the woman he loved was coming home. The only thing that cast a shadow on his joy was the unanswered question: After all he had put her though, what did she feel toward him?

Although it was midmorning, the thermometer was already soaring above ninety degrees. The vast expanse of concrete in front of the hangar where the incoming fighters would park caught and concentrated the sun's rays, reflecting them back upward in shimmering waves of heat.

The excitement of the crowd was electric. Families, many carrying signs and banners, clustered together awaiting the arrival of their loved ones. Banks of television cameras sat in a roped-off area, separating them from the waiting families. All the major news stations were there.

Morgan stood behind Max and Becky. He had debated what to wear and eventually settled on simple jeans and a white polo shirt.

He had scraped off his beard two days before and Becky had trimmed his hair. He was presentable. His side was healing, but if he moved too suddenly his wound reminded him sharply it was still there.

He had thought long and hard about flowers. It would have been easy to have settled on a large bouquet—after all, that was the way things were done in this time and place, but his mind was still attuned to an earlier time when symbols had great meaning and thought carried more weight than show. He carried in his hand a simple arrangement of two roses—one red, one yellow. The memory of the florist's questioning look when he asked her to entwine the stems brought a brief smile to his lips.

A willowy, dark-haired lieutenant wearing khakis pushed through the crowds and threw her arms around Becky and then Max. *Obviously a friend of Kate.* She looked at him with open curiosity, her eyes appraising, measuring him. Max turned to make the introductions. "Lisa, this is Morgan Michaelson. Morgan, this is Kate's best friend, Lisa McKay."

Her grip was firm. "Pleased to meet you, Mr. Michaelson." Her eyes narrowed as she focused on the flowers in his hand. "Are you the man Kate told me about? Her dream guy?"

Morgan smiled. Kate would not have said much, but a perceptive and persistent friend would have been able to pry something out of her, no matter how closely she guarded her tongue.

He smiled at her. "I sincerely hope there's not another one."

She threw her head back and laughed, revealing symmetrical, brilliant-white teeth. "There's only one. If you were not here to meet her, I would have hunted you down and done you some serious harm." From her no-nonsense look, he sensed she wasn't joking. Something about Kate engendered passionate loyalty in her friends.

Lisa suddenly tensed. A young woman, baby in arms and toddler in tow, struggled toward them through the crowd, the toddler obviously having a different idea than his mom about where they should be going.

"Who's that?" Morgan asked.

Lisa leaned close so as not to be overheard. "That's Kim Otis, wife of Kate's problem child. She's a real piece of work. Been busting her husband's chops about being in the navy and being away from home so much. He's the guy Kate almost died trying to save, but who ended up saving her instead."

Morgan watched with curiosity as she approached Max. The toddler tried to pull away from her. It was either let him go or drop the baby. Before he knew what he was doing, Morgan stepped up. "May I hold her for you?" he asked.

She looked at him in surprise, eyes red-rimmed, face haggard, drawn. Gratitude softened her features. "Thank you," she replied, handing him the baby.

Morgan rocked her gently as wide eyes stared trustingly up into his.

Kim caught up her son into her arms, and his struggles immediately ceased. "Mr. and Mrs. Trenary?" she asked.

"Yes." Max nodded.

"I'm Kim Otis. I don't want to intrude on your reunion, but I had to stop by and say thank you. Commander Trenary saved my husband's life. He's too junior to join the fly-off, so I wanted to thank you on his behalf. Because of your daughter, my children will grow up with their father. That's a gift no one can repay."

Morgan suddenly saw it all, knew it with rock-solid certainty. God had altered time and rearranged the fabric of the universe, not so that Kate could single-handedly win the air war over Iran, but so that the baby girl in his arms could grow up in a family of faith. He suddenly saw a small portion of the tapestry God was weaving, knew beyond a shadow of a doubt Kate's selflessness would ultimately lead their father to Christ. A sense of awe at being part of something so grand, so elaborate, so sacred, washed over him, and he held tight to the tiny, infinitely precious bundle in his arms.

He watched as Becky and Max embraced the young woman.

"I think we owe you and your husband the same debt of gratitude," Max said, dabbing at an eye.

"I don't want to intrude any further," Kim said. "I'll wait over there"—she gestured toward a patch of shade by the hangar—"and hopefully catch Commander Trenary before you all leave."

"Nonsense," Becky said firmly, putting her arm around Kim's shoulder. "You're not intruding, and you will stay right here with us."

It was amazing, Morgan thought, how easily the Trenarys' circle grew and brought in those in need, just as they had brought him in a few days before. He was going to be marrying into an amazing family. *That is, if Kate will have me,* he reminded himself. He continued to rock the baby, whose eyes were growing sleepy. He turned slightly so his head and shoulders would provide her a modicum of shade.

A staff car drove up and disgorged a captain in service dress, an older woman—obviously his wife—and another younger woman and two boys. They stood a little distance apart, not mingling with the other family groups. The younger woman stood with a boy on each side. Morgan guessed the older to be about fifteen and the younger ten. Her eyes were red and puffy, as if she had been crying. Her sons stood stoically by her side. The captain and his wife stood protectively by her, warning off those who would approach.

Morgan instantly understood. She had lost someone dear—probably her husband. Yet, for closure, she needed to be here when his squadron came back.

"Is that the skipper's wife?" Morgan leaned over and whispered to Lisa. He already felt a closeness to her. She was dear to Kate and therefore was to him as well.

She nodded. "That's Carol Nelson. Her husband went down on the second day of the war. It takes a lot of courage for her to be here to welcome his squadron home."

Morgan felt a flood of compassion as he saw the TV cameras starting to point at her, capturing her standing strong in her grief. A reporter ducked under the rope separating the press area and started to approach, only to be intercepted by a pair of seamen providing security. The reporter turned back to the press area. The navy had just looked after one of its own. He hoped they would be as diligent when the media came after Kate.

"Five miles out." The announcement made him jump. He scanned the sky off the approach end of the runway and picked eight tiny dots out of the haze. Four followed by another four. That was it. The Outlaws had deployed with twelve aircraft. Only eight were coming home. The thought was sobering. For many at this base, and others across the country, there would be no joyful reunion. Only grief and tears.

He shot another glance at Carol Nelson. She had spotted the approaching Hornets, was pointing them out to her younger son. The older boy stood stoically, his shoulders hunched, hands in his pockets. His dad was not coming home, and Morgan could well imagine the thoughts running through his mind.

Instead of the traditional diamond fly-by formation, the squadron entered the traffic pattern four aircraft line abreast, at tactical speed and tactical spacing, the second division precisely spaced two miles behind the first. Morgan gave a mental nod of approval to the flight leader. He was symbolically acknowledging his squadron had been in combat.

He was so intent on watching the approaching fighters, wondering which one was Kate, he scarcely noticed Lisa taking the sleeping baby from his arms. His hands free, he raised one to shield his eyes from the sun.

The roar of eight engines was deafening as the first division flew over the crowd. The lead jet pitched out at midfield, vapor streaming from its wingtips throughout the high-g turn to downwind. The other three aircraft followed until they were strung out in a line parallel to the runway, each aircraft following precisely three thousand feet behind the one in front. The trailing division pitched out, perfectly timed to fall in sequence behind the first.

Morgan's heart was full. God was so good. He had allowed him to come home, come back to the woman he loved. As he watched the small puffs of smoke from the first Hornet's landing gear kissing the runway, a certainty settled into his heart. No more transitions. His work was done.

The wait seemed endless—eight fighters de-arming took time. So too did the long taxi back from the end of the runway.

Precisely spaced, eight Hornets taxied onto the ramp in front of the waiting crowd, where ground crew marshaled them into position. Morgan noted several of the jets had green, white, and red flags painted under the canopy rails. His eyes were riveted on the fifth jet, which was just turning toward its parking spot. It sported five flags. His gut told him it had to be the one Kate was driving.

Several moments later, in a display worthy of the Blue Angels, eight aircraft shut down simultaneously and eight canopies opened.

He saw a flash of reddish blond in the fifth cockpit as the crew chief took the pilot's helmet. He was right. He felt a surge of pride. She had been leading the second division, a privilege by all accounts she had more than earned.

He hung back slightly, drinking in the radiant smile on Kate's face as the crowd surged forward to envelop the pilots standing by their jets. She was even more beautiful than the mental image he had carried these past two years. Her bulky survival gear made her seem small, almost frail. She looked tired, drawn. Deep lines etched the sides of her face where the oxygen mask had pressed into soft flesh. Her hair was matted with sweat. His heart pounded so hard he was afraid it would burst. He wanted to run to her, but with a herculean effort, restrained himself. It was only right to let her parents greet her first.

He was aware of a commotion, and suddenly a TV camera was beside him, lens focused directly on Kate. A reporter babbled something into a microphone. As Max and Becky approached Kate, he saw a flicker in her eyes as they darted over the crowd. Was she looking for him, afraid he was not there? Was that a flicker of disappointment he saw cross her face?

Max caught her in a bear hug, lifted her off the ground, and twirled her around. He put her down and Becky joined the embrace. Kate was laughing and crying at the same time as she hugged her mom hard.

He could just see her face over Becky's shoulder. Suddenly, those extraordinary smoke-blue eyes met his. They widened, and a look of pure joy transfigured her face. She broke free from her mom's embrace and ran to him. The impact as she threw herself into his arms almost knocked him over. He held her tight for a long moment, face buried in her neck, and breathed in the faint hint of perfume buried beneath the distinctive odor of hot oil, hydraulic fluid, and burned JP-8 permeating her flight suit. Two years of pain and longing were suddenly erased. Only the present mattered. He never wanted to let her go.

He lifted his head to look into her eyes. Tears streamed down her face, tears of joy. He felt as if he were drowning in pools of liquid blue. She put her hands behind his neck, pulled his face to hers, and kissed him hard. "You really are real. You came back to me," she whispered in his ear, a note of wonder in her voice. His lips met hers again and as they did so, he was only dimly aware of the television cameras zeroed in on them. He didn't care. Kate was home, and so was he.

Epilogue

5 September
Gettysburg, PA

The weather was hot and sticky, very much as it had been on those three days that were so indelibly burned into Morgan's mind. A contrail streaked westward high overhead. Crows squabbled in the trees nearby.

Morgan put his arm around his son's shoulders. He was seven, perhaps old enough to begin to understand what had been accomplished on these fields and soft, rolling hills. "It's right over here," he said, leading the boy to a granite obelisk near the roadside.

The monument was tall, approximately fifteen feet high. He led Junior to the side away from the road, the side that faced across an open field to a line of trees a couple hundred yards distant. That side had a simple brass plaque—a representation of a battle flag displaying the seal of the State of New York. A ribbon above the seal proclaimed "172nd Regiment, NYSV"; a ribbon below contained the single word *Albany*. The flag was not intact. It bore representations of holes and tears, injuries representing a dozen battles. Inscribed into the monument below the flag were the words, "172nd Regiment, NY Volunteer Infantry."

The left side of the monument bore the names of those who had fallen on this field. Too many of them. Their faces swam through his memory. For a moment, he was gone from here, back in another time. Tears came to his eyes, but he brushed them away and forced himself back into the present.

His son, who had a perceptiveness beyond his years, looked up at him. "You okay, Dad?" he asked.

"I'm fine, son. Just thinking of these men, what they did on these fields, their hopes and dreams and the families they left behind. Come over here and look at the other side."

He shot a glance back at his wife, standing by the car, her arms around three-year-old Max, who was leaning against her legs. Her pregnancy was showing now. In a few months, the boys would have a sister. It had been a difficult pregnancy so far and the doctors had warned that, in a couple of weeks, Kate might need to go on bed rest. He pushed the thought from his mind. They'd deal with that, as they had the other struggles in their life, if and when it became a necessity.

Kate gave him a smile of support. He had walked these fields with her several years before when the memories were fresh and the emotional wounds still raw. Her presence had gone a long way toward healing those wounds. Time and a plentitude of good memories had brought the healing even further. He could look around him now without seeing the wreck of human and animal life, without hearing again the screams of the wounded and dying.

He pointed again to the monument. He could do this. This side was easier. "These are the officers and the strength of the regiment by company. A regiment was normally about a thousand men, but during the Civil War, they were almost always understrength. As you can see here"—he pointed to the monument—"the 172nd New York entered Gettysburg with 578 men. It left with 442. It lost almost a quarter of its strength on this field."

He pointed to an inscription on the monument. "There's your great-great-great-great-grandfather, George Maxwell. He was the regiment's lieutenant colonel, the second in command, but he led on this field."

His son looked impressed. "That's a lot of greats," he said quietly.

"It was a hundred and sixty years ago. Now come and look over here." He maneuvered his son so his back was against the monument and they were looking out over the field. "This would have been the center of the regiment's line. If you look to your right and left, you can see little markers showing where the right and left flanks were. The regiment stood in two rows facing those trees over there. On each side of them were other regiments of the 3rd Brigade.

"The enemy came out of those woods several times that day, and the battle raged back and forth across this field, before the brigade were forced to retreat to the ridge behind us. The important thing is, they slowed the rebel advance, giving the main body of the army time. Your grandfather was a hero. At one point when the regimental flag went down, he lifted it up, rallied the men, and led them forward again."

Kate came over to them. She wore her hair shorter than when they had first met, and strands of gray were beginning to appear. Even after so many years of marriage, her beauty had the power to take his breath away.

"Son, history is more than names and dates. It is about what happened and why, and most importantly, how it made us what we are today. The Army of the Potomac broke the back of the rebellion on these fields and hills. As a result, the Union was preserved, and from that moment forward, all Americans were able to live in freedom. We have a long way to go still, but what happened here made what we have today possible."

His son stood a little straighter as he surveyed the monument.

"When his country called, your ancestor stood up and said, 'I will go.' He left both our country and our family a legacy. He was truly an extraordinary man. After the war, he became a businessman. He was never rich because he gave away most of his money to help others. He served in state government and continued his charitable work until he was well into his nineties. He married a beautiful young woman, and they had seven children.

"Every child came to know the Lord. In turn, they passed on their faith to their children, and so it went until today, all the way down to you and your brother.

"George's descendants may not have been rich or famous, but they let their light shine, and many of them have made a difference in this world. And that's the key part of the story, Son. Life is not necessarily about the things you do. It's about the people you touch.

"George left a tremendous legacy in this world. Your mom and you boys are part of that legacy. As you live your lives, do as he did, and make a difference."

His son stared solemnly up at him. "I'll try, Dad," he said softly.

Junior had his mother's looks and fair complexion. He looked a little as George must have in his youth. George had been gone now these past hundred years, but he lived on in Kate and her sons and would live on in the daughter yet to be born.

His wife took over the narrative. "Sweetheart, you're only telling part of the story. If you're going to tell the story of George's legacy, you have to start with the name above his on the monument."

He shot her a chagrined look, and she flashed him one of her brilliant smiles in return.

He thought back over their life together. Eight years now. They'd been good years, but not without conflict, as two strong personalities blended to become one. He'd thought his former life was over, gone for good, but some tiny niggle of doubt lingered at the back of his mind, disturbing his tranquility. But it was nothing he could put his finger on—it was a hunch and nothing more. With an effort, he forced himself to concentrate on the here and now.

"Merlyn was the regiment's commander," Kate was saying. "George was a troubled, directionless young man. Merlyn led George to the Lord and helped him develop the character that led him to become the man he grew to be. Without Merlyn, George would have been a vastly different man, and who knows how our family history would have turned out.

"Legacy is not the material things parents pass along to their children. It's the difference we make in the lives of other people. For some, it's helping the poor. For others, it's leading people to faith or helping them reach their potential in the Lord. That's what Merlyn did for George. That's what your dad and I hope to do with you kids and the people God brings into our lives."

Junior looked thoughtful. "What did Merlyn do after the war?"

Kate looked back at her husband. "You take over, dear."

"The brigade commander was severely wounded, and Merlyn took over the brigade. George took command of the regiment. Merlyn went missing during the battle of Cold Harbor a year later. His body was never found. George followed in Merlyn's footsteps and became one of the youngest generals in the army."

Kate interjected again. "What your dad's not saying is that George's legacy really began with Merlyn. So if you want to look at it that way, we're all Merlyn's legacy as much as we are George's." She looked at him and smiled sweetly. "Isn't that right?"

How like her to build me up, even if the boys would never understand the true meaning of her words, he mused. Before he could reply, she continued, "I know you boys want to play soldier until it gets dark, but Beltway traffic will already be backing up. I need to put in a couple of hours work tonight on the chief's testimony before the House Armed Services Committee, so we really must be going."

He put his arm around her, pride swelling in his heart. "Aye-aye, Cap'n," he said cheerily.

He looked over his shoulder at his son, who was still staring up at the monument. "Come on, Son. Your mom's got work to do."

"Wait a minute, Dad. I just noticed something."

"What's that?"

"Merlyn has our last name. Could we be descended from him too?"

"I don't know about that, son. Remember, he died at Cold Harbor."

The boy looked disappointed as he walked back over to join them. Suddenly his face brightened. "Colonel Michaelson. Sounds just like you, Dad."

Morgan put his arm around his son. "I guess it does, Son. I guess it does."

As he turned back to the car, he heard thunder rumble in the distance. It was a rumble not too far removed from the sound of the guns that had roared here more than a century and a half ago. The noise caused his stomach to tighten slightly, but it was not a reaction to memory, more an anticipation of what was to come.

He saw Kate staring intently at him, concern written on her features.

"What is it?" she asked.

He tried to keep his tone light. "Nothing, just a fragment of memory. Come on, let's get everybody back to the car."

One arm around Kate, the other around Junior, he prayed a silent prayer as he walked his family back to the old Mercedes parked in the pullout. *Lord, protect them from what is to come.*

It was hard to feel anxious on such a beautiful day, though. As he walked across the grass, Morgan felt his sense of foreboding evaporate. *God is so good,* he thought, as joy once more filled his heart.

Get a Free Short Story

Building a relationship with my readers is one of the best parts of being a writer. I occasionally send updates about new releases, special offers, and other news about the books I'm writing. And when you sign up, I'll send you a free short story.

Sign up at <u>robertezelle.com</u>

Like This Book?

You can make a big difference!

I am so grateful for my loyal and committed readers. Your reviews are one of the best thank-yous I can receive.

Reader reviews are the most powerful tool I have as an author when it comes to bringing my books to the attention of other readers.

If you enjoyed this book, I would be very grateful if you could spend just five minutes leaving a review (it can be as short as you like) on the book's Amazon page.

Author's Note

Much has been written about the American Civil War. Historians have chronicled its campaigns and battles. Generations of novelists have attempted to put us there, on the fields and in the lines, helping us imagine the sounds and smells, the heroism of those who served, and, of course, the awful carnage of those years.

It was not my intent to write another book to compete with the monumental works that already dot the landscape of American fiction. For me, the Civil War was a vehicle to tell the story of a relationship and God's work in that relationship.

All characters and actions in this story are fictional. The 172nd New York is a fictional regiment. In reality, it existed for a time on paper but was never mustered into service. The reader should not attempt to draw a parallel between it and any regiment that served in the Army of the Potomac, for none is intended. A student of history might assume from circumstances that in one episode, the 172nd would have been a regiment in Hancock's II Corps, and in another chapter, it would have served in Sickles' III Corps. Again, my intent was to give a flavor of those terrible years, rather than provide a historically accurate account.

Moving to the present, fighter pilots are a rare breed. Prospective pilots must pass a rigorous battery of physical, practical, and psychological tests before they are ever offered a rare pilot training slot. Of those so fortunate, only a small percentage rise to the top and earn the privilege of flying high-performance jets.

A fighter squadron is a unique institution with a unique culture. It is a testosterone-charged environment that is the haven of the ultimate adrenaline junkie. Perfection in the air is relentlessly pursued, and there is no room for weakness or error. There cannot be. The stakes are too high. Alfred Gilmer Lamplugh is attributed with the quotation, "Aviation in itself is not inherently dangerous. But to an even greater degree than the sea, it is terribly unforgiving of any carelessness, incapacity, or neglect." This statement is exponentially true when flying aircraft at insane speeds close to the ground or mixing it up in a fifty-aircraft furball. Many friends I flew with are no longer with us, due to a minute misperception, channelized attention, or the almost always fatal g-induced loss of consciousness.

In these pages, I have tried to give a sense of what it is like to climb into the cockpit and blast off into the wild blue in one of our nation's most advanced fighter jets. The systems the pilot operates are highly classified, so I have skimmed over capabilities and employment techniques. I have deliberately stayed away from employment parameters, and all capabilities and tactics I have quoted can be found in open-source materials.

I have striven to be as accurate as I possibly can within the boundaries described above. If I have erred, the fault is mine and not that of the many friends who provided advice and guidance.

I hope you enjoyed reading this work as much as I enjoyed writing it. May God bless and keep you, and may he always be the wind beneath your wings, as he has been mine.

Acknowledgments

I owe a humble debt of gratitude to the many people who believed in this book and gave of themselves to make it a reality. First, and foremost, to Angel, my loving and ever-patient wife, for bearing with the long absences, the frequent moves, the uncertainty that accompanies a high-risk profession, and for always being my greatest cheerleader. To my editor, Erin Healy, for her sage guidance and gentle touch. *Coming Home* is much stronger due to her insight and encouragement. To Lisa Jackson, for her unflagging support and belief in this project. And, of course, to the many friends, in uniform and out, who provided help and words of wisdom along the way. You were all instrumental in making *Coming Home* what it is today.

About the Author

Robert Ezelle makes his home in the Pacific Northwest with his
wife, Angel, and two Old English Sheepdogs.

Glossary

The fighter community is a subculture of the greater US military. It has its own acronym-laden language that the uninitiated would find almost impossible to understand. Following is a compendium of terms found in this novel. They are drawn from fighter pilot slang, commonly used acronyms, everyday military life, and technical terms pertaining to the world of the fighter pilot. Items marked with an asterisk denote terms found in *Brevity, Multi-Service Tactics, Techniques, and Procedures for Multi-Service Brevity Codes*—a standardized language for communicating complex information in as few words as possible. I have modified some definitions to provide context.

AAA: Anti-aircraft artillery. Spoken as "Triple A."

Air Combat Training: Air combat training progresses at several levels of intensity and complexity. BFM—Basic Fighter Maneuvers—One V. One dogfighting, comprises the first building block. ACM—Air Combat Maneuvering is next, in which two aircraft employ as a team to defeat a single adversary. ACT—Air Combat Tactics—is the third tier of aerial combat training. In ACT, formations of aircraft, generally in pairs or fours, employ together to defeat varying sized formations of adversaries. A *D* preceding the mission type (DBFM, DACT), indicates that the mission will be flown against a dissimilar aircraft, i.e., an F/A-18E Super Hornet fighting an F-15C Eagle.

Angels*: Altitude in thousands of feet above mean sea level.

Aspect Angle: The angle from the nose of the aircraft or radar to the flight path of the opposing aircraft. If both aircraft are pointing directly at each other, the aspect angle is 180 degrees. If the radar contact is tail to the fighter, its aspect is zero. In brevity code, a radar contact's aspect angle is communicated by "Hot," "Flank," "Beam," or "Drag."

ATFLIR: Advanced Targeting Forward Looking Infrared, the F/A-18's targeting pod incorporating electro-optical and infrared sensors and a powerful laser designator.

AWACS: Airborne Warning and Control System. The E-3 Sentry aircraft is a modified Boeing 707 with a disc-shaped radar dome mounted above the fuselage. Its mission is to provide airborne surveillance and command, control, and communications.

Bandit*: An aircraft identified as an enemy in accordance with established identification criteria. The identification does not necessarily give authorization to engage.

Bingo*: Fuel state needed for recovery. A bingo fuel is established for every mission. It includes the fuel needed to bring participating fighters back together and return to base with a safe fuel margin.

Blind*: "I do not have visual contact with friendly aircraft." Opposite of "Visual." Visual/Blind are normally used to convey that I see/do not see my flight-lead/wingman.

Bogey*: A radar or visual air contact whose identity is unknown.

BRAA*: Tactical control providing Bearing, Range, Altitude, and Aspect angle of an adversary aircraft or formation to a friendly fighter. Pronounced as a word.

Brevity Code: Standard terminology used by US military forces to convey complex information or provide direction in as few words as possible.

Bullseye*: A reference point from which the position of an object can be established using bearing and range.

CAG: Commander Air Group. Although the title was officially changed to commander air wing in the 1960s, the traditional usage continues.

Call sign (Radio): Every airborne or surface radio transmitter is identified with a unique radio identifier, a "call sign," in common parlance. The call sign identifies who is transmitting on a particular frequency. A formation will operate under the same call sign, with sequential numbers identifying individual flight members. Examples: Outlaw 31 through 34 for a division (four aircraft). Chevy 11 through 14, and Chevy 21 through 24, for two divisions operating together.

Call sign (Personal): A nickname that normally follows a pilot throughout his or her career. Often derogatory, call signs are normally awarded for an act of buffoonery, can be a play on the awardee's name, or can be completely random. Examples: Joe

"Chunks" Smith (awarded because of his inability to hold his liquor), Paul "Notso" Sharp (play on name).

CAP: Combat Air Patrol. A defensive patrol to protect a location or asset against enemy air threats.

CVIC: The carrier intelligence center. Its primary functions are mission planning and intelligence fusion.

Data link: In its most basic sense, data link is a radio network over which participating entities exchange data. The US military and its allies use it as their primary means of cross-platform information sharing to enable participants to see the battle space, thereby improving situational awareness and combat effectiveness.

DDI: Digital Display Indicator. See Multipurpose Display Group.

Division: A flight of four aircraft. Normally led by an experienced flight lead, a division is the basic element with which fighter aircraft employ. A division is made up of two sections.

Dog*: Towed decoy. The ALE-55 Towed decoy is a radio frequency countermeasure that protects a fighter from radar-guided missiles. Deploying a decoy is referred to as "walking the dog."

Drag/dragging*: The radar contact's aspect angle is zero to sixty degrees from the tail. In other words, the contact is moving away from the fighter. Also used as a directive call to turn tail toward an incoming flight of aircraft or to signify one is turning tail. In this case, it is to decline a merge or to preserve spacing.

Drop*: Directive/informative call to stop monitoring a specified emitter/target and resume search responsibilities. In other words, "Break lock on the target you are tracking."

Fence In/Out*: Pilots perform a fence check when crossing the fence, the line between friendly and hostile territory. The check involves setting all switches/systems for combat during ingress and setting all systems safe when egress is complete.

Float*: Widen the formation laterally while maintaining visual contact.

FNG: Derogatory reference to a new pilot.

Fox 1, 2, 3*: Launch of air-to-air weapons. 1=semi-active radar-guided missile. 2=infrared-guided missile. 3=active radar-guided missile.

G-Force: Simply known as gs. A pilot turns a plane by rolling to the desired bank angle and pulling back on the stick. The harder the pull, the tighter the turn. The turn creates acceleration in the vertical axis of the plane (top of canopy to belly of aircraft). This acceleration is measured in multiples of the force of gravity, or gs. Modern fighters are capable of sustaining turns generating nine times the force of gravity. A 180-pound pilot in essence weighs 1,600 pounds when in a 9g turn. To put it mildly, it is painful and requires a herculean effort to maintain blood flow to the brain.

Greenie Board: A prominently displayed scoreboard showing the grades of every squadron pilot's carrier landings. Green is good. Anything else is not.

HARM: High-Speed Anti-Radiation Missile. The AGM-88 is a tactical missile designed to home in on the radar beams of enemy surface to air defenses. Pronounced as a word.

Heater: Slang for heat-seeking missile.

Helmet Fire: Slang for task saturation in the cockpit. Often leads to loss of SA.

Hostile*: A contact identified as an enemy upon which clearance to fire is authorized in accordance with established rules of engagement, or ROE.

HUD: Modern fighters are equipped with a heads-up display, commonly known as a HUD (pronounced as a word, not as individual letters). It displays basic flight information such as airspeed, altitude, and attitude. It also displays employment data such as ranges, parameters, and all importantly, the aiming point for weapons release. Pilots know this aiming dot as the pipper. It shows where bombs or bullets will impact. The purpose of the HUD is to allow the pilot to have access to all the information needed to fly and employ the aircraft without burying her head in the cockpit.

IP: Context dependent. IP in day-to-day parlance is short for instructor pilot. Alternatively, IP, or initial point, when used in a tactical context, is the reference point from which a pilot begins an attack profile. Depending on the threat environment, a pilot may simply fly to the IP, or may navigate to it by following a preplanned route.

JDAM: Joint Direct Attack Munition, pronounced "Jay-Dam"—a general-purpose bomb mated with an inertial navigation system/global positioning system guidance kit. The guidance kit provides the capability of all-weather weapons delivery as well as expanding the envelope from which the weapon can be employed. An added benefit is that it provides the pilot a fire and forget capability.

Knock It Off*: A directive call used in training—cease maneuvering, attacks, activities. During BFM or ACT, the flight lead or IP will make a "knock it off" call to end each engagement.

LSO: Landing Signal Officer—an experienced aviator who assists pilots with the final approach and landing on the aircraft carrier. They provide a pilot with corrections to alignment, glideslope, and airspeed to compensate for the movement of the flight deck. They also grade each landing to improve pilot proficiency.

Magnum*: Friendly launch of an anti-radiation missile.

MANPAD: Man-portable air defense system, a shoulder-fired surface-to-air missile. Spoken as a word.

Merge/Merged*: Aircraft have come together within the visual arena or radar returns have come together. In the former sense, it can also signify aircraft passing close aboard in a visual engagement.

Miller Time*: Completion of air-to-ground weapons delivery. Slang for mission complete, time to go home.

Multipurpose Display Group: A set of displays consisting of Right and Left Digital Display Indicators (DDI), Multipurpose Color Display (MPCD), Up Front Controller (UFC), and the Heads-Up Display (HUD). Aircraft computer systems integrate information from a variety of sensors to generate symbology that present navigation, attack, and aircraft attitude information to the pilot.

Naked*: No RWR indications. Opposite of "Spiked."

No Joy*: "I don't see the nonfriendly aircraft that is being called out to me." Opposite of "Tally."

Notch*: Aircraft is in a defensive position and maneuvering with reference to an air-to-air threat.

Nugget: First-tour aviator.

NVG: Night vision goggles.

O-4: Officer pay grades are numbered from O-1, Ensign, to O-10, Admiral. O-4, pronounced "Oh-Four," is the pay grade for lieutenant commander, the next rank above lieutenant. Officers are addressed or referred to by rank, but when rank is being discussed, sometimes pay grade is substituted for brevity.

Pickle Button: The red button on the stick which, when depressed, launches missiles or releases bombs. In fighter pilot slang, the act of dropping a bomb is often referred to as "pickling it off."

Picture*: When transmitted as an interrogatory, is a request for information pertinent to the mission. It can also be used as an announcement that information follows. Picture clear means simply that there are no factor aircraft in the area.

Pipper: See "HUD."

Reset*: Proceed to prebriefed area of operations. Reset CAP would mean proceed back to the assigned area of operations or CAP.

RWR: Radar Warning Receiver. A fighter aircraft is covered by a network of sensors to detect electromagnetic radiation. The signals are collected, analyzed, and presented in a display in the cockpit. RWR detects and categorizes both friendly and adversary radiates to tell pilots what is looking at them.

SAM: Surface-to-Air Missile. Always pronounced "Sam," never spelled out.

Section: A flight of two aircraft. Normally comprised of a flight lead and a wingman, a section provides mutual support and employment capability between two aircraft. Two sections combine to form a division.

Situational Awareness: Commonly known as SA. Pilots who have SA have an accurate mental picture or understanding of the environment around them. It encompasses what is happening with their jets, what is happening within their formation, and what is happening in the air around them both close in and at range. It includes weather, ground, other friendly aircraft, and, of course, what adversaries are doing. It takes in and rapidly processes changing information. Pilots who have SA are able to effectively and safely employ their jets to accomplish their mission. A pilot who lacks SA is a danger to self and others.

Slapshot*: Directive call to employ a HARM against a specified threat at a specified heading.

Slammer: Slang for AMRAAM.

Snap*: Directive call to turn to a heading.

Sorted*: "I have fulfilled my targeting responsibilities within the group." More simply put, "I have radar-locked the correct adversary in accordance with pre-briefed targeting and sorting plan." **"Locked"*** would be a radio call indicating that a radar lock had been achieved, but the pilot making the call is unsure whether sort criteria have been met.

Spike(d)*: RWR indication that the aircraft is being tracked by an air-to-air radar. Spike(d) Mud indicates being tracked by a surface-to-air radar. Opposite of "Naked."

Splash*: Airborne target destroyed.

Strafe Rag: A circular piece of cloth strung between two poles and used as a target for air-to-ground gunnery. Slang for an aircraft that has run itself out of airspeed and is essentially hanging in the sky, an easy target.

Tally-Ho*: Sighting of a nonfriendly aircraft. Opposite of "No Joy." Often shortened to "Tally."

Visual*: "I have visual contact with friendly aircraft." Opposite of "Blind."

Vul Time: Vulnerability Time. The time a flight needs to remain on station performing its mission. For example, a pair of Hornets are fragged to defend a lane for a four-hour vul time.

WESTPAC: Western Pacific theater of operations.

Winchester*: No ordnance remaining.

A note on how numbers are spoken: The rule of thumb is that numbers should be read out individually, instead of being spoken normally. Buick 11 would be "Buick One-One." However, rules are made to be broken and a mishmash of how numbers are read is the result. A direction is always read out. 170 is always "One Seven Zero." Distance should be read out, but often is spoken normally. The bearing and range, 360 for 125, will usually be spoken as "Three Six Zero for One Twenty-Five." Altitude should be read out but is often spoken normally. One will hear both "Angels Two Seven" and "Angels Twenty-Seven." Time is also a mixture. 0200 hours, 2:00 a.m., would be spoken as "oh two-hundred." 1300, 1:00 p.m., would be "thirteen hundred."

Technically the word *hours* should be included but is seldom used in conversation.

Made in United States
Troutdale, OR
08/10/2024

21890319R00246